THE
COCONUT
AFFAIR

John de Caynoth

By

John de Caynoth

ISBN-13: 978-1515090038

ISBN-10: 1515090035

DEDICATION

This book is dedicated to Claire, my wife and companion, without whose support, help, and encouragement this novel would not have seen the light of day.

CONTENTS

PART 2

ACKNOWLEDGMENTS

I must thank Claire Lilley, my wife, for her help editing my original manuscripts and prompting me when I got stuck in a story line.

The Coconut affair is set on the fictitious Caribbean Island of Kaeta. This story is entirely fictional and any similarity to real people and events is unintended and coincidental, but if you know, or have visited, the eastern Caribbean and experienced the wonderful islands, you may recognise aspects that I have borrowed to add reality and atmosphere.

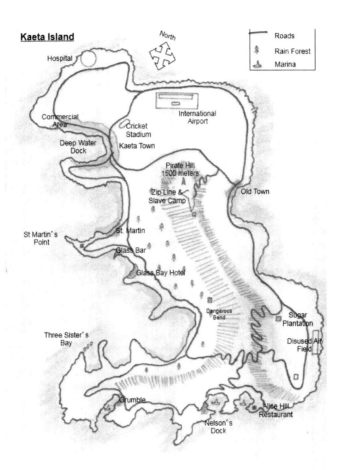

Kaeta Island

Hospital

Commercial Area

Deep Water Dock

Cricket Stadium

International Airport

Kaeta Town

Pirate Hill 1500 meters

Zip Line & Slave Camp

Old Town

St. Martin

St Martin's Point

Glass Bar

Glass Bay Hotel

Dangerous Bend

Sugar Plantation

Three Sister's Bay

Disused Air Field

Grumble

Nelson's Dock

Alice Hill Restaurant

North

Roads

Rain Forest

Marina

Prologue

On 3rd November the Federal Drugs Administration in Florida received the following communication from the Drug Control Section of the Dutch Police.

'We have information that a shipment of amphetamines destined for the United States of America will be dispatched within the next few days using the Caribbean corridor. The carrier is identified as a white middle-aged male who will be carrying a rucksack and camera bag.'

The next day the Federal Drugs Agency sent the following message to its police contacts across the Caribbean. 'Code Name, Coconut: we have received the following information from a source in Amsterdam. We have information that a shipment of amphetamines destined for the United States of America will be dispatched within the next few days using the Caribbean corridor. The carrier is identified as a white middle-aged male who will be carrying a rucksack and camera bag. Please be on alert for the carrier. He should not be detained unless absolutely necessary. Please observe all contacts and movements and report back to us. We require this route to be closed and the organisers to be apprehended.'

Bernard Shrewd, the Detective Inspector for the Kaeta Island Police Force, who was responsible for drug issues, received this communication. He notified immigration officials at Kaeta International Airport and Kaeta Town Docks to watch out for a middle-aged white male carrying a rucksack and camera bag.

PART 1

Chapter 1

Douglas Jay; Friday 7th November

I looked out of the aircraft window as we circled over the shimmering north coastline of Kaeta Island. The land was brown and parched, separated from a vivid blue sea by a rocky fringe, pounded by white surf from the Atlantic rollers.

For a few moments I was lost in a reflective daydream, wondering what the world had in store for me. Just days before I had been the finance director of a veterinary drug manufacturing company, but I had lost my job when the sale to a large American pharmaceutical company completed. With no commitments, I was taking a long holiday to give me time to sort out my life and to decide what to do next; at least I had made a bit of money over the last few months. Also the Americans had given me a good redundancy payment, plus honouring the remainder of my employment contract. Enough, perhaps, if I liked it here, to buy somewhere on Kaeta Island, and turn a hobby into a business. I watched as the landscape changed beneath me. The sweeping sand-fringed bays and calm, blue waters of the Caribbean Sea replaced the rocky coastline. The buildings of Kaeta Town came into sight as the aircraft completed its approach to Kaeta International Airport.

I was startled back to reality as I heard the instruction to the crew to take their landing positions. The aircraft bumped slightly as the undercarriage descended and the engines took on a more urgent note as the arid ground, which shimmered in the afternoon heat, rushed up towards us. The landing was so smooth that I hardly felt it. I anticipated reverse thrust and braced myself for the rapid deceleration as the plane slowed down and turned towards the arrival buildings. I was now feeling a sense of anticipation and excitement. For the first time in many days I was looking forward to something new.

The aircraft had now come to a halt and passengers were gathering up their belongings ready to disembark. From experience I guessed there would be a long wait for immigration, so I had reserved a seat towards the front of the Boeing 747 Jumbo as I intended to leave the plane as quickly as I could. The aircraft door opened and I started to move forwards. As I stepped out of the door, a wall of hot air hit me. I love that feeling of warmth, after the winter chill of England, that lets you know, in no uncertain terms, that you are on holiday. I had arrived and I was excited.

I hitched my rucksack on to one shoulder and camera bag across the other and followed the line of passengers being ushered across the black tarmac towards the airport arrival building by a couple of airport staff, who perspired in their dark uniforms. The heat bounced back off the tarmac as we walked the few hundred yards to the entrance. I made my way into the arrivals hall. It was not a particularly large room, with a low ceiling, and was painted totally in a light grey colour. It was cheered up slightly by the posters advertising the local mobile phone operator and tourist board selling 'Paradise by the beach'. There were toilets to one side of the hall and doors to the other marked 'Staff Only'. At the front of the hall, it was divided from the rest of the arrivals area by a line of four immigration gates. Only two were manned. I had a short wait before being beckoned forwards by a large, dark-skinned lady in her custom officer's uniform.

On taking my passport and immigration paper, she looked at her list, looked at me, and looked again at her papers.

'Please wait here for a moment,' she said as she beckoned a security guard over to block the exit. She disappeared through a one of the doors at the back of the arrivals hall. I was feeling nervous now. The excitement had been replaced by concern. My chest tightened as my stress levels rose. I wondered what the problem would be. The immigration official returned about ten minutes later with another security guard.

'Follow me please,' she instructed, and led me towards the same door and then into a small windowless room painted in the same grey colour, with no posters this time, and furnished only with a steel table and two plastic chairs. A CCTV camera lurked menacingly in the centre of the ceiling, looking at me as I was directed to one of the chairs. 'Wait here sir, someone will attend to you shortly,' she said as she disappeared.

She was gone before I gathered enough wits to ask why I was being detained. The security official stood guarding the door. He was over six foot and heavily built, not a man to tangle with, I assessed. 'Can you tell me what the problem is?' I politely asked the guard.

'I have no information, sir. Please be patient. Someone will attend to you soon.'

I was tense now. I hoped this was just some mistake or misunderstanding which surely could be sorted out quickly if I could speak to someone in authority.

After fifteen minutes I was beginning to get a little more tense and worried. I said to the official, 'Please can you get someone in charge that I can speak to so I can get this sorted out? I have done nothing wrong.'

'Please be patient, sir. Someone will be along shortly.'

No joy there then. *Okay*, I thought to myself, *just sit here calmly and wait.* I wondered what was going on. Had they found something in my luggage?

An hour passed and any calm resolve I had possessed was beginning to melt. I was getting very stressed. My chest felt as though it had a bag of concrete sitting on it and I also had a headache. *What could they have they found?* I kept thinking. I was rehearsing in my head what I would say when the 'someone' did eventually appear.

There was a knock on the door and the guard stepped to one side as it opened, and a stunningly beautiful woman walked into the room. I guessed she was in her mid- to late thirties. She was wearing blue jeans and a loose blouse top, which together showed off her tall, slim figure: about five foot eleven at a guess. She was very pretty, with clear Asian-coloured skin, dark brown shoulder-length hair, not tight and curly but with a slight wave to it, and large brown eyes with a hint of European features, a small nose and straight lips. I guessed she would have a warm smile if she did not look so stern. I could see the shape of her breasts outlined through the thin material of her blouse as she squared her shoulders to confront me. I must have sat open-mouthed as she apologised for keeping me waiting.

'I am Sergeant de Nouvelas of the Kaeta Island Police and I am extremely sorry you have been detained like this and have had to wait for so long. You are, of course, free to leave now.'

I was momentarily stunned. When she said she was a policewoman, I thought she had come to arrest me.

'I would like to know why I was detained,' I stammered as I recovered some semblance of composure.

'It was a simple mix up of names,' she replied. 'Your name was misspelt on our passenger manifest and we had to check that out. It's all because of the anti-terrorist procedures.' She continued, 'I realise you have been considerably inconvenienced so please let me make some gesture of compensation and give you a lift to your hotel.' She did not wait for an answer as she instructed me to follow her.

She led me straight through the arrivals hall where passengers were still queuing, and then into the luggage hall where she pointed at a carousel and asked me if I could see my suitcase. She had a soft voice with an English accent and I had difficulty hearing her through the noise. 'Yes, it's that brown one there,' I told her. She picked it from the conveyor belt and passed it to a porter, and then walked purposefully towards the exit at the far end of the hall with myself, and the porter, following. People parted to make way for her as she strode through the crowd.

Outside was pandemonium, with tourist representatives standing by little tables looking for their customers, and tourists milling around looking for their holiday representatives or transport. Taxi drivers and porters were prowling hopefully through this melee hoping for a fare or tip. The policewoman marched straight through all this with me in tow and made towards a white unmarked Suzuki Grand Escudo, four-wheel drive, parked immediately in front of the taxis. As she approached, the driver climbed out of the vehicle and disappeared quickly into the crowd. She opened the back door of the Suzuki for the porter to load my suitcase. I briefly saw an array of emergency equipment, police cones and ropes as she closed the door. She opened the front passenger door for me and then moved round the vehicle to the driver's seat.

The engine had been left running to keep the air

conditioning on so the car was comfortably cool.

'What about the driver?' I asked as we put our seat belts on.

'He will be okay; he has to get back to the station,' she replied.

'I am staying at the Hotel Glass Bay,' I told her.

'I know,' was the reply. I was puzzled, why would she already know where I was staying?

Chapter 2

Joelle de Nouvelas; Friday 7th November

It was late afternoon and I was sitting at my desk in the police station headquarters building, and it was just beginning to get uncomfortably warm. The headquarters were still located in the old British Police Station and the air conditioning was unable to keep the old building really cool. For years there had been talk of a new police headquarters out of town but we were still here in this old building on the edge of the commercial part of Kaeta Town. I share the general office with Constable Merv Land, and an administrative assistant. My boss, Inspector Bernie Shrewd has an office adjacent to the general office. Also on this floor are an interview room and incident room, which we rarely use. The top floor is occupied by the commissioner and his staff and on the ground floor is the public reception area and waiting room, the duty sergeant's office, an open plan area where the duty officers work, a small canteen and rest room, locker rooms and toilets. The cells are in the basement with all the archives.

I was thinking about packing up for the day when Bernie called me into his office. I was the Sergeant on his team. 'Got a little job for you,' he smiled. This was his usual opening when he passed down some job to me, which he did not want to do himself, and as he neared his retirement more and more jobs were being referred. He passed me a slim file marked 'Coconut'.

'Read that and then get over to the airport where Immigration has detained a suspect,' he instructed. I read the file and groaned. If this guy is a courier this case has the makings of a long, drawn-out surveillance which promptly will be taken over by the Americans if it turns up anything. I was wary of working with visiting detectives. They were all too loud, too self-important, considered themselves God's gift, and always chatted me up trying to get me into bed, and I do not like that! Not after the experience I had when I met my first husband while I was at university. He took me out for dinner and then to bed and got me pregnant. He did the right thing and married me, although I now suspect that was only when he discovered my father owned valuable land on Kaeta Island.

I called my partner, Merv. 'Bring a car round; we are going to the airport. He drove, and I explained what we were doing. 'I will go in and talk to the guy, you stay with the car and when you see me coming towards you with him, have a good look at him but disappear quickly. It is best he doesn't recognise you as we may have to set up surveillance if he is the courier.' I did not say anything to Merv but I thought it best for me to see the suspect by myself. He was probably extremely cross and aggressive by now, so a woman may take the edge off it, I hoped.

When we reached the airport I first spoke to the immigration officers.

They explained that the man in question was the only passenger with a rucksack and camera bag. They had by now disembarked all the passengers and discreetly inspected their hand luggage as they queued for immigration. Only Douglas Jay carried the camera bag and fitted the description. I checked with the aircraft crew. They were not sure what hand luggage each passenger had carried and they confirmed that when the plane had been cleaned for the return flight no other bags had been found on the aircraft. Nevertheless I asked that the aircraft be given a thorough inspection as soon as possible to see if anything had been hidden.

I instructed immigration to get the camera bag and rucksack over to the police station for examination, and to identify Douglas Jay's baggage and put it through the x-ray machine to see if there was anything in it. They found the suitcase and we took it over to an x-ray machine in Departures. We could see nothing suspicious. Immigration also confirmed that the hand luggage had been x-rayed and was on its way to the police station.

Time to confront Douglas Jay, I thought. I watched him for a few minutes on the security camera. He was sitting quite calmly, and in black and white he looked very tired. I noticed he had his hands on the table and was twisting his fingers. I wondered if this was due to nerves or anger.

I knocked on the door and walked in. Douglas Jay started to rise but then fell back onto his chair. He looked surprised and did not say anything. *He looks a nice sort,* I thought, as I saw a slightly overweight, white, middle-aged man, probably early 50s, six foot tall and about 95kgs. He had light brown receding hair going grey at the temples. A pleasant, kind face looked at me, with light blue eyes, with stress marks beneath the eyes and round the mouth. He appeared surprised, very pale, tired and needed a shave. Before he recovered his composure, I started speaking.

'I am Sergeant de Nouvelas of the Kaeta Island Police and I am extremely sorry you have been detained like this and have had to wait for so long. You are, of course, free to leave now.'

He did not say anything immediately but then very quietly and politely asked why he was being held, and his voice confirmed my first impression. I expected this question, so explained it was simple a misunderstanding over the spelling of names. He appeared to accept this without question and followed me out. I had expected more anger and I wondered why he had appeared so calm, but I was grateful he had not created an angry scene and that he had just accepted explanation, just saying, 'These things happen, it's not your fault.' We retrieved his case and headed for his hotel.

He responded well to small talk and while I think he guessed I was questioning him he responded openly to my questions. I only once hit sensitive ground; he tensed up visibly when I asked about his family. *Oops!* I thought, *have I alerted him to something?* I was puzzled. If this man was a courier I would have expected to see anxiety and stress or a display of feigned anger, but he appeared calm and was even relaxing. He was friendly but not pushy and not trying to get off with me.

When we reached the hotel I was anxious to get away. I went across to where he was sitting and apologised for the inconvenience, and held out my hand as I said goodbye. He hesitatingly took my hand to shake. His grasp was firm and reassuring but, unlike other men, he did not try to squeeze my hand hard to prove how strong he was. I turned and walked briskly away, wondering why this man made me feel both uncomfortable and excited at the same time.

Chapter 3

Douglas Jay: Friday, 7th November

Why would the local police be concerned where I was staying? I wondered, so I asked the lady in front of me. 'How did you know I was staying at Hotel Glass Bay?'

'You put it on your immigration form.' She paused and told me it was about a forty-five minute drive through Kaeta Town. 'It's near the village of St Martin, where I live,' she went on. 'Glass Bay is a lovely bay with a half-mile sandy beach fringed with palm trees. The hotel is at the furthest end of the beach away from St Martin, which is on the opposite side from the northern headland called St Martin's Point. It's one of the best hotels on the island. It was built a few years ago in area that used to be a bit of a swamp. They created a number of artificial canals and lakes to control the water and set the whole complex in a beautiful tropical garden, which has now matured, with tropical flowers and foliage in shades of red and green complemented by the vibrant colours of bougainvillea and other tropical flowers. All the rooms are in little cabins set discreetly round the gardens with the main restaurant, bars and lounges looking out over the beach. You will be very comfortable there I am sure.'

We sat in silence for a few minutes as she negotiated the traffic leaving the airport complex. The airfield itself was separated from the main road by an eight-foot wire fence topped with barbed wire. As we pulled out of the main airport gate I saw a small black child, more or less naked, sitting on the ground watching a couple of tethered goats looking for something to eat. Sergeant de Nouvelas did not seem to register this as she accelerated along the main road, avoiding most of the potholes.

After a while she asked, 'How long are staying on the island?'

'I have booked the hotel for three weeks but I might stay longer if I like it here.'

'You do not have a job you need to get back to?' she queried in her rich and cultured mellow voice.

I explained that I had just lost my job and I was visiting the island to get my head together and work out what I wanted to do next.

'No family to go home for?' was the next question.

'No,' I replied shortly.

Thankfully this killed the conversation for a while. I was still wary of her questions but was now beginning to feel more relaxed. As we entered Kaeta Town, Sergeant de Nouvelas, for that was the only name she had given me, started to point out the points of interest in the town.

That is the main tourist market down there, and over on your right is our old cricket and athletics stadium. Our two most popular sports.'

I looked but all I could see were narrow streets with run-down looking buildings crowded together and shimmering in the late afternoon heat. Deep gutters down the side of the road hinted at the intensity of tropical rain, but at the moment were just full of discarded litter and squashed fruit over which the flies swarmed. The walls of the old stadium loomed darkly over the whole area scene.

She continued. 'Shortly we will see the main port where

the tourist ships come in. The bay is an old volcanic crater, now flooded. It is one of the deepest harbours in the Caribbean and it was recently extended, so we can now accommodate up to four large tourist ships,' she told me proudly.

The area around the harbour area looked more prosperous. The roads were still narrow but they were cleaner here, and full of street traders. The shop fronts looked newer and better presented than in the town. There were also lots of bars and restaurants, mostly with outside tables wherever space could be found. The harbour buildings themselves looked quite new, and as we drove along, I glimpsed shops and market stalls crowding the area immediately in front of the immigration barriers. Beyond this, a cruise ship dominated the harbour like a tower block.

She continued, 'There is only one ship in the moment so it's not very full but when there are four large cruise ships in the harbour it gets very crowded. It's a nightmare for us patrolling the area to keep the tourists safe and the local touts at bay.' She smiled.

Pointing out more sites, we drove through the town and as we were leaving she asked, 'Is there anywhere on the island you would like to see?'

'I don't really know yet,' I answered. 'I plan to do some photography…' I paused. 'I have left my rucksack and camera and all my equipment back at the airport. The immigration officer took it all from me when I was held in that office.' I felt worried.

Sergeant de Nouvelas immediately picked up the radio microphone and contacted her radio controller.

'Car 15. Isaac,' she called.

'Hello, Joelle,' the radio responded. 'What can I do for you? Not in trouble again are you?' the operator joked.

I noted her given name and though it pretty and it suited her, although I did not feel I could address her in such a familiar way.

'Can you contact Immigration at the airport and check if they have Mr. Jay's camera equipment and hand luggage and then arrange to collect it and return it to him at the Hotel Glass Bay?'

'Will do,' was the friendly reply.

'Don't worry.' She turned to me and smiled again. *I was right*, I thought to myself, she did have a lovely smile. 'We will find it and let you have it back by tomorrow at the latest.' She paused. 'You were going to tell me if there was anywhere you particularly wanted to visit,' she continued. It occurred to me that I was being questioned by her. She had a very relaxed way about her now and I was beginning to feel comfortable and finding her easy to talk to, so I replied.

'I don't have any plans yet. I am going to relax at the hotel for a few days and get my bearings before I decide what to do and where to go. My only ambition at the moment is to play with my new camera and try and get some stunning pictures of your island.' She changed tack and asked about my photography and I explained that I was very much an amateur but I did enjoy taking pictures.

'I might make up a portfolio of my best pictures some time,' I told her.

'Have you been doing photography for long?' she asked.

'On and off for years, but I have just bought a new camera and I am looking forward to trying it out on this holiday.'

She was quiet for a few moments and then said, 'I saw some photos of Holland once, Amsterdam I think it was. It looked very pretty with its tall buildings jutting out over the water. Have you ever been there?'

'Fairly often, but always for business. In my last job, I

had to visit the accountants and consultants handling the sale of the company and their head office was in Amsterdam.' I paused. I did not want to get into that.

Sergeant de Nouvelas considered this for a few moments before she started chatting again about the countryside, and the town of St Martin's, which were just passing through.

The arid, parched land had given way to a much greener semi-tropical landscape. I recognised coconut palms and banana trees but there were lots of other trees and lush green large-leaved plants as well. Interspersed with this were small fields, some with grazing cattle and others with small horses. I asked about the horses and was told that horse riding was quite popular, and many of the stables in this area catered for tourists who wanted to trek up into the rainforest interior of the island.

Joelle pointed to her left. 'If you look over there you can just see the top of Pirate Hill, that's its local name. It is about 1,500 metres high. It is an old volcano, now extinct, but you can still see mud and sulphur wells bubbling up in the centre. The hills stretch down the spine of the island ending in some spectacular cliffs on the south coast. It's all now covered with tropical rainforest but in the past, on the Atlantic side, it was mostly given over to sugar plantations. You can still see the remains of some of the slave villages in places. Nowadays they are a tourist attraction. In later years, spices were harvested on the Caribbean side of the island and were exported, mainly to Europe.'

A few minutes later she pointed to a hill in the distance. 'We are nearly there now, just a couple of minutes. That's where I live, just the other side of that hill overlooking the sea.'

I felt a twinge of disappointment that the journey was nearly finished. I was enjoying just sitting next to her, watching her drive and occasionally just smelling a hint of the perfume she wore. I noticed she had long, straight fingers and wore no rings. She pulled in to the hotel entrance and flashed her police warrant card at the guard who waved her through. We drove for another quarter mile through the semi-tropical, landscaped garden. There was a golf course on one side and a small lake with a water feature on the other. The reception building was set discreetly in the gardens with the main hotel buildings just visible beyond.

We climbed out of the Suzuki and I was ushered by the receptionist to a seat, where I was given a cold, refreshing towel and glass of champagne. Sergeant de Nouvelas unloaded my suitcase and gave it to the hotel porter. She walked across to me.

'I am really sorry you were so inconvenienced at the airport. I hope it will not spoil the rest of you holiday. I will personally see that your camera and hand luggage are returned to you as soon as possible.'

She held her hand out to me as she said goodbye, and I reached my hand out to shake hers. Her touch was firm and she held my hand briefly before she turned and walked quickly back to the Suzuki and drove away.

Chapter 4

Joelle de Nouvelas; Saturday 8th November

It was Saturday morning and I decided to go into the police station for a few hours.

As usual these days, Bernie was not in, but usually dropped into the station at some point on a Saturday to see what was going on. I used the time to check the bags and camera equipment. The camera and lenses worked normally. Immigration had x-rayed the bags and emailed me the pictures but there was nothing suspicious. I filled in more time by writing up a report. When Bernie arrived he called me into his office to update him. I went through the events of the previous evening with Bernie and told him that from our superficial examination of his baggage we had not found anything suspicious.

He thought for a few moments and asked, 'Did you do a body search?'

'No, that would have alerted him and we were trying to maintain a low profile.'

'Then he perhaps could have hidden the drugs on his person.'

'I suppose so,' I responded, 'but he was relaxed and he did not act is if he was concealing anything, but you are right, he could have cleverly hidden something in his clothing somehow.'

Bernie rifled through a pile of papers on his window ledge. 'Are, here it is,' he said, pulling out a single sheet of paper. 'That pusher we nicked a month ago said he got his drugs from a dealer, who told him there was a warehouse operation on this island. He did not where and claimed the dealer only contacted him when they had a surplus they needed to move. If this is good information, your Mr. Jay could well be a courier, and if he is as cool as you say he could be even more important. This is all circumstantial at the moment, but he has no job, no commitments apparently, and he fits the description of the carrier!'

'I suppose,' I said, again doubtfully. 'We have nothing concrete as yet, and his replies were all very reasonable.'

'Right,' said Bernie after more thought. 'Get as much information as you can about his background, check out his story. Keep him under surveillance. Go with Merv and I will find someone else as well to help you. Do you still have contacts in the hotel that can get them in? And you, Joelle, keep close to him, find a way to question him further – discreetly – we don't to frighten him off.'

I confirmed that I could probably get two people into the hotel as gardeners to watch Douglas Jay through the day. But thought, resignedly, getting close to him would mean getting familiar with him, and I didn't want to get involved with anyone.

Chapter 5

Douglas Jay; Saturday 8ᵗʰ November

It was my first day at the hotel and I rose early to explore the hotel and grounds.

The guest entrance to the hotel was secured by a gate, which was operated electrically by a security guard from a hut. There was a drive, about a quarter of a mile long winding through landscaped gardens with a small nine-hole golf course set back on one side. At the end of this drive was the guest reception building with a car park hidden behind bushes and trees. Behind this building were three paths which radiated out across more gardens and small lakes connected by a series of canals, all of which eventually drained into the sea. The central path led down to the main hotel buildings containing a restaurant, bar, shops, guest information, library and lounge, and administrative offices, all built just behind the beach. The two side paths led to the guest chalets, which were built in the gardens and along the beach. Each chalet contained one, two or four guest rooms. To one side of the main hotel building was an outdoor complex with two connected swimming pools, a tennis court, games areas, and another restaurant and bar. The hotel gym and health spa were adjacent to this area.

After breakfast, I walked through the garden making my way to the guest information desk.

'Do you have a phone number for the local police station?'

'Yes, Mr. Jay. Would you like me get them for you?'

The lady behind the reception desk pressed some buttons and handed me the receiver.

They must have the local police on their speed dial, I mused as I took the receiver and listened to a ringing tone.

'Kaeta Police,' I heard.

'Please could I speak with Sergeant de Nouvelas?'

'Who is calling?' I gave my name. 'Please hold; I will see if I she is in.'

As she spoke I thought, *She has the sexiest voice I have ever heard.*

'De Nouvelas. How may I help you?'

'You may remember me from yesterday, Douglas Jay.'

'Of course, how may I help you?'

'I am sorry to bother you, you are probably very busy, but I was wondering if you knew where my camera and travel bags were and when I might be able to get them back?'

'No problem. I have them in front of me now. I will bring them round to your hotel later this morning.'

'There is no need, I would be happy to collect them if that would be easier.'

'Not at all sir, I have to come out your way today so it's no inconvenience at all to drop them off. I will see you in about an hour if that's okay?"

That's good, I thought. I had not expected to see her again and the thought pleased me. I did not have anything to do or read, it was all in my travel bags, so I found a lounger in a shady part of the garden where I could see the reception desk. After a while it occurred to me that she would probably just leave the bags at reception and I would miss her. As I started walking through the garden, I spotted her walking through reception with the bags. She was swearing white calf-length slacks and a black tee-shirt today. I walked towards her and we met near a bar area.

'I thought you might like to check the bags and contents are all there,' she said as she handed me the two bags.

'Hello,' I replied and she did not respond. 'Yes,' I continued, 'I think I should. Shall we sit over there?'

We moved towards the bar area and sat at one of the tables. A waiter walked up and I ordered a coffee for myself. I looked at Joelle; I still did not have the courage to call her Joelle out loud but I that's how I now thought of her. 'Can I get you coffee?' I asked.

'Thank you,' she said, looking at the waiter. 'Could I have a lemon tea?'

The waiter bustled off and Joelle sat silently watching me as I checked through the bags. 'All seems present and correct,' I reported.

She said nothing so I got the camera out and checked it. I fitted the 70mm-300mm lens and took a picture of a tree at the opposite end of the garden. *That's OK*, I thought as I looked at the camera's LCD screen. I fitted the 20mm-80mm wide angle and zoomed to wide angle and took a picture of Joelle.

She said nothing but her look could have melted an iceberg. *That's blown it*, I thought, as I apologised to her.

'I am sorry, that was a very insensitive thing to do. I will delete the picture,' I said.

She paused and made an effort to smile and sipped her tea.

'Do you have any plans for your holiday?' she asked me.

'Well not really,' I replied, 'I think I will just spend a few days relaxing round the hotel. I have a free daily spa session with my holiday package so I will take advantage of that, but for the moment just reading and sleeping really…' My reply trailed off as she regarded me with a frosty stare.

'I love the spa here,' Joelle said after a few moments. 'When I get time, I come over for a massage myself. It's very relaxing.' She sipped more tea. 'Have you thought of anywhere you should visit?' was her next question. She continued, 'I can suggest some ideas. There is the old sugar cane works.' She paused and looked at me and then suggested, 'Or the Zip Line station built around the old slave camp, that's worth a visit. And there is always the old airport on the Atlantic side of the island. It closed as the runway was too short for modern jets, but there a couple of old airplanes still there.'

I wondered why she was studying me so intently so I simply said, 'I expect I will eventually find them all. They all sound interesting places to take some pictures.'

She looked away and took more tea, and we chatted for a few minutes about the hotel and what there was to do in St Martin, which was not a lot, as it is only a small town. She did tell me that her father had originally owned the all the land behind the beach. He had bought it when it was worthless marshland, but had recognised the potential for tourism and had drained the area and built the original hotel complex. 'We leased it to the hotel operator after he passed away,' she reflected. She then announced that she really must be moving and finished her tea.

'Of course, there is one place you must visit. Glass Bar. It's that place at the far end of the beach.' She pointed to a building set back among the palm trees, which I could just see at the far end of the bay. 'It's my mother's place,' she informed me, 'but she serves the best fish on the island. It's very popular with tourists. They come from all over the island specially to eat there.' I promised her I would give it a go soon.

She got up to leave saying, 'I will look forward to seeing you there soon, I hope.'

What do I make of that? I thought. *She is a bit of a cold fish, and what is that invitation to see me in the bar all about? Just pushing her mother's restaurant I suppose.*

Chapter 6

The meeting with Douglas Jay last Saturday had been a difficult for me. I was trying not to encourage him but equally I was trying to get him to slip up and reveal information about… what? I was very aware that I had been instructed to get close to him and find out what he was up to. In a way that was the easy part as he was a good listener, but I cautioned myself to be careful and not let my guard down again.

After leaving Jay in the bar I found the hotel manager and arranged for Merv, Denzel, and Isaac, the constables who had been assigned to the operation, to be given gardeners' uniforms and tools and start the surveillance. I phoned Merv and told him to find Isaac and report to the hotel, and work out a schedule so they could maintain full daytime surveillance. In the evenings I hoped Jay would visit the bar so I could keep an eye on him. I then left to find Bernie and brief him.

'I returned Jay's bags this morning and invited him to look through them, which he was quite happy to do in front of me. He checked the contents of his bags and that his equipment was working. I noticed nothing unusual. I questioned him about his intentions and he gave nothing away; just said he was going to take it easy for a few days. I have set up the surveillance at the hotel and hinted that he might visit my mother's bar where I can keep an eye on him in the evenings.'

'What happens if he does not go to Glass Bar in the evenings but slips out somewhere?' questioned Bernie.

'Well he can't really go anywhere without transport and I have contacts in the hotel who will let me know if he books a taxi or anything like that.'

'Hmm,' sighed Bernie.

'We still have nothing positive to link him to drug smuggling, but equally we have nothing to prove our suspicions were wrong.'

He pulled out a sheet of paper and spoke as he wrote down: 'He is the only identified match with the tip-off. We have information that Kaeta Island is the centre of the warehousing operation. He appears to have no job, no commitments, but enough money to buy about £4,000 worth of new camera equipment and stay in one of the most expensive hotels on the island for as long as he pleases.

He's cool, does not respond to being detained as we might expect. He has travelled frequently to Amsterdam over the last few months.'

Bernie studied his list and then wrote: 'And we have no tangible evidence that he is not the courier.'

Bernie said nothing for a few minutes while he studied he sheet of paper.

'Is there anything I have missed?' he asked me. I thought for a moment, and shook my head.

'OK,' said Bernie, finally, 'I will make a Coconut status report and see what our American friends say. In the meantime you maintain the surveillance and see if you can get anything more out of him.'

He was right: the circumstantial evidence was building up but we had nothing at all tangible. *Tomorrow*, I thought,

'I will chase up London and see if they have any information on Douglas Jay.'

Tuesday 10th November

I got to the office early, as London is five hours ahead of us. I rang Scotland Yard and spoke to a Sergeant Munroe who complained they only had a couple of days to dig up 'the dirt' but he told me that so far they could confirm that Douglas Jay was a Chartered Accountant, he had a rented flat in Wandsworth, South London, which he had recently given up and a cottage in Wiltshire which he still owned. He had been the finance director of 'VP Ltd', a veterinary drug manufacturing company, which had recently been bought by a large American drug company and had received a substantial pay off on losing his job. And he is divorced as well.

He finished, saying, 'He has no police record. We got all this information from the internet.'

I considered whether this added anything to Bernie's list and added:

Connections with a drug company.

Confirmation that he appears to be relatively wealthy.

I went to report to Bernie and he told me he had heard back from the USA who asked for the close surveillance to be maintained.

'I expect him to come to the bar tonight,' I told Bernie. 'Perhaps I can get something more from him if I speak to him again.'

But he did not come to the bar.

The next day, I visited the hotel, but kept out of sight. I spoke to Merv who confirmed that Jay had spent the last few days around the grounds. He had breakfast and then sat reading for a couple of hours. He swam, had a beer at lunchtime and ate in the restaurant on his own. He went for a spa treatment after lunch, read some more and went into the bar late afternoon. He usually drank three or four beers before going back to his room. My contact in the bar confirmed that he ate in the hotel restaurant on his own, had a brandy after dinner and retired to his room early. 'He is friendly enough,' he said, 'but is making no effort to join in with the other guests.' In other words, he was doing exactly what he told me he was going to do.

I hoped he would come to the bar that evening. He did not, nor did he come the next evening.

I will have to think of a new strategy to get to him, I was thinking.

Chapter 7

I spent most of the first week at the hotel basically doing nothing. I got into a simple routine. Get up, walk round the gardens, have breakfast, find a sun lounger on the beach or under the trees and read using my Kindle. If I spent time in the garden I had a favourite spot that I found the first morning, behind the buildings housing the gym and spa centre, looking out over the gardens past the reception buildings towards the rainforest and Pirate Hill, which I found intriguing – I must find out why it is so called. I also decided that at some point I would have to climb it as I might get some good photographs up there. Joelle said it was near the Zip Line, which I wanted to visit as well. *No hurry though*, I thought, *I have plenty of time.*

To the side of the main hotel buildings there was a swimming pool complex comprising of two pools, and a splash pool for children. The main pool was used for the water sport and fitness sessions. There was a bar and a snack cabin serving the bathers. I kept away from the pool area, as I found it crowded and too noisy.

The beach, on the other hand, was very relaxing. It was naturally sandy, and fringed with palms and coconut trees, which provided some shade. The Caribbean Sea was deep blue and clear, and one of my great pleasures was just lying in the water watching the sky. You had to watch for the current though, it was strong and once nearly caught me out by drifting me away from the beach and up towards the northern headland.

I had found a spot far enough from the hotel to get away from the mass of bathers and shaded by a couple of palms where I set up my lounger most mornings.

The hotel maintenance team was very diligent, I noticed. There was always at least one guy attending the gardens and checking along the palm fringe, picking up dead leaves and so on. I realised I had seen this particular gardener before over the last few days; he was often working near where I was sitting. *A pretty boring job*, I thought.

I had more or less dismissed the thought of Joelle. Time drifted by and as the end of the week approached, I had been in the hotel for six days now. It was time to explore a little further and for the time being Glass Bar sounded about far enough. I decided to take a walk along the beach for an early evening beer.

Glass Bar was situated right at the northern end of the beach just below the headland that separated Glass Bay from St Martin's Bay. It was a ten-minute walk along the beach from the Hotel Glass Bay. It was actually built on an area of raised ground which jutted out into the bay, and separated the main beach from a much smaller little cove immediately under the headland. The bar itself was built slightly towards the rear of this area backing on to the palm trees. There was a small car park in the trees and an access road, which ran up a shallow hill to join up with the coast road running down the Caribbean side of the island.

The bar had been extended out along the spit and into the bay by a wooden structure which was open on three sides and was furnished with dining tables. A stone building with a tiled roof housed the kitchen, toilets, and bar. It had a wood tile roof and roller blinds fitted which could be pulled down to prevent sun or rain bothering the diners. Beyond this was a small restaurant on an open decking area, with only twelve tables, and I reckoned it had a capacity of about thirty people.

I arrived at about 6.00pm. There were not many people in the place as I looked round, moving towards a bar stool in the corner of the bar with a view out over Glass Bay.

There were a couple of older men, who looked like locals, sitting on the veranda drinking beer and smoking, and a man and woman also sitting on at a table on the veranda drinking a rather green-looking cocktail in a tall glass topped with a paper umbrella. There was a girl, who looked about fourteen or fifteen years old, sitting on her own absorbed in writing in an exercise book at a table in the restaurant area.

An elderly woman saw me from the kitchen as I walked in and came out to offer me a drink. I ordered a rum cocktail and looked around the bar. I noticed it was clean and well decorated and well stocked with drinks. The lady, who I guessed was Joelle's mother, came out and started to write the evening menu up on a blackboard on the wall.

I watched as she wrote:

Starters

Black Bean Soup with hot roast pepper cream

Green banana and celery soup

Chilled avocado with crab

Caramel-lime chicken wings

Mains

Baked Spiced Sea Bass with aubergine, spring onion and coconut

Kaeta Island Rundown
Spicy Mackerel and green bananas
Caribbean Fish pie
Coconut chicken curry

Sweets
Lime and orange jelly
Pineapple in lime, vanilla and rum syrup
Mango Honey ice cream
Coconut Crème Brûlée

Reading the menu as it was being written up my mouth began to water as I decided I was definitely eating in Glass Bar this evening. What to have was the question.

As I pondered on this problem I saw Joelle arrive and walk into the kitchen.

After a few minutes she emerged into the bar and served a young couple who had just walked in. I watched her as she walked toward me.

To start a conversation I told her I recognised her as Sergeant de Nouvelas. She told me she was off duty and I should call her Joelle. *Good start*, I thought, as I told her that she had a pretty name. That earned me an icy look and I realised I had put my foot in it again. Fortunately her mother walked out of the kitchen, wanting to be introduced to me. Introductions were made and Joelle retreated into the kitchen as Mary pointed out her grandchild, Jasmine, the teenage girl who was sat at a table doing her homework, I guessed. I wondered if Jasmine was Joelle's daughter or whether Mary had other children.

Mary politely asked me if this was my first time on the

island and whether I had any particular plans, and then asked me if I was going to eat in the bar. I said I was, but had not made my mind up yet.

The bar was still quite empty when Joelle came out of the kitchen. There was no one waiting for drinks and she came over to me and asked me if I was enjoying my holiday. I explained, 'Yes, I am thank you. Not that I have done much yet. I have spent the last few days around the hotel, just sleeping, reading, with the occasional dip in the sea.'

'Nothing exciting, then,' she said.

'No,' I agreed, 'but I do intend to get out a bit more now and see the island.'

'Anywhere in particular?' Joelle enquired.

'Not really,' I answered, 'I have not planned anything yet.'

'Are you here on your own?' she asked next.

'Yes,' I answered, thinking that she had already asked me that once at least.

'No friends on the island you are planning to visit?' she queried.

'No, no one,' I told her. To change the subject I turned my attention to the menu and asked her, 'What is Kaeta Island Run Down?'

She explained it was based on the fish Mary got from the boat that day, usually mackerel, stewed in a coconut milk with onion, yams, tomatoes, and so on, flavoured with thyme, limes and Mary's own all-purpose seasoning.

'She keeps her recipe for that a secret but she sells pots and pots of it to the tourists.' She pointed to a stack of small glass jars on the other end of the bar.

I thought about this but decided to have the Black Bean Soup and Caribbean Fish Pie.

Joelle took my order and went back to the kitchen, saying she had to help Mary.

The place was beginning to fill up now and Mary, Joelle, and the waitress, whose name I gathered was Belinda, were kept busy cooking, and serving food and drink.

Joelle, in a friendly mood, brought my meal out to me, spoke to me for a couple of minutes and invited me to enjoy my meal.

The fish pie was delicious but unlike any fish pie I had ever had before. I could taste it was made with coconut but the other flavours were new to me.

Mary cleared the plates when I had finished so I asked her what was in the dish.

She explained it was made from white fish and shrimp stewed in coconut cream with butter, flour and lime juice. She finished explaining the recipe:

'Coriander and spinach are added when the fish is cooked and the dish is then covered with mashed sweet potato, topped with cheese and grilled until the cheese melts over the top. I am pleased you enjoyed it. Will we see you here again, do you think?'

'Indeed you will,' and I thanked her.

I skipped the sweet and had another beer. Joelle came out of the kitchen, picked up a beer for herself and came over to speak to me. She introduced me to Sean.

'Our part-time bar man who comes in when the place is busy,' she informed me, and went on to explain that she did not usually work in the bar all evening as she had liked to get Jasmine home at a reasonable hour. She, again, questioned me about my family and plans and what I intend to do on the island. *I really don't want to talk about England and family such as it is*, I thought, *but I suppose she is just making conversation*. I changed the subject and asked her if she was still driving round in the Suzuki.

'No,' she smiled, 'that's a police vehicle. We have an old Toyota Starlet and new Suzuki SZ3 Wagon which Mary and I use. I usually drive the Toyota but I also have a big Triumph motorcycle that I like to ride. I love it, it's fast and the only one on the island,' she told me enthusiastically. I had not placed her as motorcycle lover so I was a bit lost for words, but was prompted to explain that I needed to hire a car or something so I could start to get round the island.

'Any idea what you want to see?' she asked.

I thought, and replied, 'Well, you mentioned the Zip Line; I would like to try that, and the slave village sounds interesting. I must go Pirate Hill as well as I should get some good pictures from the top. And then there is the old airfield.' I shrugged and smiled at her and continued, 'But, I think the first thing would be to arrange a guided tour of the island. That would be the quickest way to learn about the place and decide where I want to visit again.'

Joelle had finished her drink by now and glancing at the clock she rather abruptly rose to her feet, saying, 'If you will excuse me I must go now and take Jasmine home. Goodbye.' And she walked out.

Chapter 8

Joelle de Nouvelas; Thursday 13th November

'That Englishman you were telling me about, the one you wanted me to look out for, I think that must be him sitting at the end of the bar.' Mary whispered to me as walked into the kitchen of Glass Bar.

Mary is my mother, now in her late sixties, although she will not admit it. She owns Glass Bar and runs it virtually on her own. As well as Sean, she also employs a waitress, Belinda, who works most evenings. I come in and help behind the bar sometimes. Mary loves cooking and the bar has built up an excellent reputation for its local fish dishes.

Mary has silver hair, which she ties in a bun at the back of her head. She was born on Kaeta Island, as were the previous generations of her family, and she takes great pleasure in telling the tourists that her forebears were slaves, although she has no proof that this was so, but I suppose it's a good bet that they were. Like many Kaeta Island women she has put on a bit of weight over the years. She does not need to work: my father was a shrewd investor on the island, and when he passed away a few years ago, with the exception of a bequest to me, she inherited all his wealth. She likes people, she enjoys company, and, as she says, what better way is there to meet people than running Glass Bar?

I peered round the kitchen door looking towards the

end of the bar.

'Yes, that's him,' I confirmed as I pulled back into the kitchen to consider the situation. 'Be polite but not too friendly. Try to find what his plans are for the rest of the holiday. But Mary,' I instructed, 'I have him under surveillance: you must not say anything, but I want him to feel comfortable here, so please be friendly.'

'I am always friendly,' Mary answered slightly archly. 'Anyway, what is he supposed to have done to be under surveillance?'

'We think he may be involved with drugs.'

Mary responded doubtfully, 'Oh, you know what I think of drugs, I don't what anything like that in here.'

'It's all right Mary,' Joelle assured her. 'I am sure he does not take drugs or bring them in here, we are just keeping an eye on him as we think he may lead us to people on the island who we want to speak to.'

I realised I had probably said too much so I reassured her again.

'Just be normal, Mary. Please don't say anything to anyone, just let me know if you see anything you think is odd.'

I went out to the bar and served cocktails to couple standing there. As they went to a table to sit down I moved up the bar and asked Douglas if he would another drink.

'Hi,' he said to me, 'it's Sergeant de Nouvelas isn't it?'

Of course he knew it was me, so in an effort to appear friendly I said, 'I am off duty now so please call me Joelle.'

'Joelle.' He savoured the name out loud, saying, 'That's a very pretty name.'

Here we go, I thought, *the chat up line*. Fortunately Mary came bustling out of the kitchen at this point.

'Joelle, introduce me to your friend.'

'He's not really a friend, Mother. I met Douglas at the airport over a mix-up on the passenger lists.'

'Well,' she said, pushing past me to talk to Douglas, 'you are very welcome here.' She looked at his empty glass and went on, 'And Joelle is a poor bargirl. Your glass is empty, what can I get you?'

Douglas replied, 'I will switch to beer, thank you.'

I gratefully retired to the kitchen as Mary started pointing to Jasmine, who was sitting at a table drawing, and telling him that Jasmine was her granddaughter.

Mary came back into the kitchen to carry on cooking and I returned to the bar.

There was no one waiting for a drink so I went over to talk to Douglas. I asked him what he had done so far and if he had plans go visiting anywhere. He was non-committal and changed the subject, asking me about the menu. I took his food order and went back into the kitchen.

By now the bar was getting full and we were all busy, so there was no immediate opportunity for further discussion with Douglas. Mary cleared his meal away and brought the plates into the kitchen as I was washing up.

'He enjoyed the meal,' Mary was pleased when customers liked her dishes, 'and he says he is coming again back soon.'

I finished the washing up and went back out to the bar, pulled a beer for myself, and went over to talk to Douglas again and introduce him to Sean.

I asked Douglas if he was on his own or had family with him and asked about his holiday plans. He said he was on his own this holiday and immediately changed the subject by asking me if I always drove the police Suzuki.

Again I noted he always changes the subject rather than discuss anything personal. It surprised him to learn that I enjoyed riding a powerful motorcycle. I love riding that bike and I remember how, when I was a little girl, I used to love riding round the island on the back of my father's motorbike and him telling me to hold on tight. He had a Triumph as well.

He asked me about car hire as he wanted to travel round the island, so I asked him again if there was anywhere particular he wanted to see. I noted that he referred to the Zip Line and slave camp and the old airfield but did not give anything away, and then he said he would like to arrange an island tour. I thought he might be getting too friendly and was dropping hints. It was time to leave before I got too involved so I said, 'If you will excuse me I must go now and take Jasmine home. Goodbye,' and walked out.

Friday 14th November

I arrived at the police station just after 9.00am. I was supposed to start punctually but Bernie allowed me to be a little late as I usually took Jasmine to school on my way to work. In any event Bernie usually arrived late himself, and this morning was no exception.

I waited impatiently for him to arrive. I gave him time to collect his first coffee of the morning and then put my head round his door. 'Can I speak with you Bernie?'

'Come in.' He waved me towards a chair.

I explained that Douglas had not really moved from the hotel yet and had not made contact with anyone. Merv's reports from his surveillance at the hotel confirmed this.

I told Bernie that Douglas had started visiting Mary's Bar and this had given me opportunity to talk to him. 'He is vague about his plans, and changes the subject when I ask personal questions,' I explained, 'but on more than one occasion he says he wants to visit the Zip Line and old airfield.' I continued. 'He wants to hire a car so he can get round on his own but first he says he wants to find a guided tour of the island.'

Bernie reflected for a few moments and then said to me, 'You haven't seen the recent report from London have you? The say they have nothing more specific on Douglas Jay, but one of the employees at the veterinary drug company he used to work for was arrested for drug dealing a few months ago. Apparently he was stealing pills from the production line, carrying them out in his pocket and then selling them. There is no evidence that Jay was connected with this at all, but the arrested person did work in the internal audit department which reported to Jay.' We both thought about this and eventually Bernie said, 'We must be careful not to jump to conclusions. I think we need to carry on watching Jay to see what he does.'

He looked directly at me. 'You once worked for a travel company and know as much about the island and its history as anyone, don't you?'

I guessed where he was going with this, as I reminded him that I had only spent six months as a travel courier and only once conducted an island tour when the official guide was sick.

'I think you should take Jay on his island tour and show him where he can hire a car. See if you can get a tracker put on it.' I really was not sure I wanted to do this, and I realised that I would have to be very careful to avoid getting too involved with Douglas, and that I would have to have a very good story to be believed. I decided to embroider my travel rep experience a little and tell Douglas that occasionally I filled in for a friend organising island tours when he got busy. I would tell Douglas the cost would be US$75. Sean runs sailing trips for tourists. I decided to tell him to back up the story if Douglas asked who the friend was.

Chapter 9

Douglas Jay; Friday 14th November

This morning, I sat in the garden trying to read a story on my Kindle, but my concentration was distracted by thought of the previous couple of evenings. I had certainly enjoyed Glass Bar and I liked Mary. She was friendly and welcoming and a very good cook. *Yes*, I reflected, *I could certainly make a habit of spending my evenings there.*

However I was not sure of Joelle. She bothered me. Being a policewoman, asking questions comes easily to her, but I did get the impression that she was interrogating me at times. She is certainly not exactly friendly, but comes across as reserved. *A pity*, I thought, *'aloof' is the word that describes her. She is attractive and obviously intelligent and it would be nice to get to know her better.* Another reason for going back to Glass Bar. I was surprised when she admitted she enjoyed motorcycling and had a powerful bike herself. *That says something about her*, I thought, *there is more to her than meets the eye.* That made me think. I enjoyed motorcycling myself and had an old 1960s BSA Gold Star bike in my garage back in Wiltshire. With the pressures of work I had not even seen it for the last couple of years, but I reflected it might be fun if I could hire a motorbike rather than a car. I'll ask Joelle if that's possible.

Late afternoon, at my usual time, I showered, changed, and set off to walk along the beach to Glass Bar. There was someone sitting in my usual seat, so I got a beer from Belinda and went out to sit on the terrace. Looking directly out across the terrace is the Caribbean Sea and I watched a couple of cruise ships coming up from the south, presumably making for Kaeta Town. To my right lay the headland, separating Glass Bay from St Martin's Bay, while to my left I could see down Glass Bay to Trigs point at the southern end of the bay, and beyond to the higher ground at the end of the island as it curved round into the Caribbean Sea. I did not notice Joelle as she walked up.

'May I join you please?' she asked.

'Of course,' I replied. She sat down without saying anything initially, as we both watched the cruise boats move slowly north.

'They are docking in Kaeta Town for a couple of days,' she informed me. 'Tomorrow the passengers have an option of an island tour or watching a cricket match; ship's crew versus passengers, in the international stadium. And the next day they have a free day before they sail on the St Lucia overnight. Sunday is going to be a nightmare as we will have four cruise ships in at the same time.'

'You are well informed,' I commented.

'I have to be,' she replied, 'I plan the town security when the cruise ships are in.'

'That must be a big job.'

'Not too bad most of the time. When all the ships are in town we just have to put extra patrols on around the markets in the evenings to watch out for pickpockets and drug pushers.' She said watching me carefully. I was expecting her to slip back into her police mode, but she did not. Instead she said, 'Are you still interested in taking a guided tour of the island?'

'Yes, but I have done nothing about finding a guide yet.'

'That's OK,' she continued, 'I sometimes fill in for a friend when he is busy and take island tours around. I could show you around if you like. The tour costs US$75, I am afraid.'

I was pleased, I did not know if $75 was cheap or expensive but I did not really care. This was an opportunity to get to know Joelle a bit better.

'That would be very kind of you,' I said, 'and I would very much like to take you up on that.'

'Not a problem,' Joelle replied, 'I have a day off in a couple of days. I will pick you up on Monday at 10.00am from your hotel reception.'

'Thanks,' I said, to confirm the arrangement and continued: 'One more favour, if I may ask you?'

'Go on.'

'Would you know where I might hire a motorbike for the rest of my stay?'

Joelle thought for a bit and said, 'There is Rusty Rick's, sorry, that's what we call him, it is really Rick's Auto Shop. He mainly sells cars and does repairs, but usually has a few bikes and scooters as well. He might rent you one. He works out of a workshop in the commercial area outside Kaeta Town. We could call in and ask him when we do the tour if you like.'

'That would be great.' I thanked her. We talked a bit more about the weather and the cruise ships and she quizzed me about where I would like to visit on the island. I told her I would leave it completely to her to decide where to go. She said she would put an itinerary together. 'Are you coming over here tomorrow?' she asked me. I said I would be and she said she would meet me and show me her tour plan. Belinda brought us out another couple of beers which we sat drinking and talking. Joelle finished hers before me and apologised that she had to leave to take Jasmine home.

'She still has homework to do and she gets distracted too easily here,' she explained

When she had left I went in and ordered a prawn and green banana curry for dinner, thinking that had gone well.

Chapter 10

Douglas Jay; Saturday 15th November

I had used the last of my sun block. I went into the hotel shop to buy some more and exchanged pleasantries with the girl who runs the shop. She asked the usual questions such as: 'Are you enjoying your holiday?' and, 'Have you been to the island before?' But then she commented that I seemed to spend all my time in the hotel.

'Not for much longer,' I replied. 'I have booked a guided tour of the island on the day after tomorrow.'

She looked at me and said, a little nervously, 'Will you be going to the Zip Line and sugar plantation?'

'I expect so,' I replied.

'I would be very grateful if you could do me a huge favour.'

'As long as it's legal!' I joked.

'Oh! Yes, of course it is. It is just that I have these new advertising brochures for our gift shop in Nelsons Dock. They were delivered here and I have to get some up to the Zip Line and sugar plantation for their tourist information stands, but I am on my own here and can't leave the shop. There is a bundle of them and if you could just deliver them to the receptionists they will know what to do with them.'

I agreed I would take the brochures but, I thought, perhaps not with Joelle escorting me around. I was looking forward to meeting Joelle again, and I wanted to look my best, hopefully to impress her. I spent time that afternoon showering and choosing what to wear. I opted for a dark blue polo shirt and light blue slacks. They were both just a fraction on the tight side and as I looked in the mirror, I realised how much weight I had put on over the last year or so. *I must shift that*, I thought, and resolved to start running again.

That evening I again made way along the beach to meet Joelle.

I sat out on the veranda again and watched a yacht tacking across the bay, sailing up against the evening breeze from Three Sisters Point at the southern end of the island. The yachtsman gave up in the end, dropped his sail and used the engine. Joelle arrived later that evening by which time I was well into my second rum punch. She sat down and greeted me. 'Sorry, I am late. I took Jasmine home earlier tonight and left her with instructions to finish her homework before getting her laptop out.'

That evening the sunset was spectacular. A fiery white globe of sun sinking towards the horizon, and firing out cherry-red light, which turned a vibrant orange as it fanned out in both directions. As the sun sank, the golden path it projected across the sea gradually faded until all that was left was black water with a few sparkling golden pinpricks as the wave tops caught the last reflections of the setting sun. The purple clouds darkened as they slowly rolled across the sky, taking on an orange glow as the sun dropped lower in the sky. Joelle and I sat together in silence watching this panoramic display of colour unfold before us.

'I think the conditions are right this evening for us the

see the green flash as the sun sets. If you look carefully at the moment the sun dips below the horizon you should see a green flash as the light is refracted.'

'There,' she exclaimed a few moments later, 'did you see it?' I admitted that I had missed it. Gradually the colours faded as night marched up from the east pushing the last hues of orange below the horizon. 'Sunsets are so romantic,' Joelle whispered as she looked out across the now dark sea, and rather forlornly whispered under her breath, 'it's a sight lovers should watch together.' On hearing this, I looked at her in surprise and thought I saw her blushing. I was about to reach out for hand and say something romantic in return, but I think she realised I had overheard her private thoughts and she rushed off to turn the veranda lights on. Assuming her usual reserved demeanour, she returned with a tourist map of the island, which she laid out on the table in front of me.

'I thought we would drive up from your hotel and round St Martin's Point. It is the posh, expensive part of the island where the millionaires and film stars have their villas. We will then drive through St Martin's and round the bay to Kaeta Town. If we have time, and you want to, we can stop and I will show you round the spice and fish markets. We will detour to look at the cricket stadium but then we have to go back into Kaeta Town and out past the oil storage depot to Rusty Rick's.'

She traced the coast road past the hospital and airport at the northern end of the island saying, 'This bit is a bit boring. The soil is very poor here and it's just flat scrub land. We follow the coast road round to Old Town where we stop for bit. From there we head up towards Pirate Hill, at 1,500 metres it's our mountain, and on to the Zip Line. We can stop there and look at the old slave camp if you wish.'

'Is it possible to get up to the rim of the volcano?' I asked.

'It is,' Joelle informed me, 'but only by foot. There is a path leading up from the above the top station of the Zip Line but it's quite steep and difficult in places. We won't have time to climb it on the tour.'

She continued to trace a route on the map back through Old Town and then travelling towards the south along the Atlantic coast road.

'We have a choice here. We can either take this road, which goes to the sugar plantation and then winds up through the hills, or we stay on the Atlantic coast road and stop at the old airfield. There is not much there except a couple of old derelict aircraft and some tumbled down buildings.' She was watching me carefully as she explained this.

'I think the sugar plantation sounds more interesting,' I replied.

Joelle continued. 'We stop for lunch at Alice's restaurant and then go down the Nelsons Dock. If we have time we can drive round the southern end of the island past Grumble and the marina there and Three Sisters Bay on the Caribbean side. The Spice Farm is up in the rainforest here,' she pointed, 'but I don't think we will have time to go there as I want to follow the Caribbean coast road back to your hotel.'

'Perhaps we could go there another time,' I said and agreed, 'that looks like a good day out to me, thank you.'

'It will be a full day,' Joelle warned me, 'can you be ready earlier, say 9.30am?'

I agreed I could be.

'I just need to sort out a car now. I will try and get hold of one with air conditioning,' she concluded. Joelle started telling me that one of her favourite places was Three Sisters Bay. 'It's very secluded and usually deserted as you can only get there by boat. There is a track down from the road but it's very narrow and quite steep, but you can just get a motorbike down it.'

At this point Mary came out and told Joelle that she needed help in the kitchen and asked me what I would like to eat.

I ate my meal and had a couple of beers but did not see Joelle again that evening.

I asked Mary where she was and she told me she had helped in the kitchen through the busy period, but then gone home.

I thought we had broken the ice a little that evening and I was disappointed she had left without at least saying goodbye.

Chapter 11

Douglas Jay; Sunday 16th November

I saw on the room television that it was 16th November. I was now nine days into the holiday and definitely relaxing and looking forward to the Island Tour and getting some transport, as there were things I wanted to do on my own.

I spent the morning as usual, and went for a run before breakfast. I was serious about the need to get more exercise and shift some of my waistline. After breakfast I took the Kindle into the garden for a reading session.

After lunch I went for a massage in the hotel spa and then called into the shop to pick up the brochures. I was presented with a big bundle held together with an elastic band. It occurred to me that it would be much easier to deliver to the Zip Line and sugar plantation if I wrapped them in separate parcels. The shop only had large carrier bags so I got some brown paper and sticky tape from reception and took it all back to my room to wrap later.

I checked the camera equipment, put a charged battery and empty memory card into the camera ready for tomorrow's trip. I then spent an hour or so downloading the pictures I had taken so far into my laptop. I wrapped the parcels and then I ran through all the pictures full size on the screen, deleting the slightly out of focus and the shots that did not work.

While I was doing this, the gardener decided that the shrubs outside my chalet window needed cutting back and the window cleaning, much to my annoyance as he kept peering through the window and disturbed my concentration. Eventually I went out and asked him to go away.

After this I went for a swim in the sea and dried off by lying on the beach sunbathing. As the sun cooled off I decided it was time to shower and change and make my way up to Glass Bar.

My stool at the back of the bar was empty and so settled myself on it and ordered a cold beer. I looked round. It was 6.30pm and the bar was beginning to fill up. There was group of four, two overweight men with two equally overweight women, sitting on the veranda noisily talking and drinking gin and tonics. I listened to them giggling about something while the two women pulled their market purchases from bags to show each other who had grabbed the best bargain in the Kaeta Town Market that day. *Definitely English*, I thought, as I turned my attention to the other couple sitting on the veranda. They were much younger, drinking beers and holding hands whispering to each other. *They are either newly married or about to get married*, I decided.

My surveillance moved further into the bar where there were a couple of men sitting. The older man was slightly overweight with long but receding hair tied in a ponytail, wearing bright red shorts and an orange shirt undone at the front in order to display his large gold medallion. The younger man was also wearing shorts, very short ones, with a tight vest through which his bodybuilding efforts and suntan were clearly visible. He wore his blond hair in a sort of shaved crew cut. I decided he must bleach his hair, as it was an unnatural shade, almost white in colour. *He must also wax his chest*, I thought, as I decided they were probably gay. A couple of local Islanders sat at a table in the bar area drinking beer and playing billiards. I had seen them in the bar before and recognised the smaller of the two as the fisherman who brought fish in for Mary each day. Jasmine was sitting in a corner concentrating on her homework. *She is a younger version of mother*, I thought. She had much paler skin than her mother's and her hair was lighter in colour, but they had the same eyes and facial features. I guessed she was about fifteen years old.

A middle-aged couple accompanied by an older lady walked into the bar. All three were conservatively dressed: the man in a white shirt and light fawn cotton trousers and the two women in floral print dresses. The two women had similar features and I decided they were probably mother and daughter. They paused to read the menu, which I noticed was the same as it was yesterday, while the man asked what they would like to drink. The women sat at a table while he made his way over to the bar.

There was no one behind the bar and after he had waited patiently for some time he rapped on the bar surface and called out, 'Service please!' Mary rushed out of the kitchen looking very hassled and apologised to them as she served them drinks.

She immediately ran back into the kitchen. After a few moments there was a tremendous crash. Followed by a few moments of silence before we heard a sobbing noise. Everyone in the bar turned to look, but it was Jasmine who reacted first and ran into the kitchen. I followed and heard Jasmine say she would clear the mess up. A large pan of soup had fallen on the floor and the soup was spreading out around Mary's feet. Mary was crying. Jasmine went out to the back to get a mop and bucket while I went up to Mary, took her by the arm and led her to a chair in the corner of the kitchen. 'What on earth is the matter Mary?' I asked.

Mary was trying desperately, and unsuccessfully, to compose herself. 'I am working all my own in the kitchen,' she sobbed. 'I have people in the restaurant and at eight o'clock I have a party of sixteen coming in. I just don't know how I will cope!'

'Where are Belinda, Sean and Joelle tonight?' I asked.

'Belinda is sick. She phoned in earlier. I have tried to get Sean but he is not answering his phone and Joelle has just phoned in to say she has to work tonight. Jasmine can help but she has a lot of homework to finish and I won't have her working behind the bar anyway, she is too young.'

'I could help you?' I volunteered.

'No, you are a visitor.' She smiled at me. 'I can't let you work here.'

'Actually,' I retorted, 'I think you can't not let me work tonight.'

Chapter 12

Joelle de Nouvelas; Sunday 16th November

It was the morning after I had watched the evening sunset with Douglas and I was still thinking about that evening. Sitting next to Douglas, I had felt emotions that had been dormant within me for some time, and thinking about it now I realised that, while I loved Jasmine and Mary dearly, it was not the same as having someone to love and share my life with. For a moment, yesterday evening, I had felt very alone. I could like Douglas and I knew he had overheard me, and I thought for a moment he was going to say something in return. I must stay professional and not get involved. I had to shake myself away from these melancholy thoughts. It was going to be a long, hard day.

There were already two cruise ships in Kaeta Town and another two were docking during the day. Two ships would be leaving after dinner about 10.00pm I was told, and the other two were scheduled to leave before breakfast next morning.

The evening would be the worst time as the markets would stay open for the tourists and all Kaeta Island lowlifes would be on the prowl. Everyone, even Bernie, was on duty today. First things first, though. Bernie wants to see me about the Coconut surveillance. I walked into the office and reported, 'Not much has developed since we last spoke. The guys who were watching him at the hotel say that he still follows the same routine every day except that he has started going for an early morning run. They don't know where he goes as they have trouble following him without being seen.'

Bernie interrupted me. He wanted to know how I was going to handle the Island Tour with Douglas. We went through my proposed route and Bernie said he would get some officers stationed around the island in case I got into difficulty.

'I don't think I will, I am not exactly on an undercover stakeout!' I joked.

'Nevertheless,' he ignored my joke, 'it's better to be safe, and if he does do anything you will need backup, fast.' He had further thoughts. 'I think you need to take a police vehicle. At least then you have a radio and equipment if necessary.'

'I can hardly drive round the island in a marked police car,' I said.

'No,' he agreed, 'but you could at least take the Suzuki Jeep.'

I agreed it was not marked, but pointed out, 'It's hardly discreet – it's got a bloody great aerial and two blue lights on the roof!'

'Hmm.' He drummed his fingers on the desk. 'I wonder if we could borrow the commissioner's car for the day. He has that new Lexus GS: that's unmarked, but it has a radio, and the blue lights are hidden behind the grille.'

'Yes,' I cautioned, 'and everyone on the island will recognise it, with its little bonnet flags waving in the wind. And anyway it's Sunday and he will be at home.'

'That's not a problem,' countered Bernie, 'I will phone him at home. We will get the flag taken off and make up some window stickers. You are using Sean as a cover, you said, so I will have a sign made up, 'Sean's Island Tours', to go in the window. Perfect, that's agreed then.'

I said no more as he picked up the phone and dialled the Commissioner's number. I listened while Bernie apologised for bothering him and explained that we wanted to borrow the car for an undercover operation tomorrow. 'We only need it for a day.'

'You could use our Suzuki Jeep if you need transport,' Bernie told the Commissioner, grinning as he spoke.

'Thank you sir, I will arrange to pick the car up today so we can get it ready.' He hung up and smiled at me. 'All sorted, but he was not keen, especially on using the Suzuki.' He chuckled.

'You can pick the car up tonight when you finish. I suppose you can drive an automatic?'

I mumbled something and wondered what I had let myself in for.

I left Bernie still chuckling to himself about having requisitioned the Commissioner's new car and I went down to find the desk sergeant to see about today's rota for patrolling the town with the docks full of cruise ships. He informed me, 'We are OK for cover during the daytime but I think we are going to need everyone out this evening. It is going to be very busy in the town all evening.'

I groaned to myself. I knew what this meant; overtime and extra duties, and that would include me. I made a mental note to phone Mary, when I had a chance, and let her know I would be working late and would not be able to help in the bar this evening. I needed to ask her to pick up Jasmine and that I would pick her up from the bar when I was finally off duty. Hopefully it would not be too late.

I spent the rest of the morning reading Merv's reports on his surveillance of Douglas. They did not tell me much, other than he more or less stuck to the same routine each day. I wondered if the early morning runs were significant, but all Merv reported was that he ran through the gardens and then along the road to St Martin's, reappearing about forty-five minutes later running back along the beach. I supposed that he could be meeting someone but I thought it more likely he would wait until after the Island Tour when he had a better understanding of the geography of the island, and he would probably not make any contact until he had his personal transport.

I went to speak with the duty sergeant to see if he had found a tracker for me. He had not and said he did not think he'd get one in time.

'The nearest source is Florida, and I will have to buy one and there is no budget,' he told me.

'Forget it,' I said, 'I will tell Merv to just follow him.'

I went out at lunchtime for a break away from the office and ate a sandwich on my own in the cathedral grounds. The Anglican Cathedral was built by the British at the end of the 19th century and is a typical Victorian mock Gothic structure, but it is situated only a short walk from the police station. It's built on higher ground than the rest of the town so it has some spectacular views across the Market and over the docks. What I like, though, is the cemetery behind the cathedral. It is a place of peace and quiet where I like to sit on one of the benches and eat my lunch in tranquillity.

After lunch, I thought, I would go for a walk around the markets. As I expected they were not at all busy. It was too hot for most of the tourists, but come six o'clock, as the heat of the afternoon gave way to an off shore breeze and the town cooled, they would all be out in force.

When I returned to the station later that afternoon, Merv had just come in to ready for the evening's patrols. We spoke for a few minutes and I told him that when Douglas Jay got his own transport we would drop the hotel surveillance, but I wanted him and the two constables assigned to the surveillance to follow Douglas Jay and see where he went and what he did on his trips round the island. I told Merv he had better hire a car so he could be discreet. He updated me with the latest surveillance report.

'This afternoon he went into his chalet and did some work on his computer. I could not see what he was doing and I aroused his suspicions, being outside the chalet for such a long time. He came out and asked me to move on. Anyway, while I was looking through the window I did see him wrapping up something in a brown paper parcel and sticky tape. I could not see what it was.'

My immediate thought was that he was preparing for a drop at long last. I doubted it would happen tomorrow but as soon as he had his own transport he would make his move. I walked down to the staff rest room, which was filling up as additional officers came in for the evening patrols around the market. I made myself a large white coffee from the newly installed coffee machine. The Commissioner had presented into the station one Christmas, proudly informing us that it used real coffee beans! It certainly made a better coffee than the old machines on the detectives' floor.

I bought a ham roll from the sandwich machine in the corner and remembered I had not yet phoned Mary. I drank the coffee and ate most of the roll. I returned to my desk upstairs and made my call to her. She did not sound very happy.

Chapter 13

Douglas Jay; Sunday evening, 16th November

Mary actually looked relieved as I said, 'Don't argue just tell me what I can do first to help. I do have some experience working in a bar you know!'

I did not tell her that it was thirty years ago when I was a student working in the local pub.

'Perhaps you could set the tables: you need to push some of them together to make up sixteen places, and could you watch the bar as well. If you could do that I can get on with the cooking.'

I found Joelle's apron, I thought I had better look the part, and walked out into the restaurant. I looked at the table layout and realised that the only way I could push six tables together was to put them down the sidewall of the restaurant, and even that would be a tight fit. At this point I heard the loud English group bellowing for a waiter. I walked out to veranda and up to their table.

'Took your time didn't you!' I was greeted by the larger of the two men.

'Two large beers, pints mind, and two large gins and tonics, slim-line,' I was instructed.

I knew there were no marked pint glasses left in the bar so I used the largest glasses I could find and pulled a couple of large draft beers. I prepared a couple of double gins and went into the kitchen to get some ice and lemon. Mary was busy so I asked Jasmine if she knew where the ice and lemons were. She filled an ice bucket for me and showed me where the lemons and limes were. I went back to the bar, put ice and a slice of both fruits into each glass, put the drinks on a tray and took them out to the veranda. The two men looked at the beers and the belligerent one said, glaring at me, 'We asked for pints.'

I returned to the kitchen. Picked up a measuring jug and walked back to the foursome. I measured a pint of 'Mr. Belligerent's beer into the jug, threw what was left in the glass over the side of the veranda, refilled his glass and placed it in front of him. I repeated the exercise for the second glass of beer, and walked back to the bar before they could say anything. As I walked past the young couple they nodded and smiled at me and as I walked into the bar room I saw Jasmine giggling.

The two gays had empty glasses so as I passed them I asked if they would like another drink. 'Please,' they said, 'a couple of large beers, and we don't mind how full the glasses are!' They gave me a friendly smile. I looked around the bar to find where everything was kept. I put some white wine bottles into the fridge behind the bar to cool and topped up the beers in the tall glass-fronted beer chiller. I found price list behind the bar with a note pad on which the drinks for each table were recorded, I added the drinks I had served and noticed that Mary had forgotten to note down what the middle-aged couple had been served.

Wearing my apron and with a tea towel slung over my shoulder I was beginning to feel like a barman. Mary peered around the door. 'I forgot to tell you, Douglas, the party of sixteen asked to sit on the veranda.'

I looked out to the veranda and saw 'Mr. Belligerent' and his party finishing their drinks. *I bet they are going*, I thought. I knew from my previous visits that all drinks and food were entered into the till so I asked Jasmine if she knew how it worked. She came over and showed me how to call up the different computer menus. Each menu had a picture of the drink and description and all that was need was to touch the picture and the till did the rest of the transaction. 'The price of drinks are all preloaded,' Jasmine told me, 'I set it up for Grandma, but you have to enter the food prices separately as they are all different.'

Simple, I thought, as I ran off a bill for 'Mr. Belligerent' and took it out for them.

I was right, they were leaving and were already halfway out when I reached the veranda. I stopped them and gave them the bill. They produced a credit card and, as the card reader was not a portable one, I had ask them to come back to the till so I could process the card. They did not leave a tip. It was a good job they left when they did as I would have had to have moved them to make up six tables. Jasmine told me where the table cloths, cutlery and condiments were kept and started laying tables with me. I thanked her and told her I could manage and to go and finish her homework. I spent the next forty-five minutes preparing the tables and working the bar. The restaurant was getting busier even though the big party had not turned up yet.

At one point Mary came out and wrote up the day's menu. There was no soup today, so she had substituted a starter of melon with Parma ham.

'I hope it not too popular as I could only find one packet of ham,' she whispered to me.

The main courses today were a green and red pepper salad with snapper fish.

'I have made the dressing but we need to cut the peppers when it's ordered so they are nice and fresh,' she told me. The fish of the day was hot roast snapper with coconut, chilli and lime salsa. 'I have got all the fishes prepared and ready go into the oven. I will part cook them ready for when someone orders,' Mary told me as she wrote up the menu.

'The fish pie is the same as you had the other night. That's all pre-cooked and portions prepared in the freezer. We just microwave that when it ordered.'

The last dish on the night's menu was roast salmon with a lime and coriander butter, with salad.

'The salad is all made. The salmon is out of the freezer and will only take ten minutes to cook.' She looked round the bar area and nodded. 'Good,' she said, 'I think we are ready to go,' and disappeared back into the kitchen.

I was being beckoned over by the table of three. They ordered two starters and two hot snapper dishes and a small portion of salmon and salad. I took the order into the kitchen. Mary looked at it and said, 'That will be ready in ten minutes. As you take orders, pin them up on that bar so we don't get in a mess.'

There was a bit of a lull at that point so I went over and sat down with Jasmine. I had noticed earlier that she had been frowning and chewing her pencil.

'Something the matter?' I asked her.

She looked up and said, 'It's my maths homework: we have started algebra and I just can't get the hang of it. I did my best last week but got it all wrong so I had to stay behind again tonight while Miss Stevens, the maths teacher, explained it to me again, but I still don't understand and I don't know how to do these ten equations!' she cried.

'Let me look,' I said. 'Perhaps we can work it out together.' Unfortunately, at that point the party of sixteen turned up. 'Put that to one side,' I told Jasmine, 'and finish the rest of your homework, and we will do the equations together later when the bar is less busy.'

I went back to the bar as the party began to assemble,

discussing what they wanted to drink. They all decided to start with cocktails. Now, I can cope with three rum punches, and a rum and Coke, but when they asked for two Blue Hawaiians I had to go and ask Mary. She pointed at an old dog-eared cocktail recipe book and advised me that if they wanted something not in the book to tell them we did not have the ingredients. The Blue Hawaiian is made from rum, pineapple, Curacao and coconut cream. A Havana Cooler was next and this one turned out to be rum, with ginger ale and ice and topped with a sprig of mint. A couple of ladies in the group wanted martinis which sent me off searching for a jar of olives, while three men in the group wanted Manhattans, made with rye whisky, vermouth and biters. I was kept busy at the bar preparing and serving drinks, and passing food orders through to Mary while the party adjourned to their table.

More people came in and the place was getting quite full and noisy. Indeed at one point I thought we were going to run out of tables, but fortunately we did not.

Jasmine had finished her homework. 'We will do my maths won't we? I must hand it in tomorrow,' she asked as she went into the kitchen to help Mary. I promised her that we would.

I had heard the big party talking about a birthday, so I guessed this was someone's celebration and it occurred to me to find some champagne and put it in the cooler.

Most of the diners inside the restaurant had, by this time, ordered their food and Mary was about halfway through preparing and serving their orders.

'See if you can delay the big party order for a bit so I can finish off the orders in the queue,' she whispered to me as I collected a couple of meals from the kitchen.

After serving another two customers with their meals I

went out to the veranda and asked if the sixteen would like some more drinks. A lot of the group had switched to beers, some to gin and tonics and only a couple of requests for cocktails this time. I took their drinks out and told them I would come back for the food order shortly. They nodded in agreement, but shortly afterwards called me over to take the food order. Mary looked at their order and asked me if I could help with the preparation. Fortunately, as most customers were eating, the demand for drinks had fallen so I had some time. Mary pointed me to a chopping board and knife and told me to make the green and red pepper salads.

'Cut up a green, yellow, and red pepper into slices with some chopped coriander leaves,' she instructed me. 'Add a little demerara sugar and some olive oil, salt and pepper. Grill a couple of fish and flake over the peppers, and drizzle that dressing over the top.'

I did this while keeping an eye on the restaurant. The big group called me across and ordered ten bottles of champagne. Lucky, I thought, as I had already put twelve in the cooler. I served them and topped up the cooler, anticipating the demand for replacement bottles, which did not take long to come. When I returned to the kitchen Mary was ready to serve starters and had almost finished the main courses for the sixteen diners. Jasmine and I carried the dishes out. She asked me to make the coffee, which I did, having got to grips with the machine, while she prepared sweets for those who had ordered. By now it was getting on for 10.00pm and I was busy in the bar again, serving last drinks of the evening and teas and coffees. Mary had finished in the kitchen and had come out into the restaurant area and bar and was talking, joking and amusing the diners, much to their delight and Mary's, who had taken over control of the bar from me.

I went into the kitchen and Jasmine and I started attacking the mountain of washing up and cleaning up.

Jasmine had now got over her initial shyness with me and we chatted jokingly away, as worked together, talking about the evening and the variety of customers. I asked Jasmine about her mother and whether she had a man in her life. She told me that Joelle had once had a boyfriend but it had not lasted.

'Mum says that being in the police she has to be careful who she has for friends. She sometimes meets the people she works with at the police station and goes for a night out.' I wondered where this would put me on Joelle's scale of acceptable friends.

Chapter 14

Douglas Jay: Sunday night, 16th November

It took Jasmine and I about an hour to clean up in the kitchen and when we had finished by about 11.00pm there were still a good number of people in the bar drinking and the group of sixteen were very merry.

I beckoned Jasmine over to a table in the corner and told her to bring her maths.

'I found algebra quite difficult when I first started learning it,' I told her, 'but then I worked out a system. Right, let's look at the problem.' She showed me the ten equations she had to solve. The first one was a simple equation: '$2A-5=A+15$'.

Jasmine explained her problem. 'Miss Stevens just fiddles the numbers around and, takes out the letters giving an answer, but I just can't get the logic and I keep getting them wrong.'

'Well.' I looked at her. 'This is the way I learnt to do them. Think of a set of scales and the point of balance is the equal sign. They must always be in balance so if you take something from one side you must put it back on the other side to keep the balance.' We worked through an equation together. 'Firstly, you have two 'A's on one side and only one on the other, so take an 'A' off both sides. Now you have an equation that says, '$A-5=+15$', see?'

I watched Jasmine as she thought about this. 'Yes,' she said, catching on, 'I see, so if I take the '5' off the right hand side I must also take it off the other side, so 'A=10.''

'Yes, you have got the right idea,' I told her, 'but you must watch out for the signs. The '5' on the right is a minus so it is making the 'A' on the right hand side heavier. That means that you have to add '5' to the other side to keep the balance.'

She looked doubtful so I explained, 'Keep it simple, the other way is to remember that if you take a number off one side you have to put it on the other side with the opposite sign.'

Jasmine looked at the equation for a bit and announced, 'So A=20 then.'

'That's right,' I congratulated her, 'and you can check it by putting the value of 'A' into the original equation and see if it balances.' I demonstrated.

We worked through another couple of equations and Jasmine, looking pleased with herself and said, 'It simple really isn't it. I will do the rest of them now if you would not mind checking them for me.'

I left Jasmine to finish her homework and went over to help Mary who was beginning to clear the bar and restaurant as the last few customers finished their drinks.

The last ones to leave were the group of sixteen and they did not go until after midnight. As Mary and I cleared the tables and put them back in their original places Mary said to me, 'Douglas, for the first time tonight you looked happy and at peace with yourself.' I was thrown off guard and Mary went on, 'Why did you come here to the island? Any particular reason?' A very perceptive lady is Mary, and, I felt comfortable talking with her. 'I suppose I am looking to find myself and discover what life holds next for me.' I explained further. 'I have just lost my job, been through a messy divorce, and in the middle of all that, my last close relative, my father, passed away. I suddenly went from being busy and occupied to having nothing to do and no one to talk to. I suppose I am partly responsible for my marriage failing, I had been working long hours over the last few years and really we had seen very little of each other and rather grown apart. I could understand if my ex-wife had left me for another man, but I was stunned when she left to go live with another woman – that made me begin to doubt myself. The last straw was having to have my old dog put to sleep when he could not cope with life any longer.'

Mary sat down and looked out to sea and did not say anything for a bit but then she turned to me, saying, 'You like Joelle don't you?'

I replied, 'I would like to get to know her better, but I am not sure she likes me much. I find her a very reserved person. Jasmine just told me she is careful who she chooses to be friends with.' Mary nodded and said assured me that was just Joelle's way.

'She has had her problems and been hurt by life, and so, yes, she is careful and she is very dedicated to her job but when she does choose someone she is very loyal. Really she is a lovely kind-hearted person; don't give up on her too soon.' She paused and rested her hand on my arm. 'Be careful, don't get hurt,' she said to me. 'You have not eaten all night. Would you like a meal? I could cook you something light, an omelette maybe?' I realised I was hungry and thanked Mary.

I took a bottle of beer and went across to Jasmine to see how she had got on with the homework. Mary went into the kitchen. I checked through Jasmine's answers and they were all correct. 'Well done,' I congratulated her.

'It's easy, you just have to remember the set of scales,'

she said, pleased with herself.

'You wait till you get to quadratic equations,' I warned her. 'They are a bit harder, but the principle is the same.'

'What's a quadratic equation?' she asked.

'It is where you have more than one letter in the equation to solve.'

'Oh.' Jasmine looked doubtful, wishing she had not asked. 'I expect I will manage when I get to that stage.' It was well past midnight by now and as she waited for Joelle to collect her she started to tell me about her school and her ambitions. 'I did OK in my NCSE exams last year and I am working for my GSECs now. I need to get the grades so I can go on to do my CAPEs.'

'What are CAPEs?' I asked.

'Caribbean Advanced Proficiency Examinations, the equivalent of your English 'A' levels. If I can get good enough grades I would like to go to university in England. Mum does not talk about my dad at all so I don't know him, except that he sends me presents every year for my birthday and Christmas. I would really like to meet him but Mum won't hear of it. She says she never wants see him again but if I went to university in England then perhaps I could spend some time with him.'

We both contemplated this for a bit. I did not know what to say and Jasmine broke the silence. She smiled and started describing her teachers to me.

She had good powers of observation and was a natural mimic. She soon had me laughing with her as she verbally caricatured the school staff. She got as far as Taffy Jones, the Welsh geography teacher who had been on Kaeta Island for years but still retained his Welsh accent. As she mimicked a perfect if rather broad Welsh accent we heard a car pull up outside, and few moments later Joelle walked into the bar.

When she saw Jasmine and I sitting together laughing she glared at me furiously and before Jasmine could say anything angrily demanded, 'What are you doing here with Jasmine and where is Mary?'

I started to explain Mary was in the kitchen, but Joelle interrupted and turned on Jasmine, and still angry, accused Jasmine, 'Why do you ignore everything I ask? I have told you before not to get involved with the customers and I find you after midnight entertaining them!'

I tried to explain to Joelle that it was entirely my fault and Jasmine was not to blame but she turned on me then said, 'And you should be ashamed of yourself, what do think you are doing with my daughter…?'

She paused, visibly angry and about to hurl more verbal abuse at me.

I held my hands up and simply said, 'OK. Sorry, I will go now,' and walked out.

Chapter 15

Joelle de Nouvelas: Sunday evening, 16th

November

I go on patrol dressed in plain clothes and this evening I was wearing red denim jeans, a loose fitting long sleeve white blouse and white trainers, with my sunglasses resting across the top of my head. In order to avoid looking too obvious I only take the barest minimum of equipment with me, most of which I keep in a shoulder bag which doubles as a hand bag, the contents of which are a lipstick, sun cream, tissues, purse and keys, a small police radio, my mobile phone, which was usually more reliable and easier to use than the police radio, a pair of handcuffs, and a small lead pellet filled cosh, which I had never used and which was not police issue. I also carry two pepper sprays, which I had used in the past. I keep one in the bag and one in my pocket, and finally, also in my pocket, a personal alarm siren with a pull cord clipped to my belt, one of those devices that would almost burst the eardrums of anyone in the vicinity. The siren was not police issue either but it made me feel safer. Thus equipped, I set off for an evening around the markets.

The police station is located on the higher ground near the cathedral, the law courts, old town hall and office buildings. It was a short walk down to the main shopping areas and markets, which were adjacent to the main docks. The shops in the dock area would all be open tonight. These shops catered for tourists and sold a variety of goods, ranging from tourists trinkets and gifts, to good quality, if expensive, clothing, leather goods, ceramics and pictures from local artists, and electronic goods, supposedly at duty free prices. In the middle of all this was a large old warehouse, which had been converted into the Spice Market. The original front of the building, facing the docks had been closed off and the building turned round so that now it was entered from a small square into which spice stalls had overflowed. This was St Peter's Square, named after the church on the far side.

Just north of St Peter's Square lay the Fish Market in the narrow streets of the oldest part of town. Beyond this area was the newer commercial port area. Tourists very seldom got that far and there was nothing for them up there anyway.

To the south of St Peter's Square was the general market area. The buildings tended to be newer and streets a bit wider, with market stalls spreading down both sides. This area served local people as well as tourists. Some stalls sold the usual tourists' gifts and trinkets, others sold garishly coloured Caribbean shirts for tourists to take home. Mixed in were stalls selling more practical everyday items. Household necessities, groceries, fruit and vegetables, fresh meat (fresh being a loosely applied term and personally I would not touch this meat), and fish could all be found. The shops in this area also tended to serve local needs as well as tourism and so grocers, bakers, iron mongers, chandlers and butchers had their shops in this part of town. There was also a small supermarket in this area.

I started my patrol in the general market area. This tended to be busy during the day and the early part of the evening but as the shops and stalls tended to close earlier here, by mid-evening it would be quite deserted. The Spice Market would keep going all evening but the Fish Market would be where the main action took place between about nine and midnight. The whole area would close down between eleven and midnight. The cruise ships sailing overnight would leave about ten p.m. while the tourists leaving in the morning would drift back to their ships around eleven o'clock at night.

Patrolling the general market are was more a process of being seen, exchanging pleasantries with stall holders, and keeping up to date with the gossip. Of course, this evening, I was particularly interested in anything drug-related. I did hear one snippet at Marge's fish stall. Marge's is one of the better stalls and her fish is always fresh, as her husband is a local fisherman. He lands his catch about lunchtime and, while most of his fish is sold through the local co-operative, Marge takes her share to sell on the stall. By the time I reached her she had sold just about all her fish and was very happy to gossip while she packed up. She told me that her husband had been talking with some other fisherman who had told him that coastguards between Bermuda and Miami had stopped a powerful motorboat a few nights earlier. They found thousands of dollars' worth of drugs concealed on the boat. Apparently the haul included cocaine, heroin and ketamine pills.

'No, they did not tell him where the boat had come from nor what had happened to two crew members, but I expect they are in jail in Miami now,' Marge concluded, answering my question. I made a mental note to add this information to the Coconut file. If the story was true perhaps Bernie could get more information about it.

I slowly made way back through the streets to the Spice Market. Again I strolled around slowly mainly to be seen by the stallholders and to pick up any gossip going round.

One of the most difficult crimes to deal with in the markets is shoplifting by the tourists. The stallholders are not rich people and can ill afford to lose their stock, but it's difficult because it is a crime where we are reluctant to make an arrest. To do so inevitably means that the culprit, and frequently their travelling companions, miss their ship's departure so we often end up having to find somewhere for them to stay while bail is posted. They then either want to re-join their cruise or fly directly home and look to us to assist them. Embassies get involved, which means more paperwork, and then at the end of the process the culprit fails to turn up in court to face the charge. All a waste of time and energy and the stallholders understand this so rarely press charges. Most patrol officers have their own ways of dealing with these crimes.

So it was that I while I was in St Peter's Square, I was called into the Spice Market. I went across to see what was going on and was confronted by two large stallholders holding a middle-aged white woman by the arms. She was a large, overweight lady in blue shorts that were too tight and over which hung her belly. She wore a loose round-necked, multi-coloured blouse which more than fully exposed her ample cleavage and she had a large shoulder bag which she carried in her hand with it hanging by the strap.

'We have been watching her and she was trying to leave the market with a bag full of spice jars for which she has not paid. She also took an item of jewellery from the Diamond Emporium stall.' They did not sell real diamonds.

I asked the woman if this was true, and she said she meant to pay for the items, but she just forgot.

We cleared a space on one of the stall tables by the exit and I asked the lady to empty the contents of her bag. Out fell her personal effects together with two tee-shirts, and six containers of spices.

'Those all came off my stand,' one of the stallholders told me.

'Well?' I questioned the woman. She shrugged and said

nothing. 'And these tee-shirts?' I asked.

'Can't remember which stall they came from but I paid for them.'

'And the item of jewellery?' She looked shifty and I just caught her glancing down.

'Don't know what you are talking about officer,' she said, trying to be polite now.

'I believe you have jewellery concealed down your cleavage,' I told her, 'and if you don't produce it now I will remove your blouse and brassiere and search you.'

She glared at me and put her hand down her cleavage and pulled out a pair of gold earrings and a gold pendant. I thanked her for her co-operation and said, 'Firstly you will pay these stall-holders for the items you have stolen.'

By now the owner of the Diamond Emporium had been told what was going on and had come across. The two stallholders took their money from her. She went to pick up the items, but I stopped her and told her I was impounding them as evidence. I put them in my bag. I fastened my handcuffs around the woman's wrists and told her I was taking her across to the church where it was quieter to process her arrest.

A man I took to be her husband came up to me and pleaded with me not to arrest her.

'She has never done anything like this before and she has paid for the items now.'

I ignored him and marched the woman across the square, for maximum embarrassment, hoping the other passengers on the ships would see. The man followed us into the church, still pleading reasons why she should be released. I told him to be quiet. I took the woman's name and address and gave her my lecture about how we had a crime-free island and we did not like visitors abusing our delightful island and robbing our community. 'However,' I said in conclusion, 'if you leave the island immediately, and as this appears to be your first such offence,' but I did not believe this for a moment, 'I may not have to arrest you on this occasion.'

I paused for this statement to sink in and then said, pointing to a collection box, 'You may care to make a generous donation to St Peter's orphan fund.'

The woman produced a five-dollar bill and I got my notebook out again, checked the time, and started writing. I pulled out the police radio. It was not switched on as I pretended to ask for assistance in at St Peter's Church. The man stepped forward and said, 'Please officer, we would like to help but she has no money and I only have a $100 bill.'

'$100 will do fine sir. I am sure St Peter will find it in his heart to look favourably on this incident.' He opened his wallet and, as he extracted the $100, I briefly saw that he had more money than I could hope to earn in a month. I removed her handcuffs and the pair made off over the square faster than a Formula One racing car. I smiled and walked back to the Spice Market to return the impounded items to the stallholders.

I noted a couple of beggars in the square. We tolerate a few beggars as long as they are behaving and not bothering the tourists by getting too pushy. We only move them on if they are being aggressive or there are too many of them in any one place.

I spent a few more minutes around the St Peter's Square. I nodded in recognition to a couple of uniformed officers as they patrolled into the square and then I made my way back into the Spice Market. The point had been well made and everything was very quiet in the building. Tourists were in orderly queues to pay for their items and as I walked past the stall targeted by the shoplifter, the wife of the owner slipped a jar of nutmeg into my bag, thanking me for my help.

I made my way into the Fish Market, and what a contrast it was to the now quiet Spice Market. Crowded, narrow streets, and lots of noise with vendors shouting out their offers and competing with loud music of every genre blaring out from the buildings on either side of the streets. Because it was so crowded and there were so many stalls, the Fish Market appears much larger than it actually is.

The market itself covers about a quarter of a mile along the main roads of Saint-Pierre Rue and Poudre Voie, and fills the smaller alleys between them. These two main streets connect St Peter's Square with the Place de la Vierge de Houx. This is the oldest part of Kaeta Town originally built by the French when the island was a French colony, and most of the streets still have their old French names. The Place itself is dominated by the old cathedral, now the Catholic church of Sainte-Marie, the oldest church on the island and also originally built by the French.

Although the area is called the Fish Market it used to be the main island market three hundred years ago, and everything from fish to guns and ammunition could then be purchased there. Many of the streets took their name from the merchandise sold, hence Poudre Voie, where gunpowder suppliers traded.

Today the market operates largely for the tourists. Fish can still be purchased but mostly in cooked form, sold in small paper dishes with plastic forks and spoons, to be eaten at tables crammed into every available space. Every sort of fish dish is available somewhere here. Lobster, crab, squid, fish curry and seaweed, fishy pizzas, fish and pasta, even fish and chips (normally made with sweet potato) are sold somewhere. Interspersed with the fish stalls are vendors selling everything from CDs, DVDs and even old vinyl LPs, to fruit and vegetables.

Everything was vibrant. The stalls had brightly coloured awnings and streamers while the stallholders dress in vibrant shirts and scarves. There were people everywhere, tourists of course, but also residents and locals, sitting gossiping on door steps, old men and women sleeping on chairs, young men swilling bottled beer and wolf whistling at pretty ladies, and young lovers holding hands, momentarily existing in their own private world.

The noise, smells, and sights of the Fish Market at night assault every human sense. It was through all this that I moved, watching, gossiping, directing lost tourists, and ignoring the smell of hash floating out through the open windows of some of the buildings.

I took note and action only when these drugs moved into the open market, which seldom happened. Unfortunately the market was also the hunting ground for pickpockets and small drug dealers offering their wares to the tourists.

Hence, when I spied Light Foot Lionel, so called because he was the fastest 200-yard sprinter on the island and a known pickpocket and small-time dealer, I followed him discreetly. He was engrossed in his trade, looking for open bags and wallets hanging out of trouser pockets and selecting likely customers for his small paper packets. I was too far away from him as he took $20 in exchange for a couple of packets off one couple, but I got closer as he approached a large white man with a shaven head. I was behind him as he palmed another packet and held out his hand for another $20 bill. I already had the cuff round my wrist and snapped the other cuff on his before he could sprint off. The white guy instantly realised what was going on, snatched his $20 and ran off. 'Awe, Joelle.' Lionel knew who I was. 'I have lost a packet and $20 now.'

'And you are under arrest as well,' I told him. 'How much more have you got on you?'

'Nothing I swear!'

I towed him to the old church where it was quieter and I could more easily deal with him, and also more discrete than the market for when I called the wagon up to take him back to the station. I asked him again what he was carrying.

'Just a couple of packets for personal use,' he said, delving into a pocket.

'It does not really matter at the moment; you will be stripped and searched back at the station.'

I got my mobile phone out to call for assistance.

'Joelle, I can do a trade with you, if you let me go?'

'What trade?'

'Information, I know you are asking about drugs and I have valuable information.'

'How valuable?'

'How about where they are stored?'

'On the island? How do you know this?'

'Yes, on the island.'

I paused, trying to assess how much he really knew, if he did indeed know where the warehouse operation was it could be worth doing a trade. If I did arrest him I knew he would be out in the morning. He only ever carried small quantities and claimed it was for personal use, usually getting off with a caution. Also, he had given me good information before and I would lose a valuable informer if he told me something and I arrested him anyway.'

'If your information is any good I will think about it.'

He looked around furtively, but we were alone in the church. He moved closer to me to whisper and I got a whiff of unpleasant body odour.

'They keep the stuff at the Zip Line place in one of the disused huts on the old slave camp.'

'How do you know this?'

'I recognised the guy who supplies me and collects money.'

'Who is he? What is his name? How do you contact him?'

'He works at the Zip Line; he is one of the station attendants and I don't know his name.'

'How do you contact him?'

'I don't, he finds me and asks me if I want any.'

'What does he look like?'

'Like any other coloured man.' Lionel shrugged and I prompted him.

'Yes, go on.'

'Big, shaven head and ugly with a big scar on his face.'

'Who else do you know? Any of the organisers?'

'My guy is just a go-between,' he told me. 'I don't know anyone else.'

'Have you ever heard of a white man called Douglas Jay?'

His eyes flicked briefly round the church and he quickly said, 'No, never heard of him.'

'Are you sure?'

'Yes, quite sure!' he said more confidently.

I was pleased with the information. It confirmed our information that there was something on the island and now we knew where it might be. I took the cuff off Lionel and told him to disappear. 'And don't let me see around the market again, or next time I will arrest you.' He was out of the church and sprinted off before I dropped some coins into the collection box.

It was nearly 11.00pm now and I decided to go back to the station and talk to Bernie to see if he wanted to change tomorrow's plans in view of what I just learnt. Bernie had gone home so I phoned him as soon as I got back to the police station. His wife answered and did not sound too pleased, as she asked me if I knew what time it was. I apologised, and said it was urgent. Bernie listened to my summary of Lionel's story.

At the end I added, 'There was one thing. When I asked Lionel if he had ever heard of a man called Douglas Jay he looked nervous as he denied any knowledge so he might have been lying.'

Bernie thought for a moment. 'He may or he may not have been lying but I don't think anything changes for tomorrow. Take Jay round the island and see what he tells you, he might let something slip. I don't think he will make a move until he has some independent transport. You say you are going to see if you can find him some tomorrow?'

'Yes,' I confirmed. 'He says he would like a motorbike so I am taking him to Rusty Rick's to see what he has got.'

'Hope he does not kill himself on it,' grunted Bernie.

'Get him fixed up as soon as possible and then you and Merv's team need to work out how you can follow him. Joelle, be discrete. Operation Coconut is just surveillance as far as we are concerned. Our instructions are not to do anything which might alert the ringleaders.'

I assured him I would be careful and we ended the call, Bernie to go to his bed and me to spend time at my desk writing up a report.

Chapter 16

Joelle de Nouvelas: Early hours, Monday morning, 17th November

It was after midnight and I was dog tired as I walked out of the station to the police compound to pick up the Toyota. I saw the Lexus parked near it and remembered that I was supposed to collect it for the island tour, which I remembered was today.

I went find the duty sergeant to get the keys and returned to the car. Someone had done a good job on the disguise. The bonnet flags had been removed and large magnetic signs saying 'Sean's Island Tours' with a phone number were attached to the sides of the car. I thought the Commissioner would not be pleased if saw his car now, and hoped that they could be removed later without marking the car.

As I drove away, I realised the sign writers had put my mobile number on the side of car. *Very funny*, I thought sarcastically.

I drove straight to Glass Bar hoping Mary would still be there. I needed a drink and to relax before going home and bed.

I walked in and was horrified when I saw Jasmine talking and giggling with Douglas. Thoughts of Lionel and drugs flashed through my mind as I shrieked at them both, fearing that Douglas had given Jasmine something.

She started to say something but I shouted over her voice. I said something to Jasmine, I don't remember what; I was too angry, and turned on Douglas. I don't know what I was going to do, but I did not have time to decide. He stood, held his hands up defensively, apologised and walked out. I stood frozen for a moment and Mary walked out with an omelette on a plate. I looked at the plate and said, 'I am not hungry.'

Mary started saying, 'It's not for you,' and looked round the room as Jasmine burst into tears.

'Mother,' Jasmine sobbed, 'you are horrible, look what you have done, why can't you keep your mouth shut and let someone else talk?' She tried to control her tears.

I was confused, dumfounded and hurt. Jasmine had never spoken to me like that before and I did not have time to react before Mary turned on me and said, 'Joelle, I could hear you in the kitchen. Your reaction was unforgivable. As a police officer, you of all people should know to hold you temper until you know what's going on!'

I was still hurt and angry and even more confused. 'Please explain then.'

'No one turned up for work this evening and I was on my own. The place was full and we had over forty covers to serve. Jasmine could not help: she's not allowed behind the bar and she had her homework to do. So I was on my own and Douglas stepped in. I could not have managed without him. He looked after the front house and bar all evening while I did the cooking.'

'I helped!' chipped in Jasmine.

'Yes you did.' Mary smiled at her and continued, 'Douglas worked hard for over six hours and I had just made this omelette for him when you chased him out.' She put the plate down.

Jasmine spoke. 'And he helped me with my maths and algebra equations and explained how to do them, and was interested in what I do at school, which is more than you ever do!' She glared defensively at me.

'And something else,' Mary took my arm and walked out on the veranda out of Jasmine's hearing. 'I am a good judge of people and I don't think he has done anything wrong. I spoke with him tonight, as you asked, to try and find out what he doing here and he has a perfectly reasonable story.'

'He does not tell me anything,' I said sulkily.

'I am not surprised, the way you talk to him and treat him like a suspect,' Mary retorted as she stalked off. I felt crushed by her remarks and I sat mulling this turn of events over in my mind. Clearly, Douglas had endeared himself to both Mary and Jasmine and there had to be a side of his character I had yet to find. Was he a nice decent person, or just devious and clever? Equally clearly, whatever sort of person he was I needed to apologise for my behaviour. I looked down the beach thinking I would do it now and get it over with, but he had disappeared. I wondered about today. Would he still want an island tour with me?

Chapter 17

Douglas Jay; Monday 17th November

I arose late on the morning of the tour, skipped my run, and went straight in for breakfast. I usually go for breakfast either very early or very late to avoid the busy times. Today I hit the busy period.

The hotel serves a buffet breakfast. It is a very good buffet, presenting Continental, English, and American style breakfasts. My preference is simple eggs and bacon.

I was shown to empty table and served with a coffee. I got up to go and find breakfast and had to queue for juice, eggs, and toast, which made me grumpy. When I returned to my table I found I was now sharing with two English people.

They introduced themselves as Irene and Geoff Handley and they were a likeable enough couple, but they did try and make small talk with me. I guess they were in their sixties and they told me they were on holiday here for the week, having arrived yesterday.

Irene whispered to me, 'We are here with our daughter Jean, she is a freelance scriptwriter and she has not had a proper holiday for years. She has just finished writing a big six-part serial script for the BBC; she finds it very stressful and we thought the break would be good for her. I am sure you will like her, I will have to introduce her.'

I was not really listening and I was not in the mood for company that morning. I was worrying about how to handle my next encounter with Joelle, if indeed, she actually turned up.

I was mystified by Joelle's aggressive reaction and why she had got so upset with me for talking to Jasmine. I had not expected her anger and I was genuinely puzzled as to why she had reacted the way she did last evening. I mentally shrugged and decided I would go to reception at 9.30am as planned and see what transpired.

I got to reception a few minutes early and sat on one of the sofas with a view of the drive as it swept down through the gardens and around in front of the reception building. It was bright sunny morning; relatively cool still but with the promise of a hot day to come. I was travelling light with just my camera and lenses in the camera bag, and a straw hat. I was looking at the arrangement of flowers and different coloured foliage planted to form a green island in the centre of the driveway where it circled round in front of reception. I was mentally composing a photograph when a metallic white Lexus limousine with darkened glass windows appeared. Some rich guest arriving I supposed. It glided round the flowerbed and rolled gently to a halt in front of reception at precisely 9.30am.

I had expected Joelle to arrive in her Toyota or Suzuki and was surprised when I read 'Sean's Island Tours' on the side of the car. *Sean must be doing well*, I thought to myself. Joelle climbed out of the car and walked towards me. She was wearing white shorts and a lime green short-sleeved top with a square-cut neck. She had tied her hair in a ponytail. I thought she looked nervous, I was nervous as well so to break the ice I said, 'You told me you would get a car with air conditioning but I was not expecting a limo.' She looked very attractive that morning and I complemented her. She smiled. *Definitely nervous*, I thought, so I joked, 'You don't expect me sit in the back all day do you?'

With the merest hint of a chuckle she replied, 'No, I expect you to sit in the front next to me all day.'

We walked to the car and Joelle opened the front passenger door for me. I noted she almost helped me into the vehicle the way the police do when they arrest someone, but stopped herself in time. She sat in the driver's seat; the engine was still running to power the air conditioning and before driving off Joelle turned to me, looking serious.

'I am really sorry for the way I behaved last night. I was terribly rude to you and completely out of order.'

I started to tell her not to worry but she interrupted me. 'No, please let me explain. It was just that I had a long and difficult day and was tired and feeling tetchy, and I have told Jasmine not to get involved with customers so when I saw her with you, well I spoke without thinking. I am not trying to excuse my behaviour and I am really am sorry.' She paused for breath and wiped her eyes with a tissue.

I twisted in my seat towards her. 'Thank you for saying sorry.'

We looked at each other for a moment. Joelle spoke first. 'Shall we do the tour now?'

'Yes, let's go! I have been looking forward to this day.'

We clipped on seatbelts and Joelle fumbled a little, unaccustomed to the automatic gear selector. Once in gear the Lexus moved forward smoothly.

We turned left past the hotel security cabin, where the security lady on duty gave us a cheery goodbye wave, and headed along the coast road towards St Martin's and Kaeta Town.

At this point the road skirted along the edge of the rainforest, with, to my left, the deep blue Caribbean Sea glimpsed occasionally through the palm and coconut trees that grew back from the shoreline. After about a quarter of a mile Joelle slowed and pointed out a small road heading towards the sea. 'That's the way down to Glass Bar. In a few hundred yards we will take the St Martin's Point road and have a look at the millionaire's houses.'

We turned left and at this point the road was just a narrow track, not wide enough for two vehicles to pass, made from crushed gravel. As the track climbed away from the beach it became a slightly wider tarmac road. Before long Joelle started her commentary.

'If you look to your right, up there, that villa belongs to a Greek shipping millionaire and over there down by the cliff, that house belongs to a film star.'

As we drove round the point I saw a beautiful brick-built, older style, two-storey house set in a mature garden full of bougainvillea set against shrubs with multi-coloured leaves ranging from silver green to deep red and purple in colour. Amongst this planting there were lawns surrounded by rose beds. The usual palm trees provided shade but also this garden had what looked like lemon and orange trees planted as well.

'That's a beautiful house up there,' I commented, 'who lives there?'

'I think it's one of the nicest on the island.' She said nothing more as we carried on driving slowly round the headland.

Approaching St Martin's village the houses became less grand and the grounds much smaller, eventually giving way to more mundane dwellings. These were usually constructed of concrete blocks, most had tin roofs, and all had large verandas at the front, usually furnished with seats and tables. All were painted in vibrant colours, pinks, yellows, light blues, orange, and purple, had gardens, and most had spaces for parking vehicles. I assumed that Kaeta islanders occupied these houses, and remembering that Joelle had told me she lived in St Martin's near the headland, I wondered if one of these might be her home. St Martin's, the village, is quite small, although it has three churches: an Anglican church, a Catholic church and a Baptist chapel. Joelle assured me they all had full congregations. Some of the dwellings in the centre of the village also doubled as bars and shops and an old wooden shed was obviously the local car repairer judging by the derelict vehicles surrounding it and the blue flashes of an arc welder visible inside. The only other building of any note was the primary school with its neat, well-kept playing field. Joelle explained that the children start school as young as three or four and move from the local primary school to secondary school in Kaeta Town.

'The Caribbean has one of the best education systems in the world and is amongst the leaders for the literacy levels achieved by its students,' she proudly told me.

As we drove on round St Martin's Bay the landscape changed. The long sandy beach was still fringed with palms but we had descended from the lush valleys and hills of the central and southern areas of the island and were entering the flat, less fertile plains at the northern end. Joelle warned me that she thought the northern end of the island is not nearly as pretty as the southern end and that the approaches to Kaeta Town were particularly unattractive. I did not wholly agree with her about the Kaeta Town outskirts, and the suburbs I saw that morning were of mixed quality.

Modern brightly coloured concrete blockhouses were set in their own small yards. You could not call them gardens, although occasionally there were areas of planted vegetables, but generally they were concreted or just bare earth covered with old cars, fridges and items ejected from the dwellings. Adjacent to these buildings were poor quality timber-walled and tin-roofed shacks usually stretching back from the main road down rutted alleys. They had no defined boundaries and shared communal yard space. Interspersed with the domestic buildings were more modern retail structures housing furniture and DIY retailing warehouses, supermarkets, vehicle distributors and dealers with second-hand car sales. There were even some very new-looking American-style shopping malls housing a variety of shops and offices.

As we approached downtown Kaeta, Joelle asked me if I wanted to stop and have a look at the markets.

We walked through the general market area, through the Spice Market and into the old Fish Market. The stallholders usually greeted Joelle as we strolled past. More than one shouted across to her.

'Not working today! Who is the new man you have?'

I thought she blushed as she explained to me, a little irritably, that this was just their way of being friendly.

Joelle explained that the Fish Market was the oldest part of Kaeta Town originally built by the French on the site of the original Spanish settlement.

'That was called Quita,' she explained, 'and the present name of Kaeta is a corruption of that old, Spanish name.'

The next stop on the tour was in the commercial area near the oil depot to visit Rick's Auto Shop where Joelle introduced me to Rick and explained that I would like to hire a motorbike. Rick examined me. 'Have you ever ridden a motorbike before?'

'Yes, I have one back in the UK.'

'Mm,' muttered Rick, 'follow me.' We went round to the back of the workshop to a wooden shed. Rick pulled the doors open and we walked in. 'These are all for sale,' he said hopefully, thinking I might buy one.

'Not that one,' he said as Joelle walked up to a gleaming Harley Chopper. 'That's mine.'

'Would you let me rent one of these for my holiday?' I asked him.

He looked at me carefully again. 'I am not renting out the two Harleys or this one,' he said as he walked past a big Suzuki. 'Nor this one.' He pointed out a Honda track bike. 'There is probably something at the back that might suit you.'

Out of the gloom at the back of the shed he pulled out a small Honda moped with pedals and put it to one side saying, 'This one is knackered, but this one is OK.'

He pulled out a Honda motorbike. It was one of the step through kind of bikes, with an under slung frame, rather than a traditional motorbike where the tank is mounted in front of the rider's saddle.

'This should get you round the island OK. It has a 70cc motor so it has enough power.'

I looked at it and shrugged. It was transport and would give me some independence and would be easy to park and conceal if I needed to.

'How much?'

'US$25 a week, or part week and a $100 deposit.'

'Will you check it over and give it a service before I take it?'

'Of course, nothing leaves here without being checked.'

'How soon can I pick it up?'

'Tomorrow, if you like.' I looked questioningly at Joelle, who had been silent.

'If you want a bike that one is as good anything else,' she said with a shrug. I looked at Rick and asked if he had any crash helmets.

'I can hire you one for $5 a week,' he said.

We concluded the conversation with me agreeing to the deal and confirming I would pick up the Honda the next day. As we left Rick asked if I wanted insurance.

'You have to have third party, I will have to organise that for you, but do you want full comprehensive as well?'

I agree that I wanted to be fully insured and Rick said he would fix it but it would be an extra cost.

As we walked back to the car, Joelle spoke. 'Douglas, don't use one of Rick's helmets. They're all second hand and who knows what has happened to them in the past. I have a spare one you can borrow.'

'Thank you Joelle, but I can buy a new one.'

She looked doubtful and assured me, 'It's no problem. It's a spare I am not using. It's a good quality one I got from America and has never been in a crash. I am not sure what you would get on the island even if you found a new one to buy. The wearing of crash helmets is not compulsory on this island. I will bring the helmet round to your hotel in the morning.' She paused. 'Actually, I could pick you up in the morning on my way to work and take you round to Rusty Rick's to collect the bike.'

'Are you sure? That's really kind of you Joelle.'

We reached the car and climbed in.

I thought about Joelle; she was being friendly this morning and I was enjoying her company. I wondered where I stood on her scale of acceptable friends. I guessed I would soon find out.

Chapter 18

Douglas Jay: Monday 17th November

We drove on in silence for a bit while Joelle found her way out of the industrial estate. When we reached the main road again she quietly admitted, 'Mary told me about yesterday evening and how you helped out. I did not realise that she had been left to manage on her own.'

I replied, 'I think that was just an unfortunate combination of circumstances; you were working, Belinda was poorly and you already said that Sean was busy elsewhere. Anyway, I quite enjoyed the evening. It was good to be doing something rather than sitting round doing nothing.'

'Well, thank you anyway, I don't know what Mary would have done if you had not stepped in when you did. By the way, that reminds me.' Joelle fumbled around in her pocket while driving. She produced an envelope, which she handed to me. 'Mary asked me to give you this.'

I took the envelope and opened it. There was a note inside together with a wedge of US dollar notes. The note read:

'Dear Douglas, thank you so much for your help in the bar. Here are your tips from the evening.'

There was $53 in the envelope. 'I can't take this,' I said to Joelle.

'What is it?' she replied.

'Tips from yesterday according to the note.'

'Why can't you take it?'

'Well, it does not feel right, I was helping Mary out of a problem, not looking for a reward.'

'I think you will have to sort that out with Mary. It's nothing to do with me.' Joelle glanced at me and smiled as she drove.

I put the money into a drink container beneath the dashboard.

'Please give this back to Mary for me and thank her, but tell her I can't accept it.'

'Please Douglas, don't leave the money there; we will both forget it. You must give it to Mary yourself.'

I did not pick up the notes and after a short silence Joelle said, 'Jasmine says you helped her with her homework and explained how to solve algebra equations.'

'You have a very capable daughter there,' I said, 'I did not really do much, I just gave her a few clues – she worked it out.'

'Well, whatever you did, she is in awe of you now, and you seem to be her latest hero!'

'How embarrassing.' I chuckled. 'She will get over it,' I assured Joelle and then continued. 'She told me she wants to go to university in the UK. She says she does not know her father and would like to meet him one day.'

After a few seconds of silence Joelle spoke quietly. 'I never want to see her father again.'

'I know,' I responded, 'Jasmine told me.'

'I have never really told her about her father. It was the biggest mistake of my life marrying him. I don't think we were ever really in love or anything. I had just had my twenty-first birthday and was in my final year at university doing a postgrad doctorate and he was a tutor. I suppose I was a bit in awe of him when we met. You know what it is like living in such a small, intense community with a group of immature girls. Someone older and handsome pays you attention and you fall for it. Anyway, he took me out for dinner to celebrate my twenty-first birthday, I got drunk, he took me bed, and I got pregnant.

'Shortly after that we came out to Kaeta Island on holiday and to see my parents. He found out that my father owned a lot of land on the island. That was at the time the tourist industry on the island was just taking off and land was rocketing in price. Anyway, he realised I might be a good investment, so he married me. It was good at first. We lived in his flat and I finished my doctorate. Jasmine was born soon after we married and things changed. I think he resented her.

'We were living in a single bedroom flat so she was sleeping in a cot next to me and waking up regularly through the night, so neither of us got much sleep. Our relationship soon hit the rocks and he started blaming me for everything. He started threatening Jasmine, but the last straw came when a friend told me he was having an affair with a student. I was not working and had no money so I used the housekeeping credit card to buy a ticket home for Jasmine and myself and left him.'

She pulled over to the side of the road, stopped the car, and put her head in her hands. After a few moments she looked at me and said, 'Sorry, I did not mean to burden you with all that, it just came out. I never told anyone before how bad it was, not even my parents.'

'Are you still married?' I asked.

'Technically I suppose,' she replied. 'I asked for a divorce but he prevaricated and asked for money, but at that time I had no money and was working as a travel rep here on the island and living in my parents' home. He even tried to get some money out of my parents. I am rid of him now and I never want to see him again.'

We sat in the car in silence. I could think of nothing appropriate to say, but what I wanted to do was to give her a hug and tell her that not all men were like that. I didn't give her a hug, I just said, 'I am sorry, it must have been bad.'

After a while Joelle twisted round in her seat to look at me. 'Mary told me you are divorced as well.'

I took a deep breath before replying, 'Yes, that's right.' I paused, wondering how much to tell her.

'You don't need to talk about it if it hurts.'

'No, it's OK, I would like to tell you.' She was looking at me and I felt she was being sympathetic rather than questioning this time.

'I was working as the finance director at the time,' I started telling her. 'It was a family-owned business, but was quite large and the family had financed the expansion of the business by taking capital from a venture capitalist company. It was through them that I got the finance director job. Anyway I was working very long hours, leaving before six in the morning and not getting home until nine or later. I frequently had to go in at weekends as well, so my wife and I hardly saw each other and when we did we had nothing to talk about. I suppose we gradually grew apart. I came home one night and she was gone. Left a note saying she had met someone in the gym she went to and had gone to live with them. She took her clothes, her credit card, and the emergency money we kept in the house.

'Not long after she left she served divorce papers on me citing mental cruelty. I did not contest the divorce so the decree absolute was declared about six months later. The real trouble started when we got to the financial settlement. I knew she was entitled to half of the assets but she was claiming much more than that and was also looking for a substantial maintenance order as well. Eventually it was all settled in court. She got the old family house in Ewell, half my pension and a substantial cash settlement as well. That was a problem, I had to find some cash quickly to pay her off. Anyway it's all settled now and she is out of my life.' I paused.

It was Joelle's turn to say nothing this time and we sat in silence again until she looked serious, not her stern policewoman look, and just said, 'I'm sorry.'

I was grateful for her sympathy and we were silent for a minute or so until I said, 'Thank you.' I paused and added, 'Come on, we are both beyond all that now. Let's get on and see the island.' Joelle smiled and put the car in gear.

'This is the boring bit,' she said as we drove past the hospital. 'That's quite new and was built by an American healthcare company,' she told me. 'In a minute you will see the Atlantic Ocean as we drive round. After that we join the main road just before the airport. You will recognise it from when you arrived.' Silence followed as we contemplated the circumstances of my arrival on the island.

We were not far past the airport when Joelle pulled off the road into a small car park. 'Come on,' she said, 'I want to show you something, bring your camera.'

We walked a short distance over to the cliff edge. A small paved area had been created near the edge of the cliff and a safety rail erected on the cliff edge. The area was surrounded by a few windblown scrubby trees and a short way off I could see three goats grazing on the short spiky vegetation.

'This is called Carib's Leap,' Joelle informed me. 'The story is that towards the end of the 17th century a British militia, sent to control the island on one of the many occasions it changed hands from French to English, decided to deal with the troublesome native Carib Indians once and for all. They fought a spasmodic running battle across the northern plain and eventually cornered the remaining Carib warriors and their women and children on this cliff. Rather than surrender and be enslaved the men, women and children committed group suicide by jumping off the cliff.'

I looked over the edge. It was a long way down and at the bottom was just rocks, over which the Atlantic rollers were breaking. I looked round to see if there was anything interesting to make a picture. Joelle was the only thing with any photographic merit. This time I asked if I could take her picture. She agreed so I got her to pose, leaning on the rail, looking out to sea but twisting slightly towards me and took a three quarter side shot. I took two pictures, one with the flash to catch the features of her face and the other using a filter to enhance the sky and clouds, showing Joelle in silhouette. I showed her the pictures on the little screen on the back of the camera. We stood very close together, our bare arms touching, and this time she did not pull away from me.

The second picture was the best one and I was pleased when Joelle asked if she might have a copy.

Chapter 19

Joelle de Nouvelas; Monday 17th November

I rose late the morning of the tour and had a panic attack wondering how I was going to handle meeting Douglas and get through the day, if he actually turned up after last night.

I expected him to be very formal with me, and probably angry at the way I treated him. I was nervous and feeling sick. As I showered I thought, *At least I can wear my favourite clothes, that might give me some confidence.* I choose my lime green top; it was made from a lovely light floaty material, and simple white shorts to show the top at its best. I wore my hair in a ponytail as it is cooler that way. I began to feel a bit better as I checked myself in the mirror. I skipped breakfast, drank a glass of orange juice and went out to the car.

It was not far from the house to the hotel and realised I was going to be very early so I pulled up just before the hotel to wait. That was a mistake as the longer I waited the more nervous I became. The minute hand on the car's clock took hours to tick off ten minutes but at precisely 9.26am I set off for the hotel.

As I headed down the drive, rehearsing an apology speech, I saw Douglas waiting for me. I was almost disappointed; if he had not been there I could have called the whole thing off; the tour, and my involvement in the surveillance. But he was there and I had to force myself out of the car to meet him. I thought, *He does not look angry, he looks a bit nervous as well.* I was so relieved when he said, in a very friendly way, 'You told me you would get a car with air conditioning but I was not expecting a limo and pretty driver,' and then joked about sitting in the back seat. I smiled at him, relieved. Perhaps it would not be so difficult.

We got into the car and I knew I had to say something. My carefully rehearsed apology speech had completely gone and I started saying how sorry I was, and then realised I was just making excuses. Fortunately I stopped myself before I told him about my drug fears. I thought for a moment I was going to cry but he responded in the nicest way possible, thanking me for saying sorry. After that I started to drive and relax.

I pointed out the houses of the rich and famous on St Martin's Point, skipping over our house as I did not want the conversation to get personal. We stopped in Kaeta Town and I showed him round the markets. Unfortunately some of the more familiar stallholders chose to tease me. I hoped Douglas would not get any ideas. I explained some of the history of the town to him and told him a bit about policing problems in the markets. He was fun to talk to, a good listener who asked the right questions. Next, I took him out to Rusty Rick's to see about hiring a motorcycle. He seemed to know what he was doing and I lost interest after a while. I was pleased that the tour seemed to be going well and was actually quite fun, but I was still thinking about Jasmine.

We got talking about last night and I was genuinely grateful to him for stepping in and helping Mary. I had not planned to tell him about my first marriage though, it just slipped out and that was one of my problems with this surveillance. He was easy to talk to and standing closely together, our bodies touching as we peered at the camera, sending shivers down my spine. He did however tell me about his marriage and I noted that he had needed to get money quickly to pay off his wife. *Could be a motive*, I thought.

After we had left Carib's Leap, Douglas observed that we were leaving the flat plain of the north and moving into a more hilly landscape. Although the vegetation looked scrubby there were more bushes and trees with cactus plants more evident. I pointed out a tamarind tree and an almond tree in blossom. He asked me whereabouts the sugar cane was grown originally.

'Well more or less from here on,' I explained. 'We are moving towards the part of the island where most of the sugar cane was grown. It used to be much more forested but on this side of the island the forest was all cleared to make way for the sugar plantations. They have all gone now and the land is gradually reverting back to a natural flora. There is really only one active sugar plantation on the island now and that is further to the south. They make Kaeta Island Rum there but it is really run as a tourist attraction these days. We are about to enter Old Town now,' I concluded.

Douglas pointed out that the dwellings we saw as we drove into the town were very similar to those around Kaeta Town, a mix of well-kept, colourful concrete block houses living side by side with more basic wood and corrugated iron houses.

I pointed out that although some of the houses look untidy and run down on the outside, on the inside they are all clean and well furnished. All the houses will have TVs, video recorders and DVD players, fridges, washing machines and probably dishwashers as well.

We were by now nearing the centre of the town, which

was distinguished by having larger buildings, a church, a municipal office, and some shops. We rounded a corner and pulled into a square, surrounded on three sides by stone-walled buildings, one of which displayed a faded sign saying 'Hotel' and had some tables set out in the square, some of which were occupied by people eating or just drinking. The forth side faced the sea and served as the town's quay. There was a motor yacht and fishing boat tied up to it.

I parked the car in the square and Douglas walked over to the quay. Beyond it was a harbour bounded to the north by a headland and to the south a heavy stone quay about a hundred yards long and curving round to create a sheltered area of water. There were a couple of sailing yachts moored there. Douglas walked back to me as I waited, leaning on the Lexus watching him. He took my hand, saying, 'Come on, I am thirsty, I will buy you drink it the hotel.' He led me across to a spare table under the shade of an umbrella and after few moments a waiter came out to us. I ordered a large glass of lemonade with ice and Douglas ordered a beer.

We finished our drinks and I said we should move on as I wanted to show him the Zip Line and old slave camp. He did not hold my hand this time; instead he stood slightly behind me and momentarily put his hand on my waist, allowing me to walk out in front of him.

We drove out of Old Town on the main interior road across the island and, after about a mile, branched off on the minor road, which led up to the Zip Line. Initially the road followed a valley leading up into the mountain. As we climbed the rainforest became more apparent, with giant ferns, different indigenous tree species, bushes and wild flowers all growing in abundance. Soon the road climbed up the side of the valley in a series of zigzags and sharp hairpin bends. We did not say much as I was concentrating on driving and Douglas was busy looking at the rainforest for the first time. I asked him if he was enjoying the trip.

'Yes, very much. Are you enjoying it too?'

I said I was. 'It's a long time since I have driven round the island like this and it's quite relaxing.'

However, I was not feeling that relaxed. Douglas was getting too familiar. But my best chance of getting him to talk was to make sure he stayed relaxed with me and as the Zip Line was next on the tour I decided to play along with him, as I wanted to see what he did at the Zip Line.

Chapter 20

Joelle de Nouvelas; Monday 17th November

I parked the car and said, 'We don't have time to go on the Zip Line today but if you want to walk around and have a look I will wait for you by the car.'

'I would like to take a quick look round if we have time.'

I gave him fifteen minutes. 'Any longer and we won't have time to drive down to the slave camp,' I warned.

Douglas wandered off to look at the plan of the Zip Line track. The reception building was immediately adjacent to the car park and next to it was the gift shop. Running up the side of the reception was a road with a barrier across it. The access by foot was through the reception and up a footpath behind the building. On one side of the path was a restaurant and on the other was a changing room where they kitted out the Zip Line riders with a helmet, gloves and harness. There were five Zip Lines in total and they ran round in a circle, with the last line finishing near the car park. It was a short climb up some steps to the first landing station.

I followed Douglas through the reception and saw he was in conversation with the attendant who was sitting on the station steps smoking. I overheard part of their conversation. Douglas passed the time of day with him and asked how long it took to get round the lines. He said about half an hour but it depended on how many people were on the lines.

'Where do you finish?' he asked.

'Just over there.' He pointed to a path, which emerged behind some trees. 'It takes about ten minutes to walk back up from the last station.'

'It looks as if one of the stations is near the old slave camp,' I heard Douglas say, but some people started talking near me and I did not hear the rest of the conversation, but I did see the attendant pointing out some of the old slave camp buildings on the map of the site. As I watched, Douglas spotted me and came over to where I was standing, and we walked back to the car together. It only took a couple of minutes to drive down to the old slave camp. On the way I started to explain, 'The original camp was built here towards the end of the 18th century. One of the large plantation owners wanted to improve the quality of his slave stock. The West Africans straight off the boats were usually sick and weak after their sea crossing and the mortality rates were high. Also the demand for slaves was high because of the number of plantations on the island, so consequently the prices had risen. This owner decided to start breeding his own slaves. He installed the strongest women from his workforce up here in dormitories, they were just rough-thatched sheds really, and used the biggest, strongest men to get them pregnant.'

'Seems a pretty remote place to set up a breeding colony,' Douglas observed.

'That was the idea. It made it harder for the women to run away and enabled better control over the men selected for breeding. Also the cooler mountain air was supposed to be conducive to the conception and rearing of young children.'

'Must have taken a long time to establish a work force,' he said.

'Not really. The children were taken from the camp as young as five or six years old, as soon as they could use their hands effectively, and put to work along with the adults.'

'It sounds very inhumane,' Douglas concluded.

'So was slavery,' I replied.

In practice there was not much to see at the slave camp. One shed houses a reception and pay desk together with a small museum displaying some of the paraphernalia of the slave trade, and another shed had been set up as a dormitory showing the conditions the women lived in. I did note that Douglas was interested in two derelict-looking sheds near a Zip Line platform and asked me if I knew what they were. 'They were supposed to part of the original slave camp and I believe one was once used to house a generator before mains electricity was run up here. I don't think they are used anymore.'

We did not stay there long. I found the inhumanity of the place upsetting so suggested to Douglas that we move on. I suggested that we continue round the island using the prettier hill road past the sugar plantation and then on to Alice's Hill for lunch.

The hill road was quite narrow with sharp bends as we climbed above the rainforest and out on to a ridge. I stopped the car for to admire a view across the South Eastern corner of the island.

As we moved off again I told Douglas that Kaeta gained its independence on 22nd November 1967. 'We adopted a British-style parliamentary democracy and judicial system based on British common law and our titular head of state is the British Monarch. We have a President which is more of a ceremonial appointment and the real political power rests with the Prime Minister, who leads the majority political party elected every five years.'

'Has your family always lived on the island?' Douglas asked me.

'Mary has, and my father's family is descended from an old French family who once farmed on the island. My grandfather left Kaeta as a young man and went to England in the 1930s. He married my grandmother there and they lived in London where my father was born. My father was in the British police and when Kaeta was granted independence he came back here to organise the new independent Police Force. He married my mother, stayed on the island, and eventually became the Commissioner of Police.'

We pulled into the sugar plantation car park and I checked my watch. 'It's half past one now. We could spend ten minutes here for you to have quick look round and then head down to the Alice Hill restaurant for a late lunch, or we could skip lunch and do the tour which takes about an hour.'

'What would you prefer Joelle, are you hungry?'

'It's entirely up to you Douglas, you are the customer.'

'Right then, I think it would be nice to go and have lunch together.'

My alarm bells rang, Douglas really was getting the wrong idea and I could not let this go on.

Chapter 21

Douglas Jay; Monday 17th November

Joelle drove on towards the south. The vegetation changed and was now dominated by cactus-type plants mostly with long, spiky, fleshy leaves, grasses and small thorn trees. She stopped by one of the cactus plants and showed me how slaves had used them as a means of communication.

'They were not allowed pens or paper so they would take a sharp thorn and scratch onto the leaf as a way of keeping record of events and so on. The scratch would scar and remain visible for the life of the plant, about six years.'

'What happened when the plant died?'

'They transferred any permanent messages to another younger plant.'

The road climbed upwards in a series of curves as it crossed over the range of hills that formed the backbone of the island, stretching from Pirate Hill right down to the southern end of the island, abruptly meeting the sea in a series of tall cliffs and deep inlets.

It was on top of one of these cliffs that we found the restaurant on Alice Hill.

It was nearly 2.00pm when we arrived and we were the only people there. We went into the bar, I took a beer and

Joelle a soda water and fresh lime, and we went out to the open terrace on the cliff top. The view was spectacular. Joelle pointed out a headland in the middle distance. 'Just in front of that headland is a large inlet with Nelson's Dock. That's where we are going next. It is the only 18th century working dockyard in the world.'

The owner, who everyone called Joe, came out to take our order, but first he greeted Joelle with a big smile and hug saying, 'Joelle de Nouvelas. What a pleasure to see you again, I remember the little girl who used to come here with her father clinging on to the back of his motorbike like a little monkey.' He teased her and, shaking my hand, said, 'And this time you come with your new man. We were expecting you.'

He looked intently at Joelle, clearly expecting to be introduced. 'This is Douglas. He is on holiday and I offered to show him round the island.'

'Pleased to meet you Douglas,' he said as he winked at Joelle, who I could see was not amused.

'Joe, we are in a bit of a hurry, so could we order now?' Joelle changed the subject.

'Do you have your chicken and pineapple casserole on today? It's delicious, no one else makes it like Joe,' she said, turning to me.

'That will do for me,' I said as Joe took an order for chicken and pineapple.

While we waited, I took some photographs of the view and talked about what we seen that morning. Joelle, however, was silent and thoughtful. Her mood seemed to have changed. Eventually, she asked me what sort of work I did that took so much time.

'I trained as an accountant but my last job was as the finance director of a private company. The role was very consuming. The company had been financed by a venture capital company and part of their finance deal was that the company employed a finance director of their choice, so as well as being a part of the management of the company I was effectively working for the venture capitalists as well.'

'What did the company do?' Joelle asked me.

'It was primarily a medical company manufacturing veterinary drugs and consumables, bandages, dressings, that sort of thing. We had two factories, one making the consumables and the other the veterinary drugs. It was the finance needed to refit and expand the drug factory which got the venture capitalists and me involved.'

'Mm, drugs,' Joelle contemplated, 'did you ever have any trouble? You know, theft, that sort of thing?'

I was on my guard now. *That was an odd sort of question,* I thought. She had her police enquiry attitude on now and I wondered where she was going.

Guardedly I replied, 'As a matter of fact we did have some trouble a short while ago. One of the employees was caught stealing tablets which he was selling on the black market.'

'How did he do that? Surely you have tight controls and checks to stop that sort of thing?'

'We do, but this person worked in the internal audit department and was in a position to access records and alter them to hide the loss. He was actually caught selling the drugs in a night club that was raided by the drug squad.'

Joelle nodded and then asked me, 'Have you ever taken drugs yourself?'

Fortunately our lunch arrived before she could pursue this further and I avoided answering.

The meal was excellent, just as Joelle promised it would be, and as we sat drinking a coffee she went back to asking about my work. 'You described the veterinary company as your last job, so what do you do now?' she asked.

'I am not working at the moment,' I replied.

'Oh!' Joelle responded, and was silent for minute before she looked at her watch and said, 'Time is pressing on, we should move.' We went back to the Lexus.

It was a short drive round the cliffs before we dropped back down to sea level and followed a narrow road round the side of an inlet, before pulling into a car park on the left hand side. It had a sign up advising that this was parking for the Nelson Dock Experience. There was a coach, two taxis and another car already there.

Joelle walked with me across the car park and into a reception building and walked up to a window marked 'Tour Guides'. She returned to me and handed me a ticket.

'There is your entry ticket. Go through that barrier and your guide will meet on the other side. His name is Winston. The tour takes about half an hour and I will see you back at the car when you are finished.'

'Aren't you coming with me?' I queried.

'No, they only allow in-house guides to escort parties. See you in a bit,' she said as she walked off.

I felt deflated and dismissed. *Oh well, never mind*, I thought and went off to find Winston, who was a smart, enthusiastic young man in a uniform blazer.

'This is the oldest working dock yard in the world,' he informed me as we walked down the road between two brick walls, 'and the only way in and out of the yard is through this entrance.'

'Unless you have a boat,' I commented.

He ignored the interruption and continued. 'When it was a working navel dock in the 18th century this was heavily guarded to stop the slaves escaping. The navy started using the inlet at the end of the 17th century. It was well-protected from hurricanes and ideally situated for strategic purposes. The original dock was built on the east side of the inlet.' Winston pointed. 'The development of the dock on this side was first started about 1743 when a row of wooden store houses was erected and land reclaimed to form a wharf. The buildings you see now mostly date from between 1785 and 1794.' He pointed out the Admirals Inn, tar and pitch store, and a row of pillars on which the sail loft was erected. 'That blew down in a hurricane and only the pillars survive now,' he informed. 'Over there is Nelson's house next to the shop. Nelson was only here for three years between 1784 and 1787. He never actually lived there but it's said he designed the house but left the island before it was finished.'

We walked on towards the wharf.

'All this is built on reclaimed land, and on this spot, marked by the anchor, Lt Lord Camelford shot Lt Peterson in a duel over seniority in 1798.'

We reached the quayside and looked out over all the magnificent, and expensive, yachts moored. Winston announced that the guided tour was now finished but I was welcome to look round on my own. 'Stay as long as you like,' he invited as he walked away. I could have stayed longer, it is an interesting place and the history fascinated me but I was conscious that Joelle was impatient to press on, and so I went straight back to the car.

Joelle was sitting in the car with the engine running and the air conditioning going full blast, writing something in her notebook, which she promptly put away.

'You're back,' she said as I got in the car. I had hardly got the door shut as she drove off. 'We don't have time to drive right round Grumble and Three Sisters Bay,' she said as she headed back the way we had come in. 'We will join the main road and head down through the rainforest and pick up the coast road on the Caribbean side of the island, which will take us back to the hotel.' It was just after 4.00pm by now and Joelle drove quickly, now clearly anxious to get back. We did not say much to each other; I was lost in thought and Joelle was concentrating on the road. She did slow at one point and indicated a turning on the right.

'That road leads up to the Spice Farm and then rises up over the hills and drops down to the Atlantic coast road.' Eventually I asked Joelle if I had done something to upset her.

'No,' she replied curtly.

'Well, I don't believe you,' I said crossly. 'This morning we were friends, having a good time, and this afternoon you can barely say a word to me. If I have not done anything wrong, what has happened to change you?'

She glowered at me and I yelled at her to watch the road as we headed for a gulley on the side of a bend. She swerved back to the road and pulled up when we were back on the straight again. I watched her compose herself.

'Douglas, you have not done anything and we are not friends. You are a tourist and I am a policeman. Tourists are important to Kaeta and one of the jobs of the police is to help the tourists and see they are happy. Let's leave it at that please.'

Well, that put me in my place clearly on the bottom of Joelle's friendship scale. I admitted to myself that I was disappointed. I did like Joelle but I suppose she was right. Had anything developed between us it would only have been a holiday romance and I really had other personal matters to settle here without being distracted before I left. It would have been fun though!

Chapter 22

Joelle de Nouvelas; Monday 17th November

Sitting waiting for lunch I reflected on the morning's events, which had not gone the way I had intended. It was not that I had not enjoyed the morning, quite the contrary, I think I enjoyed it too much and had allowed my guard to drop, and Douglas had clearly got the wrong idea and thought a relationship was developing. Under other circumstances I would have been tempted but, as I reminded myself, I was on duty. I did not want to hurt him and I did not know how I could let him down gently. I reflected on the visit to Rusty Rick's where I had taken Douglas. Rick looked doubtful about hiring him a motorcycle and at first I thought he was going to try and sell him one. I was pleased that Rick said the big bikes were not available. I thought of Bernie's comment; I did not want him to kill himself either – too much paperwork!

As Rick pulled the smaller bikes out from the back of the shed my attention drifted off and I began to think about last night again and what Jasmine had said to me. I was appalled to think she might have meant the things she said, but I told myself it was just teenage talk. I decided I had handled this situation wrongly. Douglas must have impressed her somehow though; she was normally very level-headed and sensible, even cynical at times.

I heard Rick offering Douglas one of his used crash

helmets. I know they were potentially dangerous and so without thinking I offered to lend one of mine. I then made matters worse by offering to drive him over to Rick's in the morning to pick the bike up. *Oh Lord!* I thought. Why on earth did I get involved?

Then he refused to take the tip Mary gave me pass to him, which made me think about last night and Jasmine again. I was still upset about Jasmine and I asked Douglas about the homework. He complimented Jasmine, which annoyed me a bit! But then he told me she said she was planning to meet her father. I was shocked and before I could stop myself I was explaining to Douglas why I never wanted to see Jasmine's father again. I told Douglas about the divorce, and I even nearly showed him the cigarette scars, which I have never shown anyone before!

Sitting eating lunch I now reflected how stupid that was, and I was really angry with myself for letting my guard down and becoming too familiar. However, it was an opportunity to ask about his divorce and I did learn something. He told me he had needed to raise cash quickly in to pay his divorce settlement. This might be a motive, I reflected. I also noticed that at the Zip Line he had spoken with one of the line attendants; was this the contact, I wondered? I would have to check that somehow.

I decided Douglas was a really annoying person. While I am trying to be distant and professional he is friendly and easy going, encouraging me to talk and the more he encourages me the more relaxed and talkative I get. He spent all morning getting me to tell him the history of the island; well I suppose I had started it, but he encouraged me and then, and damn it, I even let him hold my hand and buy me a drink like we were lovers!

After lunch, as I drove back to his hotel, I fuelled my irritation thinking about that lunch. While we were sitting together waiting for lunch I had asked him about his work. At first he was quite open in his replies, but became guarded when I asked him what he was doing now. Each time I ask this question he clams up. *Does he have something to hide?* I speculated. When I asked about the employee caught for stealing drugs his reference to a police operation made me feel very uncomfortable as I reflected on what I was doing, and I realised he had never answered when I asked him if he did drugs.

After the lunch we travelled the short distance to Nelson's Dock. As I drove, feeling angry and uncomfortable with this whole surveillance, I started to think about my mother defending him. She thinks he looks innocent; what does she know! Some of the worst criminals I have come across looked like kindly old men! I took the opportunity, while Douglas went round the attraction, to sit in the car and log what I had learnt for a discussion with Bernie. I used my note book and summarised:

He matches the Tip Off

Opportunity; worked in a drug company, also Amsterdam connection.

Drug company employee caught with stolen drugs – any connection? In his position he would have access to alter records as well.

Motive; need cash to pay off his wife.

How: made contact at the Zip Line which Lionel says is the storage point.

Disappears on morning runs; another contact?

Seen wrapping parcels; what's in them?

Behaviour; is he hiding something?

Evades answering personal questions.

Light Foot Lionel. Denied knowing him; but?

Douglas did not stay long in the Dock. I don't think he saw what I was doing as I put my notebook away. I was anxious to get back so we drove off quickly.

It was after I pointed out the road to the Spice Centre that he challenged me about my behaviour and implied I had been leading him on. That annoyed me, I had done no such thing and then he yelled at me when I nearly crashed the car. That shook me and I had to stop and compose myself. I realised that this was my opportunity and there was no gentle way to do it, so I told him that we were not friends. He did not say a word and I felt awful. It was then I realised I actually liked this man, even though I thought he was probably a criminal. I kept reminding myself he was probably a drug smuggler and as we neared his hotel I concluded that there might be enough circumstantial evidence now to bring Douglas in for questioning, and sitting in the car next to him I felt even more uncomfortable.

After I dropped Douglas at his hotel I went to pick Jasmine up from the bar and told Mary I was having an early night. In truth I did not want to see Douglas again. I was still feeling unsettled and beginning not to enjoy this investigation.

I took the Lexus back to the Police Garage and picked up my little Toyota. As I drove home I thought, *Damn the man, he has no right to make me feel like this!*

Chapter 23

Douglas Jay; Monday evening 17th November

We got back to the hotel and I retrieved my camera and asked Joelle if she would rather I took a taxi to Rick's in the morning.

'No, I said I would take you; I will pick you up in the morning about 9.00am. Sorry, I can't make it later but I must get to work.' I thanked her and told her I would be ready and as I shut the door and walked off she called me back.

'Don't forget this!' She handed me the envelope with the tip money in it.

I did not want to meet Joelle that evening but I needed to go to the Glass Bar to pay Sean and I wanted to return the tip money to Mary. When I got there neither Joelle nor Jasmine was there but Mary came out of the kitchen and offered me a drink.

'Beer please.'

Mary pulled me a beer and put it on the bar in front of me saying, 'Joelle came in earlier and picked Jasmine up. She said she would not be back this evening.' Mary shrugged and looked disapproving. 'She looked in a bit of temper to me. How did the island tour go?' she enquired.

'It was very interesting. Joelle certainly knows a lot about the island and its history.'

I paused for a bit, uncertain whether to say anything further, but I added, 'but I think I must have said or done something to upset her this afternoon.' Mary just nodded and told me it probably was not my fault. I dismissed that thought and turned back to Mary, holding out the envelope with the tip money in it. At first she would not take it but when I suggested that she take it for Jasmine she reluctantly agreed saying she would take Jasmine shopping, 'but I will tell her where the money came from,' she warned me. I changed the subject again and asked Mary, 'Are you going to be short staffed again tonight, if Joelle is not coming in?'

'I should be OK, Sean is here and we should not be too full tonight.'

I went across and spoke to Sean offering him the money for the Island Tour. He looked mystified. *Very odd*, I thought, so I prompted, 'Sean's Island Tours.'

'Oh! Of course,' he said, 'Joelle's tour, sorry but I think you better pay Joelle, I don't know anything about it.' It was my turn to be mystified: I thought it was Sean's business. *Strange*, I thought, and felt rather depressed as I walked back along the beach.

When I got back to the hotel I went into the bar. The Handleys were there and invited me to sit with them. I accepted and was promptly introduced to Jean.

I put her in her early forties, a bit older than Joelle. She was not very tall, only about five foot four inches with mousey coloured short hair and she wore glasses. She was quite slim around the waist but this and her height emphasised the size of her chest and hips. She had obviously been in the sun and had gained a bit of colour, still pink in places, against the white shirt she was wearing.

We started talking, discussing the holiday and what there was to do on the island. Jean told me about her writing experiences and I told her about my cottage in

Wiltshire. At one point Geoff and Irene slipped quietly away, saying they were tired and were skipping dinner that night. Jean and I went into dinner together. I had smoked salmon and crab rolls as a starter. Jean skipped the first course and for a main meal we both had the sea bass with a crab sauce served on a local spinach-type vegetable. We drank a bottle of white wine with the dinner.

There was a band playing in the Caribbean bar overlooking the beach and after we had eaten we went out to the bar for a couple of glasses of champagne. People started dancing and Jean and I joined in. We started jigging around separately as the band moved through their repertoire of old Rolling Stones and Bill Hayley numbers and as the evening moved on they started playing the slower, more smoochy numbers. I held Jean's left hand and put my right hand behind her back as we danced a sort of foxtrot, but as the pace slowed down further Jean moved closer to me and slipped her arms round my neck and we started to move together in a close embrace. We broke apart as the band finished and we decided to have nightcap while watching them pack up.

'I really enjoyed this evening Douglas, it's ages since I have been dancing,' Jean told me. I said something inane like the pleasure was all mine, and then Jean said, 'I have enjoyed this so much I don't want the evening to end. Let's get another night cap and go somewhere where we can sit and watch the night.'

I asked if we could have more champagne. The bar man winked at me and gave me a nearly full bottle. 'Take that,' he said, 'it will be flat and no good in the morning.'

Jean asked me where my cabin was. I pointed it out and Jean pointed in the opposite way, 'Mine is at the other end in that direction. As a condition of coming on holiday with Irene and Geoff I insisted on having my own room.' She paused, looking at me. 'Would you like to walk me back to my chalet? We could take our bottle and sit on my veranda if you like?'

I felt a pang of regret as I thought of Joelle but then thought, *Why not? I will enjoy the company.* We walked along to Jean's chalet with me clutching the bottle of champagne and Jean giggling irritatingly at my side.

When we got to her room she went to find a couple of glasses and I moved out to her veranda and leant against the handrail looking at the sea. Jean came out with the glasses and I poured some champagne. She stood next to me, looking at the sea. We did not say anything but after a few moments she moved up and stood close to me. I put my arm round her waist and she nestled into my side turning her face up towards me. I bent my head down and kissed her, she threw her arms around my neck and returned the embrace. We stood there, caressing and kissing. I was surprised how soft and warm her lips were, quite unlike my ex-wife who always had cold, hard lips when she kissed. I briefly wondered what Joelle's lips would feel like but pushed the thought away as Jean's breasts pressed against my body and I felt myself becoming aroused.

Jean pulled away from me, saying, 'Not out here Douglas.'

She took my hand and pulled me into the bedroom.

Chapter 24

Joelle de Nouvelas; Tuesday 18th November

The next morning, I felt calmer and more in control. I found my spare crash helmet and loaded it and Jasmine into the car and drove round to the hotel to collect Douglas. I was early, and he was five minutes late. Jasmine told me not to worry, we had plenty of time, and that just increased my level of irritation and stress.

Of course, when he did arrive, he apologised profusely for keeping us waiting and I rudely said nothing, just drove off. It made my mood worse when Jasmine turned round to talk to Douglas in the back seat and started asking why we were not talking to each other. We both gave the same reply, and that made us look at each other and I nearly laughed, but then I seethed again as Jasmine apologised for me, saying, 'Don't mind Mum, she is in a stress this morning.' Jasmine then asked Douglas how he had enjoyed the Island Tour.

'It was really great,' he told her.

'What was your favourite bit?'

'Well, Nelson's Dock was interesting and I really want to have a go on the Zip Line and walk up to the top of the crater.'

That damn Zip Line again, I thought, as Douglas continued, 'I think I might go to the Zip Line tomorrow.'

And I might follow you and see what you do, I thought.

'Did you take any photos?' Jasmine asked him.

'Yes, lots. Most of them are scenery but I took a very nice one of your mother.'

'Can I see them sometime?' Jasmine asked.

'Of course, when I have sorted them out.'

'Oh, please bring them round to the bar and show me,' Jasmine asked and, annoyingly, Douglas agreed he would.

To my further irritation, the two of them chatted like old friends about the island, photography, and school, all the way into town and when we arrived at the school to drop Jasmine, she goodbye to Douglas with a barely a nod or word in my direction.

On top of all the other emotions I was now jealous of my daughter. I hated Douglas!

He stayed in the back of the car and we barely said a word to each other. To fill the emptiness I turned the car radio on. One of those chatty morning news shows, interspersed with music, was playing. I dropped Douglas outside Rick's and drove away quickly, feeling very melancholic.

An old love song played on the radio 'Everybody's Got to Learn Sometime' and I started crying as I listened to the singing about changing hearts and needing love like sunshine, and I felt desperately alone wishing that Douglas was just an ordinary tourist.

When I got back to the police station, Bernie was already in. I did not go in and see him immediately, I needed to calm down and wash my face and put some make-up on. I went into the ladies' toilet and locked myself in a cubicle to compose myself, and tried to think through what I wanted to tell Bernie. When I was ready I collected a cup of tea and knocked on Bernie's door.

'How did yesterday go?' he asked.

'Difficult,' I said and told him briefly what we had done.

'And how did you get on with the Commissioner's new Lexus, I hope you did not bend it!' he chuckled.

'No I did not,' I said stiffly, remembering that I nearly had.

'I noted three possibly significant things.' I ticked them off on my fingers. 'One, I discovered a motive; he needed cash quickly to pay off his wife. Two, I might have spotted his contact; he had a long conversation with one of the Zip Line attendants. And three, the way he sometimes clams up about his personal life makes me think he has something to hide.' I went through the rest of my list from yesterday.

Bernie rubbed his chin and looked thoughtful, eventually saying, 'It's all very circumstantial still. Until we get something hard linking him to illegal drugs we are on weak ground.'

'Could we not bring him in for questioning? I am finding this surveillance very frustrating and difficult; and he gives so little away.'

'We can't bring him in yet. The instruction from our American friends is very clear. Watch him, report back what he does, and don't alarm him.' Bernie continued, 'I think he may make a move soon now he has his own transport. I know it is difficult but carry on with the surveillance. Keep in contact with him. Keep his company and be friendly; he is bound to let more slip if you can keep him talking, see if you can get him drunk. We will give it another three or four days and then review where we are.'

I said, 'Bernie, I don't think I can do that. He was

reading too much into me being friendly yesterday and I am in danger of getting too involved. Anyway getting him drunk is not so easy, he holds his drink well, he sticks to beer most of the time and after a couple of beers he remains polite and charming, but can get argumentative.'

Bernard instructed. 'I am sorry Joelle; I have only you who can run this. The three constables are no good and anyway they are not clever enough. You don't need to go out with him or anything, just keep him in sight and talking.'

I said resignedly that I would do my best and Bernie then asked, 'Have you sufficient cover to follow him when he takes off on this motorbike?'

'Yes, I think so, I have Merv, and two PCs, Isaac and Denzel, taking it turns to hide outside the hotel in a car and follow him when he goes out. I will also use my Triumph, so if they report something I can be there pretty quickly.'

'If he has a motorbike will they be able to keep up with him?'

'They should be able to; it's only a small bike and will not go that fast.'

'Have they seen the motorbike? How will they know who they are following?'

'He has my black crash helmet with red flashes down the side. They can't miss it.' Bernie nodded his head and looked at me quizzically. 'You are not getting emotionally involved are you?'

'Certainly not,' I lied.

'Be careful Joelle, I need you to handle this. It's asking a lot, I know. Go along with him, he is either very clever, or completely innocent, and I don't know which yet. Just give it a few more days.'

'Are you going to report progress back to the

Americans?'

'I don't know yet, let's see what turns up over the next couple of days.'

I sighed and told Bernie again, I would do my best.

Chapter 25

Douglas Jay; Tuesday 18th November

Joelle picked me up and drove to Rusty Rick's. We barely spoke to each other on the journey. I don't know what Joelle was thinking, but after last night I was feeling guilty. I told myself that was ridiculous, we owed each other nothing and if I had a one night stand, so what? But I still felt like I had betrayed Joelle. Jasmine started talking to me and asked why Joelle and I were not talking. In unison we both said that we were tired after yesterday. At least that caused us to look at each other and smile.

Joelle dropped me off outside Rick's and I went in to find him. He was round the back pushing the little Honda bike out of his workshop.

'This is a nice little bike,' he said. 'It's a Honda C70 Passport. It's quite old but it has not done many miles and goes well. I got it off an American man who brought it over when he came to work here and sold it to me when he had finished. It's not governed and has a manual gear box so it has a good turn of speed. It is a four-stroker so uses ordinary petrol.'

This was the first time I had seen the machine in daylight. It was a brown colour with white knee fairings, a single saddle and a pannier box mounted on the luggage carrier. It was one of those small motorbikes that are mounted by stepping through the frame in front of the saddle rather than throwing a leg over the rear wheel. It was a tidy-looking little machine. It was quite small but at least looked like it would get me round. *Yes,* I thought, *that will do nicely.*

'It has an electric starter.' Rick demonstrated. It fired up promptly and sat purring away. Rick turned it off and said, 'It's all serviced and ready to go and I have even put a small pannier box on it for you. We just need to go into the office and do the paperwork and then it's all yours.' I asked Rick to take the Honda round to the front of his shop so I could take his picture with the bike.

We went into his office and I signed all the papers, paid for the insurance, gave Rick $100 for the deposit and bought a large-scale island map from him. I put Joelle's helmet on, started the Honda and wobbled off. I would have preferred my first ride to have been on less busy roads than Kaeta Town, and I had a few near misses as I rode through the town, until I learnt that to drive faster in the middle of the road was the best option. Fortunately I more or less knew the way from the previous day and only took a wrong turning once. Once out of town the roads were a lot quieter and I began to get more confident and enjoy riding the bike. I arrived back at the hotel just before lunch.

I left the Honda at the back of the car park. As I walked back to my room, I passed the hotel's gym and paused to look inside. The gym had large sliding glass doors, which opened on to the gardens. It was crowded early in the mornings and late afternoon but was seldom used at lunch time so I was surprised to see a person in there working hard on a cross trainer. I was even more surprised when I recognised Joelle. She had her back to me so did not think she had seen me. I walked quickly on but then stopped, wondering if I should go and say hello. I decided not, after all she had made her position quite clear yesterday afternoon so what would I say to her? And anyway, she would not thank me for interrupting her gym session. I did stand and watch her for a couple of minutes, regretting that things had not worked out.

As I walked back to my room I remembered that, as I left Jean in the early hours of the morning, I had arranged to meet her in the hotel bar and then eat lunch with her.

I showered and changed into a tee-shirt and shorts and made way over to the bar. Jean was already there, drinking a glass of wine. I sat down at the table with her and ordered a beer. 'Where are Geoff and Irene?' I asked.

'I sent them to eat lunch at the burger bar so we could be alone.'

My alarm bells tinkled faintly at this as Jean asked me where I had been that morning. I explained I had been to collect transport so I could get round the island.

'Fabulous,' Jean exclaimed. 'We can go together.'

With some relief on my part I explained that my transport was a motorcycle and it would not be possible for her to come with me. Jean started to suggest that I exchange the bike for a car and as she spoke I spotted Joelle by the guest information desk. We held eye contact and then Joelle said something to the receptionist and walked across to me. As a waiter walked up and placed a glass of soda water and lime on the table for her as she reached me, and realised that I was not alone. She gave Jean an icy stare.

'Joelle, please sit down and join us,' I invited her, and introduced her to Jean.

The two women regarded each other warily. Jean looked positively hostile while Joelle gave me a questioning look. Jean said nothing just glared first at Joelle and then at me. Joelle explained that she liked to keep fit for her work so usually came to the gym about twice a week in her lunch hour when it was not crowded. Jean asked her cattily when her lunch hour finished. Joelle ignored that and asked me if the Honda was OK.

'It's great,' I replied, 'I am going to take it out again this afternoon and top it up with petrol.'

Joelle finished her drink and stood up, saying, 'Douglas, I do need to talk to you but it will keep until a more convenient time.'

I rose to my feet as Joelle explained that she had to get back to work and left us.

Jean immediately asked, 'Who was that?'

I explained that she was the policewoman who had questioned me when I arrived on the island.

'What does she want to talk to you about?'

'I don't know.'

'Are you seeing her?'

I did not tell Jean that Joelle had taken me round the island, I simply said, 'No.'

We went into the restaurant for lunch and Jean looked considerably happier when I suggested that we meet in the bar later and have dinner together again.

That afternoon I took the Honda out for a ride and to buy some petrol, which meant a trip into the outskirts of Kaeta Town. From there I took the main island road through the rainforest and then back up the coast road. I noticed there was a white Suzuki Alto parked by the security cabin as I left the hotel. It would not have registered except that a white Suzuki Alto also pulled into the garage when I bought petrol and then it was again on the main road behind me. It only registered because I thought there must be a lot of these Suzukis on the island.

When I got back to the hotel, I showered and changed and made my way to the bar to join Jean. We had a glass of champagne and Jean asked me about the Honda and then motorbikes in general. I told her about my hobby, rebuilding classic cars. At one point she said she never ridden a motorbike. I think she was hinting for a ride on the Honda but I explained it only had one seat.

We decided to walk along the beach and watch the sun setting. Jean wanted to hold hands. We walked along the beach together and watched the colours change. At first I felt uncomfortable, remembering who I had been with the last time I had watched a sunset. As we reached the far end of the beach we sat down on the sand and watched the sun slip below the horizon. Somehow, I found myself lying on top of Jean, kissing her passionately.

We ate late that evening and afterwards decided to take a nightcap back to Jean's chalet again.

Chapter 26

Douglas Jay; Wednesday 19th November

I fell asleep after an active night, and crept out of Jean's chalet without waking her as dawn broke. There were no guests about, but the hotel staff was arriving for work as I made my way over to the Honda to collect the island map, which I had left in the pannier box, and then walked back to my chalet. It was no good going back to bed so I decided to have a shower and go for a run. I would not sleep anyway as my mind was buzzing and I needed time to think, and a good run would clear my head. After Monday I was trying to forget Joelle but seeing her yesterday lunch time had upset me again and last night, lying in Jean's bed, it had been Joelle, and why she needed to speak to me, that I had been thinking about. Also I was now acutely aware that the liaison with Jean meant far more to her, Jean, than it did to me: she was getting quite possessive and clearly intended to spend her time on holiday with me. I could see I was heading for trouble if I did not cool things with her. In the end I could think of no better solution than to keep out of the way for the day; I had already decided I was going to visit the Zip Line and I could spend the evening at Glass Bar. I might even see Joelle and find out what she wanted.

When I got back to my chalet I was surprised to find a gardener outside my door talking to one of the chalet maids. *He is always hanging around this part of the garden*, I thought; probably the maid is the attraction.

After breakfast I put the packet of brochures into the Honda's pannier and slung my camera bag over my shoulder and set off to the Zip Line. The quickest way was into Kaeta Town and out again on the main Old Town road across the centre of the island.

The little Alto was again parked near the security lodge at the end of the hotel drive.

I reckoned that I should have enough petrol for the ride, but decided to come back the same way so I could refuel on the way back. The little bike theoretically had a top speed of about 60mph but was happiest cruising at around 40mph, which was quite fast enough for me, and I made reasonable time across the island arriving at the Zip Line at about 11.30am. As I pulled into the car park I realised I had no way of actually securing the machine and leaving it in a public car park with Joelle's crash helmet, and my gear was not a particularly good idea. I rode up to reception and asked the young lady receptionist if there was somewhere more secure I could park.

'Sure, you can leave it round the side of the building behind the bushes. If you follow the path round you will see some bins, leave it there. It will be quite safe and I will keep an eye on it.'

I did just that, but my camera bag was too big to fit in the pannier box so I took it and the brochures into the reception. 'I was told to give these to Oria, the office supervisor. Apparently she knows what to do with them. And may I leave my camera with you while I go on the Zip Line?'

The receptionist took the package, saying she would see Oria got it when she came in, and took the camera, saying, 'I will be going for my lunch break soon so if I am not here when you return the bag is under the desk here.'

I took my little Canon Ixus with me, bought a ticket and headed for the Zip Line.

I was fitted out with a helmet, harness and gloves and directed to the first station. There I met the attendant I had spoken to a couple of days before. I don't think he remembered me as he instructed me on the safety aspects of using the Zip Line. He told me it would take about an hour and half to walk up to the rim of the volcano and about an hour to walk back. He also told me to keep a look out for the Jaquot birds, a species of brightly coloured parrot as there were lots of them around this part of the rainforest.

The Zip Line was great fun. Essentially I was clipped on a steel hawser slung between two hill stations. You then jump off the top station and gravity propels you down to the next station. You build up a lot of speed as you zip downwards across the treetops and on the first line I was a little worried, wondering how I would stop at the bottom station. I need not have worried as the lines are designed such that as you near the end you start travelling uphill, and this slows you down sufficiently for you to just step neatly onto the station platform. That is the idea anyway, but me being over cautious, slowed down too much, did not quite reach the platform and had to be pulled in by the attendant.

It was then a short climb up to the start of the next line to travel the next stage.

I travelled the next two lines but at the forth station I took a break to walk down to the old slave camp. I looked at the two old wooden cabins. They both looked derelict, one was falling down and had some old machinery in it but I was more interested in the other one. While it looked derelict from the distance it had been repaired recently and the roof looked new. It was locked and the windows blacked out. I walked round it and tested the doors, but they were locked, and when I had seen all I was interested in I took some photographs with my small camera, and made way back up to the Zip Line and zipped back to the car park.

As I walked into reception to retrieve my camera bag I noticed another white Suzuki Alto in the car park. *This is too much of a coincidence*, I thought, so I took a note of the number plate.

Now, I decided, I would walk up to the volcano crater. I was not disappointed; the walk took me over an hour and a half, and was indeed a difficult and steep climb in places over loose scree slopes. I climbed through the rainforest, which gradually thinned out, disappearing completely by the time I reached the top. As I neared the top the ground became very rocky with very little soil and even less in the way of vegetation. However the view from the top was worth the climb. I could see the whole island to the north and south stretched out beneath me. To the north I could see the airport and a plane coming in to land. A heat haze limited the view to the south, and looking east I had a view of Old Town with the Atlantic ocean beyond, while to the west I looked out over the different colours of the rainforest, and a thin strip of yellow sand that separated the deep blue Caribbean Sea from the greens and reds of the rainforest.

Looking into the crater was just as spectacular. I could see hot mud pools with steam bubbling out of then in great gulps. The cooler mud pools had crusted over and I had been warned not to venture into the crater as it was all too easy to step on a crust which would give way leading to certain death drowning in hot mud. There was even a sign by the path warning climbers to go no further. Everywhere there were streaks of bright yellow sulphur and pools of the stuff emitted a yellow-brown smoke. The colours were pretty to look at but the smell of rotten eggs was all-pervasive and slightly nauseating. I stayed up there just long enough to take some pictures and then made my way back down. When I got back to the car park the

Suzuki Alto was still there with a man sitting in it. I wheeled the Honda out from behind the bushes and rode back to the hotel.

I wanted to avoid the Handleys, so I went straight to my chalet when I got back to the hotel and showered and changed for the evening, and set off for Glass Bar earlier than usual.

I was a lot earlier than usual that evening; the bar was deserted and Mary was working alone in the kitchen. I did not want to sit alone in an empty bar, I wanted someone to talk to, so I asked Mary if I could help her in the kitchen.

'Of course, you can chop up some potatoes for me and then make a pepper salad.'

I followed her into the kitchen, washed my hands, donned an apron, and got work on a pile of sweet potatoes for mashing to go with the bass fish dish on the menu. After a few minutes Mary spoke. 'Now Douglas, what is on your mind?'

'Joelle, I suppose. I can't make her out at all. When we did the tour I was trying to be friendly, but she got very upset and dismissed me, telling me we were not friends and she was just doing her police duty as an island ambassador, and then at lunch time yesterday she appears in the bar coming over to sit and talk with me. I just wish I knew what was going on her head. Is it me that upsets her?'

After a few moments Mary spoke again. 'Douglas, it might not be anything you have done at all. She is a policewoman and has to deal with some very difficult situations sometimes, and if she is worried about something or feeling stressed she does go quiet and moody while she works it out.'

I was concerned and asked Mary, 'Why would she be worrying about me?'

'I did not mean that she was worrying about you specifically,' Mary replied, 'in fact, I think she probably likes you but won't admit it because she has been hurt in the past. Be patient with her, I am sure things will work out in the end.'

'You might be right,' I said, unconvinced, 'I need to think about that.'

Mary muttered quietly, perhaps talking to herself as much as to me, 'You two need to get to know each other better, go out somewhere together.' Mary moved on to lighter matters then and asked me why I had chosen to hire a motorbike.

'I have one back in England and I fancied something different. In truth I am a bit of a petrol head and I enjoy messing around with old cars and engines and things. I have a little collection of old cars at home. Not that I have had much chance to do anything with them for the last couple of years.'

'My husband, Paul, was the same. He had a Triumph motorbike that he imported from England. It terrified me the way he rode it round the island, no crash helmet or anything and sometimes with Joelle clinging on to the back of it shrieking with delight. I suppose that's where she gets her enthusiasm from. I worry about her on that motorbike as well.

'Paul also had a great big old car he used to tinker with, I am not sure what it was, a Princess I think. I remember it was the governor's state car, a gift from England when the island got independence. After about ten years it looked so old fashioned they decided to buy a new American car and as no one wanted the old limousine Paul bought it. It is still in the garage at home. Joelle says one day she wants to get it going again, but she has never done anything with it.'

'What happened to you husband?' I asked.

'He had a stroke a few years ago and passed away shortly after Joelle arrived on the island without anything, just a baby and the clothes she stood up in. He was very upset at what had happened and it affected him badly. Although he was retired by then he got her a job in the island police based on her criminology degree. I miss him a lot.'

'I am sorry.'

'Oh! I am OK now, I have Joelle and Jasmine to look after.'

I was interested in the car so I asked Mary a little more about it.

'I can't really tell you much except that it's called a Princess and it's big and it's painted grey. Speak to Joelle, she knows more about it.'

'I will talk to her and I will ask her if I could see it.'

'Well, if you want to look at it, I can show it to you. I shall be at home most of the day next Monday. Come up to the house and we will have a look.'

'I would love to but I don't know where you live.'

'Did Joelle not show you yesterday? The house is called Windrush and it is almost on the end of St Martin's Point. You can't miss it. Come round the back and find me.'

Chapter 27

Joelle de Nouvelas; Wednesday 19th November

It was now two days since the Island Tour when I got so angry, and I was sitting at my desk supposed to be planning the surveillance shifts watching Douglas's movements.

I was conscious I still had to keep my promise to Bernie and that meant I had to build a bridge to Douglas after what I had said on Monday. Yesterday, I thought I had the opportunity when I spotted him in the hotel. I suppose I had gone to the gym yesterday, half hoping to bump into him. I got a little buzz when I looked in the gym mirrors and saw him watching me and I guessed I might find him in the bar. I had not counted on him being with the woman called Jean. She certainly hated me and gave me the evil eye. I did wonder about their relationship. I told myself it was nothing to do with me but I can't help feeling a pang of jealousy when I think of them together.

I had calmed down now, I was not angry any more. I was still frustrated by Douglas and determined to find the evidence which would settle this surveillance one way or another. I realised that letting my frustration and anger show would not help and I determined to keep myself under control. After all, I reasoned, he was a charming enough person and good company, so it should not be difficult, but I knew it would be, and I knew I must keep my emotions under control.

I drifted back to the shift plans when I was interrupted by desk phone. The civilian administrator on the desk downstairs spoke. 'Joelle, I have the Tour Dock Manager on the phone. He wants to speak to someone to report some vandalism down at the dock.' The manager reported that someone was drawing graffiti on the Mall walls, which led through to the dock area.

'We have cleaned the walls down twice but this morning when I came in it had been done again.'

'No, I don't know who is responsible,' he replied to my question.

I promised him I would send someone down to take a statement as soon as possible.

I finished the shift plan and remembered I had not yet told Bernie that as there was not a suitable police vehicle available, we had hired a car for the surveillance. Unfortunately the cost was being booked to his budget, but I got it at a discounted price of $12 per day, which should be some consolation. There was no one in the office so I decided to go and take the statement myself. I took the Suzuki Escudo and as I drove across town my mobile phone rang.

'I would like to book an Island Tour please,' a voice enquired.

Puzzled I said, 'Pardon?'

'An Island Tour, I got your number of the car, and we thought a tour of the island in a limo would just suit us. How much do you charge?'

The penny dropped. Damn those jokers putting my phone number on the car.

'I am sorry; you must have the wrong number.' I hung up.

Over the next week I had five more such enquiries. *Perhaps I should start an Island Tour business*, I thought.

After I had taken a statement from the Dock Manager I drove round town and spotted more graffiti before returning to the police station. It was getting on for 5.00pm when Denzel, the PC who had been on surveillance that day came in to see me.

'I followed DJ today,' he reported. 'He went over to the Zip Line. When I got to the car park I saw him carrying a parcel and his bag with camera equipment into the reception building. I saw him later as he walked up the path to the first Zip Line station and he had neither the parcel nor the camera bag with him. He must have left them either in reception or in the changing room where he got the helmet and harness.

'Did you ask anyone where he had left them?'

'No, you told us to be discrete and not alarm him or be seen. I did go and ask the attendant at the first station how long it took to go round. He told me if they don't stop to go down to the Slave Museum if took about half an hour.'

It took DJ over an hour so I think he must have visited the Slave Museum. I watched him return from the last Zip Line station. He still had no bag or parcel. I later saw him walking up the path to the volcano rim and he was carrying the camera bag.

'Did you follow him up to the top?'

'Well, no. I think he would have seen me if I had.'

'Did you see him speak to anyone?'

'Yes, he had a conversation with the attendant at the first Zip Line attendant.'

I thought about this and said to Denzel, 'He could have delivered drugs in either the parcel or camera bag and I wonder if it was the same attendant that he spoke with when we did the island tour? I must find out what was in that parcel and what happened to it, and the camera bag when Douglas left them somewhere. I must also talk to that attendant. Perhaps we are getting somewhere now.'

I realised Denzel was wearing a police uniform. 'You weren't wearing that all day were you?'

'Yes I was ma'am. The sergeant says we must always look smart and wear uniform when we are on duty.'

'You fool!' I exploded. 'You are supposed to be on an undercover surveillance. What is the point of giving you a civilian car if you wear a uniform! You might at least have thought to cover it up. In future wear plain clothes!'

Denzel slunk off, muttering, but then turned back and said, 'There is one more thing Sergeant, I don't know if it's important, but I was talking to the chalet maid early this morning and saw Jay walking back to his chalet. The maid told me he had been out all night.'

'What time was this?' I asked.

'About 6.30 am.'

'Did he take his motorbike out?'

'I did not see, he might have done; he was walking back from that direction.'

I thought about this. The obvious answer was that he had been with the woman, Jean, and I did not like that thought at all. But then if he was walking back from where he parked his Honda he probably had been out on it and if so, what had he been doing?

I planned to take a trip to the Zip Line in the morning. I hung on at the station for a little while finishing some reports, doing overtime and expense claims, but really I was hoping to catch Bernie. He did not come in that afternoon so I finished up and headed for the bar.

Mary saw me parking the car and called me into the kitchen. 'Now,' she said, 'I want to talk to you privately. Douglas gave me that tip money to spend on Jasmine. I took her to have her hair styled and we bought some nice clothes. You are not to get cross with her, do you hear?'

'Yes Mother.'

She continued her lecture. 'And another thing. You do know you have upset Douglas. He does not understand your moods and neither do I. I don't know why you are behaving like this towards him. He is a nice man and I like him, but that is not the point. I know you have to find out if he is involved in this drug thing, and you know I think he is not, but you will never get anywhere if you keep upsetting him.'

Mary paused for breath. I knew she was right but she can be very blunt at times.

I left the kitchen to find Jasmine and admire her hair and new clothes, wondering whether this was a genuine gesture by Douglas or whether he had an ulterior motive. I was fast coming to the conclusion that I did not know him at all, and that he was a much deeper person than I had first thought, and perhaps could be a very clever drug baron. I cautioned myself to be careful.

I went to get his dinner from the kitchen, telling myself to be calm and friendly and talk to him despite the nervous flutter I could feel. Why does he do this to me?

Chapter 28

Douglas Jay; Wednesday evening, 19th

November

I finished in the kitchen and moved into the bar to sit on my usual bar stool. A very excited Jasmine bounced up to me.

'You look different this evening Jasmine,' I greeted her, 'you have had your hair done.'

'I have had it styled.' She twirled round to demonstrate. 'I had it cut. Just a bit, to tidy up the ends, so it's still shoulder length and it's been washed and straightened. Do you like it?'

'It's awesome! And, by any chance would that be a new top you are wearing?'

'And new shorts as well.'

She was wearing a burgundy-coloured figure-hugging tee-shirt with a geometric pattern embroidered with gold thread, and a pair of white knee-length cargo shorts.

'You look super Jasmine.' I did not add, and very grown up, even though the hairstyle and outfit made her look a lot older.

'Has you mother seen you yet?' I asked, wondering what Joelle would think.

Jasmine shook her head and moved closer to me, and putting one hand on my shoulder gave me a quick peck on the cheek. 'Thank you,' she said.

'For what?' I said in surprise.

'For this. Gran took me shopping after school and we spent the tip money you gave her to buy me something.'

'It was not really my money. You worked very hard that evening and deserved something as well.'

'Whatever!' Joelle said as she skipped off out the bar.

Mary emerged from the kitchen shortly after and asked me what I thought of Jasmine's purchases.

'I like them; she looks very grown up though. What do you think Joelle will say?'

'Oh, I think she will be fine. She wanted to get Jasmine's hair cut anyway because she thought it looked untidy.'

Jasmine had returned and was doing her homework, so I wandered out to the terrace. I did not particularly want to watch another sunset, memories of yesterdays were still all too vivid, but I stayed out on the terrace as I heard Joelle arrive and I watched as Jasmine showed her the new purchases. I could not hear what they said, but I was pleased that Joelle smiled at Jasmine as she disappeared into the kitchen.

Shortly after she came out and walked over to me carrying a tray with my dinner.

'Where would you like to sit?' I moved to a table in the conservatory.

Joelle served my meal, went to the bar and got a beer off Sean, and came and sat at the table with me. 'Thank you for Jasmine's shopping,' she said.

'Do you like it?' I asked.

'Yes I do. It makes her look very grown up though. I need to get my head around her becoming a young lady and not my little girl anymore.'

'Does not matter how grown up she becomes, she will always be your little girl,' I commented.

Joelle nodded and was silent for a bit before she said, 'Douglas, I owe you another apology.'

'Why?' I asked.

'On Monday, in the car, my comment about us not being friends was much too harsh and I did not mean it like that at all.'

'Oh?' I said non-committedly.

'No, what I meant was, that we really had only just met and did not know each other really at all, and,' she paused, looking for the words, 'well, I felt you were just coming on to me a bit too strong.'

I thought about that and the way I had behaved that morning. I suppose I had to admit I had pushed things a bit, hoping we might get something going together. I said to her, 'Joelle, I am really sorry if I appeared crass and pushy. I certainly did not mean to be and I would always try and treat you with respect. I was just enjoying being with you that morning and I suppose I got carried away. I really am sorry.'

Joelle thought for a few moments. 'I am glad I have got that off my chest, I really did not mean to be so cutting. Let's just leave it at that and see where we go from here.'

'That's fine with me Joelle, but I need to say to you that I don't understand your mood swings sometimes. Like now, you are charming, and good company, but then suddenly, for no reason I see, you turn morose and silent with me. I find it difficult to cope with.'

For a few moments Joelle was lost for words again. 'I

don't mean to be like that Douglas, but I think sometimes work issues come into my head and they are not always easy to banish, I suppose that's why I appear to change.'

'You could tell me about them, that might help us both?'

'Some of them I can't discuss, but I will try.'

We both sat in silence for a bit. The sun was setting, throwing glorious crimson and orange light at us, but neither of us was in the mood to see it. I was pleased that Joelle and I seemed to have a basis for at least talking to each other but I was also wondering how long it would last. I was also frustrated, wondering what magic it is that drives people to seek the company of one person, but be entirely indifferent to another. Of course, as far as I was concerned this was all about Joelle, a person whose company I sought, but had no relationship with, and Jean, a person with whom I had a strongly developing relationship, but felt entirely indifferent towards.

I sighed as Joelle broke into my thoughts. 'What sort of a day have you had?' she asked me.

I told her I had been zip lining and walked up the volcano.

'It's years since I have climbed that volcano,' she commented. 'What did you think of the Zip Line? Did you do the walk down to the slave camp?'

'Yes I did. Well I did not actually go right down to the reception and museum. I got as far as the two derelict sheds. Funnily enough one is derelict and falling down but the other has been repaired and was all locked up.'

'I wonder why?' Joelle mused. I could not answer that.

I pushed my dinner, mostly uneaten, to one side and got my wallet out and counted four twenty dollar bills out and handed them to Joelle. Sean said I should pay you.'

'What for?'

'The Island Tour. Funny but Sean did not seem to know anything about it.'

'I expect he forgot. He was very busy, and I did organise it all.'

She looked at the money. 'I will go and get some change.'

'Don't worry. Keep the $5 as a tip.'

Joelle looked at me, not angrily this time.

'I will pay you back one day,' she said, smiling as she stood, putting the money in her pocket, 'but now I must go and get and Jasmine home.'

I said I was tired and going back to the hotel as well.

As I walked along the beach I was thinking about Joelle and Jean, wondering what would develop with Joelle and worrying how to let Jean down gently.

Chapter 29

Joelle de Nouvelas; Thursday 20th November

I did not go into the station that morning. I collected my bag containing my police equipment, but also today, a small Nikon camera and notebook, and unlocked the garage where I kept the Triumph. I started him up, and headed straight for the Zip Line.

As I rode I thought about last night. I was not sure whether it had gone well or not. I suppose I had not expected Douglas to say anything when I apologised, and I was surprised when he commented on my mood swings. Of course I could not tell him the real reason was that I had to stop myself enjoying his company and focus on what I was supposed to be doing. It made me realise how difficult this job was getting.

I had read the books where the heroine police woman falls in love with the gangster and either becomes his accomplice, or changes him into a philanthropist, and I knew real life was not like that. I decided that I was not emotionally detached enough to encourage a friendship with Douglas while lying to him about the reason. I had to step back and avoid personal meetings with Douglas and focus on the surveillance and evidence gathering.

I felt happier with this thought and able to cope, even feeling confident that today I might find the evidence I needed. On the Triumph, it did not take long to get to the

Zip Line. I left the bike in car park. It was only 9.30am and there were no tourists about yet and the staff members were just opening up. I went around the side of the reception building where Denzel said that Douglas had hidden the little Honda. There was nothing particularly there, just dustbins screened from the car park by a wooden fence, in front of which were growing some well-established plants. *Why would Douglas have hidden the Honda?* I asked myself. The obvious answer was he did not want it to be seen, but why? Did he perhaps have to remove something from it? Or perhaps he wanted to throw something into the bins, and putting the bike there was just an excuse if anyone saw him poking round the bins. Then I thought, perhaps he was collecting something from the bins; he had made contact when we did the island tour and been given instructions for the drop off and where to collect his payment.

I will tell Denzel to search those bins. Serve him right for wearing a police uniform when working undercover!

I took some photos of the area round the bins and in the car park. As I walked into reception there was no one around, so I wandered about looking. There was nothing particularly interesting and I browsed through the attraction leaflets, mentally speculating that there might be a market for limousine tours round the island. I noticed that Raeni Curtis, who operated the gift shop in Hotel Glass Bay, had revamped her leaflets, and had opened a new shop in Nelson's Dock. The receptionist appeared and asked if she could help me. I showed her my warrant card and asked, 'Did you see a man yesterday,' I described Douglas, 'with a brown paper parcel,' I indicated the size with my hands, 'carrying a green bag containing a camera and photographic equipment?'

'Yes, he came into reception in the afternoon to collect the bag which had been left under the desk, down there,' she pointed.

'Did you see the package, do you know what he did with that?'

'No, I only saw him collect the bag, there was no package; but I did not see him arrive in the morning, Letta was on reception yesterday morning.'

'Is Letta around? I need to speak to her.'

'No, she is not working today.'

I thanked the receptionist and made my way up to the changing and fitting room.

The attendant there was sorting the helmets and harnesses into their sizes on the racks. Again I showed my warrant card and described Douglas. 'Yes, he was here yesterday morning, I fitted him with a helmet and harness and he went to ride the Zip.'

'Did he have a brown paper parcel or green bag with him?'

'Not that I saw.'

Next, I went to speak to the Zip Line operator in charge of the first station. There were a couple of guys on the first platform but they were wearing helmets and harnesses and explained that they were Zipping down to the next stations before the line opened and no, they did not know who was manning the first station. They sent me to see the supervisor. 'He will be in the tea room over there with some of the other guys.'

I walked across to the tearoom and asked for the supervisor. An older man stepped forward. 'Can you tell me who was manning the first Zip Line platform yesterday morning?'

'Yes, that was Zach.'

'Does he always man that platform?'

'No, sometimes he would swap with the guy on the forth station.'

'Can you tell me if he was on the first station last Monday?' He checked his work sheets and confirmed that Zach had it manned that day.

'Can I speak to Zach, where is he?' I asked, looking round the room.

A general murmur went round the room and the supervisor said, 'No. He just disappeared yesterday without saying a word to anyone and he has not reported in this morning.'

'Just disappeared?' I questioned.

'Yes, just after that policeman spoke to him. Just walked off. I had to cover the first station for the rest of day. If you find him tell him not to bother to come back.'

I thanked him, took a couple of pictures, and went back to the Triumph. Next I went down to the Old slave camp. Again I described Douglas to one of the guides there.

'Yes, I think saw him. He was here earlier this week, did not stay long. In fact weren't you with him?'

'Yes, that would have been Monday. He was not here yesterday was he?'

'No I don't think so, I did not see him anyway.'

That fitted. Douglas had told me he only looked at the old cabins under the Zip Line and did not walk down to the museum.

I walked up to check the two old derelict cabins. Just as Douglas had described, one was falling down but the other had been repaired and was locked with the windows boarded up. We would need to get in there and search for drugs but I realised it was no good me just breaking in. We would need a proper warrant and anyway a break in would not be admissible evidence. I was getting concerned though that Denzel and I asking questions would put the gang on alert. I walked slowly back to the Triumph and sat on it, forming my theory.

Douglas had made contact when we did the tour and got instructions for the drop. Zach, the attendant, was the prime suspect here. Douglas had the drugs wrapped up in a brown paper package. He had put that package in the bin and removed his pay off, similarly wrapped, from the bin. He had left space in his camera bag and had put the payoff into the bag at some point before collecting the bag in the afternoon. It fitted. A couple of loose ends bothered me. How had he smuggled the drugs on the island in the first place? Most likely on his person as Bernie had speculated. Why had he carried the package into reception as Denzel had seen? Why not just put them into the bag round by the bins? There were two more things I needed to do.

I went back to the Zip Line and asked the receptionist if Douglas had collected anything else in addition to the green bag. 'No, nothing.'

'Are you sure?'

'Yes.'

Next I went to find the supervisor to get Zach's address. I planned to tell Merv to go and find him. As an afterthought I asked the supervisor what Zach looked like.

'He is a big man, over six feet tall, broad shoulders and muscular. He has a shaven head, flat nose and yellow eyes; ugly with a big scar on his right cheek. Looks like a seedy night club bouncer.'

I thanked him for the information.

Time to go and see Bernie, I thought, as I sped off.

Chapter 30

Douglas Jay; Thursday 20th November

Geoff and Irene spotted me as I walked up the beach to the hotel last night and invited me to take a drink with them in the bar.

'You have missed Jean,' Irene told me. 'She said she was tired and has gone to bed early.' I did not want to say I was also tired and going to bed early. Irene was perceptive enough without me feeding her clues, so joined them in the bar. Irene wanted to know what I had been to and what I was planning.

'Jean told us you have a motorbike and like to go off on your own taking pictures.'

I agreed. Geoff was interested in the old airfield and derelict aircraft. Apparently he had been something to do with aircraft design at some point in his working life.

I had a couple of drinks with them and then made my excuses.

I had a quick thought whether to walk down to Jean's chalet and say goodnight, but even more quickly decided that would be a silly thing to do, so I went to my own chalet and to bed.

I got up late this morning and took a late breakfast.

Afterwards I sat in the Terrace Bar drinking coffee, wondering what to do, and more to the point wondering what to do about Jean. I decided it would very churlish to spoil her holiday by telling her how I felt. She would be going home at the end of the week in any event, so I thought, *I can be polite but keep a low profile.* With that thought I slowly made my way back to my chalet. I spotted the Handleys and Jean on loungers by the pool. I don't think they saw me so I pretended I had not seen them. When I got back to the chalet I lay on the bed to read, and was not far into the book when I fell asleep.

When I woke up it was lunchtime. I decided I would take a light lunch and then take a trip to one of the shopping malls on the outskirts of Kaeta Town. I had noticed a large American chain supermarket there and I knew from my US trips that this chain often had Kodak self-service photograph printing machines. *Worth a trip,* I thought, *if they have one I can get a couple of prints of that picture Joelle wanted.*

They did indeed have one, and they had photo frames as well. I cropped the picture down a bit to take out some distracting clutter in the background and printed an eight inch by twelve inch picture, which I mounted in a frame for Joelle. *I hope she likes it,* I thought.

It was late afternoon when I got back to the hotel and I decided to go for a swim and then walk down the beach with my camera, thinking I might catch some good pictures in the golden hour before the sun disappears. It was nearly dark when I got back so headed for the chalet to shower and change for the evening.

Later, I walked out of my chalet and stood uncertain, wondering whether to go the Glass Bar for the evening and risk meeting Joelle, or whether to stay in the hotel and risk meeting Jean. I was on the point of deciding Joelle was the better option when Geoff Handley walked up and clapped me on the shoulder.

'Douglas, old boy, well met,' he greeted me, 'I need to talk to you so come and join us for a drink.'

Well, I thought, *that's made this evening's decision.*

Geoff told me he had taken a taxi to the old airfield. 'Would you believe it,' he told me, 'I recognised that Dakota there. I remember working on them when I was a youngster; may have even done spanner work on that very plane at some time!'

He continued telling me about the plane. On my part I promised to take some pictures of it and if he could give me an email address I would send him copies.

Irene and Jean were looking very bored by this time and I sensed that Jean was manoeuvring to get me alone with her and away from her parents, so I suggested that we go into the dining room for dinner together. As walked in Jean whispered that there was a dance band on later and asked if I would like to dance again later. The waitress sitting us at a table saved me from answering. Dinner talk was inconsequential except that Irene kept saying what a handsome couple Jean and I made, winking at me, and telling Jean it was time she settled down. Fortunately Geoff seemed not to notice any of this and we spent most of the dinner talking about planes and engineering.

As we finished dinner I wondered how I was going to avoid getting trapped alone with Jean. Fortunately Geoff inadvertently came to the rescue. I had told him about my interest in classic cars and as we walked out of the dining room he pulled me to one side, saying, 'Let's leave the women to listen to the music, we'll go and have a beer over there and talk cars.' I was quick to accept and Jean glared at us both.

However, in the end Geoff and I felt compelled to go

back and join Irene and Jean. It did not take long before Jean pulled me up on the dance floor, despite me pleading I had no energy for dancing. While we were on the floor I saw Irene telling Geoff to finish his drink as they were going back to their chalet. She waved goodbye to us.

I started daydreaming what it would be like to dance with Joelle as the music slowed down and Jean put her arms round me for a close smoochy dance. I felt well and truly stuck now.

Chapter 31

Douglas Jay; Friday, 21ˢᵗ November

I was up at 7.00am this morning and went for my customary run round past Glass Bar and back along the beach, trying not think about Joelle and trying to forget last night.

I had danced with Jean until the band finished and packed up. Jean had said, 'Let's get a night cap and go back to my chalet, or would you rather we went back to yours?'

I told her I had already had enough to drink and really did not want to drink any more so then she suggested, 'We will go back to my chalet and I will make you a coffee or something.' In the end I told her I was planning a full day and really was exhausted and just needed to get to my bed tonight. She had looked very hurt but agreed that we both probably needed a good night's sleep. She had given me a quick kiss and we went our separate ways.

It occurred to me over breakfast that I had already been away for a fortnight and only had a week left booked at the hotel. I needed to decide whether I wanted to stay on longer, or go home. The thought of Christmas in cold, wet England with no family or friends was not very appealing.

After breakfast I remembered the other packet, which I promised to take to the sugar plantation. I put the package in the pannier box and tied the camera bag on top with a bungee strap I had borrowed from the golf instructor, and set off up the hotel drive. The Suzuki Alto was parked at the security hut again and the driver was talking to the security lady. I recognised the number and knew it was the same one I had seen when I went to the Zip Line. It amused me to stop by the driver and tell him, 'To save you following me around again today, I am going along the coast road and over the hill to the sugar plantation and old airfield to take some photographs.' *Good*, I thought. *Got you!* A look of horror spread over his face. I rode off before he could say anything.

It worried me a bit knowing that someone was interested enough to follow me around so I rode along slowly, stopping every so often to check if I was being followed and to photograph a view, or a particularly attractive plant. I did not see anyone following me, but at one point I spotted an iridescent bird and hung about for twenty minutes with the telephoto lens, waiting to get good picture of it.

When I got to the sugar plantation I thought about hiding the bike with the helmet but realised that I was being too imaginative. No one around here had any need to touch it. I took the package into reception. There was no one about and I could see where the brochures were supposed to go so I unwrapped the package put the brochures into the rack and threw the paper into the bin. I wandered around the reception and picked up a brochure for an Island Festival on Saturday. *That's tomorrow*, I thought. Eventually the receptionist came back and apologised for keeping me waiting. I asked to go on the guided tour. She charged me $10 and handed me a pair of earphones attached to a black box about the size of an old mobile phone. She instructed me to press the menu button, select my language, and then start.

'All the viewpoints are marked with large green signs.

Just follow the tour round as it plays. It takes about forty minutes to the do the tour and you will finish in the museum.' I did as I was bid and set off round the site.

It took me across to the field and told me about sugar cane cultivation, then to the windmills where I learnt how the cane was crushed. The tour took me past ruined buildings, which had once been the slave huts and the hardship the slaves endured was described in graphic terms. I felt this part of the site had a particularly sad atmosphere. Next it led me across to better preserved ruins on a slight rise away from the slaves' cabins. This was clearly a much higher quality building, which the gadget told me had been the owner's mansion. The final part of the tour was through the rum distillery and then back to the museum and shop.

After this I headed down to the main road and then turned south for the old airfield. It was not difficult to find. There was no fencing and I was able to ride straight on to an old runway and ride down it towards some buildings at the far end. Halfway down the runway was an old aircraft. I did not recognise the type but in faded red letters on the tail plane it had a winged symbol and writing in Cyrillic script. I guess the airplane was Russian and it appeared to have rolled off the runway at this point as the undercarriage on one side had collapsed one wing had broken and looked as if the other had just been cut off. The engine on the broken wing looked pretty mangled and rusty, while the engine on the other wing was missing. I looked inside and what had not been stolen had been smashed.

I rode on down to the buildings. Again they were derelict and had been ransacked as there was nothing at all inside them. However, behind them was the Dakota DC10 that Geoff was so interested in. It looked complete and was still sitting on its undercarriage, but the tyres were flat and inside most of the fittings were stolen or smashed.

One engine had been removed and it looked as if the other engine had been partially stripped. I took some photographs and was trying to compose a silhouette shot of the plane with the sun behind it when I heard an engine approaching. I did not take any notice of it at first but a few minutes later a large motorcycle roared round the corner of the building and stopped. I recognised it as a Triumph and I knew the rider must be Joelle, even though she was wearing black leathers and a full-face helmet with a darkened visor, and looked quite intimidating. I walked across to her as she sat on the bike. At one point I thought she was going to ride off but she did not. She killed the engine and took her helmet off.

'Hello Joelle,' I said. 'This is a surprise, what brings you here?'

'Actually, that is the question I am asking you,' she said.

'I am just looking round and taking some pictures. I could not see any signs which indicated I could not have a look.'

'It is private ground and you are trespassing.'

'Sorry, I was about to leave.'

'We had a report someone was prowling around the old planes. Apart from the fact that they are dangerous, removing anything from them is theft.'

'I have not taken anything,' I said, thinking, *She is being very officious.* 'You search me if you want.'

She softened her attitude a little, saying, 'No I am sure you did not take anything. Did you go into any of the old buildings?'

'No, I looked through the doors and windows but they are all empty and falling down.'

'OK,' she said as she dismounted and walked towards the DC10.

163

I decided it would be prudent to leave and so mounted the Honda and took my leave.

As I rode up the runway in the mirror I saw her entering the buildings.

Well what was that all about? I thought. *And more to the point how on earth did she get out here so quickly?* I had not been on the airfield for more than about fifteen minutes.

Chapter 32

Joelle de Nouvelas; Friday 21st November

Friday morning found me sitting in my office worrying.

The previous afternoon I had returned to the police station to see Bernie. I needed to update him with the new evidence from Douglas's visit to the Zip Line and get his opinion on my theory before doing anything else.

I was very conscious that my instructions were to observe and report back, but do nothing that might alert the suspect, but I did feel that now the evidence was building and I needed guidance. I also thought that it was time we reported back to the Americans, but I did not want to go over Bernie's head as it was his case after all.

But Bernie was not in the office. In fact he was not even on the island. He had gone to Barbados to attend a pre-retirement course; he had taken his wife and was not expected back until Monday.

So I was sitting in the office worrying.

Merv strolled in and I explained my dilemma to him. He just shrugged and said, 'It's easy isn't it? If in doubt obey instructions: so we just carry on watching.'

He was right, of course, another two days was not going to make any difference, especially a weekend. Even if we sent a Coconut report in today the Americans were unlikely to do anything with it until Monday, and anyway

Saturday was going to be a busy day as it was Festival day in Kaeta Town and four cruise ships were in.

I went through the Zip Line events with Merv and concluded by telling him to go and find this Zach character. 'You said he was ugly and had a scar?' Merv queried. 'Can you pass me the information we got from Light Foot Lionel?'

I passed my report across. Merv skimmed through it and said triumphantly, 'Here it is, big, shaven head and ugly with a big scar on his face. It's the same person, has to be.'

I congratulated Merv. I had missed that and it added another bit of evidence to the pile. Merv went off to find Zach and I started to go through the plans for tomorrow.

Denzel came to see me next to report that he had been to the Zip Line, tipped the bins out, and found this. He produced a plastic evidence bag with a brown paper wrapper inside it.

'Yes,' I said to him, 'it's coming together now. Send that off to forensics for testing to see if they can find what was wrapped in it.'

My mobile phone rang. 'Yes, Isaac?' Isaac explained that Douglas had spotted the tail.

'He stopped on his way out of the hotel and told me not to bother following him. He said he was taking the coast road and visiting the sugar plantation and old airfield.'

'How did know he was being followed?'

'I don't know.'

'Where are you now?'

'Still at the hotel. I don't know what to do.'

'Come back to the station and wait here for me,' I instructed him. Luckily I had the Triumph today so I donned my leathers and rushed off to try and see what

Douglas was doing.

When I got to the sugar plantation there was no sign of him but I reckoned I was there before him. I had gone straight across the island, riding fast. He was using the coast road and his Honda did not go that fast. I left the Triumph out of sight and waited with it. Eventually Douglas turned up.

He took a brown paper parcel out of pannier box and walked into reception. Shortly after he left reception with one of the tour recorders and set off on the tour on his own. He was not carrying the parcel, and fortunately he had not seen me either.

I waited and watched him but he just did the tour and took photographs and then left.

I went into the building and asked the receptionist if Douglas had given her a parcel wrapped in brown paper. She looked puzzled and said he had not given her anything.

'Was he carrying anything?'

'Yes, he had a camera and camera bag.'

'But no brown paper parcel?'

I thanked her and as I was walking back the Triumph she ran out after me, waving a square of brown paper. 'Is this what you are looking for? I found it in the waste paper bin and I did not put it there.'

I put the paper into an evidence bag and went back into the reception to look around. There was nothing unusual there; nothing I could see that indicated what Douglas had done with the contents of the parcel.

I went back to the bike again thinking, *It has to be something to do with that camera bag. Does he take the stuff out of the parcel and put it in the camera bag to take it to a drop point? But if he does that, why do it in the reception building? There are lots of other places he could do a transfer much more discreetly. Come to that, why wrap the stuff up in the first place only to carry it round and unwrap it again? And assuming he is going to a drop off point, where is it?* Maybe the gang knew we had discovered the slave camp drop and have set up another, possibly at the old airfield, if that is where Douglas was going next. It did not make sense and I did not have an answer. Perhaps Bernie would work it out.

I did not want to pass Douglas on the road so I waited a bit longer before I followed him, slowly, to the old airfield, presuming that was where he had gone.

I drove down the old runway slowly. I could not see the Honda nor any sign of Douglas. Had he gone somewhere else, or had he been and gone? I rode round the back of the old airport buildings and almost rode into the Honda parked on the old apron. Douglas was crouching in front of the old airplane taking a photograph. It briefly crossed my mind to ride away quickly, but I realised he had seen me and was walking towards me. I did not want to tell him I was following him so I had to quickly think of an excuse for being there. The best I could come up with was that we had received a report that there was a trespasser on the old airfield. I realised I sounded more officious than I meant to be, which caused Douglas to become defensive. I did not want to put him on his guard and thought I might recover the bad start if I tell him the history of the airfield and walk round with him. But as I dismounted he waved and said something to me and rode away.

I checked round the area but clearly nothing had been disturbed and there were no obvious places for a drop point. A complete search would be a massive exercise and I did not want to set that up without talking to Bernie first. I frowned with frustration as I made my way back to the police station. I could not figure out what he had been doing today. I caught sight of Douglas on the road ahead of me and decided to turn round and go back a different way. I thought he had not believed my explanation at the airfield and following him or roaring past him would do no good. Stopping him would be even worse! Yesterday I thought the evidence was stacking up but today's evidence did not make sense yet.

Chapter 33

Douglas Jay; afternoon and evening of Friday 21st *November*

After being seen off the old airfield by Joelle I went straight back to the hotel, arriving there just in time for the afternoon tea. Every afternoon the hotel serves a buffet selection of neatly trimmed sandwiches and cocktail nibbles for the guests. As I had missed lunch that day I grabbed a plate of sandwiches and nibbles and made way across to an empty table.

I was thinking about Joelle. She was pretty scary today, roaring up her massive motorbike dressed in black leathers and helmet. I had even thought for a moment she was going to arrest me for trespass. *Trouble is*, I thought, *I am attracted to her and perhaps under other circumstances, well, who knows what might happen; but I don't like these mood swings and it's time to back off. I will deliver the picture I have for her but maybe not spend so much time at Glass Bar in my last week, and use the Honda to extend my range and find another haunt.* My ponderings were interrupted.

'Hello Douglas. Can we join you? All the other tables are full anyway.'

I looked up and saw Geoff, Irene, and Jean. We exchanged stories of the places we had visited recently and then Irene said, 'Are you going to go to the festival and parade in Kaeta Town tomorrow?'

'I might but I have not really decided yet.'

Irene started telling me why I should go. 'It's supposed to be a marvellous spectacle with carnival floats, marching bands and music all round town and it all finishes on the town beach with a barbecue and music going on all evening. Anyway we thought we would take a taxi in and see the parade and perhaps do a barbecue in the evening. Why don't you come with us?'

Jean urged me to come as well, and as it solved the problem of how to avoid spending a romantic evening with Jean on the last night before she went home, it sounded like a good idea.

'Thank you Irene, I would like that very much.'

Irene was very pleased. Even Jean smiled.

I excused myself, saying I had some errands to run and went back to my chalet.

I had a shower and was drying myself and getting a change of clothes out of the wardrobe to wear that evening when I spotted my laptop and remembered I had promised Jasmine I would show her some of my pictures. I sat down in front of the laptop and started composing a short presentation of my best shots when there was a knock on my door. I hurriedly wrapped a towel round my waist and opened the door. Jean was standing there holding a small package in her hand.

'Douglas,' she greeted me, 'I wanted to give you a little present to thank you for making this a wonderful week for me. Can I come in?'

I said something about getting dressed first but Jean replied mischievously, 'Oh, that's OK, after all, I have seen all of you before,' as she stepped past me into the room. 'I wanted to give you this in private, and as we are going into town tomorrow and you have errands this evening, this may be the last chance we can be alone.'

She sat on the bed and invited me to sit next to her as she handed me a small gift-wrapped box. 'Open it,' she invited me. I pulled the paper off and opened the box. Inside was a small intricately sculptured silver model of a motorcycle. It was about three inches long and the wheels turned round. 'I thought it would remind you of the holiday,' Jean said anxiously. 'Do you like it?'

'Yes, I do, it is a very nice model,' I said as I turned over in my hands, inspecting it. 'It is very kind of you to give me a present but I am afraid I have nothing to give you in return,' I said, feeling very guilty.

'That's all right. I have the memory of a lovely holiday,' she replied, and I felt her hand slip under the towel and move slowly up the inside of my thigh. I put the model carefully on the floor and turned towards Jean, rolling her back on to the bed as the towel fell away.

Much later that afternoon I took the rucksack with my laptop and the framed picture of Joelle and walked along the beach to Glass Bar. Mary was there, flitting between the kitchen and bar and Jasmine was sitting at a table doing her homework. She told me that Belinda and Sean were coming in at 7.00pm and she did not know what Joelle was doing.

'I expect her to come and collect Jasmine sometime and I could do with her help, we are busy this evening but just lately she has been in a strange mood.'

I nodded and Jasmine came across to us.

'Have you finished your homework?' Mary asked her.

'Nearly, I have just a bit of reading but I will do that at home later.'

She turned to me and asked where I had been all day. I explained where I had been and told her I had taken more photographs, and that if she would still like to see them I had brought the laptop with me. I booted it up and started going through the pictures with Jasmine. I thought she might get bored with them but she seemed to find them interesting, stopping me now and then to tell me she knew the place in the picture or asking me how I got a particular picture of somewhere she knew well but made it look different. She told me that she would like a digital camera.

We got to the picture of Joelle at Carib Point and she stopped me, exclaiming, 'That's a lovely photo of Mum.' I showed her the framed version and explained that Joelle had asked for a copy and this was for her. Jasmine called Mary out to admire it as well. 'I will make sure that goes on display and not tucked away somewhere,' Mary said, and then she asked me how much longer I was staying on the island.

'I am booked in the hotel until the end of next week and I have not decided what to do then. I have nothing to go home for. It is cold and damp in England, but then again I am not sure there is much to stay here for either. One option is to visit another island but I have not made any arrangements yet.'

Jasmine interrupted, 'Oh, Douglas, you must stay. You could use our chalet along the beach over there. It is very comfortable and has a bathroom and kitchen and it is not let out to anyone until the end of January.'

I looked at Mary, who confirmed I could use the chalet if I wished.

'Come on Douglas, I will show it to you.' An excited Joelle ran into the kitchen to fetch a key. I looked at Mary and asked if it was OK.

'Of course, you must go and see the chalet before you make your mind up. My husband had it built, and we used to use it a beach home, but after he died I had it refurnished and now we let it out as a holiday home.'

Jasmine skipped along the beach in front of me and

opened the chalet.

It was a timber building with a thatch roof and a large veranda overlooking the beach. Inside were two quite large rooms, one furnished as lounge with French windows opening on to the veranda, and a second furnished as a double bedroom. At the back of the building was a passage leading to a door out on to a small paved area with access to a private road leading out past Glass Bar. To either side of the passage was a small kitchen and small shower room and toilet.

It looked very comfortable and I thought that if I did extend my holiday on Kaeta Island I would be happy to rent it. When Jasmine and I got back to the bar, Joelle was there. She gave Jasmine a hug and kiss, turning to me with a friendly, 'Hello. I see you have your photos here; Mary tells me you have been showing them to Jasmine.'

'Yes he has Mum and you should see the one he has of you.' Jasmine turned to me. 'Go on Douglas, show Mum.'

I produced the framed portrait and handed it to Joelle who took it out of the bag.

'Thank you Douglas, I don't know what to say. It is a beautiful picture, thank you.' Joelle smiled at me. Packing up my laptop I made an excuse to get away.

'Sorry Jasmine, we can look at the rest of the pictures another time. I have to get back this evening, I am eating dinner at the hotel with some friends,' I lied.

Chapter 34

Joelle de Nouvelas; afternoon and evening of

Friday 21ˢᵗ November

When I got back to the police station Isaac was waiting for me there, and also waiting for me was a note on my desk telling me that the Commissioner wanted to see me as soon as I returned. I groaned, thinking it must be something to do with the car and decided to deal with Isaac first.

I asked him how Douglas had spotted him. 'I don't know, I was parked by the security hut at the main gate and he stopped on his way out and said if I wanted to follow him he was going to the sugar plantation and old airfield.'

'Tell me, Isaac, do you always park by the security hut at the gate?

'Yes, it's the best place, we can see who comes and goes.'

I was exasperated and told Isaac he was an incompetent fool. I told him to go and change the car and to get a different model and different colour. 'And don't park by the main entrance in future. Hide the car in car park or something and make sure he does not see you.'

I walked up the stairs to the third floor and knocked on

the Commissioner's door. 'Come in and sit down,' he responded when I knocked on his door. 'Miss de Nouvelas,' he started, 'I have here a complaint about you.'

Oh God! I thought, *It must be serious if he is calling me 'Miss'.*

'It says you handcuffed an American tourist and marched her across to St Peter's Church where you coerced her husband into giving you $100. Is that correct?'

'Not quite, sir. I did arrest an American woman I caught shoplifting, and I did handcuff her and walk her across the square to St Peter's Church, where I suggested she might like to make a donation to the Orphans' Fund. Her husband kindly put $100 into the collection box.'

'And what did you do with the lady?'

'I gave her a warning and released her.' He scratched his chin and looked at me.

'I thought that there must be more to this than reported in this complaint, so I contacted her local police office, and they told me she has multiple warnings and two convictions for shoplifting.' He smiled as he put the letter of complaint into his out tray, saying, 'I will send a reply to the complainant advising that the matter has been thoroughly investigated and we find that the officer acted entirely properly and there is no case to answer.'

'Thank you sir.' I breathed a sigh of relief as I left. I did not ask about the car, though.

I went back down to my desk and, before packing up for the day, checked the plan and duty sheets for patrolling tomorrow's festival. *More overtime*, I thought, as I saw that Merv and I were together on general patrol duty round the town.

I went straight to the bar, wondering if Douglas was going to be there, deciding I would apologise if I had been a bit too sharp with him at the old airfield.

When I got there, it was deserted except for Mary in the kitchen. Neither Jasmine or nor Douglas were there but there was a laptop open on a table. Mary told me that Jasmine had taken Douglas to see the chalet. 'He thinks he might rent it if he extends his holiday,' she told me. I did not know if I wanted Douglas to extend his holiday or not. It would certainly put the pressure on us if he decided to go; perhaps I should encourage him to stay.

However there was another worry growing as I looked at the open laptop. The developing relationship I noticed between Jasmine and Douglas. I cornered Mary and asked her what they were doing and what she thought Douglas saw in Jasmine. She looked at me in surprise. 'They were looking at his pictures of the island, and I don't think he see's anything in her other than an intelligent teenager.'

'Do they go off together often?'

'No Joelle, they don't. This is the first time and it was Jasmine's suggestion, and he checked with me that it was okay before they went. In fact I would say that he has always been most proper in the way he treats Jasmine. You are being far too suspicious.' She continued, 'Actually, if there is any interest, it's Jasmine who is interested in Douglas. She is a young lady now. She has never had a father and was very young when her grandfather died, so she has no experience of men. It is quite a natural part of growing up for her to take an interest in men and I would rather she started with someone I, at least, trust.' She looked balefully at me and added, 'She needs a father figure.'

I was wondering what Mary was getting at, when Jasmine came running in followed by Douglas.

She was happy and excited and ran to hug and kiss me. I calmed down and accepted that as usual Mary was right as Jasmine told Douglas to give me a picture.

I regarded Douglas carefully, wondering about Mary's

barbed comment concerning father figures and trust, as he handed over a framed photograph of me standing on Carib Point. He had done something to the picture and it looked even better than I remembered it. I could not believe I was looking at myself. I looked far too pretty!

I was disappointed when Douglas said he had to go before I had chance to even apologise to him. I was also frustrated as I realised that under different circumstances I would like him as a friend, and sad and worried as I realised it was getting increasingly difficult to shut my emotions away and think of him as a drug criminal.

Chapter 35

Joelle de Nouvelas; Saturday 22nd November

I was not on duty until midday today so I had a lie in and then sat at the kitchen table drinking coffee. It was probably a good job Douglas had left early last night, as I reminded myself again that he was a suspect in a drug-running ring and that I had decided not to get personally involved.

Everyone would be in town today for the festival so Mary had decided to close the bar for the afternoon, and she and Jasmine had gone into town to meet some of Jasmine's school friends and watch the parade in the afternoon. I decided to go and wash the dust off the Triumph before going to work.

When I arrived at the police station it was busy with a lot of extra officers called in to patrol the festival.

Merv and I got ready, checked our equipment, and went out on patrol. Merv was in uniform and I was wearing jeans and a red short-sleeved shirt. As usual on these patrols I carried my bag slung over one shoulder, my pepper spray in one pocket and personal attack alarm in my other pocket with the ripcord clipped to my belt.

We strolled around the markets and route of the parade for a couple of hours as the crowds gathered, waiting for the start at 3.00pm. As Merv was in uniform we decided that Merv would follow me and I would be look out. If I saw anything I would make a sign to Merv who would move in for the arrest.

We were walking across St Peter's Square and Merv tapped me on the shoulder and pointed across the square. 'Douglas Jay is over there with that mousey-haired woman.'

I looked across and saw Douglas holding Jean's arm and pointing at something. I stood watching them as they talked to each other. *The rat*, I thought. *He has had a girlfriend all along.*

Merv said he knew the woman. 'She is a guest at the hotel, she seems to be travelling with an older couple but I can't see them at the moment.'

'Have you seen Douglas with her before?'

He regarded me with a quizzical look. 'No, I haven't. Is it important?'

'No, I was just asking,' I replied haughtily as I moved away.

The crowds were getting thicker now and I pointed to man wearing baggy cargo trousers and a loose shirt. 'Have you seen him before?' I asked Merv. 'He seems to be taking a lot of interest in those women with the handbags.'

'No,' Merv replied thoughtfully. 'I know all the local villains and he is not local.'

'You stay back and I will move closer and see what he is up to. Of course he may be a harmless tourist.'

I moved closer and was standing almost behind him when I saw him execute a classic pickpocket. He bumped into a tourist, pushing him sideways and put his hand out to steady the victim, saying, 'I'm very sorry man!' as he removed the victim's wallet from his hip pocket.

I instinctively shouted, 'Stop, thief – you are under arrest!' and grabbed the back of his shirt.

He turned on me, dropped the wallet, flicked open an eight inch blade and waved it front of me yelling, 'Back off, bitch!'

We just stood facing each other, and I told him to calm down and put the knife away, but he stepped forward, waving the knife in my face, shouting, 'Back off, or I'll scar you!'

I yanked the alarm out of my pocket and heard it screech. As I stepped back, I raised my hand up to give him a shot in the face with the pepper spray as he lunged forward with the knife. Instinctively I threw my arm to protect myself and at the same instant, as the blade connected with my arm, I saw, out of the corner of my eye, another large man beside me raising his fist to punch me. He hit me hard on the side of my head and I thought I was going to black out. I don't know what happened to the pepper spray; I think I must have dropped it. The guy with the knife suddenly dropped the knife and staggered backwards and I felt another blow glance off my cheekbone. My last memory before passing out was someone else grabbing my arm and pulling me over.

Chapter 36

Douglas Jay; Saturday 22nd November

I met Irene, Geoff, and Jean Handley for lunch in the hotel dining room. Lunch was a buffet meal and the selection was enormous. There were usually two or three hot dishes, a curry, a West Indian style stew with chicken or beef, and a chef's special which today was a prawn pasta. Geoff and I went for the pasta but the two ladies opted for a light salad, giggling that the food was too tempting so they were only eating light lunches to avoid putting on weight. It did not stop them having ginger, pecan and rum chocolate brownies as a dessert, though.

We had booked a taxi at 1.30pm expecting to arrive in Kaeta Town at about 2.15pm in plenty of time to make our way into town to watch the parade. The taxi dropped us on the edge of the town centre and we made our way through the general market heading for St Peter's Square. We were standing at the back of the square as the spectators began to gather round. I put my hand on Jean's arm and pointed out the route the procession was supposed to take across the square. I was telling her that although it started at St Mary's Church, the band and people in dress costume walked round the Fish Market first and assembled in St Peter's Square to wait for the floats and other wheeled vehicles. They all assembled on the other side of the Fish Market, but because the streets were so narrow, the floats had to make their way through the wider roads outside the Fish Market and in to St Peter's Square where they met with the band. Geoff moved up next to us, pointing out some sort of commotion on the other side of the square and we pushed our way over to see what was happening. Everything then seemed to happen in an instant.

I heard a personal alarm suddenly screech out. I remembered Joelle telling me she always carried an alarm and I ran forward, pushing people out of my way. I reached a cleared patch surrounded by a ring of people watching a woman being threatened by a man with a knife. I immediately recognised Joelle and I ran towards her. I don't know what I intended to do; I was being driven by instinct and adrenaline. I saw the man with the knife lunge towards Joelle and something fly out of her hand towards me as she raised her arm. I caught it and realised it was her pepper spray. By now I was almost level with Joelle, spraying pepper up her back and over her shoulder. The man with the knife made another lunge and got a face full of pepper spray. But as he dropped the knife and fell backwards I realised that Joelle had been punched on the side of the head and that this assailant was swinging another punch at her head. I grabbed her arm and pulled her away from the punch, which glanced off her cheekbone. As I supported Joelle who was about to black out I saw a police officer cosh the man doing the punching and push him down to the ground. I lowered Joelle gently to the ground and looked around for help. The nearest policeman was busy handcuffing the man on the ground and there were two policemen on the other side of the square. One was pursuing the man I had pepper sprayed and the other was heading towards Joelle and me.

Someone put a hand on my shoulder and I turned and saw Geoff. He grabbed my arm and pulled me up saying, 'Come on Douglas, we should get out of here before they arrest you as well!' I started saying that I was not one of the attackers but Geoff interrupted me. 'I know that but you know what these local coppers are like. They arrest first and ask questions later. If they catch you will spend a couple of nights at least in a cell while they sort it out.'

I let him lead me away into the crowd I heard someone shout at me, 'You, stop. I want to talk to you!' Geoff hurried me off.

Chapter 37

Joelle de Nouvelas; Sunday 23rd November

It was 7.30 am and I was lying in a hospital bed, waiting for the registrar to do his morning rounds and declare me fit for discharge. I had slept well overnight and woken up about half an hour earlier with a mild headache, throbbing arm and enormous black eye. Apart from that I felt fine as I lay in bed going through the events of the previous afternoon.

I remembered events up to the second punch and someone pulling me over but then I must have blacked out. When I came to, I was lying in St Peter's Square with Merv tying a rough bandage round my arm to stem the bleeding. I asked him what had happened and if he had caught the three assailants. 'There were only two, and yes we have got them; they are handcuffed over there.' When I looked over they were handcuffed, back-to-back, round a post with two PCs watching them balefully.

'What happened to the third one?' I had asked Merv.

'The third man was Douglas Jay and he actually saved you from a more serious injury by spraying the knife man with pepper and pulling you away from the one punching you while I overcame him.' I was so surprised I nearly passed out again. I looked around the square but all I could see were half a dozen PCs moving the crowds back and clearing an access road.

'Where is Douglas now?' I asked Merv.

'I don't know. As soon as he lifted you down to the ground he took off with an older man.'

We heard sirens approaching and a police van pulled up in the square to take the two men away, followed by an ambulance to take me away.

When I got to the hospital, I was rushed into an emergency room and hooked up to a monitor. A doctor examined me and declared that all I had suffered was a very mild concussion and black eye. A nurse came in next and cleaned up my arm.

'You were lucky,' she said, 'it was only a single slash and is not very deep. I will put stitches in and a dressing. Keep the dressing on for a week and don't get it wet.'

The doctor decided to keep me in overnight, for observation, he told me. I was moved into a private room and a nurse came in and gave me a painkiller and a pill to help me sleep. She also told me I had a couple of visitors. 'Who?' I asked. I had a crazy thought that it might be Douglas, but it was not, it was Mary and Jasmine. At first Jasmine was tearful but when she realised I was not seriously hurt she cheered up and started laughing at the black eye that was colouring up.

'That's going to be a real purler!' she giggled.

Mary was also very relieved, and when I told her what Douglas had done she just said, 'Well, he would look out for you, wouldn't he.'

What does she mean by that? I thought. They did not stay long, the sleeping pill was having its effect and I was getting very drowsy.

So here I was lying in bed thinking that I now really did owe Douglas and that was going to be a big problem for me. I felt very frustrated and bit cross. *Why*, I thought, *has he got to be so damn nice and considerate all the time and not behaving like a criminal should?*

A nurse brought me some breakfast. Not having eaten the day before, I was hungry and ate it all, so she brought me some extra toast. The doctor eventually came round at ten o'clock and examined me quickly and said I could go home. I was about to get dressed, but found my shirt stunk of pepper and my jeans were covered in blood. The nurse took pity on me and said she would find me something to wear. 'You also have a visitor, shall I bring him in?' It was Merv, who had come in to see how I was.

'I need to get a statement off you but we can leave that until you come into the station. I also need to find Douglas Jay and get a statement off him.' I told Merv I would attend to Douglas. The nurse came in with a dressing gown. She apologised and said that was all she could find. I was really grateful and told her the dressing gown was absolutely fine. Merv offered to drive me home.

When I got home I had a bath, waving my arm in the air to keep it dry, and fixed myself some lunch. In the afternoon I decided to drive over to the bar and see Jasmine and Mary. When I got there I sat with Jasmine drinking a cup of tea, deciding whether to walk along the beach to find Douglas.

Chapter 38

Douglas Jay; Sunday 23rd November

It was Sunday afternoon and I was on my own, reclining on my favourite lounger, shaded by a palm tree, watching the Caribbean Sea roll gently up the beach.

I had eaten breakfast with the Handleys that morning and said goodbye to Geoff and Irene, and promised Jean I would get in touch when I returned to the UK. Their taxi arrived, I shook hands with Geoff and kissed Irene and Jean on the cheek, thanking them for their company. It was with some relief that I watched them drive away. All day I had wanted to find out how Joelle was. I had no contact number for Mary, only the bar number, and I had phoned it last evening but Sean told me Joelle was in hospital and Mary and Jasmine had rushed off to see her, and, no, he did not how serious her injuries were. I gave him my mobile number and asked him to phone me if he had any news. He never phoned back.

By morning I feared the worst and was contemplating phoning the police station to ask after Joelle, but I had moped around all morning, heeding Geoff's final words at breakfast: 'Don't get involved Douglas. The police don't know who you are but they will if you phone them. Anyway if she is seriously injured there is nothing you can do.' As an afterthought he added, 'And don't even think of going to the hospital to visit.'

So I was still moping around and worrying. Eventually I decided to go to Glass Bar, hoping Mary would be at there.

I was walking along the sand looking at my feet when I heard someone call my name. I looked up and saw Joelle walking towards me wearing a large pair of dark glasses.

Our encounter was not like that moment when two lovers run up to each other and embrace, in fact, it was quite the opposite. We approached rather warily, wondering what to say, and stopping to look at each other when we were close enough to talk.

I said, 'Joelle, you are out of hospital then.'

'Yes, I was discharged this morning.'

'How badly were you hurt?'

'A headache, which has gone now, a small cut on my arm.' She held her arm out to me. 'And a huge black eye.' She did not remove her glasses. After another moment's silence, Joelle spoke again. 'Douglas, I came to thank you for yesterday. Merv told you were only bystander who came forward to help me, and were it not for you disabling the man holding the knife I would likely have been badly injured as he could not have tackled both men on his own.'

'Who is Merv?' I asked.

'He and I were patrolling together but we got separated by the crowd so I was on my own. I was stupid, I should have waited for him before making an approach.'

I was a little surprised by Joelle's sincerity, so I just said, 'Well, I am glad you are not more seriously hurt.' We walked together slowly along the beach back toward the hotel.

I wondered how she knew it was me helping her yesterday afternoon. 'Merv recognised you.' That puzzled me because I did not think I had ever met Merv, but I let it pass. We walked on in silence. I was not sure where we were going, I had just fallen into step beside her, and did not want to just walk off and leave her at that moment, so I asked her if she would come in to the hotel and have a drink with me. 'Yes, I would like that,' she accepted.

We went into the beach bar. I ordered a glass of wine and Joelle ordered a lemon tea.

'Did I tell you that my father built this hotel?' she said.

'I think you did mention it.'

'At one time he owned a lot of the land round here including St Martin's Point and a half mile strip of land all along the back of the beach here. He bought the land just after independence when the land was worthless. St Martin's Point was just arid scrub, worthless for agriculture, and the land along the back of the beach was just wet and marshy. The owners were delighted to get some money for what they saw was worthless land, but father saw that tourism was the future for the island and that coastal land would be worth a fortune, one day.'

I kept quiet, waiting for her to speak again. After a short silence she asked, 'Was that Jean, the lady I saw you with yesterday?'

'When?'

'I saw you in St Peter's Square just before I was attacked.'

I explained about the Handleys and going to watch the parade with them and then told her, 'Actually I never saw the parade. After you were injured, I did not feel like staying in town so I got a taxi back to the hotel on my own.'

'You were not really friends with Jean then?'

She watched me carefully as I answered, 'No, not really,

we just met this week and she has gone home now. Anyway, she was not my type at all.'

'Who is your type?'

I could have said 'you', but instead said, 'I'll know when I meet her.'

'And have you met her yet?'

'I might have done, I am not sure.'

We regarded each other carefully and then Joelle, becoming business-like, said, 'I must be going. As you are the only independent witness, we need a statement from you about the attack yesterday. Can you come into the police station sometime soon?'

I said I would, although I did recall Geoff saying that if I went to the police station they would clap me in irons. I hoped he was joking.

Chapter 39

Joelle de Nouvelas; Monday 25th November

A lot had happened since I last spoke with Bernie and I was aware that I had to tell him everything that had occurred over the last four days. I was very conscious of his instruction to stay detached from Douglas, but on friendly terms. That was getting very difficult. I had savoured the brief time we had sat together in the hotel talking, and my heart had jumped when he said he might have met someone who was his type, but I was acutely aware that we could end up arresting Douglas, as the evidence, even though circumstantial, increasingly seemed to be pointing towards his involvement with drugs at some level, and I while I longed to see him again, I did not want to be around the station when he was brought in.

Bernie was in early that morning and came looking for me. 'I hear you got mixed up with some nasty characters on Saturday.' He looked at my face and asked me if I should even be at work. I told him I was fine. 'I need to talk to you,' he said as he invited me into his office. He started by telling me that my two assailants were from Jamaica and were known thieves who worked all the islands, especially festivals and carnivals. 'They have both been in prison for GBH before, and they will go down for a good long time for this one. Have you done your statement yet?' he asked, and then commented, 'Bit of a coincidence Douglas Jay turning up like that.' He gave me a knowing look, which I ignored.

I started by telling him full reports were on the Coconut file.

'I know, I've read them.'

He must have been in early then, I thought, as he went on to ask me to go through events in my own words.

'We followed Douglas to the Zip Line and when he got there, for some reason, he left his motorbike parked out of sight behind the dustbins. He had a brown paper parcel, which he took into reception and then it disappeared. We later recovered the paper and have sent it off to forensics. He spoke with a Zip Line attendant operator who we believe may be an intermediary contact. We also believe he checked one of the old slave camp buildings, which may be where the drugs are stored.'

I went on to tell Bernie that the next day I visited the Zip Line and interviewed the staff. 'I spoke to the receptionist; she was not the one on duty when Douglas arrived the previous day. She knew nothing of any parcel and not seen anything. The attendant has disappeared. His description matches the one of the drug contact that Light Foot Lionel gave us. Merv went to find him but I have not yet had chance to follow that up.'

Bernie interrupted me, dialled an internal number on his phone and said to someone, 'Can you find Merv and ask him to come into my office?' He turned back to me and told me to carry on.

'I then checked the slave camp's disused hut. It has recently been repaired with a new roof, the windows are boarded up and it has a new and substantial door which was locked. We need to get a search warrant and get a team inside.'

'Leave that to me,' said Bernie. 'Do you have a theory?' he asked me.

'Well, one theory that fits is that he made contact when we did the tour and got instructions for the drop. Zach, the attendant, is now a prime suspect. Douglas had the drugs wrapped up in a brown paper package. He put that package in the bin and removed his pay-off, similarly wrapped, from the bin. He left space in his camera bag and put the payoff into the bag at some point before collecting the bag in the afternoon.'

Bernie nodded while he thought about what I had just said. I continued, 'However there are still loose ends and not everything fits. How did he get the drugs onto the island? He could possibly have concealed them on his person. Why would he wrap the stuff up and carry it round only to unwrap it again? When I speak to him he quite openly tells me where he has been and who he has spoken to. If this is all part of some elaborate drop I would expect him to at least gloss over such events, and finally, on Friday he visited the sugar plantation and the old airfield, again with a brown paper package which disappeared. The paper was subsequently found in a waste paper bin. The events of that day make no sense at all and don't fit with my theory, unless, the gang has found out that we know about the drop at the slave hut and quickly set up a new drop point at the old airfield.'

'Perhaps that was just a blind to throw any observation off the scent,' Bernie commented.

'Maybe,' I replied, 'or he could have made the first drop but they were alerted by us poking around, and that's why Zach disappeared. Douglas might have had to wait for a new drop before he could get rid of the second parcel.'

'In that case where did he get instructions for the second drop?' Bernie queried.

'On his morning run, or perhaps in the sugar plantation, and that's why he took the parcel in there but came out without it,' I speculated.

'This is all guesswork,' concluded Bernie, 'let's concentrate on the Zip Line end first and see what else turns up.'

'That reminds me, he spotted the team following him on Friday,' I started to tell Bernie, but Merv walked in and interrupted us.

'You wanted to see me, sir?'

'Yes Merv, did you check out this Zach character?'

'Yes, I went to the address we had for him. He rented a single bedsit room. The landlady said he came home early on Thursday, packed his bag and disappeared, even though he had paid his rent for the rest of the month. Apparently he gave her no explanation and was very agitated.'

Bernie thanked Merv, who, as he left told us that Douglas was in the police station.

'He came in asking for you, Joelle. I went down to see him, put him in an interview room and asked him to write out his statement of Saturday's events.'

'How did he seem?' I asked.

'Nervous,' Merv replied.

Bernie adopted a cunning look. 'Hm. Give him a few more minutes then I will go down and get his statement. I would like to meet him for a little chat.'

When Bernie returned from interviewing Douglas he called me back into his office and opened the conversation. 'I see what you mean about him talking openly. He certainly gives the impression he has nothing to hide. There is one thing though. This 'Geoff Handley' person. Is it coincidence that he turns up the week Douglas Jay gets his own transport? We only have Douglas's word that they were only passing holiday acquaintances. What were they doing together at the festival and why did Geoff drag Douglas away so quickly with this cock and bull story that he might get arrested?'

Bernie looked at me but I had no answer. It had not even occurred to me to question Douglas's explanation. Bernie scratched his head and picked up his phone asked the receptionist to get Detective Superintendent Passmore in Scotland Yard.

'I know him well, we have worked together before, and he is a good contact,' Bernie explained.

A few moments later his phone buzzed. He asked D.S. Passmore if he had ever come across a Mr. Geoff Handley. I gathered from the conversation that he had not. Bernie explained the possible connection and asked for Handley to be checked.

Bernie bought his attention back to me by saying, 'You won't have seen this yet, the report has just been put in the file. You asked for the aircraft Douglas arrived on to be deep cleaned. They don't actually do a deep clean but the long haul aircraft are all cleaned after each return trip. Well on its return after this trip they found, stuffed underneath one seat, a small blue bag, measuring fifteen inches, by nine by twelve deep. It was partitioned inside but was empty. It was described as being typical of a camera carry bag.'

We looked at each other and I said, 'That's strange, why would he swap bags on the plane?' Bernie shrugged. The significance of this find did not occur to me at the time.

Bernie started saying it was time to submit another Coconut report when my mobile phone rang. Bernie told me to answer it.

'Yes Denzel. He is where? Just rode his Honda up to my house!' I exclaimed. 'What is he doing there? No, don't go in just stay out of sight, I am coming up.'

I looked at Bernie, who confirmed that I should go and find out what is going on. 'And be careful,' he cautioned, 'make sure Denzel is close in case you need backup.'

Chapter 40

Douglas Jay; Monday 24th November

After I had finished giving my statement about last Saturday's events I headed for Mary and Joelle's house to meet Mary, who was going to show me her husband's classic car. I was looking forward to seeing the car and also Joelle if she was at home. In my garage in Wiltshire I had a couple of old MG sports cars which I had restored myself, and finding a new motor car locked away and forgotten in a garage gave me a thrill. I found the house called 'Windrush' and it was the older brick-built villa right at the end of St Martin's Point, which I had noticed when Joelle drove me around the island. The house was approached up a drive through mature gardens. The drive circled around the front of the house and then passed round the side to the back of the property. Mary had said I would find her round the back so I followed the drive. At the back, the house opened up onto more gardens. To one side, discreetly hidden by trees and bushes, was a paved area with a Suzuki SZ3 Wagon parked. The paved area was flanked by two smaller outbuildings and large two-storey garage, which I guessed would hold at least six cars.

I cut the Honda's engine, removed my helmet and went looking for Mary. I knocked on one door and got no answer so I walked along a veranda to a pair of open French windows and called out, 'Mary!'

'I am down here in the garden!' she called out. I walked towards the voice and found Mary cutting flowers. 'They are for the bar. I like a real flower on each table,' she explained. 'You have come to look at the car, of course. If you could hold the basket for me while I finish then we can go and have a coffee and I will show you the garage. There are not as many flowers at this time of the year so sometimes I just make up a small spray of coloured leaves,' Mary explained as we walked up to the house. She showed me into a large modern kitchen and bade me sit down as she poured two coffees.

'Milk and sugar?' Mary asked.

'Just milk,' I replied.

'Now, Douglas, you must tell me all about last Saturday. Thank goodness you were there to help Joelle.'

I explained what I had witnessed. Mary shook her head and said, 'That girl never tells me much. She just said she had been threatened and punched and that you and Merv had overcome the two men. I would have been worried sick if I had known what really happened.' At this point we heard a car pull up and a minute later Joelle flew into the room.

'Are you all right Mary?' she shouted.

'Of course I am all right. Douglas and I are just talking about last Saturday.'

She turned on me, demanding, 'What is he doing here?'

Mary admonished her, saying, 'Calm down Joelle, and remember you are in my home not the police station. Douglas is here at my invitation to see your father's old car. Joelle apologised and Mary told her to sit down and have a coffee with us. While we drank, Mary told me about her garden and how much she loved it. 'We have to get a gardener in, I could not cope with it all myself,' she explained. She looked at the clock and turned to Joelle.

'Joelle, I must get down the bar and open up for lunch. You can show Douglas the car, but don't forget to lock up if you go out again.' Joelle did not look too pleased and told her mother that she really did not have time. Mary simply said, 'Of course you have, you are supposed to be resting today and you have nothing else to do.'

Joelle reluctantly went to fetch a key and we walked across to the garage. She explained the car was a 1967 Vanden Plas Princess with a landaulette body. 'It's actually an Austin chassis and engine with a custom built body by Vanden Plas. They ceased production of these cars in 1968 so this is one of the last they would have built and being an open-topped car it is quite rare. At least that's what Dad told me,' she clarified.

She entered the garage by a side door and then pulled back the big double doors to let some light in. She pulled a large dustsheet off the car and revealed a large limousine painted in two-tone grey. Dark grey wings swept back the full length of the vehicle with the upper body panels finished in a lighter grey. It was resting on blocks keeping the weight off the white-walled tyres.

'I put it on blocks after my father died,' she told me. 'One day I would like to recommission it and drive it.'

'Did your father use it much while he was alive?' I asked.

'Yes, a bit. I remember we went for a picnic in it just before he died and he let me drive it up the drive and put it in the garage. That was the last time it moved.'

We opened a door and looked inside. It was trimmed with walnut and grey leather with grey Wilton carpets and still smelt of old leather. Unfortunately there was a burn mark on one of the seats. Joelle saw me looking at it and said, 'that was the President, he dropped his cigar one day. I am not sure it can be repaired and a new seat cover would not look right.'

'We could get that fixed,' I said, 'I know an upholsterer in the UK who would match the leather and just let in a new panel to replace the damaged one.' We opened the bonnet and I admired the massive engine. It was a straight six overhead-valve, four-litre petrol engine.

'I wonder if it would start?' I pondered.

'I don't know, shall we try? We could use the Toyota battery and there is a can of petrol for the mower somewhere.' Joelle went to get the battery while I cleaned the points, checked the oil, removed the rocker cover, and turned the engine over by hand to make sure nothing was seized up. I went to find the can of petrol and noticed Joelle's motorbike parked at the other end of the garage. I put half a gallon of petrol into the tank as Joelle returned carrying the battery. 'I hope it will be powerful enough to turn this engine over,' she said as she connected it up.

Joelle got in the car to turn the engine over while I watched. 'Turn it over without the ignition on,' I told her, 'until the oil pressure registers.' Fortunately the battery was fully charged and once it had got the engine moving it turned it over quite well.

'We have oil pressure!' Joelle called out.

'OK stop and turn the ignition on when I tell you.'

I checked that the petrol had run through to the carburettors and called out to Joelle to give it a go. We were like a couple of kids dancing round the car with excitement as the engine started on the third attempt and settled down with a steady tick over.

'Let's get it off the blocks and drive it round the house.' Joelle laughed. She went to pull a large hydraulic jack out. I switched the engine off while I helped her take the car off the blocks. It only took a few minutes. I put the rest of the petrol in the tank and we started the engine again. 'You drive it,' Joelle said.

'Don't you want to?' I said.

'Yes, but I would rather you did first.'

I got into the driver's seat and Joelle sat in the passenger seat. We could not get it into gear. 'I think the clutch has seized,' I said. 'Go and jack up the back until the wheels are just clear of the ground.'

'OK, done.' Joelle said.

'Stand back out of the way!' I instructed. When she was clear I put the car into forth gear and started the engine, I depressed the clutch pedal and then yanked the handbrake on hard. The back wheels stopped and there was a loud bang as the clutch released and the engine stalled.

'That's why I wanted you to drive it first,' Joelle laughed as she took it off the jack. She climbed back into the car, we started the engine again, and this time engaged first gear. I gingerly let up the clutch and the car moved forward with a loud grinding noise, which quietened down after we had moved a few feet. 'I think that was a seized brake,' I said. I tried the brakes and nothing happened. 'We have no brakes!' I told Joelle, but we carried on anyway round the side of the house and round the circular drive in front of the house and back to the garage using the handbrake to stop.

'It's your turn now.'

'Do you think I could?'

'Of course, just remember to use the handbrake to stop.'

After Joelle had driven the car round the drive a couple of times we put it back in the garage. 'Thank you Douglas,' she said.

'What for?'

'For getting the car running again. It's given me the impetus to get it going properly now.'

'Well, if you do any work on it while I am still here I

would love to help you.'

'I will take you up on that.' Joelle smiled at me.

I asked her for another favour. 'Could I have a look at your Triumph, please?'

She walked over to the bike, opened the door and pushed it out into the sunlight for me to admire. 'It's a road cruiser: a Triumph Thunderbird Commander. It has a 1699cc twin cylinder water-cooled engine with a six-speed gearbox.' It was a mean-looking machine, with gleaming burgundy-red paintwork and lots of chrome. The saddle was low slung between the rear mudguard and petrol tank and there was a pillion seat sitting on top of the rear mudguard. Joelle started the engine for me. It ticked over quietly but when she revved it had a deep, loud bark. 'Would you like to ride it around the drive?' she asked.

'Would I! Would you let me?'

'As long as you don't fall off it!' she laughed. I mounted the machine and very gingerly rode off. I could feel the power as I changed into second gear.

I rode back to Joelle and dismounted. She took the bike and drove it back into the garage and turned it round. As she did this I thought this was a good morning and I had enjoyed being with Joelle. I remembered Mary's comment that we should go somewhere to get to know each other and I resolved it was now or never. As she walked back to me I asked, 'I have one more request before I go?'

'Yes?'

'Please would you have dinner with me tomorrow evening at the hotel?' She did not answer immediately, just stood frowning slightly, watching me.

Chapter 41

Joelle de Nouvelas; Monday 24th November

I had really enjoyed spending the morning playing with the Princess and actually getting it running and driving it. In fact the morning was such fun that for the first time I put the drug smuggling and the investigation to the back of my mind and enjoyed working with Douglas. But, I had not expected him to want to take me out, let alone take me to dinner, and when he asked initially I was pleased. However it brought me back to reality with a jolt. I had forgotten who he was, that he was under surveillance, and that was the problem. I knew I could not emotionally cope with him taking me out to dinner when I was still supposed to be watching him. As I stood there looking at him I was thinking, *Perhaps, if this has a happy ending, and he is still talking to me then we could have dinner together.* I was in a real quandary and Douglas was expecting an answer. I did not want to say no but I could not say yes either, so I lied. 'I think I will be working late tomorrow,' and as an afterthought I added, 'and I promised Mary I would help in the bar after work tomorrow.' I felt terrible.

Douglas looked at me, crestfallen, and said sadly, 'I understand.' He stopped. I don't think he knew what to say next and I could not think of anything either. Eventually he spoke. 'I had better be going now. I am not sure how much longer I shall stay on the island, at the moment my return flight is booked for Saturday so I don't expect our paths will cross again before I go.' I felt like crying as he walked off.

At first I mooched around the house and garden alone and confused, trying to make a plan. Then, I gave myself a mental kick and thought, *Get on with something.*

Bernie had told me take the rest of the day off but I decided I needed company and the best place for that would be the police station. I wanted to take the Triumph but I decided not to. My crash helmet was uncomfortable, pressing on the bruising to the side of my head and I would not risk riding without it. As I put the battery back in the Toyota it occurred to me that Douglas was also alone and I wondered what he was doing, and realised that I wanted to go and find him to just be with him. But I did not, I hoped he was okay and drove back to the police station.

When I got there the first thing I did was to go in and see Bernie. 'I was not expecting to see you again today.'

I shrugged and said, 'I'm okay. I don't need time off.'

'Everything alright at home?'

'Yes, fine. Mary invited Douglas to come and look at my father's old car and I showed it to him.'

'Good heavens!' Bernie looked surprised. 'Have you still got that old limo your father bought? I thought that was scrapped ages ago.'

'No, I have still got it, and in fact we got started and drove round the garden this morning.' Bernie raised his eyebrows and I told him Douglas had asked me out to dinner.

He did not look particularly surprised as he asked, 'And are you going to go?'

'No.'

'Pity, you might have picked up some useful information while he was off his guard.'

'Yes, well, I don't want to get involved. Anyway, he says he is leaving on Saturday.'

'Probably sensible.' Bernie dismissed the conversation and then said, 'By the way, the forensic report on that brown paper just came in. They found nothing on the paper. No traces of drugs or anything suspicious.' Bernie looked disappointed. I was not sure that I was unhappy about this. My headache had returned and I can't have been thinking straight as it occurred to me that it would be for the best if Douglas did leave the island. Douglas would be gone, there would be no arrest and I could get back to my routine.

'Joelle,' Bernie pulled my attention back, 'you look terrible. I think you better go home and come back in the morning. Leave the Coconut file with me. I am going to do a report for the US drugs investigation people.'

Chapter 42

Joelle de Nouvelas; Tuesday 25th November

I woke up feeling a lot better. I showered and looked in the mirror at my black eye. The swelling had gone down and the colour was beginning to turn to green and yellow round the edges. I was thinking today would see the end of the Douglas Jay surveillance. Douglas would be going home on Saturday. Bernie could do a final report and I could move on.

I told Jasmine to hurry up or we would be late. As we drove into town she asked me about Douglas and what had happened yesterday. I told her we had got the old car started, and then remembered Douglas had offered to help with repairs. *Well, that won't be happening now*, I thought sadly as I told Jasmine that Douglas would be leaving on Saturday.

'I thought he was going to stay on in the beach chalet,' Jasmine queried, 'why has he changed his mind? I want to see him and say goodbye before he goes; can we go find him?' She paused to look at me and then whispered to herself, 'I expect he will come to the bar and say goodbye.' I could not say anything; I was trying to understand a drug smuggler and reconcile him with the man who had risked serious injury to prevent me being attacked, the man who had joyfully helped me get the old car started and, when I let myself, the man whose company I found stimulating and exciting. Yes, I realised I too wanted to see Douglas and say goodbye.

I got to the station about 9.30am after dropping Jasmine off at school. Bernie was already at his desk talking to the duty sergeant. I picked up the Graffiti File in an attempt to put Douglas to the back of my mind by concentrating on something else.

I had just started reading the file when Bernie put his head out of his office and called me in. 'I have sent in a Coconut report,' was his opening remark, 'they said they would let me know later today what action they want to take. You did say he was planning to leave soon.'

'He told me his return flight was booked for Saturday.'

'I thought he said his stay was open ended and he had no return plans,' Bernie queried.

'He said goodbye to me yesterday and told me that he did not know how much longer he would be on the island and his return flight was booked for Saturday,' I repeated, irritably.

Bernie gave me one of his quizzical looks, saying, 'I wonder what changed his mind, wouldn't be anything to do with you would it?' I did not answer and Bernie continued. 'Have we still got surveillance on him?'

'Yes, Isaac is at the hotel ready to follow him if he goes out anywhere.'

'Good. Keep the surveillance going until he actually boards the aeroplane. In the meantime can you have a look at this case? It's giving us grief at the moment.' He passed across a report from last night, saying, 'One of those expensive yachts moored out in the harbour. Apparently the owner and his family came into town yesterday evening to eat and, when they went to return to their yacht, someone had nicked their tender. Anyway he is in the harbour master's office creating merry hell demanding to see a senior police officer. Take Merv, go down there and see what you can do.'

The harbour master introduced Merv and I to a very angry Mr. van den Bent, owner of the schooner anchored out in the harbour, who proceeded to shout insults at everyone within hearing range. I told him to calm down as we could not proceed with him making such a fuss and if he continued I would arrest him for disturbing the peace. Initially that upset him even more but eventually he did calm down and we were able to take a statement. I asked the harbour master if anyone had yet searched for the tender to see if it simply had been moved for some reason. Apparently no one had, so I suggested that the harbour master take Mr. van den Bent out in his motorboat to see if they could spot the missing tender, while Merv and I asked round to see if anyone saw anything. The two of them went off in the motorboat and it took Merv and me ten minutes to establish that no one had seen or heard anything last night. Merv suggested that we wait in the car until the motorboat returned. 'If we are lucky they may find the tender and we can close the file,' he said hopefully.

He asked me how the Douglas Jay surveillance was going. 'Bernie is organising a search warrant for the shed at the Zip Line and he is running a check on the man, Geoff Handley to see if there is any connection, but nothing new really since last week at the Zip Line. Bernie has sent a report off to the USA and is waiting for their reply.'

'I don't know why Bernie doesn't pull him and question him,' Merv said. 'After all he matches the description, he has a motive and we saw him deliver the parcels. I bet when we search that locked cabin we find the stuff.'

'The paper wrappers were clean,' I reminded Merv.

'Yes, well, the stuff was probably in plastic bags or something so the paper would be clean. I think he is our man,' Merv replied.

He was about to expand on his reasoning when we saw the motorboat returning across the harbour with an inflatable tender in tow. We walked across as they came into the dockside and the harbour master explained they had found the tender beached just outside the harbour entrance. Probably joy-riders taking it for fun, he speculated. I was inclined to agree and was telling Mr. van den Bent so when Merv heard our call on the car radio and rushed back to take it. Van den Bent was reluctant to leave matters to rest and was demanding that we make every effort to catch the culprits. I assured him we follow up all leads and was asking him how long he planned to stay on Kaeta Island when Merv called me back to the car for an urgent message from Bernie to return immediately.

I made my apologies and got in the car as Merv turned the blue light and siren on and sped off out of the harbour. 'What's so urgent?' I asked.

'Nothing,' he said, 'I just thought you needed rescuing, although Bernie does want to see us when we get back.' I saw Douglas walking along the road as we approached the police station. I lurched inwardly, wondering why he was here but also secretly hoping he would come in. I really did want to see him again and I told myself that it was because I wanted to make sure he was okay after yesterday. As we walked in I lingered at the public desk waiting for him. He did not come in, he walked straight past without even looking.

I caught up with Merv and we went straight into to see Bernie. 'I have heard from the Florida Drugs team,' he told us. 'They are sending an officer, a Mr. Tony Choizi, over to us to review the evidence we have collected and advise us on the surveillance.'

I groaned, saying, 'That's all we need, a Yankee drugs officer stomping round the island upsetting everyone.'

'Joelle!' he admonished. 'That's not the attitude, we will co-operate fully, understand?'

'Yes sir!' Merv and I said in unison.

'When is he arriving?' I asked.

'Thursday afternoon, he is flying in from Bermuda,' Bernie answered. 'Merv can go and meet him at the airport and bring him back here.'

I was grateful; Bernie knew I had personal reasons for not wanting to get mixed up with visiting police officers, and had let me off that hook at least.

'We do have a small problem.' Bernie looked at me. 'I have been instructed to make sure Douglas Jay does not leave the island before Tony Choizi has completed his investigation. They have told me not to tell him he is a suspect in this drug smuggling, but to find a reason to confiscate his passport.'

All three of us were silent while this sunk in. I was thinking that I had really wanted Douglas to go away, while Merv and Bernie were thinking of a plausible reason to detain him. Merv suggested, 'Why don't we tell him we are still investigating the attack on Joelle and until that is completed we need him to stay on the island?'

'Good, good,' said Bernie, picking up on the idea, 'we can keep it low key without actually having to take his passport, just ask him not to leave the island. If we alert the border police he can't get away anyway. I like it. I will ask him to come into the office at his earliest convenience. On a brighter note, I have a search warrant for the locked cabin at the Zip Line. Joelle can you organise a search for tomorrow?' I left Bernie's office with a feeling of dread. Things were not going to get easier; they were about to get a whole lot harder.

That evening I went to the bar feeling rather sorry for myself. I realised that it would be better for everybody if I did not see Douglas, but I was still hoping he would there sitting in his corner with a beer and his cheery welcome as he greeted me. He was not there and he did not come to the bar that evening.

Chapter 43

Douglas Jay; Tuesday 25th November

I woke up on Tuesday morning not in the best of tempers. My mood was a mix of anger, rejection, and a bit lonely. From what Mary had said, I had assumed Joelle would have agreed to have dinner with me, especially after we had worked so well together getting the old car going. She had not actually said no but her excuses for not saying yes were pretty thin, and it was now obvious to me that any contact we had was purely at a policing level, and that any thoughts I was harbouring of developing a more personal relationship were not going to happen.

Oh well, I thought, *no fool like an old fool when it comes to love!*

It is probably for the best; holiday romances never last and if Joelle and I had got something going together someone would have ended up hurt. Best to keep out of her way.

I thought perhaps I should have paid more attention to Jean Handley, but quickly put that thought to one side; Jean definitely was not my type. However this thought led me to comparing Jean and Joelle and I thought about Joelle asking me who was my type, and I nearly telling her.

I daydreamed, wondering what it was about her that made her my type of girl. I admired her self-reliance and confidence, which in some strange way rubbed off on me, giving me more self-assurance. I also admired her sense of justice, based on what she considered was right, and I liked her tomboy streak and desire to be just a little different without being too obvious about it. Also I thought she was a very attractive lady. I had to kick myself away from this line of thought. I had just decided to keep out of Joelle's way, and thinking of all the reasons why I should not, was not helping.

What shall I do today? I thought. *The first decision is whether I am going home on Saturday or not because if I am I need to confirm my flight booking. The next decision is, shall go for a run before breakfast?*

I did go for the run and the exercise chased away my dark thoughts, and made me late for breakfast, which was a good as far as I was concerned as the crowd had finished, and were now by the swimming pool fighting over the best-positioned loungers.

I was shown to an empty table and luckily did not have to share it with anyone else that morning. I helped myself to the buffet and sat down to decide when I wanted to return to England. I noticed I deliberately thought of 'returning to England' and not 'going home'. Curious, I then thought, and realised that thinking where I would like to make my home was going to lead me straight back to Joelle again. *Damn the woman*, I thought, as I devoured the breakfast.

On my way back to my chalet I stopped at the guest information desk and asked them if the airline had an agent in town. Yes, they told me, the airline agent is Kaeta Travel Services and they told me where to find them. I booked a taxi to take me into town to confirm the flight and have a look around. Something I had not really done before except for the fleeting visit with Joelle when she showed me round the island.

I found Kaeta Island Tours but delayed going in as I remembered how, on the airplane coming in, I had thought that if I liked the island then one option for me would be to settle down here and start some sort of business, and I had not even considered that yet. I strolled through Kaeta Town, looking round as I considered this option. The docks and the markets were definitely set up for tourism but as I walked up the hill to the newer part of the town the architecture was predominately Victorian Gothic and comfortingly British. *This would not be a bad place to work,* I thought. *I wonder if I could find a job round here, and how I could get a work permit. I must ask Joelle.* I kicked myself. *Why does every thought end up leading me back to that woman!*

I came across the cathedral and walked around the cemetery, which again felt very British. It was cool as well being well shaded by trees. I read the headstones and remembered that Joelle had told me that this was one of her favourite places and she often came over here to sit quietly on her own to eat her lunch. I wondered if she would be there this lunchtime and quickly decided to leave in case she was! I found myself walking towards the police station when a police car drove slowly past me. Joelle was sitting in the passenger seat. I don't think she saw me, but the driver looked familiar. *I have seen him before somewhere, but I can't think where.* I walked on past the police station, resisting the temptation to look in through the open door and perhaps catch sight of Joelle.

As I walked I came upon the island museum and spent the next three hours looking round. Naturally there was a great deal of information and many artefacts from the slavery period, but what I found most interesting was the archaeology room and the various items found on the island, and the geology displays describing how the island was formed and its geological and topical maps. I was absorbed and the time passed very quickly. On my way out I asked where I could find a taxi and the receptionist kindly phoned for one to come and pick me up. I was tired when I got back to the hotel and decided to eat in the hotel restaurant.

I never did confirm Saturday's flight and was beginning to think I might stay on for a little longer. I checked with the hotel and they could accommodate me for another week and I could remain in the same chalet. Unfortunately after that their Christmas season started and they were fully booked.

Chapter 44

Joelle de Nouvelas; Wednesday 27th November

The first thing I did on Wednesday morning was to send Merv off to find the two PCs assigned to assist with the search of the Zip Line cabin, and to find the equipment we would need for a full search. I had to wait for Bernie to come in as I needed to collect the signed search warrant from him. While I waited I read the report on Douglas's movements yesterday. He had clearly only been doing what any tourist would do when wandering round the town. I noted he had spent a long time in the museum and thought how typical it was of him to show such interest. I was glad that he not done anything suspicious.

As soon as Bernie gave me the search warrant we set off in two cars for the Zip Line. Merv and I went in the Suzuki and the two PCs in a police Toyota estate car.

We went straight to the slave camp reception and I asked for the attraction manager. They told me he was busy so I showed the search warrant and told the receptionist we would proceed with the search whether he was busy or not. We drove the vehicles up to the two disused cabins and the manager came running up behind us. 'What is the problem?' he asked. I explained that we had reason to believe drugs were being stored somewhere on the slave camp. 'I can't believe that,' he said. 'There is nowhere drugs could be stored.'

I pointed to the repaired cabin and he explained that he had been approached by one of the Zip Line operators and asked if it could be used to store some equipment. He told us three men had come up and repaired it and replaced the roof and door. 'These sheds are not really from the days slaves were kept here. They are much later and we just made them look old,' he explained.

I asked him for the names and details of the men.

'I don't know who the repair men were and I only know the Zip Line attendant as Zach.'

Merv called me over to the cabin. 'Look,' he said. 'The door is unlocked and shed is completely empty inside, it has even been swept clean.'

'OK, but search it thoroughly. Get down on you hand and knees and examine every crack and crevice.'

Merv and the PCs set to and I walked back to the manager and asked him if he knew when the shed was cleared, and who did it. 'No, I am sorry, I have no idea,' he said.

I walked back down to the reception and shop to ask if anyone had seen anything or had any further information. The only thing I learnt was that Zach had occasionally been seen carrying a bag into the shed but no one had seen how or when it was emptied. I also showed a picture of Douglas and asked if anyone recognised him. The receptionist said she thought she recognised him and asked if he was the person I was asking about last week.

Merv came down and reported they had searched the shed and said, 'Look what we found in between the floorboards lodged right in the corner.' He held up an evidence bag containing a small cream-coloured pill. 'I have also swept some dust out of the corners for the forensic people,' Merv explained as he showed me a bag of grey dust.

Before we finished, we looked round the other buildings but found nothing to indicate they had been used.

Merv and I headed back to the station and left the two PCs to take statements from everyone. We got back mid-afternoon and went straight in to see Bernie. We told him about the search and showed him the two evidence bags. 'It looks like we may have found where the stuff was stored but it also looks like they have moved on, probably because Zach got spooked and disappeared.' Bernie concluded and added, 'We also have not found anything new that links Douglas directly with the store.' I nodded in agreement.

I spent the rest of the afternoon writing up my report before I left for the day and headed over to Glass Bar. As I drove it struck me that after three relationships, I was not very good at picking men, yet, here I was harbouring thoughts about a man who was probably involved in the illegal drugs trade. My first marriage did not last for much more than a year, and the second time I never even made the ceremony.

That happened here on the island a year after I joined the police. The island was hosting a test match series and security was an issue, so a UK security expert was seconded out to advise the Island Police. His name was Simon Eagle and I was attached to his team for the duration of the series. We ended up having an affair and he asked me to marry him, and suggested I move into the apartment he was using. You can imagine how I felt when one evening I arrived after work to find two plastic bags with all my clothes and possessions sitting by the front door and Simon opened the door and introduced me to his wife. It was Bernie who pulled me back from that one. He never liked Simon anyway and he offered me a job as a detective constable on his team.

The third and last occasion was with an American backpacker. I met him at Glass Bar and seemed a nice enough guy. He played the guitar and sang and was very laid back. We had a short affair and then one day he just disappeared, having borrowed $200 from me. Mary rescued me from that one. She never liked him and told me I was a silly girl who should stop picking losers and find a good man.

My mind drifted to Douglas. *He is probably just like all the others*, I speculated, *and I would just end up hurt again. They all declare undying love for me within days and swear that love has to be consummated before we can be happy together. Well I am not falling for that one again! Trouble is Douglas is not like that. He has not declared love and has not tried to get me into bed. He has not even tried to kiss me. The worst he did was to hold my hand. He is gentle, treats me with respect, and both Mary and Jasmine like him. What could possibly go wrong?* I thought wryly, as I reminded myself he was a criminal, well, a suspected criminal. *Pity*, I thought, as I walked into the bar, half hoping Douglas would be there, and thinking that under different circumstances I would probably have a go at a relationship with him. He was not there and despite myself I was disappointed.

Chapter 45

Joelle de Nouvelas; Thursday 27th November

Today I walked in to the office a bit later. It was Thursday morning and the day was already warm and humid, with temperature outside already hitting 25°C. The air conditioning was not coping and the office was getting sticky. Bernie was pacing round the general office looking tetchy. 'Ah – good afternoon Joelle,' he greeted me, sarcastically.

'It's only 10.30,' I said, 'and I have been to the tourist office about crowd control for the festival next summer.' I defended myself.

'I know, I know,' he answered. 'We need to be up to speed on the Coconut case. Are you still keeping contact with Jay? Have we got anything yet to directly link him to this drug smuggling ring?'

I thought for a minute while I considered how to phrase the answer. 'Yes, to the first question. Some evenings he comes over the bar but I have not seen him since last Monday.'

'Are you avoiding him, worrying about getting too involved?' interjected Bernie, looking thoughtfully out of the window.

'No,' I responded and continued, 'and no to the second question. Since we spoke last Monday, Douglas has not done anything else suspicious. On Tuesday he visited Joseph town and the museum and on Wednesday he spent the day in his hotel.'

'Ah well,' Bernie said slowly, 'later today we have Tony Choizi coming to help us.' He paused for effect and asked, 'When will we get the forensics on what you found in the Slave Cabin?'

I know Choizi is coming, I thought, fearing the worst, but told Bernie, 'They have promised a full report later today but they have told me that the pill is an animal drug typically used on small animals as a sedative and relaxant. If taken by a person it would have a relaxing dreamy effect. The dust contains traces of heroin. They are trying to trace the manufacturer of the pill.'

'Excellent,' said Bernie, and continued, 'yes, we have Detective Tony Choizi, from the US Drug Enforcement Administration arriving this afternoon. Apparently he is based in Florida and is coming here as an observer to share the information they have on the drug ring and Mr. Jay, and assist and advise on our surveillance. I can now tell him we have found the drug store, and if we are lucky that pill will have been made by the company Jay worked for.'

'Oh good!' I said sarcastically.

'I thought you would be pleased. Don't worry, Merv will meet him at the airport and bring him here but you need to meet him this afternoon.'

Wonderful! I thought, and as I had planned to keep out of his way all day, I said, 'That might be difficult; I was planning to go round the island today and see if I can catch our graffiti merchant.'

'OK, but be back this afternoon,' instructed Bernie.

I spent the rest of the morning driving round the island in the Suzuki looking at the graffiti trying to see some pattern in the placing of the work. Whoever was doing this was quite good, I thought. Some of the work was just embellished slogans but some were very well constructed pictures. There was one of Pirate Hill, but it had been painted erupting with cherry red lava flowing down the sides, scorching the rainforest, and smoke billowing out blackening the sky. Another was a picture of a beach scene. Azure blue sea, and yellow sand with a single coconut palm, very simple but a pity it was spoilt by a woman, painted standing on the beach making a rude gesture.

It struck me that whoever was doing this, had only graffitied highly visible walls where tourists tend to go.

My last stop was the Island Cricket Stadium. This was the new stadium built by our last President to demonstrate his support for cricket and a number of international test matches had been held there. It was located about seven miles out of Joseph town on a flat, arid area just south of the airport, and as no games were scheduled until the weekend it was locked up and deserted today. To the front of the stadium were the reception entrance and visitor facilities. It was constructed with lots of glass and concrete but no convenient walls for decorating.

But on the left hand side were the administrative offices and they were of a much plainer construction, offering to one side a flat concrete wall which was visible from the car park; *Just right for the graffiti artist to decorate before the test match this weekend*, I thought, and if I was going to do that I would choose today, as tomorrow the caretaker would be opening up to let the set-up team to come in to prepare for the match.

I parked the Suzuki discreetly at the far end of the car park and settled down to watch for a bit. A couple of hours later a teenager, riding a small motorcycle, rode into the car park. He stopped outside the reception entrance and just sat there for about ten minutes before riding round the car park and then zooming away with lots of noise and not much speed.

Strange, I mused, deciding to stay a little longer and see if anything would happen. At about five thirty, just before it got dark he came back with another young-looking person. They wore helmets so I could not see their faces. This time they went straight round the side of the stadium and I watched them pull some spray cans of paint from their backpack. I called for assistance warning them to drive in quietly – no sirens.

The artists were putting the finishing touches to the picture using the headlight of the motorbike when the support car arrived and I spoke to them on the radio. 'I will go over and arrest them. When you see me talk to them, drive in quickly and grab them – they will probably try to run.' I walked across the car park; they did not see me, they were too engrossed in painting.

I took the keys out of the ignition on their bike and walked up behind them. As I did so, I heard the police car drive in behind me. The two looked round in surprise as I told them were under arrest. They dropped the cans; one ran to the bike and jumped on it. I cuffed him as he stretched his hand out to the starter button. The other was caught by the two support officers as he tried to climb over the fence at the back of the ground. 'Good job,' I congratulated the two constables. 'Take them back to the station and charge them. I will follow you.'

When I got back to the police station I was greeted by a livid Bernie. 'Don't you answer your radio?' I had turned it off while waiting for the kids. 'I told you to be back here this afternoon. I have a furious American detective on my hands who insists on seeing you immediately for an update.'

Bernie was not much calmed down by my explanation so I offered, 'OK, sorry, I will go and talk to him now.'

'Yes you will,' Bernie spat back to me. 'He has gone to his hotel and wants you over there as soon as you return.

You will find him in the bar.'

'Which hotel?' I asked.

'Hotel Glass Bay.'

My heart sank. 'That's where Douglas Jay is staying.'

'I know,' replied Bernie. 'He specifically asked for that hotel so he could observe Jay.'

Chapter 46

Douglas Jay; Thursday 27ᵗʰ November

I woke early this morning. Weather was already quite warm and humid although the sun was shining brightly. I was feeling good and decided on a long walk along the beach with the camera and to take some pictures before breakfast. I did not particularly want to lug the big SLR with me so I just took my little Canon Ixus in my pocket.

I took a few pictures of the surf breaking over the rocks just beyond Glass Bar. The bar was closed and locked, no one about, so I headed back to the hotel for breakfast, and to plan the day.

After breakfast I headed out to the little Honda bike. I was going to drive about six miles down the island to a bay called the Three Sisters, named after three volcanic plugs rising out of the bay with sheer sides. The two smaller ones had flat tops on which sea birds nested, but the third, which was the most distant one, was much taller and was crowned with a conical top. The beach itself was a deep yellow sandy colour, and was fringed with the usual coconut palms but also a number of other rainforest shrubs, which lent a secluded atmosphere to the beach. The popular tourist beaches had paved access roads leading down to them but this beach had no visible roads, just a well-concealed track winding for about a mile down through the rainforest. I bumped down the track through the trees and I left the Honda leaning on a coconut palm while I went off exploring the beach, looking for the right angle to get some good pictures. I gave up in the end. The sun was too high and the light too harsh for the picture I wanted to take.

I sat on the beach, daydreaming. I still had no idea what I wanted to do when I went home. I had given up my London home anyway so only had the holiday cottage in Wiltshire, which had always been a holiday place, not a home. *I could become self-employed*, I thought, that had some attraction as I was fed up with working for an employer, too much stress, always at someone else's beck and call. Perhaps I could be a financial consultant or maybe a corporate troubleshooter. Unfortunately all my thoughts were interrupted by daydreams about Joelle, wondering what she was doing now and debating whether I should go to Glass Bar and see her. Eventually, I stood up to go and find the Honda and return to the hotel for lunch.

I did not do anything after lunch, just sat in the garden and read. I watched the arrival of a rather large, loud man in a blue suit and white shirt sitting in the back of one of the transport buggies, gesticulating at the driver.

It was 5.30pm and time for a beer, I thought, and to decide what to do this evening. The Handleys had told me that they had a good meal at the hotel in the next bay, where a celebratory chef had opened a restaurant. I decide to give it a go and ordered a taxi.

I went back to my room for a shower and to change. Under the door was an envelope addressed to me. I opened it and saw it was short note from Inspector Bernie Strange asking me to please call into the police station at my earliest convenience, as he needed to talk to me. *I wonder what that is all about,* I thought, hoping that it was not anything to do with me personally.

I put on a pair of white cotton trousers and a dark blue shirt and went to reception where the taxi was waiting.

Romero's. That was the name of the restaurant, is in the Palm Court Hotel, which is not far from Glass Bay, situated on high ground at the southern end of Trigs Bay, the next beach down from Glass Bay.

The restaurant itself is inside the hotel but has glass doors running the full length of the room, which open on to a terrace with spectacular views across the bay. All the tables on the terrace were occupied so I was seated at a small table at the back of the room. I ordered a bottle of South American Sauvignon Blanc and looked round the room at my fellow diners while I sipped the first glass and waited to order. There was a strict dress code in the restaurant, collared shirts and long trousers for the men, and for the ladies, no beachwear.

The head waiter walked across to my table and enquired whether I would like to be joined by another single diner. I declined.

The head chef at Romero's is, apparently, a protégé of the famous man himself, who features on both American and British culinary television. I did wonder when a busy TV star, with a chain of eating houses in which he allegedly cooks from time to time, last visited Kaeta, but no matter, the menu looked satisfactorily *cordon bleu*, with prices to match.

I studied it. The starters looked delicious but I jumped to the main courses first and naturally had difficulty deciding on the 'Stuffed Chicken Breasts wrapped in Palma Ham', or 'Duck Breast served with Green Vegetables and Gooseberry sauce' or as I read the last main dish on the menu, 'Monk Fish with Curried Mussels'. A difficult choice so I looked at the starters; 'Herby Crayfish with a prawn Pilaf', 'Baked Figs stuffed with Goats Cheese', or 'Prawn, Feta and Watermelon salad.' I ordered the crayfish starter followed by the stuffed chicken breast. The food lived up to its promise and was delicious. I skipped the dessert and topped the meal off with the cheese platter and large glass of port. After the meal I had time for another beer on the downstairs terrace bar before the taxi arrived to take me back to Glass Bay.

The taxi dropped me at the hotel reception and I walked down the drive past the lake and golf course towards the swimming pool. As I reached the path to my chalet I paused to look at the full moon, which was just emerging over the horizon and casting a dappled silver light over the sea and beach, piercing the dark shade from the trees fringing the beach and the hotel gardens.

I was standing in the shadow of a large palm and watching a couple walking out of the restaurant. They were in deep shadow so I could not see them properly, but as they moved across the moonlight I was sure the woman was Joelle, but I could not see the man properly. They moved back into shadow and he put his arm round her shoulder and they kissed. The woman stepped away, said something to the man, and started walking out across the path by the lake towards the main reception and car park. The man said something to her about bourbon as she walked away. She emerged into the moonlight. It was Joelle.

Chapter 47

Joelle de Nouvelas; Thursday evening,
27th November

I got to the hotel and went straight to the beach bar, dreading meeting with Douglas. *I should be OK*, I hoped. *It is nearly seven thirty so hopefully he has gone out somewhere by now.* No Douglas in the bar, but sitting at the bar was a large black-haired, heavy-featured man, wearing shorts over which hung his paunch and a lurid floral shirt, the buttons of which strained to hold the material around his oversized stomach. He was sweating heavily, drinking a large beer, and eating from a bowl of nuts. *That must be him*, I thought as I walked across the room. 'Detective Choizi?' I queried as I walked up behind him.

He turned and said, 'Sergeant Joelle de Nouvelas, better late than never. Call me Tony,' he responded as he looked me up and down, mentally undressing me. 'My, but you are a pretty one.' I disliked him immediately as he went on. 'I am hungry so I have booked a table in the restaurant. I will treat you to dinner and you can bring me up to date.'

Dressed in the day's jeans and tee-shirt I hardly felt like dinner in the dining room, especially with him. I said I was not hungry but he insisted. 'Got to get to know each other,' he leered at me, 'and what better way than spending an evening together?' Clearly there was no escape so I said

OK, but that I needed to freshen up first.

I knew that guest information had a key to the shop in case she needed to open up in an emergency and I figured this was an emergency. I walked round and explained I needed to get a new shirt quickly. I chose a pretty dark blue blouse, which at least covered the top of my jeans, a lipstick and mascara, and left the money at the Guest Information desk on my way into the ladies' toilet to change and do my make-up, which made me feel more confident and more able to cope with the evening.

I made my way back to the bar where Detective Choizi was ogling me as I walked across the room. He took my arm and steered me through the dining room to a quiet corner.

He ordered the soup, followed by a smoked salmon tureen, with a blue steak and chips topped with a fried egg for his main course. I ordered a salmon tagliatelle for my dinner. A bottle of red wine arrived and two glasses were poured. 'Cheers,' he said, 'here's to you and I working closely together,' and he drank the glass and refilled it. I sipped mine and asked for a glass of water.

His soup arrived and as he started slurping it he told me to bring him up to date. I felt very uncomfortable telling him about Douglas as I went through what we had so far and finished, concluding that all we had was circumstantial and although it fitted with Douglas being involved we had no direct evidence connecting him with any smuggling activities or storage on the island.

'Bernie Strange tells me you have a theory?' he asked.

'Well yes,' I replied, and putting my growing feelings for Douglas aside, summarised. 'We know he has spoken with the suspected contact, Zach, on more than one occasion and that he carried a parcel to the Zip Line and left it there. He also visited the cabin which we now know was being used as a drug store. He hid the little motorbike he hired by the Zip Line rubbish bins where we suspect he might have switched the drugs and collected his payment.'

Tony nodded and asked, 'Do you know where this the stuff is being stored now?'

'No, the disused hut at the zip line centre has been cleared and we don't know where the contents was taken.'

Tony speculated, 'Probably to a boat and then to Bermuda. We know Bermuda is the final dispatch point on the way into the States. But we don't yet know the organisers. And you say he left his camera bag at the reception while he rode the zip line?'

'Yes, we have no evidence that anyone apart from the receptionist touched it.'

'Seems a pretty convincing story to me,' said Tony, pinching his bottom lip with his fingers, in thought.

'Do you have any additional information?' I asked.

'We know he worked for a veterinary drug manufacturer and visited New York on at least six occasions which he described as business. We know he visited the drug company that bought his former employer, but we don't know what else he did. I want to question him about that. We also know that some of the drugs seized on a motorboat crossing from Bermuda to Florida were animal drugs made by the company he used to work for.'

'That's all still circumstantial,' I commented.

'It's strong enough to get me out here after him,' was the reply.

His steak arrived. He sliced it in two and my stomach turned as the blood ran out, mixing with the egg yolk as it ran across the plate. He did not notice and he stuffed it by the forkful into his mouth. I picked at my tagliatelle.

After the meal, our conversation slipped into small talk. He told me about his luxury apartment in Florida "in the best part of town, I had the interior designed by the best designer in the USA, cost a fortune…" He went on and on, explaining his golfing prowess for another ten minutes.

I found my attention drifting away and I began to think about Douglas. *Actually he is quite a nice guy compared to this pig.* I thought of the dinner I could have had with Douglas and realised I would much rather have been with him. *He is fun and easy to talk with, he does not boast, and he listens when I say something. Yes,* I dreamed, *it would be rather nice to be having an intimate dinner with Douglas.*

I returned to the present conversation, which was still droning on. '…and my own car, not those crappy Fords the department give us, but a new model Cadillac, picked it up real cheap as an ex-demo, but it's top of the range,' he told me as he moved on to explain that his wife did not like it, as she felt it was too big and ostentatious. 'She hardly ever talks to me these days – doesn't understand me you know. Anyway we don't really live together anymore,' he grumbled, eyeing me hungrily.

'I really must go,' I said as I started to rise from the table.

'Please, not so soon. We need to get to know each other a lot better; in fact, I have good bourbon in my chalet, come back and have one with me.'

Here we go, I thought. *Not on your life, buster,* but I said, 'Sorry, I must go, I have to pick my daughter up and take her home to bed.'

He rose with me and grabbed my arm again, saying that he would walk me out to my car. As we got outside he put his arm round me and clumsily tried to kiss me as he said, 'Are you sure you don't want that bourbon?' I squeezed out of his embrace, said goodbye and fled, wondering how I could get taken off this investigation.

Chapter 48

Douglas Jay: Friday 28th November

I had only caught a brief glimpse of Joelle before she disappeared back into the shadow. Well, I thought it was her. As I went back to my chalet, I was certain it was her and I wondered what she was doing. If it was her, who was she with? He was in shadow but was not someone I recognised. Might he have been the man I saw arriving this afternoon?

The picture of Joelle and her unknown partner kissing haunted me, and the question of who she might be with rolled around my mind as I lay in bed, feeling lonely and betrayed, tossing and turning, eventually falling into a disturbed slumber.

By the morning, there was some doubt in my mind that it really had been Joelle I seen last night. After all it had been dark and I had only a glimpse of the woman as she moved through a patch of moonlight. Anyway, even if it had been Joelle there was probably an innocent explanation, perhaps a brother or cousin she had been with – after all it was only a brief kiss. And even if she did have a close friend it was really no concern of mine. I had no claim on her, even if I did like her.

Best thing to do was to get on with the day, I thought, and so I got my Kindle out and started a new book with a plan to get engrossed in it, but I kept finding thoughts of

Joelle interrupting my concentration. I gave up and went to the beach bar and ordered a coffee.

I sat in the bar, still pondering upon the meaning of life, when the man I had seen arriving yesterday afternoon walked up and asked if he could join me. He put his beer down on the table as he sat down and introduced himself as Tony and held his and out. I shook it but it was like holding a damp fish and I had to resist the temptation to wipe my hand afterwards.

'Douglas,' I introduced myself.

'Here on your own?' asked Tony.

'Yes,' I replied.

'So am I. We should buddy-up.' He paused. 'You could show me round the island. Have you found anywhere interesting?'

'I only have a small motorbike,' I replied, trying to put him off coming with me.

'That's OK. I can hire a car and you show me round. I hear there is a Zip Line and an old slave camp. I would really like to look round that, I am interested in those old buildings.'

He was studying me carefully, as I replied that there was a small museum, and the reconstructed hut showing typical living conditions was quite interesting, but the other buildings were just derelict timber sheds which I doubted had ever seen a slave.

He slid into small talk, mainly about himself as I finished my coffee and started making excuses to move on.

As I stood he put his hand out and rested on my arm. 'Hey, buddy.' He looked at me. 'Do you know where I can get a fix round here?'

Jesus, I thought, *what planet is this bloke on?* but said, 'I am sorry, I can't help with that. I don't do drugs,' and I walked off back to my shady seat in the garden to read again.

I noticed he had found himself a garden seat not far away from me, but he did not try to make contact again that morning. Eventually, as we neared lunchtime he made his way over to the beach bar and I watched him order a burger, so I took the opportunity to make my way on my own to the dining room now for a much needed solitary lunch. I ordered a hot shrimp and potato curry for my lunch and as it arrived I saw Tony head across the dining room in my direction.

'Hey, buddy, mind if I join you?' he greeted me as he sat down.

'That looks good,' he said, eyeing my lunch. He turned to a passing waitress and demanded, 'Get me one of those will you, honey?'

"Honey" replied that she would get someone to take his order.

Tony started asking me what I did for a living, why was I on my own, if I had ever been to America, where I had travelled in Europe. He explained he had had a couple of European holidays and knew the country well. I said very little as I ate my lunch and Tony was getting on my nerves so I pushed the remainder of my dish aside and said, 'I am sorry Tony, but I have to go into town now.' I made my escape, grabbed my helmet and went to get the Honda. As I started it I saw Tony walking across the car park after me.

'Say buddy, that's a nice little machine there. Mind if I have a look?' He stood right in front of me so I had no choice but to wait while he examined the Honda. 'Do you always park in the same spot?' as he scanned the parking area. I mumbled an inaudible answer through the full-face crash helmet. Eventually he stood aside and I rode off.

I rode to the police station, left the Honda in the police

car park, and walked into the public reception, asking for Bernie Strange. The constable I had seen with Joelle in the car came down to see me, took me into an interview room and informed me that Inspector Strange would be down in a couple of minutes. As I sat there it dawned on me where I had seen that policeman before. He was the intrusive gardener in the hotel. I thought about this and recalled that I had been followed on more than one occasion when riding round the island. I put two and two together and started worrying. This was serious, clearly the police were following me. What did they know about me? What was their interest in me? Was Joelle involved? *She must be*, I thought.

At that point Inspector Strange walked into the room. 'Good afternoon Mr. Jay. Thank you for coming down, not too inconvenient for you, I hope. I am sorry to disturb your holiday but I need to talk through a couple of things with you.'

I wondered what he wanted, as he continued, 'How long are you planning to stay on the island?'

I replied, 'I don't know yet. I have extended my stay until the end of next week but after that the hotel is full and I have not yet decided what to do.'

'I am afraid I have to ask you not to leave the island without informing us first.'

'Why?'

'We are still investigating the assault on Sergeant de Nouvelas and certain questions regarding your involvement have not yet been clarified.'

'What do mean?' I asked, certain he was not telling me everything.

'Should only be a few days, but please don't try and leave the island without permission or you will be arrested at the frontier. It's just routine, nothing to worry about.'

He tried to reassure me, telling me I was free to go now, as he rose to his feet.

When I got back to the hotel, I changed and went to the beach, keeping a low profile. I tried to take an afternoon nap, but worrying about what was going on kept me awake. I was disturbed by the greeting, 'Hey buddy, found you. Why are you hiding away right up here?'

I shook my head to make myself fully alert and said, 'Look Tony, I don't mean to be rude but I am tired and I just want to be on my own and have a sleep, if you don't mind.'

'Okay, okay. No offence taken. Just being friendly.' But at least he got the message and walked off down the beach. Some distance away I watched him pull up a lounger and settle down on it, pulling some silvered dark glasses out of his pocket and putting them on. He clasped his hands on the back his head and appeared to be looking around, for another victim to hang out with, I supposed.

I spent the afternoon reading, swimming in the sea, and sleeping. As the sun dipped down towards the horizon I decided I would go up to Glass Bar. I hoped I would meet Joelle. Aside from wanting to see her again, there were some difficult things I wanted to ask her.

Chapter 49

Joelle de Nouvelas: Friday 28th November

When I got home after the evening with Tony, I felt dirty and used. I had a long shower and cleaned my teeth twice before I felt clean again. I was upset with myself for letting Tony take advantage of me and I dreaded the thought of having to work with him. I decided I would ask Bernie if I could leave this investigation.

I went into the station next morning hoping Tony would not be there.

'He is spending the day at the hotel watching Douglas Jay,' Merv explained.

That's a relief, I thought, and my skin crawled with distaste as I remembered yesterday evening. *Why should I feel guilty?* I thought angrily.

I was brought back to reality when the desk sergeant rang for me to go down and see to the two teenage graffiti artists I had arrested yesterday.

'Their parents are in the waiting room and want to speak with you,' I was told as I made way down to the custody suite.

Both sets of parents looked good people but were clearly angry and upset, not particularly with me but they did challenge me, wanting to know why I had arrested the two boys rather than just giving them a caution. When I explained the extent of their activities they calmed down a bit and asked me what was going to happen next.

I explained that the boys had been arrested for a public disorder and trespass offence involving defacing public buildings. The decision on whether to prosecute them was not mine but would be made by the Island Prosecutor, and if so charged, the boys would have to appear in a juvenile magistrate court. In the meantime the boys would be released into their parents' custody.

The parents looked relieved and thanked me. I told them that as the boys had not been in trouble before, and given their age, they would probably just get a severe reprimand but would not be prosecuted. The mother of one of them started crying and hugged me as her husband threatened to beat the leaving daylights out of his son and not let him out of his sight.

Two very contrite teenagers were led up from the cells, much relieved to be reunited with their parents who promptly marched them out of the station, threatening them with hell and damnation if they ever did anything like this again. As they left, the boys turned round and apologised to me.

On top of my already sensitive state and lingering guilt over Douglas, my emotions got the better of me and I dashed off to the ladies' room to hide my tears. I needed some time to myself away from the police station after that, so I told Merv I was going on a foot patrol around the market to keep an eye on the tourists.

There was not much going on the town. There was only one tourist ship in and that was a small one. The passengers were happily wandering round the market and shops, the ladies looking through every clothes shop and buying small tee-shirts with a picture of a palm tree on the front and Kaeta Island emblazoned across the back. The gift shops always attracted good crowds but the most popular market stands were those selling island spices; they always did a good trade. I don't think the tourists realised that spice-growing on the island has almost disappeared and that most of the spices came from all over the Caribbean.

I calmed down as I walked around. I told myself it was not my fault that Tony had made a rather clumsy pass at me. I had behaved perfectly properly. He was just a letch. Perhaps I should make a complaint about him, but I didn't really think that this would get me anywhere. More than likely, it would backfire on me somehow.

I returned to the police station about mid-afternoon. There was nothing going on there so I disappeared and took the rest of the day off. I took my beloved Triumph out of the police garage where I had left it for a couple of days while I had been driving the Suzuki.

I was not feeling good. I still felt disgusted by the pass Tony Choizi had made last night, whether I was disgusted with myself or him I was not sure, but I could still feel where he had put his arm round me and smell his lingering body odour as he tried to kiss me. It made me feel sick, but that was not the worst. I felt that somehow I had let Douglas down. I know this notion was ridiculous, but when he stepped in and saved me from attack last weekend he had turned my emotions upside down. However hard I tried to tell myself he was a criminal drug smuggler, somewhere inside me a little voice kept reminding me that he seemed to be looking out for me, plus I rather liked him. I was feeling very emotional and need of familiar surroundings, and people I could trust.

I mounted the Triumph and pressed the starter button. The machine roared into life and it felt like a live animal beneath me as I sat astride it, but I was not in the mood to go for a joyride that afternoon, so I kicked it into gear, heading to Glass Bar to be with Jasmine and Mary.

As I approached the bar, again my thoughts turned to Douglas, and how yesterday I had felt how much nicer it would have been to spend an evening with him, and, again I cautioned myself not to get involved, but I still walked into Glass Bar hoping he would be there.

Chapter 50

Douglas Jay; Friday evening, 28th November

Tony, thankfully, had disappeared as I left the beach, going to my chalet to shower and change my clothes.

It was a beautiful late afternoon as I walked along to Glass Bar. During the day we had had some rain showers. Rain on Kaeta was not like rain back in England. The clouds blew in quickly from the east and then rain fell intensely in short, sharp showers, drenching the ground and the vegetation, sometimes for only a few minutes but never longer than fifteen before the clouds blew away over the Caribbean Sea and the sun came out with renewed heat, steaming everything dry again. By late afternoon the clouds had all gone and the sun was shining brightly, and everything on the ground looked washed and clean. When I got to the bar, Mary had pulled the shutters up to let in the sunshine, and was sitting at a table, polishing glasses. Apart from Mary the bar was empty.

I ordered one of Mary's lemon fizz cocktails and I sat in my usual corner at the bar.

I asked Mary if her beach chalet was still available. She said it was and I told her that I was booked into the hotel for another week but I might need to stay on the island a little longer so asked if it would be okay to use the chalet.

'You are most welcome,' she said, 'just let me know

when you want to move in and I will make sure you have fresh linen and stock the fridge for you.'

About a half hour after I arrived, I heard a motorbike pull up outside the bar and a few moments later Joelle walked in.

She looked sad, tired and stressed. Her eyes, which were always clear and white with light brown, almost green pupils, were dull and red today. I assumed this was due to riding the motorbike with her helmet visor up. She first went over to Mary and gave her a hug. Then she looked at me and Mary gave her a nudge in my direction. We greeted each other.

Her demeanour was reserved, as usual, but she spoke to me and told me about her day and the two teenagers she had arrested. I tried to respond, but my mind kept returning to what I had seen last night and today's events. I wanted to ask her but was fearful of what she might tell me and that she may think I had no right to pry into her private life. She excused herself and went to help her mother in the kitchen but after not very long she came back and sat opposite me, looking at me with her big, sad, eyes.

After a long pause, she asked me, 'What is the matter Douglas?'

I struggled to know how to pose the questions tactfully. I started by telling her that I had been told not to leave the island without permission. She started to say, 'Oh, that's just routine while they finish investigating the two who attacked me…'

I interrupted and asked, 'Am I being followed by the police? What is going on Joelle?'

She looked at me and did not say anything immediately so I just blurted out the question I really wanted to ask.

'Who was that man I saw you kissing last night?'

She looked absolutely shocked but eventually

murmured, 'No one.'

'It was dark but I thought I saw you at the hotel?' I questioned her.

She looked very uncomfortable and said, 'I was not at the hotel, I was working last night.'

'You just told me you had arrested a couple of teenagers for graffiti, but what were you doing for the rest of evening?'

She looked at me and she said she had been working with a visiting detective. I wanted to believe this and accept that I had been mistaken, when Tony marched into the bar announcing his presence loudly, shouting, 'Hi there!'

The moment between Joelle and I had evaporated, completely destroyed by Tony's presence. I groaned inwardly and looked at Joelle who was clearly not pleased either.

'Thought I might find you here Douglas, when I missed you at the hotel. I reckoned we might have some beers together and talk man to man.'

'Not bloody likely!' I swore under my breath as he put his arm round Joelle and stroked her backside, announcing they were old friends as he winked at me. Joelle missed this possessive gesture, but I knew exactly what he meant.

As the realisation of their relationship dawned on me, I felt like a ton weight had just hit me in the body. I muttered something about feeling unwell and walked out of the bar feeling hazy and unsure of what I was seeing and of what to do about it.

As I walked along the beach, I felt sick as I realised that not only was I under suspicion for something I was supposed to have done, but any fondness Joelle might have shown towards me was nothing more than work to her, and she was just gathering information about me. The hopes I had harboured that Joelle and I might actually become friends were destroyed.

When I got back to my chalet I sat outside wondering what to do. I watched the moon rising, reflecting its silvery light across the rippling sea, wondering what on earth was going to happen to me next. As I looked at the moon I thought, *I can't sleep now*. I needed to do something tonight. I grabbed my camera bag and left.

Chapter 51

Joelle de Nouvelas; Friday 28th November

I was horrified when we were interrupted by a loud 'Hi there!' as Tony rolled into the bar. I groaned inwardly and looked at Douglas who was clearly not pleased.

I stood up as Tony invited Douglas to drink some beer with him and talk 'man talk', whatever that is. I heard Douglas swear under his breath.

The situation then got worse as Tony smugly told Douglas we were old friends, put his arm round me and stroked my backside. I tried to pull away but he had put his arm round my waist and held me firmly against him. I am not sure who moved first, me saying I had to help in the kitchen as I fled, or Douglas who had gone very pale, and stood up saying he felt unwell and was going back to the hotel.

After Douglas had gone Tony walked into the kitchen looking for me but before he could say anything Mary told him to get out, the kitchen was staff only. He started to say that he just wanted a drink and to talk with me but Mary told him again in no uncertain terms the get out of the kitchen and that I was helping her in the kitchen that evening.

He went out and after a few moments we heard him ring the service bell. Mary went out and I heard him demand a beer and try to order a meal. She told him she was short staffed tonight and would only be serving meals that had been pre-booked. He argued, telling her she could not refuse to serve him. I have never heard her so angry as she told him that this was not America and if she did not want to serve him she did not have to, and furthermore if he continued to argue she would throw him out.

She came stomping back into the kitchen and after she had calmed down she said, 'What a rude an unpleasant man he is; such a contrast to Douglas. Where is he by the way, I saw him in here earlier and I thought he was going to eat tonight?'

I explained that Douglas had not felt well and had gone. Mary gave me a very old fashioned look and asked, 'Why would that be?'

The old witch! I thought. *She knows perfectly well what happened out there, she just wants me to say it.*

'He saw Tony make a pass at me last night and Tony made another pass at me out there tonight. I think it upset Douglas.'

'I am sure it did,' Mary said and continued, 'I wish Douglas would make a pass at you and the two of you would sort out this pussy footing nonsense between you.'

I felt like a little girl and petulantly said to Mary, 'He has already, and I turned him down.'

'What are you talking about?'

'He asked me out to dinner and I said I could not go.'

'That's not making a pass,' Mary snorted, 'that's treating you like a lady.'

I was getting cross now and I told Mary, 'Look Mother, you don't know what you are talking about. I can't afford to get involved with him. He is a drug smuggler, criminal and God knows what else.'

'You stupid girl.' Mary spoke very quietly. 'Douglas is

nothing of the sort. He is a good man. I can tell, I know about people and I do not believe he is involved in this drug business.

'Has it occurred to you that you are looking at Douglas through the wrong end of the telescope? Supposing he was not carrying drugs on that plane. After all you never found any, did you? Just because he fitted the description of the man you were told was carrying drugs you have assumed that he is guilty, and made the bits of evidence you have found fit your theory, and dismissed the bits that don't fit. 'What's happened to innocence before guilt is proved?' Mary challenged me.

I finished the conversation in a petulant voice, telling Mary she had no idea how the police compiled and reviewed evidence.

Mary just replied calmly, 'Have it your own way then,' and got on with her cooking.

There was not much we had to say to each other after that.

Sean arrived to take over the bar and I heard Tony ordering more beer and trying to start a conversation with him.

I helped Mary in the kitchen a little longer but then asked Mary if she minded if I went. I needed to think so I got on the Triumph and took off to ride round the island.

I slowly realised that she was right. I, of all people, a police officer who prided myself on being fair and doing the right thing, had fallen into the trap of making the evidence fit the theory. I was ashamed of myself and more sorry than ever about what I might have done to Douglas.

Chapter 52

Joelle de Nouvelas; Saturday 29th November

It was Saturday and because of Tony's presence Bernie had come into the station.

I went straight into see him and to tell him what had happened.

'I saw Tony on Thursday evening and he tried to kiss me in the car park,' I started.

'He did what!' Bernard exclaimed. 'Why did you not tell me this before?'

'I can handle it, and it does not matter now,' I went on. 'It's got much worse since. Douglas Jay saw Tony making a pass and trying to kiss me. He challenged me this evening and I told him he must have been mistaken, and that I was on duty. Unfortunately at that moment Tony rolled into the bar pretending we were old friends.'

Both Bernie and I were quiet for a few moments while we digested the implications.

Eventually I said, 'I think we have blown it. You told him not to leave the island and he has worked out we have been following him. I think he must have worked out who Tony is, as I told him I was seeing a visiting detective.'

Bernie said nothing but went out to the general office and told Merv to go and find Tony Choizi and bring him into the station. As he came back into the office he told me, 'Don't worry, this is not your fault. We need to sort something out but we must tell Tony about the situation before he does any more damage.'

An hour later, Tony marched through the office and waved to me as he went into Bernie's office. The door shut. I nervously sat watching the door for ten minutes until it opened and Bernie beckoned me in. Tony was sitting in behind Bernie's desk and angrily greeted me, 'You stupid bitch. You have fucked this up well and truly. Why did you let him see you and then tell him who I was – you are a brainless idiot!'

I managed to say, 'But, you were there as well…'

Bernard interrupted and Tony wound himself up for more expletives. 'That's enough you two, and turning to Tony, added, 'and you will be respectful towards my officers!' Tony glowered at both us but the atmosphere gradually cooled down.

After a while Tony said quietly in a threatening manner, 'Arrest him, bring him for questioning and we will break him and get an admission.'

Bernard signalled for me to leave the office and as went out he shut the door. We could all hear them shouting at each other for a few minutes but then the voices dropped and everyone in the office looked at me. I shrugged. After a while Bernie took me on one side and whispered to me, 'I have told Choizi that we don't have enough evidence to make an arrest stick, but he is insistent we bring Jay in for questioning. I will take over now. You keep out of the way and find something to do away from the station, but before you go I want you to do one last thing. I can't leave that man here on his own, God knows what he will do. So please will you and Merv go and find Jay and bring him in for questioning.'

This was the task I did not want and I dreaded doing it, so I said to Bernie, 'I was thinking about our evidence and it is all circumstantial and I am not sure now we have anything tangible that proves he is involved.'

'I agree with you and that's the argument I just had with Tony, but he is insisting that he needs to question Jay now. His point is that if Jay is guilty he does not want him disappearing before we have chance to question him.'

'Does it have to be me who goes to get him?' I pleaded with Bernie.

'Yes,' said Bernie. 'You know him and you can talk to him in the car and warn him what to expect, then we might get somewhere. If Tony sees him cold he will say nothing and that will play right into Tony's hands.' Having to arrest Douglas was now my worst nightmare and I was dreading having to go and find him and bring him in for questioning, but I could not argue further with Bernie, so I agreed, thinking that at least I would be able to talk to him first.

Merv drove us directly to the hotel. I checked Douglas's chalet but he was not there. I walked over to the guest information and reception desk, asking if they knew where Douglas was. 'I have not seen him this morning,' said the duty receptionist. 'He has not been in for breakfast and he not sitting in his usual place over there.' She pointed towards a corner of the garden. *Perhaps he is on the beach*, I thought, telling Merv to look round the gardens while I went and had a look along the beach.

Five minutes later we met at the information desk having seen no sign of Douglas. 'Please could we have a key to his room?' I asked.

We walked round to Douglas's chalet. We did not need a key: the door was unlocked and the chalet was empty. The bed had not been slept on. His clothes were in the wardrobe and his PC was on the desk. No sign of his camera or camera bag. I sent Merv to get a master key to the wardrobe safe while I looked round the chalet further. The bathroom was dry and had not been used for some hours. Merv returned and we opened the safe and found his passport, wallet, money, watch and open return flight ticket. I sighed miserably, not knowing whether I was disappointed or pleased we had not found him.

'Looks like he done a runner,' Merv said to me.

After finding Douglas was not at the hotel, Merv and I returned to the station and with some trepidation I went straight up to Bernie's office to update him. I expected Tony to be there as well and I was not disappointed. I reported, 'We went to the hotel where we expected to find Douglas Jay. We searched the grounds and beach and the chalet he had been using but he was not there. All his personal effects, passport, wallet, clothes, laptop were in the chalet. The only things missing were his camera bag, camera and equipment and the Honda motorbike that he hired.'

This did not bring forth the tirade of criticism and accusations of incompetence that I had expected from Tony. Instead he was grinning and looking very pleased with himself. Both Bernie and I looked questioningly at him, wondering why he had not blown up. He beamed back at us savouring the moment and then simply said, 'Good.'

'Good!' I exclaimed. 'But he has done a runner.'

Tony responded, looking even more pleased, 'Exactly. I could not have wished for anything better. By running away he has given us just the evidence I needed.'

'You were not planning this when you came to the bar last night?' I asked suspiciously.

'Not at all, I was looking forward to spending the night with you,' Tony leered, grinning at me.

I thought Tony was the most devious and objectionable person I have ever met. I was furious and about to verbally let rip when Bernie interrupted, 'Joelle, get a picture of Jay and go downstairs and get a copy out to all officers to keep a look out for him. Warn airport and dock security to keep watch. I guess we may be too late, though. I expect he had his escape plan set up with another passport and money and has slipped off the island on a small boat from one of the marinas round the island. Visit them and see what you can find.'

I moved to leave the office and Bernie followed me out. When we got to the stairwell out of earshot he rested his hand on my shoulder. I turned to see what he wanted.

'Joelle, I can see you are angry but be very careful of that American. If this case goes wrong he is looking for someone to blame and he will set you up, have no doubts. He has already told me he thinks you are incompetent and too involved with Douglas Jay. Of course I told him you were one of the best officers on the island but he is insisting that you are taken off his investigation. But I don't have the manpower and I told him I can't and won't do that.'

'Thanks Bernie,' I said, and wishing he would take me off the investigation, I walked down to the duty sergeant's desk to give him the picture of Douglas and ask him to organise the search and alert all island exit points.

'Oh, by the way,' he said as started to walk away, 'we have had a report from the hospital. A male, with no identification, was admitted early this morning in a critical condition following an accident.'

'What sort of accident and what details of the casualty did they give?' I asked as I felt a knot of fear tying itself in my stomach.

'That's all the information they gave me, I expect someone will report a missing person eventually, then we will know who he is.'

'Can you telephone the hospital for more details?'

'Okay, in a minute.'

'No, now!'

'All right, don't get excited,' the sergeant said as he picked up the phone.

I waited anxiously. It seemed to take ages for him to get connected to the right person but eventually he said, 'Kaeta Island Police here; about that male involved in an accident you reported, earlier, can you give me more details?'

I waited, straining to hear but could not. The sergeant hung up and turned to me saying, 'It was a traffic accident. He is middle-aged and is unconscious at the moment and in a critical condition. Has a suspected fractured skull, broken ribs and wrist and extensive bruising and lacerations to his trunk, arm and leg. They are doing a scan at the moment as they think he may have bleed on his brain.'

I raced out to my Triumph, desperate to confirm, or not, my worst fear.

PART 2

Chapter 53

Joelle de Nouvelas; Sunday 30th November

Kaete Island hospital is situated near the Caribbean coast with a view across the Caribbean Sea, between Kaeta Town and the airport. The particular location was chosen for two reasons. It is close to the airport and the hospital has its own desalination plant providing water used to irrigate the extensive tropical gardens that surround the building. The gardens are planted with a variety of different coloured bougainvilleas, ranging from deep reds, purples, and oranges through to light pinks and whites. The whole effect is enhanced by the multi-coloured leaves of the tropical shrubs which line the pathways that wend their way through the gardens. The paths are all concrete and wide enough for powered wheelchairs. Strategically placed around the gardens are a number of paved patio areas with seats carefully placed under the trees to take advantage of the shade but still retaining views out to sea.

The hospital was developed by an American Medical Company specialising in cosmetic and bone reconstruction treatments for rich American clients. The garden is an important part of the hospital's function. By offering patients the opportunity to sit and enjoy the gardens while recuperating the company hopes to extend the patients' stay in the hospital, thus maximising their income.

As part of the deal with the Americans to build this hospital the Kaeta Island government, at the time, insisted that the hospital should also have a facility for treating local people. Actually this suited the medical company well as they used it to establish a nurse training facility from which trained staff could then be offered the opportunity to transfer to the company's other hospitals across the United States.

The residents of Kaeta therefore have access to a top-class hospital with skilled, mainly American, doctors and state of the art equipment, offering general medical wards, a maternity ward, facilities for the critically ill and injured, an accident and emergency department, outpatients' facilities, and a morgue, all on a relatively small scale.

It was 2.00am on Sunday morning and I was sitting in a visitor's lounge nervously waiting for news from operating theatre number three.

I had arrived at the hospital at about midday the previous morning shown my police badge and asked to be directed to the individual involved in the traffic accident. I was sent to see the charge sister of the intensive care ward. She told me that the patient was currently in the theatre undergoing an emergency operation to relieve a build-up of blood in the skull cavity. I explained that I needed to see patient for identification purposes.

'Well,' explained the nurse, 'you can't see him while he is in theatre, and I will have to check with the doctor when he comes back on to the ward.'

'I'll wait.'

'You can wait if you wish, but there is no guarantee you will be able to see him while he is in intensive care.'

And after a couple of hours the nurse came to find me and told me that the patient was back from theatre but still unconscious. 'Doctor says you can look at him briefly but he is not to be disturbed. You must wear this mask and do not get to close.'

I was horrified when I entered the intensive care suite. The patient was semi-prone on a trolley bed. The lacerations to his leg and arm were visible and looked horrible. His left arm was twisted at a funny angle and his hand bent backwards, virtually at a right angle to the arm. He was attached to a heart rate and blood pressure monitor and most of his face was hidden behind an oxygen mask. His head was bandaged with a tube attached from which some bloody liquid was oozing. Nevertheless, I recognised Douglas lying there.

I felt light-headed and the nurse took my arm and led me out of the room, sat me down and gave me a paper cup of water.

'It looks worse than it actually is,' she said. 'His heartbeat is very shallow and his blood pressure is low. When his condition has stabilised a bit we will be able to clean him up and do something with the broken arm and wrist, but the priority at the moment is to stop the haemorrhaging in the brain cavity.'

After a time I had recovered enough to realise that I needed to phone Bernie and let him know I had found Douglas. I had to go outside, as mobile phones were not allowed near intensive care.

'Douglas has had an accident and is in intensive care at

the hospital.'

'What sort of accident?' Bernie asked.

'I looks like he came off his Honda bike somehow, I am guessing, I have no information at the moment. I am going to stay at the hospital. Can you send Merv up to see me? There are some things I would like him to check.'

'What things?' queried Bernie.

'Well, for a start, we know his motorbike was not at the hotel – I would like Merv to find it.' I hung up and went back inside to the visitors' lounge wondering what to do next. I asked the staff nurse if I might see his admittance registration papers.

'I guess they are still round at A&E,' she told me.

The receptionist at A&E was reluctant at first to show me the document but when I explained that this was a police investigation and I could always get a warrant sent over she said I could read the paper but not take it away. 'Anyway,' she went on, 'the receptionist on duty earlier has gone home now and I am not sure where the papers are.' She rummaged about for a bit and eventually produced a sheet of paper. It did not tell me much at all. It just recorded:

Unknown male. Approximately 50 years of age, White European.

Date: 30th November: Time of admittance; 6.39am

Symptoms: Unconscious. Traffic accident with a number of visible injuries

Treatment: Emergency medical procedures

Authorisation: Authorised by the duty doctor.

Admitted by: Ambulance crew 2

The receptionist caught my eye. 'You are in luck, that's the ambulance crew that brought him over there, just going off duty.' She called them over and I asked them to tell me where and how they found Douglas.

'We got a call about six this morning from a guy who said he was on his way to work at the docks when he saw a body lying beside the road. He thought he might be dead. When we got there the guy was unconscious but still breathing so we rushed him in. That's about it really.'

'Did you see any sign of a Honda motorbike or any other vehicle which might have been involved?'

'No there were no vehicles there that we saw,' said the driver, 'I thought it was probably a hit and run.'

'Where did you find him?' I asked.

'He was on the Caribbean coast road about five miles south of St Martin's. There is a long sweeping bend with an adverse camber and a sharp twist at the end. He was lying half on the road and across rocks at the edge of the road. It looked like he hit his head on those rocks. He was lucky he did not go over the edge, if he had it might have been days before anyone found him.'

I knew the road; it was where I had nearly lost control of the Lexus. I asked the ambulance crew, 'Did you find any sort of identification, passport, or money on him?'

'There was nothing on him, when we got him back here we helped the nurse cut his clothing off. He was only wearing a shirt and a pair of light cotton trousers and all the pockets were empty. We did not really check the scene of the accident. I don't recall seeing anything there, we would have picked it up if we had seen anything.'

As I thanked them, I heard a commotion and a lot of shouting going on somewhere in the hospital. As I headed back to intensive care it got louder and I was soon confronted with the sight of Bernie trying to make himself invisible and a doctor and staff nurse confronting Tony, threatening to call security and have him physically thrown out if he did not leave immediately. Bernie made to leave with Tony ungraciously in tow threatening to be back, instructing the doctor to let him know as soon as Douglas woke up so he could question him.

'What was that all about?' I asked the nurse when we were on our own again.

'That American,' she answered. 'He is unbelievable. First he asked us to wake the patient up so he could be cautioned and questioned. When we refused, and anyway you can't wake someone from a coma, he told us that the patient was a criminal and if he looked in danger of dying, not to resuscitate. I have never seen the doctor so angry. Unbelievable man,' she muttered as she walked away.

A bit later Merv arrived. I told him that I wanted to stay at the hospital for a bit longer, at least until Douglas's condition stabilised. I explained what the ambulance crew had told me and asked Merv to drive down the road and find the where the accident had occurred, examine it carefully, take some pictures and see if he could find the Honda and camera. 'Look particularly for a passport, money, travel tickets, any sort of documentation,' I instructed.

For a long time I sat brooding about Douglas. I felt guilty, thinking that somehow it was to do with me that he had been riding the motorbike round the island all night but also I was concerned he might die and that was not because he might escape justice by dying, but because I realised that I felt affection for the man.

Towards the end of the afternoon I remembered I had not eaten all day and had only drunk a couple of machine coffees. 'Is there anywhere I could get a meal?' I asked a nurse.

'Yes dear, if you walk over to the private room building there is a restaurant for the patients. You can eat there. It's that way,' she said, pointing down a corridor.

As you might expect, the restaurant only offered healthy food, so I chose a barbecued chicken salad, a cup of tea, and a large bottle of water. The salad was good and as I ate it I started thinking again. What if Douglas was not running away at all but had just gone out riding the Honda, perhaps to take pictures? After all, why take the camera but nothing else if he was running away? But it would have been dark; he could not take pictures in the dark could he? I made a mental note to find the camera and see what pictures were on the memory chip. I knew, because Douglas had shown me, that the camera recorded the date and time and GPS location of every picture.

After all, I reasoned, all that we knew was the Honda, camera, and camera bag were missing. The passport and money were just supposition by Tony to support his theory that Douglas was escaping. I rolled this thought around as I walked back to intensive care. The nurse saw me coming and told me that Douglas had improved a bit. His heart rate had settled down and was stronger.

I returned to the visitors' lounge, pleased with the news of Douglas's improvement.

My thoughts returned to Tony's escape theory. If it is correct then it is quite likely that any documents would be with the Honda. *We must find it*, I realised. But then, if he was running, surely he would have taken more clothes with him than just what he was wearing. Perhaps he did and there is a travel bag with the Honda. If Merv found nothing with the Honda, assuming he could find it, then my theory that Douglas had just gone out for a ride and to take photographs was equally valid.

The next thought was, why go out in the middle of the night and ride a motorbike around with just a camera, and wearing unsuitable clothing? Here, I agreed with Tony. I knew the events in Glass Bar earlier that evening must have distressed Douglas. I saw his expression as he rushed out and he had looked shattered. He must have gone out on the Honda while he was not thinking straight. I realised why I had been feeling unsettled all day. Guilt. All this was at least, in part, my fault, I thought.

I thought some more about the midnight bike ride. No one had mentioned the helmet. I asked a passing nurse if she knew if he had been wearing a helmet. She did not, but directed me back to A&E.

The night receptionist had just come on duty and she remembered booking Douglas in. She confirmed he had been wearing a crash helmet. 'We had to remove the remains of it before we could treat him. He was lucky to be wearing a good one, as it undoubtedly saved his life, but it was shattered by the impact. She dug around under her desk and produced a black bin bag with the remains of my helmet inside. I was horrified. It had split into three pieces with deep scrapes and gouges down one side, and was covered in blood. The chin piece had been cut away, as had the retaining strap, I presumed when the helmet was removed. I walked back to the waiting room feeling sick and even more guilty as I remembered I had once begrudged lending him the helmet, but thanking God that I had.

I was pulled out of this morose line of though by a commotion coming from intensive care. I rushed out, expecting to find Tony again, but instead it was Douglas on his trolley being rushed down the corridor with a nurse running along beside, holding a drip. They clattered into theatre three again. There was no one about to ask what was going on so I just stood there for ages until a nurse came out of the theatre.

'What has happened, is he all right?' I shouted at the nurse.

'He took a turn for the worse,' the nurse replied. 'He is stabilising now, but the doctor thinks he is still bleeding in the skull cavity and he may need another operation to relieve the pressure.'

That's why it's 2.00am in the morning and I am sitting here in the visitor's lounge nervously waiting for news.

Chapter 54

Joelle de Nouvelas: Monday 1st December

My thoughts turned to Mary and things she said to me. It seemed like days ago but was really only just over twenty-four hours ago. She had accused me of assuming he was guilty and making the evidence fit. I thought, OK, suppose it was not Douglas who was the courier on that plane. We were not told which plane the drug courier would be on and we never found any drugs in Douglas's bags. But I could mentally hear Bernie saying that he fitted the description and could have smuggled in drugs on his body; we had never actually searched him personally. Then I remembered the bag that was hidden on the aeroplane. Probably Douglas's, we thought, and we had dismissed it without consideration, but supposing it was not Douglas's bag but had belonged to someone else who had used the bag to smuggle drugs on board, but had then moved the drugs to another bag, or something, to smuggle them in. *That's a bit far-fetched*, I thought, but that second hidden bag was bothering me now.

Then I thought how we had seen those parcels as significant in tying Douglas into the Zip Line drug store, but we had never actually found out what was in the parcels, just assumed it was drugs. I remembered I had thought at the time, why wrap them up only to unwrap then again somewhere else? And then there were two parcels, one of which he had left at the sugar plantation and there was no connection that we knew of. Bernie's explanation that it was probably a diversion was just a little too quick and convenient.

Also, there was the discussion with the Zip Line operator, Zach. We were pretty sure that Zach was a go-between but we did not know what Douglas had spoken about with him. He just could have been asking about the Zip Line or something else completely innocent. Unless we could find Zach and ask him we would probably never find out. I began to realise that, as usual, Mary was right. We had been sloppy and not followed up on a number of things that we should have done.

The growing conviction that Douglas might be innocent lifted a great weight from me and cheered me up quite considerably, but I also realised that I now had a lot of work to do. I hoped it would not be too late for Douglas, and the thought that it might be too late and I could lose Douglas for good catapulted me back to a state of anxiety and worry.

Eventually a nurse came to find me and sat down next to me. She took my hand and told me, 'He is back in intensive care. He had a second head bleed and needed another operation to relieve pressure on the brain.'

'What sort of operation?' I asked.

'It's quite simple really, the surgeon just drills a small hole through the skull to where the blood has collected. We attach a drain and relieve the pressure. He has stabilised now and we think that he should be OK.

'He has suffered a major bang to the skull but luckily the crash helmet saved him and he suffered only a minor fracture. He is in an induced coma now and hopefully we have stabilised the bleeding and he should make a full recovery when we bring him out of the coma. He has suffered extensive damage to his arm and wrist and has multiple fractures to his radius bone and wrist bone as well as some fractured ribs. We have straightened out his wrist and arm but when he is stronger he will need further operations to reset the broken bones.

'He has suffered extensive lacerations and bruising on one side of his body, arm and leg and may need some skin grafts. His heart beat is now stronger and blood pressure is recovering.' She paused and looked at me. 'You have been here all day and half the night. There really is nothing more to be done now except wait until he recovers consciousness. Why don't you go home and have some rest? I promise I will phone you as soon as there is any change.'

She was right, I was not doing any good here so I gave her my mobile number and, again, made her promise to phone me, night or day, as soon as there was any change.

Chapter 55

Joelle de Nouvelas; Monday 1ˢᵗ December

I got home shortly before 3.00am, had a shower and went to bed. I slept fitfully that night for about four hours before I got up to go into the station.

I had two black coffees instead of breakfast and told Mary what had happened the previous day. She was quite upset. She liked Douglas and ever since he had helped her in the bar that evening she had always believed he was too genuine to be mixed up with drugs.

I thought about wearing a skirt and pretty blouse but decided that jeans and a tee-shirt would be more practical for the day I was expecting. I did put make-up on to hide the bags under my eyes and stress lines across my face. It did not really work!

We got Jasmine ready for school. She also liked Douglas and was upset as well and did not want to go to school, but Mary persuaded her by promising that as soon as Douglas was well enough they would go and visit him. I started the Triumph and headed off to the station.

The first thing I did when I got to work was to ring the hospital to enquire after Douglas. Bernie came out of his office and stood by the desk, listening. 'How is he?' he asked as I hung up.

'Stable, still unconscious but showing signs of recovery.

What was yesterday all about?' I responded.

'Our American friend wanted to make an arrest and made a scene when the doctor told him it would be at least two weeks, maybe three, before Jay would be well enough for any questioning and arresting him in hospital in his present state is quite impossible. He threw another tantrum with me when I told him were not making any arrest until Jay is discharged and we have had chance to question him. The hospital however have agreed to put Jay in a private room and let us place a policeman outside as long as we don't approach him until they tell us he's fit enough.'

'Where is Tony now?' I asked.

'Don't know,' replied Bernie, 'I dropped him off at his hotel yesterday evening so I suppose he is still there. What are you working on today?'

I replied, 'I want to find the Honda, and search the accident scene and find out if Douglas was actually running away or not.'

Bernie cautioned me, 'OK, but stay low-profile and only report back to me, and keep out of the American's way; he is insisting I take you off this investigation right now.'

'Bernie, give me more time, please, there are things I need to follow up. I was thinking in hospital last night and we still only have circumstantial evidence, which we need to check out. I think Douglas may not be the person we are looking for.'

Bernie looked serious but said, 'OK Joelle, I will trust your judgement, but I don't think you will have much time; Tony wants this wrapped up quickly now, just keep out of his way and report only to me.'

I phoned Merv to see where he was and what he found.

'I am at the accident scene,' he told me, 'it was too dark

to do much last night when I eventually found the place, so I cordoned the area off, and went back first thing this morning. I have found the Honda, it had gone over the edge and is at the bottom of the ravine. I have asked for a recovery truck so we can get it out.'

'Don't disturb anything,' I instructed him, 'I am coming right over.' I used the Triumph, as it was quicker than taking a police car.

I found Merv, and the recovery truck, waiting. They were parked just before the bend. The road at this point was cut through the side of a hill. On one side was a rock face, above which was rainforest growing up the hill. The rock was not particularly stable and was wired back with netting in places to prevent slides. On the outside of the bend was a narrow verge before the ground fell away into a ravine, which was about seven metres deep. The road had a pronounced negative camber and there had been a number of accidents at this point involving vehicles taking the corner too fast and going over the edge.

The three of us, me, Merv, and the recovery truck driver walked round the bend and Merv pointed out where the accident had happened. On the verge were some large rocks, obviously from a recent landslide, which had been pushed off the carriageway on the verge. Merv pointed out blood on one of rocks. 'I reckon that's where he hit his head,' he said, 'and if you look at the carriageway just in front you see traces of material, and blood on the surface, so I reckon he took the corner too fast, the bike went over and he slid about five feet along the road and hit his head on that rock, and look there is more blood in the grass just in front of the rock.' He walked a few paces along the road and pointed to where the verge was torn up as the Honda went over the edge on its side. The bike is just down there.' He pointed.

'Can I get on now?' asked the truck driver tetchily.

'No,' I replied, 'not until I have had chance to examine the whole scene.'

I noted that Douglas was headed back in the direction of St Martin's and Glass Bay.

I asked Merv if he had seen anything that looked like a passport, or money, or travel bag. He replied that he had not. I told Merv to check round the whole area of the bend and see if there was anything else or evidence of another vehicle involved.

I scrambled down the ravine to look at the Honda. The damage was all to its near side. Scrapes on the cowling and bent handle bars and footrest were all consistent with Merv's theory that he had come off just on the corner. There was nothing on the bike; no papers, passport, or money and, as far as I could see, no evidence that anyone before me had been down the ravine. I cast around the area looking to see if there was anything lying about. There was quite a lot of litter, empty water bottles and Coke tins, but nothing connected with the accident. A little further back, just under the ravine slope I spotted a broken bungee cord and just beyond that I was Douglas's camera bag. I picked it up and looked inside. There was his camera and couple of lenses, but that was all. The equipment did not look damaged so I switched the camera on and pressed the button to see what pictures were in the memory. The last picture was a dramatic shot of the "Three Sisters" with the moon on the horizon just behind them. It was dated two nights previously at 2.43am.

'So that's what he was doing,' I spoke out loud. I retrieved the bag and camera equipment and scrambled back up the ravine. I told Merv to take pictures of the whole scene before the Honda was recovered and headed back to the office.

I took the camera into Bernie and explained my theory. 'He was not running away, he was upset and had gone off on the bike, not thinking clearly, to take photographs of the moon. We could find no passport, tickets or any other documents anywhere at the scene of the accident, and there were none on his person when he reached hospital.

'He probably went round the corner too fast and simply lost control. Also he was headed back to the hotel, not away from it.' I showed Bernie the pictures and the dating record.

'Looks like you are right,' he commented. 'And that blows Tony's theory away anyway. He won't like that.' He chuckled.

Chapter 56

Joelle de Nouvelas: Tuesday 2nd December

Again this morning, Mary offered to take Jasmine to school so I could leave home early and go to the hospital. When I arrived I went straight to the intensive care ward and asked how Douglas was and if I could see him. The charge nurse looked at me and said, 'You are the police woman who was here last Saturday aren't you?'

'Yes,' I replied.

'I am sorry, but my instructions are that he is only to be visited by close family members. No other visitors, especially police, and any enquiries regarding his condition are to be referred to Dr Leonard, the supervising consultant.'

'But can't you at least tell me how he is and let me see him?' I was about to cry, this was too much.

'I am sorry dear. The doctor was very specific.'

'But I am his fiancée,' I blurted out.

'Oh, I am sorry,' said the nurse. She looked round, clearly troubled. 'I will ask someone for you.'

She picked up the telephone and after a few moments she said, 'The patient in intensive care who is not allowed visitors. His fiancée is here and wants to see him.'

She paused, listening. 'Yes, I will ask her.'

Another silence. 'She is a policewoman, the one who was here on Saturday… No, she is local police, I recognise her… Well, she says she is his fiancée and she looks upset… No she is on her own… Ok, I will ask her, thanks.' The nurse hung up and turned to me. 'Dr Leonard is coming down as soon as he can. He asks if you would please wait for him.'

For half an hour I sat in that visitors lounge where I spent most of last Saturday waiting for Dr Leonard. I started to cry as I daydreamed about being Douglas's fiancée. Perhaps one day it might happen, probably not.

Dr Leonard surprised me. He was about the same age as Douglas: tall, athletic-looking, with a kind face. One of those people you immediately like. He looked carefully at me, studying my face where crying had made my make-up run, my eyes bloodshot and face blotchy. His opening question was, 'Are you really Douglas Jay's fiancée?' I knew I could not carry off the lie so I told the truth, 'No, but I think I might love him.'

He was silent for a long time looking at me. Eventually he said sternly, 'I will not have the police dictating to me how I should care for my patient. Nor will I have him disturbed by a police presence while he is in a critical condition. Is that understood young lady?' I nodded, about to cry again.

'However,' Dr Leonard spoke more softly, 'I think even I can see that you obviously feel something for this man so you, and you alone, are permitted to visit.' I really did burst into a full flood of tears at this point. Dr Leonard just passed me a tissue and waited for me to compose myself.

He then explained, 'Douglas is recovering as well as we can expect. The most serious injury is the blow to is head which has resulted in a fracture to the skull and caused cerebral oedema and subarachnoid haemorrhaging which we have relieved through surgery.'

'What does that mean?' I asked.

'It is basically a build-up of fluid around the brain. In Douglas's case he also suffered bleeding inside the skull cavity. It causes pressure on the brain resulting in a condition similar to a stroke. Essentially, we relieve the pressure by drilling a small hole through the skull and draining the fluid.'

I shuddered. It sounded grotesque as Dr Leonard continued, 'He is on oxygen and is being kept in a medicated coma until the swelling of the brain subsides. We are also keeping his body temperature artificially low to help reduce the swelling. He may suffer some memory loss and loss of brain function, although I am hopeful that over time this will be minimal.

'The injury to his left arm is serious. He has multiple compression fractures of the radius bone and fractures of the carpal bones in his wrist. We have straightened the arm as far as we can at the moment but he will need further surgery when he is sufficiently recovered to take an anaesthetic. He has also suffered serious bruising and grazing with loss of skin to his back and leg.'

Dr Leonard took me into the intensive care room to see Douglas. He was hooked up to various life support tubes and monitors. He was still unconscious and looked very pale and ill.

As I looked at him I had realised that I had found someone with whom I could be happy, but he might be snatched away before I could test that. I was also very aware that we had not got off to the best of starts together, and that he well might not want anything to do with me. On top of all this I was afraid there was a nagging doubt still about the drug smuggling. I was beginning to believe we had identified an innocent person, but I knew I had now to discount the evidence we had found that might implicate him. I so wanted him to wake up and tell me he was not involved. I wanted to cry again.

Dr Leonard took me out of the room, saying, 'There is nothing you can do for the moment, but he will need you when he comes round, to explain what has happened and fill in any memory gaps. This will help him recover. Now I am afraid I need to ask you some administrative questions if you feel up to it.'

I suppose I was looking pale and shaken by now, I certainly felt that way as the doctor said, 'We have administered treatment so far using our emergency fund budget but I can only do this for treating life-threatening conditions. I do need to know how the hospitalisation and further treatment will be paid for.'

'I will pay,' I said without hesitation.

'He does not have insurance?' queried the doctor.

'Oh, I don't know, he might have. I will have to look and let you know.'

'Also,' Dr Leonard continued, 'I need to contact his closest relative to get their permission to continue treatment.'

I explained that Douglas was alone on the island, and as far as I was aware had no close relatives left alive.

'Well,' said the doctor 'That probably makes you the closest person he has, so if you would not mind I will ask you to sign the consent forms and payment guarantee as his responsible friend.' He turned to the nurse and asked her organise the forms for me. As he left he turned and said to me, 'If you do find any insurance, take it to the hospital administration and they will arrange to bill the insurance company directly.'

As I signed the consent forms and payment guarantee the implications of being Douglas's only and responsible friend came home to me.

Chapter 57

I left the hospital and walked back to the car park where I had left the Triumph.

I sat on the bike and phoned Bernie to tell him where I was and that I intended to go straight to Hotel Glass Bay to see about insurance.

He asked how Douglas was. I told him what the doctor had told me and asked him if he knew what this ban on visitors was all about.

'Yes,' he said 'How did you manage to get in?'

'I told them I was his friend and I have signed the treatment consent forms and so on,' I said.

Bernie did not answer for a moment then warned me, 'Hmm. I am not sure you should have done that. You can't afford to become emotionally involved and you must remain objective.'

'Well,' I replied tetchily, 'it's too late now, and being objective has not been one of our strengths so far. Anyway what is this ban all about?'

Bernie let the first point pass and said, 'Our American friend barged into the hospital yesterday demanding they bring Douglas round so he could question him. I believe they got hotel security to escort him out.'

'Where is now?' I asked.

'I don't know,' replied Bernie before saying, 'if you are going to the hotel I would like you to search Jay's room again. Choizi is saying it was not properly examined for evidence last time and wants it done again. I will tell Merv to meet you there.'

I got to the hotel before Merv and picked up the key to Douglas's chalet. I entered the chalet and it looked just as we had left it last Saturday morning. *Bloody American*, I thought. *What does he mean, not searched properly?*

An assistant hotel manager entered the chalet behind me and asked, 'Is it true that Mr. Jay is in hospital critically ill?'

'Yes.'

'He is not likely to need this room again is he?'

'No, I would not think so,' I agreed.

'In that case we will cancel the reservation. Do you know who will pay the outstanding account and clear the room? The account is not much as most of the stay was prepaid. Just some shop purchases and three days' room rental if the room is cleared today.'

I said I would pay the account and clear the room.

He left, and I walked across to the safe, which was not locked. *Funny*, I thought, *I am sure we locked that after we left last Saturday.* I opened it, nothing had been taken but something new had been placed in the safe. I immediately shut the door and left, locking the chalet on my way out.

I lurked around the garden area, where Douglas used to sit, waiting for Merv. I was distracted by my name being called out.

'Hi there, Joelle. Just the person. Have you been avoiding me?'

Tony Choizi waddled his way across the garden

towards me in his swimming shorts and shirt straining to hold in his beer gut. My skin crawled as he leered at me.

He waved a copy of the Coconut file at me and said, 'I have read this now; you have collected some very good evidence here. It's just what I need. There is not really much more for me to do until Jay comes round. Are you here to search his room?'

'Yes, Bernie asked us to do a second search.'

'Good, good,' he repeated.

I started to say to him that I thought that the evidence we had was all very circumstantial and that there was some doubt that Douglas was actually the drug courier.

Tony interrupted me and said, 'What you have is strong enough, but you don't get the point do you?' he said nastily. 'I don't really care if Jay is innocent or guilty. This end of the smuggling line is closed down now and I want an arrest to take back to the USA and Jay fits the bill.'

I was horrified and speechless as Tony continued, 'I will just hang around long enough to see what other evidence you turn up then I might go back to Miami until Jay comes round and that fucking doctor lets me talk to him.'

He came close and I got a whiff of body odour and sun tan lotion as he put his arm round my waist and squeezed my breast, saying, 'Unless you have something here to entertain me?'

I slapped his face as hard as I could and reeled away from him. He just laughed and walked off.

I was furious, I felt sick, but most of all I was worried, for I could now see what I was up against, but I was not going to let that man treat me like he just did, and I was going to fight for Douglas. I just did not know how yet. *Please hurry up*, I willed Merv.

Chapter 58

Joelle de Nouvelas; Tuesday 2nd December

When Merv arrived I took him straight over to Douglas's chalet and told him to lock the door. I did not want to be disturbed by Tony.

'Did you bring a camera?' I asked him

'Yes,' he replied, producing one from his case.

'I want you dust the safe for fingerprints. The only ones you should find are Douglas's and mine. You did not touch the safe last Saturday did you?'

'No,' he said, as he did as I asked him.

'There are lots of different prints all over the safe and door,' he said after a few minutes. 'I guess they belong to previous guests and the safe door and knob is never cleaned. It is going to be very difficult to get a decent set of prints of this safe. One thing though, some of these prints have been badly smudged, possibly as someone pushed clothes into the wardrobe.'

'OK, Merv, open the door now and take a picture of the inside. Make sure you get that brown paper parcel at the back in the picture.'

Once Merv had got four pictures of the inside of the safe I gingerly reached in and retrieved the brown paper parcel. 'Does this look familiar?' I asked Merv.

'Should it?'

'Is it like the parcels you saw Douglas wrapping up?'

'Well, not really, I think the paper is a different colour and this parcel is smaller.'

'Take its picture,' I instructed as I placed it on the bed. I carefully unwrapped it, knowing, somehow, what I was going to find. Merv and I stared at the contents sitting on the bed in the now opened and flattened brown paper. I took a deep breath and asked Merv if he had seen the parcel in the safe on Saturday.

'You checked the safe on Saturday. I did not really look,' he reminded me.

I remembered seeing Douglas's wallet, passport, some money, flight ticket and wristwatch, but as I looked into the safe now I also saw a pair of cufflinks and under the flight ticket another envelope. I was pretty sure there had been no parcel in the safe, but we had been in a hurry that Saturday and I could not be one hundred percent certain.

I looked back at the bed at a small plastic bag sealed with a plastic-covered wire twist containing white powder, about the size of a golf ball. I tasted a grain and I knew it would be heroin when analysed. The other item on the bed was a plain white carton about the size of a cigarette box. I asked Merv to open it and see what was inside. He did and held out two small cream-coloured pills, identical to the ones we had found in the old slave cabin. We were both silent for a long time, just staring at the bed.

I did not want to believe what I was seeing. I realised I was breathing in short gasps and was nearing panic point. I took control of myself and my brain seemed to start working again as Merv said, 'Well, there is our evidence.'

'Yes,' I said, 'but who put it there?'

Merv looked at me, puzzled. 'What do you mean, it's obvious Douglas split up the drugs he carried into three separate parcels. He delivered the first two and here is the final drop waiting to be delivered. He probably could not make the drop because his contact Zach has disappeared and we have closed down the store at the slave camp. That's why he done a runner now.'

'Why would he do a runner and leave that lot behind?' I asked.

'I don't know, I expect he did not want to risk getting caught with them on him.'

'That does not make any sense, if he did not want to get caught with them why leave them in his room where they are bound to be found? And where has the powder come from? He supposedly only carried the tablets.' As I said this, I realised no one had actually spoken to the receptionist on duty the day Douglas had supposedly dropped the first package at the Zip Line. She was only a teenage girl, I remembered her name, 'Letta', and she was not on duty when I visited the Zip Line. I made a mental note to go and find her.

'Right,' I said to Merv, 'put that lot in an evidence bag, paper and all, and give it to Bernie, no one else – only Bernie, and tell him I will see him as soon as can to explain. He will need to send it for forensics for testing.

'You search the rest of room, take everything apart, look under the mattress, behind all the drawers, you know the drill, a thorough search. I will go through Douglas's clothes and pack them up. We are taking everything of his with us.'

I pulled Douglas's suitcase down from the top of the wardrobe first. There was nothing else up there. I searched the case thoroughly. There were no secret pockets or compartments, it was a perfectly ordinary soft case and I could feel there was nothing concealed in the lining. In the front pocket I did find some travel papers, itinerary, camera insurance, and his travel insurance documents, which I put in my pocket. All the other papers I placed in a large plastic evidence bag with his wallet, money, passport, and the envelope.

I looked inside the envelope and saw it contained a single sheet summary of the camera instructions which he had written himself. There was also a small four by three-inch picture in the envelope which I assumed must be his ex-wife until I looked at it properly and saw it was of me. It was the picture he had taken that first day when I had returned his camera to him. *The rat*, I thought affectionately, he told me he had deleted that picture. It was a very intimate moment holding that picture and his handwritten camera instructions, I could not bear to put them into the evidence bag so I slipped them into my pocket while Merv was not looking.

I examined all his clothes, checked all the pockets, folded them all carefully, and placed them in the suitcase as Merv looked on amused.

'I have never seen you take that much care in a search before,' he laughed at me.

It was a strange feeling, folding Douglas's clothes up and I glared at Merv, saying, 'This is different, the poor man is nearly dead.'

We finished the search and found nothing apart from the small paper parcel.

I helped Merv carry everything back to the police car and told him again to take it all to Bernie in person.

Merv drove off and I walked back to the reception desk. I returned Douglas's chalet key and paid the outstanding account on my credit card. I remember noting that they still used old fashioned keys, probably because of the way all the chalets are spread out over the grounds. Most hotels now use electronic locks and cards. I noted that she hung the key on a rack down beside the reception desk. I asked her if any of the other guests had asked for Douglas's key over the last few days.

'Yes,' she said, 'as a matter of fact one did. Yesterday, that American gentleman, Mr. Choizi, but naturally I could not let him have it. That would be against the hotel rules, we only let the guest occupying the room have the keys.'

I thanked her and thought about the implications of what she had said. I looked at my watch. I still had time to get to the Zip Line before it closed, especially if I pushed the Triumph.

I walked through the garden to the car park and saw Tony sitting by the swimming pool smugly watching me. He did not say anything, and I ignored him.

I had left my leathers and helmet with the Triumph. I dressed, mounted the bike and started the engine as Tony wandered out into the car park. I did not hear what he said, but it gave me great satisfaction to do a power-turn with the machine and to project a spray of gravel towards him as I roared off up the drive.

When I got to the Zip Line I went straight into the reception and asked for Letta.

'I think she is around,' said the receptionist, 'she has been working in the shop today.'

I went over to the shop and asked again for Letta.

'She's restocking shelves for tomorrow,' the cashier told me. She shouted, 'Letta, come here a minute. Someone wants to speak with you!'

Letta walked over and I showed her my warrant card and asked her if she remembered Douglas. She thought for a moment and said, 'Yes, he was the man who delivered the brochures.'

'What brochures, can you show me?'

'Yes,' she said, looking at the cashier for permission.

We walked over to the reception and Letta went to the tourist brochure rack and pointed at Raeni Curtis's brochures for her new gift shop at Nelsons' Dock.

'He delivered them for Raeni all wrapped up in brown paper.'

'Did you unwrap them?'

'Yes.'

'Was there anything else in the package?'

'No. Just the brochures.'

'You are telling the truth aren't you?'

'Yes.' Letta was affronted at that suggestion.

I was not taking any chances now so I asked for a pen and paper and got Letta to write out a statement which she signed for me. I asked if many of the brochures had been taken.

'No, it doesn't look like it,' Letta told me.

I measured the dimensions of the bundle and they pretty well matched the size of the parcel Merv had described, then left, taking the statement and a couple of brochures with me.

As I rode back over the island I was more worried than ever. Now I knew what the original suspect package contained I was certain that the parcel of drugs had not been in Douglas's hotel safe last Saturday, but I could not prove it. I deeply feared what I thought was going on and realised it had the power to overwhelm me.

When I got home I went to the Glass Bar, I wanted to see Mary and just talk to her. She was busy though so I sat at the bar, on the stool Douglas used to use and started thinking. I had not been there long when I saw Tony roll in. There was no escape, he came over and sat next to me.

'Nice bike you have, I used to have a Harley; American

bikes are the best,' he said as he put his hand on my knee.

I felt icily calm as I carefully picked his hand up and moved it like it was something dirty I was picking out of the gutter. He laughed and I ignored him.

'How is the investigation going? Find anything interesting in his room?'

I told him he would see my report in due course. Still icily calm I said, 'Now, please go away, I want to sit here quietly on my own.'

He called me a stuck-up bitch and walked off, saying, 'It does not matter anyway, I will go and see Bernie and I will soon have the evidence I need and then I will have Jay back to the States to stand trial, and there is nothing you can do about it.'

But I will try, I thought.

Chapter 59

Joelle de Nouvelas; Wednesday 3rd December

The next morning I went straight in to see Bernie.

'Well, we have found the evidence we needed,' was his greeting.

'Yes, but I do not believe it is as obvious as it looks,' I countered.

'Explain?'

'I can't be one hundred percent certain but I am pretty sure that the packet of drugs was not in the safe on Saturday when I looked.'

Bernie pulled the pictures Merv had taken from an envelope. 'These pictures show the packet right at the back, partially hidden by the ticket and envelope. The safe is in the wardrobe so there is not much light and as you were not searching on Saturday, is it possible you did not notice the packet?'

I had to agree with Bernie that it was possible, but I also pointed out that the first thing I noticed yesterday when I opened the safe was the packet, and had it been there on Saturday I would have seen it.

'The envelope was empty, was there anything in it?'

I had to own up and I gave Bernie the sheet of camera instructions and my picture. 'Sorry Bernie.'

He gave me one of his looks, peering over the top of his spectacles. He did not say anything, he just studied the sheet of writing and the picture and then placed them back in the envelope. He looked at me again and said, 'I am going with your instincts on this one Joelle, don't let me down.'

'No sir, I won't. Thank you.'

'What else have you got for me?'

'We found nothing else when we searched the room and when we finished we cleared all Douglas's belongs out of the room.'

'I know,' said Bernie, eyeing the suitcase now standing in the corner of the room. 'I don't know whether the case is evidence or not, so I suppose it had better stay here for the time being.'

'It's just clothes, Bernie. His wallet, passport, papers and so on are in that big evidence bag.' I pointed to the bag on his desk and went on explain what else I had discovered. 'I spoke to the receptionist and she told me that Tony asked for Douglas's room key on Monday. She did not give them to him but, the key rack is easily accessible to anyone by just leaning over the desk.'

While Bernie thought about this I excused myself for a moment and went out to get the brown paper we had recovered from the Zip Line rubbish skip. I took it into Bernie's office and put it on his desk. 'I also went to the Zip Line again yesterday and spoke to the young girl called Letta who was on reception when Douglas delivered the first parcel.' I gave Bernie her statement to read and when he finished I pulled the brochures out of my bag and placed then on the brown paper. The folds exactly matched the size of the brochures.

Eventually Bernie said, 'This changes things a bit, but not that much I am afraid. Finding the drugs in his room puts him right in the frame. You need more than this to prove he is not the courier.'

'Does Tony Choizi know about this latest stuff?'

'He caught me yesterday evening in the bar and asked how the search of the room went. I told him he would get my report when it was ready. I have not told him about the safe or the brochures. He said he was coming in today to talk to you about the evidence and arresting Douglas.'

'I shan't arrest him until the medics say he is fit enough, which gives you a bit more time to dig around.' Bernie rummaged through the pile of papers on his desk and handed me a single sheet report. 'That's from the police garage, their report on the Honda. As you can see they believe the cause of the accident was brake failure. Apparently the front brake cable was broken.'

I speculated, 'He must have tried to brake going into that corner and the cable snapped. That would certainly make him lose control. He must have hit the corner fast so he probably applied more pressure on the brake than normal and that was enough to cause the cable to give way.'

'About right, I agree,' Bernie concluded. 'You better go and write up your reports, I would like them before Tony comes in.'

It did not take me long to write up my reports. I printed a copy for the file and emailed than to Bernie, and then I sat at my desk deciding trying to decide what to do next. I made a list:

The concealed bag on the plane – whose was it?

Source of the veterinary drugs, how were they obtained, was Douglas involved?

Douglas' trips to USA, and Amsterdam. Who did he contact?

Douglas needed money quickly. Where did he get it from?

What was in the second parcel?

What did Douglas say to Zach? Need to find Zach!

Geoff Handley; is he involved?

Did the pills we found come from Douglas's factory?

The drugs in Douglas's safe. Where did they come from?

The Honda and broken brake cable. Rusty Rick said he checked the bike!

I decided that I had more than enough to do and, while I was wondering where to start, Tony Choizi walked into the office and came over and sat on my desk. I turned my screen off as he picked up one of Merv's pictures of Douglas's open safe, and studied it for a few moments. He did not say anything immediately but then turned and leered, 'We could have had a good time yesterday evening. But I won't be able to see you again this evening, I am headed back to Miami, I have a few things I need to clear up.' *He never looks me in the eye when he talks to me*, I thought, *and today he is just staring down my cleavage.*

I suppressed a shudder and took the opportunity to ask, 'You said Douglas had visited America on a number of occasions?'

'That's right.'

'Do you know what he did there?'

'It was to do with the sale of his company.'

'Is that a guess or have you checked?'

'Of course we have checked. We have spoken to the lawyers handling the company purchase and they confirm the dates he arrived and left.'

'So he would not have time to have seen anyone else then.'

Tony switched attention from my breasts and became wary. 'Why, what are you getting at?' he asked.

'Did he travel alone?' I asked, avoiding his question.

'It's me who does the interrogating,' he growled at me, getting to his feet and heading for Bernie's office. He was not there long and when he left he marched through the office without speaking to anyone, clutching an evidence bag.

I went in to see Bernie. 'What did Tony say?'

'Not much, he reckons Douglas is probably a drug user and was high on heroin when he came off the motorbike and finding drugs concealed in his room clinches it for him. He wants Douglas arrested, but I told him we could not. He took the brown paper, he says he wants it properly forensic-tested back in the States, and he says he is going back to Miami this afternoon to sort things out and he will come back with the necessary papers to arrest Douglas regardless of what the medics say.'

'How could he do that? Did you tell him about the brochures?'

Bernie shrugged and grinned. 'Do you know, I forgot to put your last report into the file he snatched to take with him. We will just keep that up our sleeve, I think.'

I smiled back and then asked, 'Remember when you questioned Geoff Handley's connection. Did you ever get an answer?'

'No, I will chase that up.'

I left Bernie, telling him I would be out of the office for the rest of the day.

I wanted to go back to Hotel Glass Bay and then call on Rusty Rick to check on the broken brake cable. I found Merv and asked him to go round all his contacts and see if he could find Zach.

My mobile phone rang. It was the hospital telling me that Douglas was regaining consciousness.

Chapter 60

Joelle de Nouvelas; Wednesday afternoon, 3rd December

Following the phone call, I went straight to the hospital to see Douglas.

The nurse told me he was waking up but was disorientated and confused at the moment, and was not making much sense. She allowed me to go in and see him.

He was still in intensive care and hooked up to various machines but was no longer on oxygen. His head was bandaged and his face looked bruised. His eyes were open and he peered at me then turned his head away and closed his eyes. I don't think he even recognised me.

'I expect he has drifted off to sleep again,' the nurse told me. 'He will be going for another CT scan shortly so the doctor can see how the cranial swelling is progressing. I should come back tomorrow. Hopefully he will be more awake then.' The nurse was right; I would do more good following up the evidence, so I set off for Hotel Glass Bay.

When I got there I went into the shop. Raeni Curtis was not there and so I spoke with Ayida who was in charge of the shop that afternoon.

'Raeni is hardly ever here these days,' Ayida told me, 'she is busy getting her new shop at Nelson's Dock up and running. She more or less leaves it to me to run this shop nowadays.'

I showed her a picture of Douglas and asked her if she remembered him.

'Yes, I remember him, Douglas, the nice Englishman.'

'Did he by any chance take some parcels off you?'

'Yes he did, it was very kind of him. He said he was doing an island tour and visiting the Zip Line and sugar plantation so I asked him if he would drop off some brochures for Raeni's new shop for me.'

'How many brochures did you give him?' I asked.

'I don't know how many, I just gave him a stack.' She held her hands about six inches apart to indicate the quantity and told me, 'I remember he wanted some bags or something to wrap the brochures in so they would not get dirty. I only have the big carrier bags here so he went to reception to see if they had anything smaller.'

I thanked her and asked if she could write out what she had just told me and sign it.

'If you could do that now it will save you coming down to the police station to make a statement.'

I walked over to reception. 'Were either of you here a couple of weeks ago on Sunday 16th November?'

The two women thought for a moment and one of them said, 'Yes, I was on duty that day.'

'Do you remember this guest?' I showed her Douglas's picture 'Douglas Jay, coming and asking for a bag or something with which to wrap up some brochures.'

'Yes, I gave him a sheet of brown paper and some sticky tape,' she confirmed.

'Thank you,' I said. I went and collected Ayida's statement and asked the receptionist to note what she had just told me on the paper. I was pleased with this. I had now statements from two sources confirming what was in both parcels. I now just needed to ask Merv to go over to the sugar plantation shop and check they had a stack of brochures as well.

My next visit was to Rusty Rick's.

'Hey Rick! How are you doing man?' I greeted him.

'I heard about that customer of yours, the one who took one of my bikes. Heard he smashed it up and put himself in hospital,' Rick grumbled.

'Good job he paid for insurance then isn't it?' I reminded Rick, wondering if he had actually bought the insurance or just pocketed the money. Rick just grunted.

'It's about that Honda that I have come to see you.'

'Is this an official visit then?' Rick asked, looking a bit shifty.

'Yes. You told us, when Douglas looked at the Honda, that you would service it and check it was all good.' I did not really expect Rick would admit to not having looked at the bike and he did not disappoint me.

'Yes I did, and I checked the bike over carefully. It was good when it went out.'

'The crash was caused by the front brake cable breaking.'

I was surprised by the strength of Rick's answer. 'No way man. You're accusing me of sending out unroadworthy machines? I replaced both the brake and clutch cable because they were both worn. There is no way that cable would have broken.' Rick was very indignant.

'Calm down Rick, I am just checking. I think we need to go and inspect that Honda ourselves.'

'Too right we do. I don't want to be stitched up for supplying bad machines.'

Rick closed the shop and wheeled out one of his Harleys, and followed me back to the police station. We went straight into the garage and I found the garage supervisor and asked to see the Honda. Rick and I looked carefully at the cable.

'Look,' he said. 'You can see it's a new cable by how clean it is.

He looked at the end where the cable joins the brake-operating lever. There should be a rubber gaiter round this end to stop the dirt getting into the cable, but it's missing.'

'Could it had fallen off in the accident?' I asked.

'Unlikely,' said Rick, 'but look at this.' He held up the broken end of the steel cable for me to look at. 'If that cable had broken through damage or wear, the ends of the individual strands would be splayed, showing signs of rust and slightly different lengths. And look at the scratch marks just above the break. The ends of this cable are all exactly the same length and are clean and shiny. I would say that this cable was cut with a hacksaw, leaving only one or two strands which would have parted as soon heavy braking was applied.'

I called the garage supervisor over to look at the cable and after a brief examination he agreed that the cable had been deliberately cut.

Chapter 61

Joelle de Nouvelas; Thursday 4th December

It was Thursday morning and almost a week since Douglas's accident. I decided to go to the police station and speak with Bernie before I went to the hospital. I wrote up the reports from yesterday but I wanted to talk to Bernie before adding them to the Coconut file.

My mobile phone rang. It was Merv telling me that he was in the reception of the sugar plantation and there was a stack of Raeni's new brochures in the rack. 'The receptionist here does not remember putting them there but confirms that she found a brown paper in the bin which she assumed they were wrapped in. She says she gave the paper to you.'

I thanked Merv and made a note for the file while I waited impatiently for Bernie. He came in later than usual that morning and was growling at everyone. I judged it wise to let him get a coffee and settle down before I asked to see him. I put my head round the door and grunted to me to enter and sit.

'Bernie,' I explained, 'I have confirmed that both parcels contained brochures and Merv has just confirmed that the sugar plantation has a similar stack of brochures to the Zip Line.'

'Doesn't change yesterday's conclusion,' Bernie grunted

as he continued to look through the pile of reports on his desk. 'Ahh. Here is an interesting one. Forensics has traced the origin of that pill you found in the old slave cabin. Guess where it came from?'

'VP Veterinary, the company that Douglas used to work for?'

'Right first time,' Bernie said, 'and I think we can assume that the pills found in Douglas's chalet safe are also from VP.' Bernie looked at me. 'Joelle, I know you have disproved the theory that the two parcels contained a drug delivery, but that is just circumstantial. If you really think he is innocent you need a lot more because finding those drugs in his room is the one bit of hard evidence that supports all the circumstantial stuff you have found.'

'I know,' I said, 'but there are some other things you don't know about yet. First, I don't trust Tony Choizi. He told me that he did not care if Douglas was innocent or guilty. He said he wants a quick arrest to take back to the States. And the second point is that we re-examined the Honda bike and the front brake cable had been hacksawed, leaving only a couple of strands intact, so someone deliberately sabotaged Douglas's motorbike, presumably with the intention of causing an accident.'

Bernie interrupted, 'That is most likely the drug gang trying to silence him before we get chance to get anything out of him.'

'How did they know we were getting close?' I asked Bernie.

'Tony Choizi, turning up and throwing his weight about was a pretty big signpost,' he replied.

I had no argument against this theory and was about to continue when Bernie spoke again.

'If this accident was a drug related execution, they will probably try again. We better get someone up to the hospital to make sure they don't get to Jay to finish the job.' He phoned the Duty Sergeant with his instruction. 'I don't care if you are short staffed. Both Isaac and Denzel are no longer on the Jay surveillance, send them. Yes twenty-four hours, starting immediately.' He slammed the receiver down. 'Is that all Joelle?'

'No. I just want to say that someone could have planted those drugs in Douglas's room.'

'Now you are clutching at straws,' Bernie told me.

I let that pass for the moment, but I hit him with my last request. 'I would like you to approve me visiting the UK. I want to follow up the passenger listings and see who brought the second camera bag on to the plane.' This did get Bernie's attention.

'Joelle, why would I approve that when we have the suspect with enough evidence for a conviction?'

'Because I think we have got the wrong person and Tony Choizi does not care as long as he gets an arrest and the credit, but I care about getting it right and so do you.'

Bernie rubbed his chin, like he does when he is thinking, and looked out of the window.

After a while he turned back to me. 'OK Joelle, you can go but in your own time and I have no budget so it has to be at your own cost. I will hold Choizi off as long as I can to give you chance to find something.'

'Thank you Bernie,' I said with relief. 'Can Merv carry on supporting me here on the island and can we keep the reports off the Coconut file for the moment?'

'Yes, you can have Merv but it is my decision what goes on file or not.'

I went over to our admin assistant and booked a week's leave, starting next Monday, and asked her to get me on the Saturday evening flight to Heathrow with an open return for the end of the week. I gave her my credit card to pay for the trip.

'How lovely,' she commented. 'Going Christmas shopping in London.'

'No I'm not. It's urgent and I am tidying up some loose ends in London, so if you have to, use an official police priority to get me a seat on the flight.

I found Merv and told him I would be away for a week and explained what I was doing. Merv was not the cleverest detective but he was reliable and discreet and we worked well together. I told him I would stay in contact with him but he must work alone and only talk to Bernie.

I asked him how he was getting on finding Zach.

'Word is he has gone deep underground. Apparently the drug gang is after him as well as he took off with a bag of heroin for his pension, but now he's scared to come out of hiding and can't get off the island,' Merv replied.

Bernie came out of his office and handed me a folded piece of paper. On it he had written, 'Go and see Detective Superintendent Passmore at Scotland Yard. He is expecting you on Monday morning and will help set up what you need.'

It was now Thursday afternoon and just two days before I departed for London. I wanted to see Douglas as I desperately needed to ask him some questions. I decided to go to the hospital and then Glass Bar and tell Mary and Jasmine I had to go away for a week.

At the hospital the nurse told me Douglas was making good progress. He was fully aware of his surroundings and able to speak, although he was a bit slurred and mixed up his words a bit. He was still a bit confused but his memory was improving, but he seemed a bit hazy about the last couple of weeks.

She took me to his room. He had been moved from

intensive care and was now in a private room on his own. I nodded at Isaac who was sitting in chair outside his room.

I went in and looked at Douglas. He did look much better. He was only connected to one machine now, monitoring his heart and blood pressure. He was still heavily bandaged but his eyes showed he was aware of his surroundings.

He said, 'Hello, I know you don't I? Are you Tamzin?'

'No, I am Joelle.' I found out later that Tamzin was the name of his ex-wife.

'Joelle?' he repeated looking puzzled. 'You are not Tamzin?'

'No, I'm Joelle,' I repeated.

'Where do I know you from?'

'Kaeta. Do you know where you are?'

'Yes, I'm in hospital on Kaeta. They tell me I had a motorbike accident but I can't remember.'

'You met me on the island. I am a policewoman and my mother runs Glass Bar. Do you know why you are on Kaeta?'

He looked puzzled and muttered, 'Yes I remember, Glass Bar just along the beach from the hotel.' He closed his eyes and looked like he had dropped off to sleep and I still did not know whether he remembered me or not.

I went out to see the nurse and she told me not to worry. 'His memory is returning well, he knows who he is and so on. Doctor is very pleased with the CT scan, which showed the swelling has almost completely subsided and with luck he should recover his memory quickly now.'

As I was leaving, Isaac came over to me and took me to one side. 'Joelle, I don't know if it's important or not, but when I arrived the nurse in from intensive care told me that Tony Choizi came to see Douglas yesterday afternoon. She said he was very polite and just asked how he was. She told him he was recovering well but that he was not seeing visitors. Tony left without any argument.'

I thanked Isaac and told the nurse I would come back tomorrow. I set off to find Mary and Jasmine.

They were at Glass Bar and I explained why I had to go away. Mary told me I was doing the right thing and if I needed money to let her know, but be very careful, she added. I thought Jasmine might be tearful but she surprised me by saying she wanted to help.

'I will ask around school and see if anyone knows this Zach person,' she said.

'No you won't, I don't want you getting involved.'

'OK, Mother.' She smiled knowingly at me.

I stayed with them and we chatted about what I should take and that sort of thing. I promised Mary that I would buy a thick coat, and Jasmine that I would bring her a Christmas present from Harrods.

I wanted to go to the hotel again and ask if anyone had been seen interfering with the Honda. It was too late tonight, I would have to do it the morning, and so I sat silently in the bar wondering why Tony Choizi had tried to visit Douglas the afternoon before he left for Miami.

Chapter 62

Joelle de Nouvelas; Friday 5th December

Next morning I went straight to Glass Bay Hotel. I started in reception, asking if they had seen anyone in the car park near where Douglas parked his motorbike or acting suspiciously. Neither receptionist had seen anything out of the ordinary but they reminded me that the footpath round the lake passed through the car park, so it was not unusual for guests to walk through the car park. I asked the same question at the guest information desk, the shop, the spa, and fitness centre, with the same response. I also asked if anyone had been seen entering or loitering near Douglas's chalet and again nobody saw anything out of the ordinary.

I walked round the hotel complex putting my questions to any staff I could find, gardeners, waiters, and administration staff, but again nobody had seen anything unusual. Finally, although I knew it was a bit of a long shot, I walked round the swimming pool complex asking the guests there if they had seen anything. Again I drew a blank, except for one person who pointed at a couple of elderly ladies who were sitting outside the terrace bar overlooking the sea. 'You should ask those two. They are a nosey pair who spend all day watching everyone and gossiping.'

Just the sort of people I need right now, I thought, as I headed across to them.

'Excuse me for interrupting you.' I showed them my warrant card. When I was at university I read all Agatha Christie's Miss Marple books and I had to suppress a grin as these two old ladies reminded me of Miss Marple.

'Sit down dear,' the first "Miss Marple" invited me. Her name was actually Jac. 'Now let me see,' she said, as she turned to the second "Miss Marple". 'Carol, which day was it we saw that American gentleman? Was it before or after that nice policeman was here asking about Mr. Jay's motorbike?'

I waited patiently while Jac and Carol debated the day. They decided it was Friday, a week ago.

Jac took up the story. 'That American gentleman, he introduced himself as Tony. Well I remember him specifically because he came over and was talking to everyone and asking lots of questions. We are in one of those semi-detached chalets, next door to his, and he snored loudly every night. What was I going to say?' Jac paused for thought. 'Perhaps he was visiting someone as we saw him walking along by the chalets over there,' she pointed to the path leading past Douglas's chalet, 'stopping and looking at each chalet as he walked past. We thought it was strange, didn't we Carol?'

I asked, 'Did he enter any of the chalets?'

'No dear, that was what was so strange. Our chalets are right at the other end of the hotel. Of course we did tell him we had seen him and asked if he was looking for anyone, and he told us he was just going for a walk and did not know anyone. Well that was strange because we saw him eating with that quiet Englishman so he must have known him.'

I was not sure if what they had told me was relevant or not. After all, he is a detective so it's very likely he would have walked round learning the geography of the hotel.

'You mentioned a policeman had also been asking about Mr. Jay?' I queried.

'Yes dear,' Jac answered. 'He was not in uniform but he was a local policeman and had a warrant card just like yours. What was his name?' Carol shrugged.

I was about to leave when Carol said, 'My dear this is so exciting, please tell us what has happened.'

'I am investigating a motorcycle accident last Friday night.'

'Ooh!' Exclaimed the Miss Marples in unison, and Carol then said, 'We heard that the English gentleman, who was staying here, was in hospital. Was it him? He used to go round the island on a motorbike.'

'It was,' I confirmed.

'Now that is a coincidence,' Jac exclaimed. 'That other policeman was interested in that motorbike.'

'How is he? Is he badly injured?' Carol asked.

'Quite badly, but he is out of intensive care now,' I explained. The Miss Marples then wanted to know every detail of Douglas's injuries and I found I was getting quite upset explaining it to them.

'He was such a nice man as well,' Carol said, as she and Jac discussed Douglas with great enthusiasm.

She turned to Jac, who was sitting watching me, and said, 'Do you remember that night, just after we got here. There was a band playing and we were going sit and listen and watch the dancing but there was only seat and Douglas, that was his name,' she informed me, as she thought of what she was trying to say, 'yes Douglas, he picked up his seat and carried it over and gave it to us. He was dancing with that girl, the Handley's daughter. You remember don't you Jac? Such a nice man. I would have danced all night with him if I was twenty years younger!'

I was getting quite emotional thinking of Douglas's injuries and listening to Carol ramble on.

Jac noticed and said, 'Shut up Carol. Can't you see you are upsetting the lady?' She was very perceptive and she turned to me, saying, 'You are fond of him aren't you dear? He is the real reason you asking all these questions isn't he? We will ask around and if we find out anything we will let you know. How can we contact you?'

I thanked her, anxious to excuse myself, and gave her a police contact card.

Before leaving I decided to hunt round the car park where Douglas's Honda had been parked. There was nothing obvious on the car park surface, so I picked up a stick and was poking round the bushes to see if anything had been thrown there when one of the gardeners came up and asked me if I had lost something. I showed him my warrant card, explained what I was doing and asked him if had seen anything out of the ordinary.

'Not in the car park,' he said, 'but a couple of days ago I was cutting back the bushes and strimming along the footpath over there and I found this.' From the tool bag in his barrow he produced a small hacksaw with a moulded, yellow plastic handle.

'Can you show me where you found it?'

We walked about 100 metres down the path and he pointed to a bush that he had cut back. 'It was right under there,' he said. 'I only noticed it because of the yellow handle.'

I thanked him and asked him if could keep the tool. I wondered if it was possible for forensics to tell if it was the saw used on the Honda's brake cable. At least they might get some fingerprints off it.

I was planning to go to the hospital and had promised Mary I would pick her up as she wanted to see Douglas.

Typical Mary, I thought affectionately, as she produced a large basket of fruit for Douglas.

'Even if he can't eat it I am sure the staff will enjoy it,' she told me as we drove to the hospital.

I introduced Mary as my mother and we were allowed to go in and see Douglas.

'He seems much better this afternoon, talking sensibly and not so confused,' the nurse told us.

He knew who Mary was straight away. 'Hello Mary, it's lovely to see you.' He nodded in my direction and just said, 'Joelle.'

'You look terrible,' Mary told him.

'Yes, I even scared myself when they showed me a mirror,' he joked.

They chatted on like this for a bit, ignoring me until I interrupted and asked, 'Do you remember what happened, Douglas?'

'Not quite yet. I am beginning to piece together the holiday and what I did but the last thing I can remember is walking out of the bar and leaving you and your boyfriend, Tony.'

Ah, I thought, *he still thinks I am Tony's girl and a policewoman spying on him. How am I going to explain this to him?* I needed to ask him some questions and I desperately needed him to trust me and to tell me he was not the drug smuggler.

Chapter 63

Joelle de Nouvelas; Saturday 6th December

Late yesterday afternoon, after we left Douglas, I dropped Mary in town. She wanted to do some shopping and she offered to get the essentials I would need for going away. I wanted to catch Bernie before I left and make sure we were both up to date. I gave Bernie the hacksaw to send to forensics and told him about the Miss Marples' observations of Tony.

'I am inclined to think it does not mean much, other than he is curious, but note it on the file anyway,' Bernie commented, and then told me, 'I have got a report back on Mr. Geoff Handley. There is only one thing on file. He was arrested at a student party in his university days for possessing amphetamines. He claimed they had been planted on him and he was never actually charged. Nothing since then so I think we can assume he is not involved.'

Bernie then told me that they had now had chance to look at Douglas's laptop. 'It is obviously fairly new and there is not much on it apart from photographs. We got into his emails and they are all advertising rubbish except for one from a company called Stripe Financing, whose website say they specialise in corporate refinancing. They are asking Douglas to come and see them about new opportunities when he returns from his holiday.'

'Sounds like the venture capitalist company who put him into his last job,' I told Bernie.

'He also kept a diary of his holiday on the computer. There is nothing in the diary that we don't already know, but he mentions you a lot.' Bernie winked at me. 'Obviously found you quite attractive.'

I am afraid I blushed.

Bernie took a deep breath and frowned. 'But there is one thing that's interesting, there is an unnamed file that's password protected. We have not managed to break into it yet.

'The last thing you should know is that I have had Tony Choizi on the phone this morning. He says he has been through the Coconut file in detail with his prosecutor and they believe there is sufficient evidence to secure a conviction, and they want Douglas Jay arrested. I have held them off for now by telling them he is still very ill in hospital and that we have a twenty-four hour police guard on him. Tony wants to be told when he is well enough to be arrested and questioned so he can return to oversee, as he put it.'

I thanked Bernie and asked him to hold Tony off and give me as much time as he could. I then said to him, 'Bernie, it bothers me that I can't remember seeing that packet of drugs in Douglas's safe on the Saturday when I looked. Do you think it's possible that someone planted the drugs?'

Bernie considered this possibility and replied, 'Anything is possible, but in this instance, I think very unlikely. I can't think of anyone who stood to gain or would have a motive for planting drugs. The only possibility would be that it is connected with the drug smuggling gang somehow, but I can't see what they have to gain by putting Douglas in the frame. In fact they have a lot to lose if Douglas talks. I know you have doubts, and I will let you run with them for a long as I can, but the best theory at the moment is that the drugs are what is left from the consignment and he is having trouble getting rid of them.'

I was not convinced. If Douglas could not rid of the drugs, why leave them in the safe where they were sure to be found? But then he was not expecting to have an accident. Then there was also the powder we found in the packet, which I suspected was heroin. We knew he was only supposed to be smuggling amphetamine tablets so if the drugs were his, what was he doing with heroin?

Tony thinks he was high on heroin when he had the accident but he does not look like a heroine user to me. I will ask the hospital. They will be able to confirm if he uses drugs.

As I left I paused and asked Bernie if knew anything about a policeman looking for Douglas's motorbike. Bernie was disinterested and said it was probably Merv or Isaac.

I caught up with Merv in the general office and asked him if he had had any luck finding Zach. He had not. I then said to him, 'Just assume for a moment that those drugs were planted in Douglas's safe. How would you go about proving it?'

'Ask round if anyone saw anything.'

'I have asked around and no luck.'

'Fingerprints on the safe?' Merv suggested.

'You did that, and it did not help,' I reminded him.

'Trace the origin of the drugs to where they came from,' he suggested.

'We have done that as well and they matched the ones in the slave hut,' I said.

'Well,' said Merv, 'does that not blow your planting theory away?'

Possibly, I thought, but still felt uncomfortable.

I headed for the hospital. I wanted to see Douglas and tell him I was going away. I also had some questions I wanted to ask him.

I asked if Dr. Leonard was available. The nurse said she thought he was doing his rounds and put a call out to him. Ten minutes later he walked in and asked me what I wanted. I asked him if there was any evidence that Douglas was drug user, heroin or anything else.

'Why are you asking?' he looked at me suspiciously.

'You are aware of what he is accused. Well I think he is innocent and I am trying to prove it.'

Dr. Leonard nodded and explained, 'Of course, he is full of drugs at the moment to help the healing process and relieve the pain, but as far as the drugs you are asking about, he is as clean as a whistle and there is no evidence he used any of those drugs or other illegal substances. As is our standard procedure in vehicle accidents, we tested his blood for alcohol and drugs when he was admitted. There was a small amount of alcohol present, nothing that would impair his judgement, but no drugs.

Douglas was awake watching an American TV programme when I walked into his room.

'Hello Douglas, how are you feeling today?' I asked.

'What do you want Joelle?' he greeted me.

Oh dear, I thought, *this is not going to be easy. Where do I start?*

'Douglas, I know you think I have come to spy on you but I want to help you if you will let me?'

'I thought you were being friendly before, but you were just checking up on me, why should I believe you are helping me now?' I could not think of an answer to that so he went on, 'OK, if you want to help me, tell me why I was being followed and why there is an armed policeman guarding my room door?'

I took a deep breath and told him everything, from the tip-off we had about a drug courier coming in by air to the packet of drugs we found in his hotel safe.

I concluded, telling him it was serious unless I could find evidence to prove his innocence. I expected him to say he was innocent and it was all a mistake. Instead he asked me, 'Why would you want to prove me innocent?'

'Because all the evidence is circumstantial, apart from the drugs in your safe, which I believe were planted, and I do not believe you are involved with drugs.'

'I am not involved,' he said vehemently.

'Douglas, will you swear to me that you are innocent and those drugs are nothing to do with you?'

'Yes, I will swear on a stack of bibles if you want. I am innocent and I have never had any involvement with the drug trade. Well, except legitimately when I worked for the veterinary company.'

'Thank you Douglas, I do believe you, but now I must ask you some questions please?'

Douglas retorted, 'Is this not where we just started this conversation? You are investigating me. Tell me why I should trust you now after you have been spying on me for the last month.'

'Oh, Douglas,' I said in desperation and sighed, wondering what I could do or say to reassure him. 'You said to me once that you could not understand my mood swings and asked me what you did to upset me. Well, you did not do anything. The real reason was because I was torn between liking you and enjoying your company, and knowing that I had to be detached to do my job. When I thought I had lost you for good after the accident, Mary made see sense and I realised how much I liked you, and I looked again at all the evidence we had. I have just explained it to you, and it is all circumstantial, and I do now believe you when you say you are not involved, and I want to help you. I would like to be your friend if you will have me.'

Douglas looked at me for a long time before he said, 'OK, I will tell you what I can. Anyway, stuck in here, I have no choice but to trust you.'

But before I asked my questions, I pleaded, 'Please trust me.'

He nodded so I asked, 'Can you think of anyone who would want to set you up?'

'No, I can't think of anyone.'

'Did you see anyone else on the plane with a camera bag?'

'I can't really remember, but no, I don't think so.'

'When you went to America, were you on your own?'

Douglas closed his eyes and I thought he had drifted away but after a while he said, 'I am sorry Joelle, I still feel confused and my memory still gets all jumbled up sometimes, but no, as far as I remember I always travelled with the accountants supporting the due diligence and lawyers negotiating the sale.'

'Can you give me their names?'

He seemed to drift off somewhere again and lose concentration, and then asked me to repeat the question.

'I am sorry, but I can't remember any names. It's on the tip of my tongue but it's gone.'

'Don't worry, I can find out. Do you remember talking to a Zip Line operator? His name was Zack. Do you remember what you said to him?'

'Not sure,' Douglas said. 'I remember speaking to someone, but my memory is playing tricks and I can't sort things out.'

He drifted off again but eventually he said, 'Can I ask you a question?'

'Yes, of course.'

'What happened after I left you and your boyfriend that evening? All the nurses can tell me is that I had an accident on a motorbike. I remember the bike. You helped me hire it, but I can't remember anything after I left you and Tony in the bar.'

He paused and then abruptly jumped back to my previous question. 'I remember I did not say anything to him really, just asked him how long the Zip Line took to get round and where was the path up to the volcano.'

'You mean that is what you spoke to the Zip Line operator about?'

But Douglas had drifted off, deep in thought. But not for long, for he suddenly looked at me and said, 'That American, your boyfriend, just how close are you?'

I was going to explain but he closed eyes and seemed to drift off to sleep again. I waited as long as could but in the end I had to leave to catch the plane. I said goodbye but I don't know if he heard me or not.

Chapter 64

Douglas Jay; Sunday 7th December

I am lying in a hospital bed, in a little pain, but being dosed up with heavy duty painkillers. There is a police constable outside the door, guarding me and I am worried.

The nurse tells me it's Sunday morning, December 6th, and I was brought to the hospital, unconscious, a week ago, early last Saturday morning. Apparently I fell off my motorcycle, but I don't even remember why I went out in the middle of the night riding it. It's a funny experience, completely losing a week of one's life. I am not even sure how long I have been awake. I vaguely remember someone coming in to see me, or perhaps I dreamt it. I thought it was my ex-wife but apparently it was not.

I do remember the day before yesterday. Mary and Jasmine came to see me. I remembered them from Glass Bar and the beach and talking with them helped me remember the last few weeks. Joelle was with them but she did not say much that day, but she did come back on her own the next day. The last thing I can remember from before the accident is Joelle standing in Glass Bar with her boyfriend, that obnoxious American.

Mary left a large bowl of fruit for me but don't really feel like eating at the moment.

I am on a pretty high dose of painkillers, I can't really move by left arm as it is in a heavy plaster cast, and I seem to have lost all the strength in my right hand. I am also told I have some pretty severe grazing and bruising which is quite painful as well. My head is heavily bandaged where they tell me I have had an operation.

The reason I am worried is because of Joelle yesterday. Apparently I am suspected of drug smuggling. It is not true and I did tell Joelle that when she came in to see me yesterday. That girl really confuses me. When I first met her there was something that attracted me to her, still does actually, but when I discovered she was spying on me to collect evidence and she has that American boyfriend I felt very bitter, confused and let down. Yesterday though, she comes to see me and explains that the police think I am a drug criminal, but since my accident she has changed her mind, and says she wants to be my friend. She said she believes me when I say I am innocent and that I don't know what they are talking about. When she explained the evidence they have, I can see why I was a suspect, but, stuck in hospital, I am not sure what I can do except to trust Joelle when she says she is trying to gather information to discount the evidence they have built up. I am very suspicious though. Her change of mind seems very convenient and I really wonder what she is up to. When I feel more clear-headed, I will try talking to that policeman outside. He might tell me more. In the meantime though I think I am stuck with Joelle as my main hope. I hope I can trust her.

Another thing is that American boyfriend just turning up; they seem pretty close. Funny that, I would not have thought he was her sort at all. She never answered my question. She just picked up her bag and rushed out saying she had to catch a plane.

So here I am stuck in hospital, suspected of smuggling drugs, trying to remember what has happened to me and dependent for help on a woman whose motives I'm not sure I can trust.

Chapter 65

Joelle de Nouvelas; Monday 8th December

It is Monday morning, my second day in England, and I am sitting on the Heathrow Express on my way to see Detective Superintendent Passmore at Scotland Yard.

I had landed at Heathrow early yesterday morning after a sleepless overnight flight from Kaeta. I had booked a room deal at the Heathrow Sheraton for the week and I headed straight there and went to bed, which is where I spent most of Sunday.

This morning I caught an airport bus back into Heathrow and found my way underground to the London Express train link.

On arriving at Paddington Station I fought my way down to the London Underground. It really is quite disorienting and I am not used to the hundreds of people all pushing and shoving to get through the system. The ticket machines in the Underground station defeated me; I had no change and could not get my credit card to work. I was starting to panic as the queue behind me started to get impatient and tell me to get on with it. Fortunately a kindly old lady came to my rescue and pointed me to the ticket office.

The man behind the glass window sold me a ticket and told me to go on the Bakerloo Line to Baker Street, change to the Jubilee line to Westminster, and then change to the Circle line to St James's Park. That's the nearest tube station, he told me, but then he said that if he was me he would get off at Green Park and walk through the park, which brings you out near the back of Scotland Yard.

That's what I did. I was feeling so claustrophobic by the time I got to Green Park I could not stand it anymore. Although it was sunny, I had forgotten how cold the winter sun in England could be, and it was chilly but very pretty in the park and quite different to home. With only a light coat I was frozen and shivering by the time I got to Scotland Yard and asked for DS Passmore.

I guess DS Passmore ('Call me Derek.') was a man about Douglas's age. Tall and fit-looking, with grey hair, slightly receding, and a ready smile. I immediately felt comfortable with him. He shook my hand, said he was pleased to meet me, and invited me to sit down. He asked about Bernie and explained they were old friends and he had met Bernie when he was a cadet and Bernie was on secondment in London. He knew my father as well; he told me my father told everybody what a clever little girl he had.

'Now, what can do to help you? I understand that you need access to the CCTV at Heathrow?' he asked.

'That's right.' I explained that I wanted to check the passengers who flew out to Kaeta on the Airways flight on 7th November.

'That's easy enough. I have already arranged with the Heathrow police for you to be given any access you require. Is there anything else?'

'Yes, I would like to visit a company called VP Ltd. It's a veterinary drug company whose offices are near Crawley in Sussex. I am not sure what else, it depends what I turn up at the airport.'

'Let me know when you want to go to Sussex and I will

arrange for someone to accompany you. Makes life easier for us all that way.'

That was fine by me. I realised that I was a visiting detective and that they would want to keep an eye on me and know what I was doing.

'When do you want to start?' Derek asked me.

'Soon as I can,' I replied.

He picked up the phone and asked for Inspector Brix at Heathrow.

When he finished the call he told me that Jon Brix was expecting me in a couple of hours and he would look after me at Heathrow. As I left his office he wished me good luck.

'And don't forget, anything you need just call me.'

I had forgotten how cold it could be in England in December so the first thing I did when I left Scotland Yard was to walk up Victoria Street to the Army and Navy Store. In the Jaeger shop I bought a warm fawn-coloured wool jumper and a couple of long-sleeved shirts, one white and one dark brown. In Country Casuals I found a pair of woollen trousers. In a sports shop, I also bought an orange four-season ski jacket and some silk vests.

I put the ski jacket on immediately. I hailed a taxi back to Paddington.

When I got to Heathrow I went back to the hotel and changed into my new clothes and then went back to the airport to find Inspector Jon Brix. I soon got lost but fortunately Derek Passmore had given his phone number and I rang him for directions. He, too, was friendly and helpful. He explained that it was not often that they were contacted by a Special Branch Superintendent for assistance but he was very pleased do what he could for me.

I explained what I wanted, so he took me to a computer terminal and showed me how to use it. The system was amazing. Completely digital, allowing me to look at any of the archive images from any camera round the airport. I just needed to know which camera location, date, and time I wanted to see.

'Of course,' Jon explained, 'you still have to look through miles of pictures if you are trying to find something specific.' He also showed me how to access flight details, departure and arrival gates and maps of the airport.

I started by looking at the pictures of the departure gate through which Douglas would have passed on his way to the Kaeta Island flight. I soon found Douglas; he was one of the first passengers through. I then paged carefully through all the other passengers on the flight, but this camera only showed the head and upper body of the passengers, which at this stage did not tell me much.

Jon Brix came in to see how I was getting on and suggested I switch to the camera outside the corridor gate exit.

'That camera should give you a better view of the passengers as they board the coach.'

I asked him if I could get paper prints of particular frames.

He showed me how and said the prints would come through on the general office printer.

I started going through the frames from the outside camera. Again I found Douglas amongst a group of passengers boarding the coach. He was carrying the rucksack and camera bag that I remembered examining a month ago.

I carried on frame by frame, looking at passengers boarding the bus. I was looking for a picture of who had carried the second bag on the plane. It was possible that

Douglas had hidden it but I was anxious to see if someone else had boarded with it.

I was getting drowsy and almost missed it as I flicked through the frames. I flicked back to a picture of a crowd of people pushing onto the bus, and there in the centre, was a middle-aged dark haired woman with a small wheelie-case carrying a square blue bag over her shoulder. I went back another frame and at the edge of the picture got a better view of her and the bag.

I zoomed in and saw a clear picture of her carrying a square blue bag, which looked like a camera bag. I took a print of the picture and was looking to see if there was a better picture of her face when Jon Brix walked in and gave me the prints I had made that afternoon.

I explained that I wanted to find out who the woman was and asked him if there was any way I could get hold of the bag that she had been carrying, which I believed might be the one hidden on the aircraft.

'Yes, possibly, but it's six thirty now and everyone has gone home. We will have to look in the morning.'

Chapter 66

Jon Brix told me he was usually in by eight in the morning so I caught an early bus and was waiting in the office for his arrival. He suggested I look through the camera on passport control and see if I could spot the woman.

'It might take some time but that way we will be able to get her passport details.'

It took me all morning trawling through hundreds of pictures but eventually I did spot her.

Her name was Elizabeth Bruce, married with an address in Epsom, Surrey.

The passport control camera only showed a head and shoulder shot and I noticed that she had no shoulder strap visible. I switched to a camera with a general view of the security hall and as I knew what time she would pass through I soon spotted her. She had the wheelie-bag but no camera bag. *Strange*, I thought, *what has she done with it?*

I found two other pictures of her walking through the departures shopping halls and in neither did she have the camera bag.

I switched back to a camera showing the seating in the gate departure lounge. There she was with a clear view of the bag on the floor by her feet. I backtracked through

320

each of the corridor cameras on the route she would have to have taken to the gate. There were two clear shots of her walking down the corridors with the camera bag.

I went back again to the shopping hall and eventually found a further picture of her, but this time without it. I reasoned she must have acquired the bag somehow in the shopping hall. It would be very easy for to sit down next to someone who had carried the bag in, pick up the bag and walk off with it.

I explained my theory to Jon Brix. He agreed that such a swap would be easy but said, 'They could not have got through our security checks with a bag full of drugs, so they got into the airport by some other means, and the most obvious is that they flew in from another airport as a transit passenger.'

Jon also told me that he had spoken with the aircraft cleaning company and the bag would have been disposed of by now, but they were sending the cleaning report through which would give details of the bag.

I said to Jon, 'If they came in as a transit passenger, in view of the Amsterdam connection we know about, it is likely they started their journey from a Dutch airport.'

Jon nodded in agreement and wished me good luck looking through the hundreds of pictures on arrivals from Holland. 'Use the arrival gate corridor cameras, you will get a complete body picture from that camera.'

I started with the Amsterdam flights arriving up to two hours before the woman was seen in the shopping hall. I had no luck. The passengers were all carrying bags, but not a blue camera bag.

After an hour or so Jon came into see me and said, 'I have been thinking, smuggling the drugs into one of the major Dutch airports would be as difficult as getting them into Heathrow. So my guess is that the passenger came through one of the smaller airports, probably one accommodating private aircraft as well as scheduled flights. If I was going to smuggle drugs I would look to the smaller airfields for a way of bypassing security checks.'

I agreed, that made some sense, and Jon continued, 'There are twenty-five airfields in Holland handling civilian passenger flights, but don't worry, there are only eight handling scheduled airlines.' He gave me a list to work down.

I skipped Schiphol and Flamingo airport, that was in the Caribbean Netherlands anyway, and Eindhoven was next on my list. Luckily there was only one Heathrow flight from Eindhoven that fitted the timing. I switched to the arrival corridor camera.

Bingo! There he was, a middle-aged man with a brown coat, wearing a cap and carrying a rucksack and blue camera bag.

I had spent all day getting this far but now I had a more or less provable theory. The drugs had come through Eindhoven Airport to Heathrow carried by a passenger with a transit ticket. They had been switched in the shopping hall and carried to Kaeta by the dark-haired woman. She had disposed of the camera bag en route and probably secreted the drugs in her wheelie case and carried them straight through the airport on Kaeta. There was our drug smuggler, and we had missed her. I resolved to phone Bernie that evening.

I was fed up and cross-eyed looking at pictures so I phoned Derek Passmore and asked him if it would be possible to visit VP Ltd tomorrow.

'No problem, a surprise visit always works, they don't have as much time to think of a good story,' he chuckled. 'I will get someone to pick you up in the morning – say about ten when the traffic has cleared.'

When I got back to the hotel, I phoned Bernie. Joseph Island is four hours behind the UK so it was mid-afternoon when I got hold of him and explained what I had discovered.

'Good work,' he complimented me, 'it certainly helps cast doubt but we still have the problem of the drugs found in Douglas's room.'

'I know,' I said, 'but I don't know how we can get round that unless we can prove they were planted.'

I asked Bernie to get Merv to do something for me. 'Tell him to go to the airport and see if he can see this woman arriving, find out where she is staying and better still see if she is still on the island.'

I asked Bernie if there was anything new at his end.

'Only that hacksaw. We got two thumbprints off it. One is quite clear but the other is a bit smudged. Merv has gone get to get the gardener's prints so we can eliminate his.'

I said I would phone back tomorrow.

That evening I phoned the Glass Bar. Sean answered and called Jasmine over, who told me in great detail what she had been doing for the last three days and excitedly asked me what London was like.

'Cold!' I exclaimed.

'I don't ever remember being really cold, what's it like?' We had another long conversation about English weather, with Jasmine concluding that she would love to visit England.

I spoke to Mary next. It was a shorter conversation, mostly about keeping warm and looking after myself, although she did say she had visited Douglas a couple of times, and he had asked after me. I wanted to phone him but felt strangely reluctant. I was not sure how he would take a call from me and I was frightened of being rejected.

Chapter 67

Joelle de Nouvelas; Wednesday 10th December

As arranged I was waiting in the reception of the Sheraton Heathrow. I was wary of just sitting around on my own. Twice already, I had been approached by men on the prowl, once, on the Sunday evening when I went into the Sports Bar to order a snack, and again yesterday evening. The Sky Bar is built round a swimming pool and decorated with tropical plants so I went in for a drink, thinking it would remind me of home. I was just sitting working through what I still needed to do when some flash character came up with his drink and asked me if he could join me and get me a drink. I said no, and he went off in a huff. Too bad!

I eat in my room and watch television now, or go for a work out in the gym. It is one of the safe places with no one in it most of the time. I was musing on this and watching guests rushing in and out when Derek Passmore walked up to me. 'Hello Joelle. Ready?'

'Derek,' I said in surprise, 'I did not expect you.'

'I decided I spend too long in the office these days so the chance to do a bit of leg work with a pretty girl was too good to miss.'

He led me into the car park and as we approached a BMW 7 Series it flashed and blipped at us. Perk of the job, he explained, but only borrowed for the day. We headed out for the M25 and I asked if we could go via Epsom. I explained I wanted to check out the dark-haired lady who carried the camera bag on to the plane. We pulled up at the address and we both got out of the car.

Derek rang the doorbell and a woman with greying hair, and on the wrong side of middle age, answered the door. Derek showed his warrant card, introduced me as a colleague and asked her if we could come in.

'Yes, just let me shut the dog away. How can I help you?'

Derek stepped back and I took over. 'Is Elizabeth Bruce here?'

'I am Elizabeth Bruce,' she said.

She was about the same height and build as the woman I had seen on the CCTV but the woman I was looking for had dark hair and looked much younger. I asked her if she had been away at any time over the last month to six weeks.

'I went up to London a couple of weeks ago to do some Christmas shopping but apart from that I have been around Epsom.'

'Have you visited Heathrow at all?'

Not since we went on holiday last summer. What is this all about?'

I explained we were trying to trace a woman who passed through Heathrow Airport in early December using a passport in the name of Elizabeth Bruce living at this address.

This Mrs. Bruce nodded and said, 'I think I can explain. My husband and I took a Caribbean cruise holiday in January of this year and visited a number of the islands. Anyway we always took a walk around the places we stopped; we like to get a feel for the places we visit. I keep my passport in my bag; I like to carry it with me all the time. I was not until we were heading back to Barbados to fly home that I found my passport was missing.'

'Did you report it?' I asked.

'Well, not really. We told the ship's captain that I had lost my passport and he said not to worry, it happened all the time. He would contact the holiday operator and they would arrange for someone from the British Consulate to meet me in Barbados and issue me with temporary travel papers. He said he could give me a travel authorisation which I just needed to show the airline people when they came to the liner to check us in and they would look after me and make sure I got home alright.'

I heard Derek mutter, 'A bit irregular. Do you have the name of the holiday operators?'

Mrs. Bruce told him it was a bargain offer cruise and the whole package, cruise and flight was run by the same foreign company.

I asked, 'Out of interest, did you visit Kaeta?'

'Oh, yes we spent a couple of days there.'

We drove out of Epsom, with Derek muttering about lack of security and how easy it was for people to get into the country without a passport. We cut across country, through a suburban town called Banstead and a busy little English town called Reigate, and then through the Surrey countryside, past Gatwick airport to Crawley where we found the enterprise park we were looking for and VP Ltd.

Again Derek took the lead and marched into reception showing his warrant card and asking to speak with the Managing Director.

'He is not in, sir.'

'Who is the most senior manager on site then?'

'That would be Mr. Herbert, our Finance Director.'

'Good, please tell him we wish to speak with him?'

'I am not sure he is available, sir.'

'I am sure he would prefer to speak with us here rather than in a police interview room,' Derek threatened.

The receptionist, looking extremely agitated, spoke to Mr. Herbert's secretary. After some whispered conversation she turned to us and said, 'If you wouldn't mind waiting for a few moments his secretary has gone to find him.' It only took five minutes before the secretary appeared and showed us the Mr. Herbert's office.

Mr. Herbert was a smart, six-foot, dark-haired American in his late thirties with a cultured transatlantic voice. Derek apologised for barging in unannounced and thanked him for seeing us.

He replied, 'No problem. What can I do for you?' Unlike the receptionist and his secretary he did not look in the least bit threatened. Derek stepped back and I took the lead again.

'How long have you been in this position?' I asked.

'About three months. This business was recently acquired by the American conglomerate, Prospect Manufacturing and I was appointed by the new owner. I took over after a sort handover with the retiring Finance Director.'

'Can you give the name of your predecessor?'

'Yes, Douglas Jay. We got on very well. We were both involved with the takeover, on opposite sides of the table of course.' He smiled at me, waiting for the next question.

'Do you have details of payments made to Mr. Jay please?'

'We have his salary records and I know the amount of his terminal payment from VP Ltd.'

'May we see those details please?'

'Yes, I will get the Chief Accountant to print out the salary summary for you and I have details of the terminal payment here. Do you wish to look at any other financial records before I call the Chief Accountant?' asked Mr. Herbert.

'Possibly,' I said, 'I understand one of the drugs manufactured here is called "KetVet". Can you tell us about that?'

'KetVet as is a ketamine-based derivative drug. It's not one of our major lines. We make it in pill form, in various strengths, and an injectable drug. The pill is for use with animals as an anaesthetic and analgesic. In its injectable form it would typically be used with larger animals, for pain control and combined with other drugs as an anaesthetic, particularly for equine surgical procedures.'

'I understand that ketamine can be used as recreational drug?'

'I understand that as well,' Mr. Herbert replied. 'There have been a number of deaths resulting from its illegal use,' he continued, 'I am sure you know as well as I, that it is used on the club circuit where it induces a mild out-of-body trance with hallucinations, and in its stronger form it has been used by some individuals to induce what is known as the 'K-Hole', a severe form of dissociation from the physical world. It is also one of the date rape drugs. I assume your interest is to do with reports of the drug being used illegally in the US.'

We did not answer that one and Derek asked, 'Have you had any of these drugs stolen and would it be possible for them to be, ah, misappropriated from the factory somehow?'

'There was an incident before we acquired the business of an employee falsifying records and stealing drugs, but the quantities involved were minimal – small-time dealing only. Following that incident all our procedures were reviewed and tightened and it would be impossible for anyone to steal the quantities which have been found in the USA.'

'How do you think KetVet got into the illegal trade?' Derek asked.

'I would look a vet's usage. We supply to vets all over the world but have no control over how they use the drugs.'

'Could we see you customer records for KetVet sales?' I asked.

Mr. Herbert pulled out a report from his desk. 'You are not the first to ask for this, the Dutch police have also visited us,' he commented as he pointed to the name – Cordite Veterinary Group, Best, Netherlands. 'He uses considerable amounts of KetVet, significantly more than anyone else, even the large multiple practices.'

I noted down the name and address of the vet who was based in Best, a small Dutch town just outside Eindhoven. I asked, 'You said Mr. Jay received a terminal payment?'

Mr. Herbert pushed a paper across to me. Douglas's payment covered payment for the early termination of his contract plus a bonus for his final nine months with the company. In total £750,000 but I noted it was not paid until after his divorce and financial settlement with his ex-wife.

'Did Mr. Jay receive any other payments?' I asked.

'Not from us, but I believe that Stripe Financing, the venture capitalists who were behind the sale of this business, had an arrangement with him to pay a bonus on the successful completion at the various stages of the acquisition. He was also a shareholder and would have received Prospect shares in exchange for his holding, which he could have sold.'

I finally asked Mr. Herbert if he knew if Douglas had

any enemies. 'Not to my knowledge,' he answered, 'but you could ask Linda, my secretary. She worked for Mr. Jay before me.'

We thanked Mr. Herbert for his help and left. As we walked out I thought of something. 'You would not have details of Mr. Jay's bank account would you?'

'I have details of the account to which we made our payments. That's all and I am not sure I should give them to you.'

Derek assured him it would be a great help and we would be very discrete. He gave us the information.

On the way out I stopped at Linda's work station and asked her, 'I understand you worked for Mr. Jay when he was here.'

'Yes,' she confirmed. 'I worked as his PA for many years. I was sorry to see him go. He was a really good boss and kind man.'

'You knew him quite well then?'

'Yes, I suppose I did. He was very busy for the last year while the company was being sold and his divorce went through, so I got involved with a lot of his personal stuff. He was very upset when his father passed away and he had to travel so I made all the funeral arrangements and dealt with solicitors for him.'

'Did he have any enemies that you know of?'

'No not really, in fact not at all. Everyone he dealt with had very great respect for him. He was always honest and straight up with everyone.' She paused. 'His ex-wife did not like him much; she used to ring and was really quite nasty about him sometimes. He was devastated when he discovered she had left him and gone to live with another woman.'

'Did he ever get involved with recreational drugs, do

you know?' I asked.

'No, I am sure he did not. He was very anti-drug abuse. You probably already know that some of the drugs we manufacture have been misused, and after one of our staff was caught stealing KetVet, it was Douglas who organised staff training sessions showing the effects of drug abuse. He was very upset over that incident.'

I thanked her and said I had no more questions and turned questioningly to Derek, who confirmed that he, too, was finished.

In the car on the way back to Heathrow I told Derek that I now wanted to visit Holland and check on the man we know had flown into Heathrow. I also wanted to visit the Dutch vet.

'You also need to see his bank account and confirm the monies he received,' Derek reminded me.

Thursday 11th December

We got back to the Sheraton late afternoon yesterday.

It was too early to phone Bernie, as I knew he would be out of the station until late afternoon. I decided I would phone the hospital and see how Douglas was. I had phoned the hospital a couple of times this week but had not plucked up the courage to talk with Douglas personally. When I got through to the hospital, a nurse answered the phone. I explained who I was and asked after Douglas and if I could speak to him. The nurse said she would put me through to him in a minute but first she needed to talk with me. I wondered what had happened.

She explained that Douglas had the operation to

straighten and reset his arm and wrist. His head and other injuries were healing well and later today, or tomorrow, he would go for a medical assessment. 'Assuming the assessment goes well we hope to discharge him over the weekend or early next week. As you are his fiancée and on his record as his next of kin we need to discuss the arrangements for discharge with you as initially at least he should not be on his own.'

I told the nurse I was abroad at the moment but I would speak with my mother and we would make any necessary arrangements. When I got through to Douglas I asked him how he was. He replied in neutral tones, telling me that he had had another operation to reset his arm.

'I have a temporary plaster cast up to the elbow and it hurts like hell,' he told me.

I said, rather inadequately, that I was sorry and wished I could be with him, explaining that I was still in London. He asked how I was getting on. I explained what I had been doing but I did not want to say too much in case Tony questioned him, and I did not want Tony to find out what I was up to until I was ready. Douglas said very little, and I don't know whether he was pleased or not. He did ask if I was on my own or with a friend. I think this was his way of fishing to see if Tony Choizi was with me, and I remembered that he still thought we were close. I was still upset over Tony's advances but, more upset that I couldn't share with Douglas what I thought of the man and how he made me feel, but it was not something I felt I could discuss on the phone so I just assured Douglas I was on my own, lonely, and missing home. I nearly said "and my friends" but stopped myself in case he misinterpreted that.

I told him the nurse had said he might be discharged soon and that if I had not returned home by then I would ask Mary to look after him for me. He thanked me for that and said he had been worrying what would happen. He asked me how long I was staying in London and I told him

I was not sure yet. I said I still had some leads to follow up and probably needed to visit Amsterdam. He was surprised at that and asked me why. I just said I needed to clear up a couple of issues that had come up. He sort of grunted and wished me luck. He told me that Mary and Jasmine had been to visit him and how kind they had both been.

'Jasmine has been round all the paper shops in Kaeta buying me magazines to read. She is a really good kid. You are lucky, I wish I had a daughter like her.' He sounded very wistful and as I could feel myself getting emotional again, I ended the conversation, telling him that I wished I was with him and would see him soon. I told him I would phone again as soon as I could.

I was in a very melancholy mood and feeling lonely and missing home. I wanted someone to hug and love me but there was no one, so I just sat on the bed feeling sorry for myself. Eventually, I said to myself, *Come on girl, you're no good to anyone like this, go and do something.* I went down to the gym and worked out hard for an hour.

There was only me and a middle-aged, balding businessman in the gym. After a while I noticed that whatever equipment I worked out on, he followed me to use the adjacent one. He got the message after I stared him down a couple of times and quickly left the gym and me in peace. After an hour I was exhausted but felt much better.

When I got back to my room I showered and then phoned Mary and told her Douglas might be discharged soon, and asked her if she would look after him if I was not home. She said of course she would and that he must stay at Windrush, our home, until he was well enough to move to the beach house on his own.

After speaking with Mary I tried to phone Bernie. He was not there so I spoke with Merv instead. The most interesting development was that they had managed to access Douglas's password protected file. With some concern I asked Merv what was in it, fearing it might be something to do with drugs.

'All personal stuff,' Merv told me, 'passwords, access codes, phone numbers, National Insurance numbers and IR numbers – that sort of thing.'

'By any chance, are his banking details there?'

'Yes, everything.' Merv read out his bank details and account numbers. There were three altogether, two current accounts and one savings account.

I asked Merv if he had any luck tracing the woman on the plane. 'I have been through the CCTV at the airport and there is a clear picture of her standing in the queue for immigration. No camera bag, just the wheelie-bag. She looks a little nervous, keeps looking at her watch. On her immigration questionnaire she has put that she is here on holiday and staying for week at the Atlantic Lodge over on the other side of the island. I have also matched one of the prints on the hacksaw to the gardener. The other print has been smudged by the gardener and so far I have not found a match.'

'Any luck with the prints on the safe door?'

'Not really, there are a lot of prints on the door and so far I have only identified yours.'

I told Merv what I had done today and he promised to let Bernie know I had phoned.

Before I hung up Merv said, 'You will never guess what his password on the file is.'

'Go on, tell me.'

He spelt out, '?4JOEL#me.'

I did not get it at first, I thought it was just a random digit password but then its significance dawned on me.

It was Thursday morning now and I was finishing breakfast. One good thing about this hotel was the breakfast, which was served as a buffet in the restaurant and you could find everything from English egg and bacon through to tropical fruits.

I needed to phone Derek Passmore later. He had promised to find a contact for me in Holland and get a warrant so we could get to see into Douglas's bank accounts.

I decided to spend the day at Heathrow looking at more CCTV to see if I could track the man from Eindhoven and see what he did.

I was pretty sure the switch must have taken place in the shopping hall. The first thing I did was to ask Jon Brix if there was someone who could walk round the shopping mall with me and point out any areas not covered by the cameras. He got one of the IT engineers to walk round with me. He explained that coverage was not that simple. The whole area could be observed with the cameras, but because they were fitted with variable focal length lenses, and were operator controlled, at any time parts of the area may not be visible if the operator chose to zoom a camera to somewhere else. The good news, however, was that the area was laid out with the seats grouped together at either end of the hall, and normally three cameras were focused at any one time on each group, which gave full coverage of the area.

I went back to my terminal and chose the period between the woman entering the shopping hall and boarding the plane, and started to go through the pictures from the first camera. On camera two I briefly spotted the woman walking past the seats with just the wheelie-bag in tow. I saw nothing more on that set of seats, and as it was late morning I decided to phone Derek Passmore.

He told me he had made contact with Inspector Willam Ince who was working with the Drug Squad in Amsterdam and had agreed to meet with me first thing the following Monday morning at his office in Holland. He had also arranged for a warrant and had made an appointment for the pair of us to visit Douglas's bank in the City of London. He told me to meet him at his office at ten and we would travel together to the bank.

I booked a flight to Amsterdam on Sunday afternoon and went on the internet to find a hotel near the police station, before returning to look at the second seating area.

I had looked through hundreds of pictures before I found one of the man from Amsterdam still carrying a rucksack and camera bag. The cameras used a time-lapse system for recording so the movements were jerky, but by switching cameras I was able to watch the man walk round the seats. He occasionally glanced up, looking directly at the cameras. He sat down in full view of one of the cameras and placed the rucksack on his knee and started to rummage through it, and placed the camera bag on the floor next to him. I waited, watching the picture carefully, when suddenly it switched focus and swung round, zooming in on a woman who had dropped a carrier bag full of bottles. There was liquid running everywhere. The camera stayed focused on the scene until a cleaner arrived with a bucket and mop. When the camera switched back to the seats the man was gone and so was the camera bag.

I spent the rest of the afternoon searching pictures but found nothing more. Late afternoon, I phoned Bernie. I brought him up to date and told him I was going to Amsterdam. He told me he had two developments to report.

'The good news is that I think we have found Zach. Jasmine phoned me and told me one of her school friends had told her that another girl in the class was not allowed to come to school because her uncle was on the run and hiding at her house. That was Zach's sister's house in Grumble. The bad news is that Tony Choizi is returning next week, as he says, to sort things out, and has instructed us not to bring Zach in, just to watch him until he arrives.'

'But we need to ask him about Douglas,' I protested.

'I know,' Bernie replied, 'but Tony is insistent that that we wait until he arrives.'

After finishing that call, first I was not sure whether I was cross with, or proud of Jasmine, after I told her not to get involved, and then I decided that I really did not trust Tony Choizi, and I was going to keep a detailed personal diary and file of all this stuff.

Chapter 68

Douglas Jay; Friday 12th December

I have been in hospital now for two weeks, all but a day, and Dr Leonard is pleased with my recovery. The head injuries are healing well, I have emerged from swathes of bandages, and even my hair is beginning to grow again and my drug intake has been reduced. Last Wednesday they operated on my arm and wrist to straighten it. It's now all held together with metal pins with a temporary plaster cast. At the moment it is quite painful but should ease as the swelling goes down. The bruising and grazing is also healing and now, not so painful, and I have been allowed to get up and even walk round the garden accompanied by a nurse and the policeman.

There are two police who take it turns to watch me. Denzel is a bit serious and taciturn. He does not say much, but the other policeman, Isaac, is OK. He is quite chatty and often now comes into the room and sits with me, talking. I have tried to get him to tell me what is going on but says he does not really know. He does speak about Joelle and obviously has a lot of respect for her. He says she is a good detective and a kind person.

I specifically remember our conversations this morning which started when he told me about Joelle's father. 'He came back to the island after independence and set up the police force here, eventually becoming Commissioner. But he was also an astute businessman. He bought a lot of the land to the south of Kaeta town when it was worthless scrub and swamp. Of course he saw tourism would become the island's main economic activity and that that land would rocket up in value as a result. He made a fortune selling building plots out on St Martin's Point, where he built himself a villa, and then sold beachfront plots on St Martin's Bay to hotel operators. He built and operated the island's first luxury hotel, Glass Bay, which he owned himself.'

'Joelle told me had owned land but I did not realise he had made that much money,' I commented.

'Yes, indeed, and of course when he died he left it all to his wife and Joelle. Between them they are amongst the richest families on the island. Joelle still owns Glass Bay but I believe it is run by one of the Caribbean hotel chains now.'

'Joelle must be quite rich in her own right,' I speculated. 'I am surprised she carried on with policing.'

Isaac looked thoughtful and said, 'Well, rich in the sense that she owns the land but I guess she needs her police income for day-to-day living. Anyway she is a very unassuming person and I think she enjoys what she is doing.' Then he said, and this is why the conversation was important to me, 'You know she thinks you did not do this drug stuff, don't you?'

I nodded.

'She has taken a week's leave and, at her own expense, gone to London to find evidence that you not involved. You must have made quite an impression on her.'

Now that surprised me and made me think. Isaac had said quite clearly Joelle had gone to find evidence that I was not involved in this drug business and to do that in her holiday time and pay for herself; that must mean something. Perhaps I have misjudged her. Perhaps she really meant what she said when she explained she had found it difficult, as she liked me, but had to remain detached and collect evidence. Maybe I have been a bit harsh in judging her.

While I enjoyed this thought and it gave me hope that if this mess ever got sorted out I might be able to make a friend of her, I also remembered that she already had a relationship with that American, Tony Choizi, not that I could imagine what she saw in him, he is just a loud-mouthed bully as far as I can see. These conflicting thoughts festered and left me still feeling confused about what sort of relationship I had, or could have with Joelle.

She phoned me yesterday and I now thought that perhaps I had been a bit off-hand. She told me what she had been doing and alluded to new evidence but was not very specific. I thought of thanking her for helping me, but I did not, as I was not totally sure whether she was actually helping me or gathering more evidence against me. I nearly asked her about Tony but that did not feel like a conversation to have on the phone, but I was pleased Tony was not with her in London. It was a relief when she told me that I might be discharged soon and that Mary would look after me. I had been worrying what would happen when I was discharged.

I got fed up lying in bed trying to think through all this until eventually I resolved that if she phoned again I would be more friendly, and I hoped that she soon would come back as there were now things I needed to say to her.

Mary has been a real friend; she has visited me every day this week, once with Jasmine but usually in the mornings when Jasmine is at school. Her talking casually about the island has been a great help in bringing back my memory. I find my thoughts drift around a bit but I more or less remember everything now, and even snatches of memory about the evening of my crash are coming back.

The nurse had just been in to attend to me and to tidy the room. She said that I would shortly get a visit from Dr. Leonard and a psychiatric doctor. Apparently they wanted to carry out some cognitive tests to see if I had any lasting mental impairment from the crash.

Chapter 69

Joelle de Nouvelas; Friday 12th December

I used the Heathrow Express to travel into the centre of London but this time took a taxi from Paddington to Scotland Yard to meet Derek Passmore.

He said we would get the tube into the city; it would be quicker, he assured me. We got a Circle line train from St James's to Canon Street and then walked up to Douglas's bank. We were shown into a small customer room where we joined by one of the bank's managers. He examined Derek's warrant closely and then asked us what we would like to see. We confirmed that Douglas operated three accounts with them and asked to see statements going back for the last two years.

While we were waiting for the statements to arrive Derek asked me about the investigation and whether I was finding the information I needed. I went through the evidence we had built up and explained to him that it was all circumstantial, and despite pressure from the US Drug Enforcement Administration to arrest Douglas, I was not certain that he was guilty.

After a few moments' thought he said, 'Well, I can understand why the Americans are looking for an arrest. The circumstantial evidence that you have combined with finding drugs in his room safe would certainly point to his guilt. However, if you can explain and knock down all the circumstantial evidence it rather leaves the drugs in his safe standing alone as evidence, and you are right to look for other explanations.'

'Don't forget the motorcycle accident looks like deliberate sabotage,' I reminded him.

'Yes, that is curious. It does not make any sense at all, unless Douglas is concealing something from you.'

'I agree with you but so far everything he has told me has checked out one hundred percent. Remember what his old PA told us. She said he was straight up and honest.'

'Yes, it certainly begins to look like you are on the right track with this one,' Derek mused. He started saying he had never met the US Detective Choizi and he sounded a difficult person, when he was interrupted by the arrival of the bank records.

We confirmed his salary payments went into his main account and quickly found the £750,000 paid into the savings account. He had transferred £50,000 into his current account just before he left for Kaeta. From this amount we could see he paid for his holiday.

His second current account had only been open for a year and it had an opening balance of £105,623, which the manager explained had been transferred from previous savings accounts. He confirmed Douglas had consolidated all his savings accounts and had then transferred them into this new account and that he had made his PA, Linda, a signatory on the account.

Over the last year there were four further receipts into this account, three at £50,000 and the most recent one, three months ago for £100,000. These four amounts had been transferred into the account by Stripe Financing. There were six small payments out of the account of £1,500 each and one payment of £15,000 just before he went away. These were all to a firm of solicitors. There was also a payment of £8,000 out of the account to a name we did not recognise. There were two large payments from the account. The first, six months ago for £100,000, and a second for £200,000 three months ago just after the final receipt. These were both paid to a different London solicitor firm. That left a balance of £23,590 after bank charges and other small payments.

The manager told us that all the payments had been authorised by Linda.

I insisted that we get a taxi back to Scotland Yard as I found the underground too claustrophobic, and while we travelled Derek summarised the visit.

'That all checks out, exactly what we expected to find except I was surprised that his PA had authority over that amount of money. I think we should ring her when we get back and see what she says.'

She confirmed that Douglas had opened the account specifically to give her authority to deal with the payments associated with his divorce, including those due to his ex-wife. He did this so there was no delay, as he was travelling so much over the last year. The smaller payments were to his solicitor, and the two larger ones his ex-wife's financial settlement paid to her solicitors. Linda commented bitterly, 'She did all right, she got the old family house worth over three quarters of a million and half his pension as well as the cash settlement.' Finally we learnt that the £8,000 was paid to the funeral directors for Douglas's father's interment.

'Well,' Derek commented when we finished the phone call, 'that's where the money he paid to his wife came from, and it rather destroys the motive that he smuggled drugs as he needed the money to pay off his wife.'

Happily, I agreed but I did wonder if there was more than just a working relationship between Douglas and Linda; *I must ask him*, I decided.

By mid-afternoon I had finished at Scotland Yard so decided to go for a walk round London to clear my head.

I will have tomorrow to myself, I decided. *I will go Harrods and get Jasmine and Mary Christmas presents. I must take Bernie and Merv back something as well,* I thought. *I should get Belinda and Sean something too.* I also decided I would buy Douglas a Christmas present, but what?

I was walking around the back streets near Covent Garden when I saw a specialist second hand bookshop and I went in out of curiosity. There was a book on the history of writing and calligraphy, which I bought for Bernie as I knew he was interested in that sort of thing.

I asked the shop owner if he had any books on motorcars, specifically the Vanden Plas Princess. He took me into a room behind the main shop, explaining that this was his engineering and mechanical collection, where all the car books were. He went along the shelves where he had hundreds of old books.

'I don't have anything on that particular model,' he said, 'but I do have a book on the Austin Princess.' He passed it to me and it was history of the Austin Princess, covering all the cars Austin had made with that name. 'You will find that book covers the model you are asking for. I also have these two books,' he said. 'They are very rare and it would be wrong to split them up. They would be very valuable to someone who restores these old cars.'

He handed me an original Austin workshop manual and an original Austin illustrated spare parts manual for the Austin Princess model 1953 to 1960. The books had a stamp inside the front cover declaring the books to be the property of "Dart Motors, Exeter, Devon. Not to be removed from the Service Department". They were in exceptional condition and the bookseller explained they would not have seen much use, as there would not have been many Princess cars in Devon.

'I am afraid the two manuals are rather expensive,' he apologised, 'they are in almost unused condition and I doubt you will find any others like them anywhere.'

I asked him what he would take for the three books together. He looked at the prices pencilled on the fly sheets of the books and said that together they added up to £250. I did not say anything, just looked at him, and eventually he said, 'You can have them for £225.' I pointed out that the books might be rare but then there would not that many people wanting to buy them, and offered him £200.

I bought all three books for Douglas.

Chapter 70

Joelle de Nouvelas; Monday 15th December

The previous day, Sunday, I had flown into Schipol airport and took the train into Amsterdam arriving late in the afternoon.

I was told that Inspector Ince worked in an office just off Munnikenstraat, and checked on the internet and found a mid-range hotel, Hotel Dauphin, near Munnikenstraat. I had no idea how to get to the hotel so I took a taxi. When I gave him the address he looked surprised and asked if I was sure that was the correct address. His English was impeccable. I confirmed that was correct address and he just shrugged and drove off.

He dropped me in Munnikenstraat and pointed to the Hotel Dauphin, which was down a narrow passage in a building that stood on the corner.

I walked down to the hotel and into a small reception area and rang the bell on the reception counter. A man emerged from the back and I gave him my name and told him I had reservation. He took my credit card, wanting payment in advance before he would let me have the room key. The room itself was on the third floor, it was quite small and modern-looking, painted white and grey and furnished with a double bed, a chair and desk, and an ensuite bathroom. I sat on the bed and looked round. On the back of the door was the fire escape map and a room-rate card. I was surprised to see the room could be rented on an hourly basis.

I had not eaten all day and was hungry. This time a woman answered the reception bell and I asked her where I might get some supper.

'You are English?' she asked. I nodded, it was easier than explaining I was Kaetian.

'There is a small cafe just round the corner,' she pointed the way, 'I should go there, it is simple but good.'

I went to walk out and she handed me a two-day-old English newspaper.

'It is OK,' I said, 'I just want to sit and eat.'

'No.' She insisted I take the paper. 'It's best you look busy.'

In the restaurant there was one woman sitting at a window table drinking coffee and two men eating at another table. I was shown to a table at the back of the cafe. I ordered a glass of wine and spaghetti bolognese. It was when a man beckoned through the window and the woman got up and went outside to him that I began to realise what was going on. Then I noticed the two men were looking expectantly at me and saw why I had been given a newspaper to concentrate on. I spread it out on the table and pretended to read, hoping my order would not take too long. It did not, and ate as quickly as I could and left.

I walked the hundred yards back to the hotel. It was cold and raining and I was feeling lonely and miserable. I got back to my room and sat on the bed thinking of home, and Douglas.

Oh, how lonely I felt and how I wished he was here with me.

It was Monday morning, 7.00am and I was just finishing my continental breakfast served in the dining room. I left the hotel with time to take a walk around the area and find the police station. I knew roughly where to go as I set off. At least the rain had stopped, but all the buildings looked a bit drab. There was a lot of graffiti on walls and there was a mix of new grey concrete buildings and older brick, but equally grey ones. It was not a bit like the pictures I had seen of Amsterdam, with its tall buildings overhanging sunny canals, with lots of trees. I had an arrangement to meet Inspector Willam Ince first thing this morning and that meant 8.00am to me.

I duly arrived at his office, in a run-down looking concrete and glass building, promptly at eight o'clock and asked for Inspector Ince.

'Is he expecting you?'

'Yes.'

'Name please.'

'Sergeant de Nouvelas of the Kaete Island Constabulary.'

A telephone conversation in Dutch followed and part way through the lady I had spoken to turned and asked me what my meeting concerned.

'An ongoing investigation into drug smuggling,' I replied.

More discussion followed in Dutch, on the telephone. When she had finished she invited me to take a seat in the waiting room while they tried to contact Inspector Ince.

An hour and half later a very tall man towered over me, and introduced himself as Willam Ince. He was at least six foot three inches tall and of average build. He looked quite young with open, boyish features and was dressed in grey slacks with an open-necked blue shirt and dark sports jacket. He wore a pair of heavy, brown, rubber-soled shoes on which he squeaked his way up to his office on the first floor with me in pursuit.

He apologised for keeping me waiting and asked me if I would like a coffee. He served me with a thick black concoction in a small cup accompanied by a small plastic container of condensed milk and a coffee biscuit.

Inspector Ince invited me to call him Will, and talking of the usual formalities and pleasantries, he asked me where I was staying. I told him.

'No,' he said, 'you mustn't stay there. It's in the middle of the red light district and has a bit of a reputation.'

I said that I was already getting that impression and he suggested that if I planned to spend any time in Amsterdam then I should change hotels.

'Rembrandt Square is quite central, I think you would like it there,' he advised, and then went on to apologise to me saying, 'I am sorry, Joelle, may I call you that? You should have been told we are in the middle of the red light district. There are a lot of drugs around here as well so it's useful to be here sometimes. It's actually quite okay during the day, lots of tourists about, but not very nice for a single girl at night. Now,' he continued, 'how can I help you?'

I explained I was investigating a drug smuggling incident on Kaete and had worked back through the chain and established that the consignment appeared to have started its journey at Eindhoven Airport, and that I wanted now to establish the identity of the man who had carried the suspicious bag and establish, if possible, the contents of the bag. I also wanted to visit the Cordite Veterinary Group as they appeared to use significantly more of the drug KetVet than anyone else in the world. As an afterthought I added, that I needed to visit Stripe Financing here in Amsterdam.

Will asked to see the prints from the CCTV pictures of the suspects passing through Heathrow and he studied them carefully for ages, but was expressionless and gave nothing away.

He turned his attention back to me and said simply, 'I can escort you to Stripe Financing here in Amsterdam, but it will not be possible for you to visit Eindhoven.'

'Why not?'

'It is a long way to the south of Amsterdam.'

'That's rubbish, I have plenty of time and it is crucial that I establish the identity of this man and what was in that camera bag,' I retorted.

'It is not possible for you to visit Eindhoven. Now shall I take you Stripe Financing?'

I agreed we should go to Stripe, but tried to insist that I should go to Eindhoven saying, 'No, this is not good enough. If you won't take me to Eindhoven I will go on my own. Even if you don't help me identify the man, you can't stop me visiting Cordite Veterinary.'

I must have looked quite fierce as he seemed to shrink back into his chair and studied me for a few seconds before saying quietly, 'If you take any unilateral actions against my wishes I will have to arrest you.' It was my turn to stare him down for a few seconds before he relented, and continued. 'So be it! Tell me what you have found and I will see if I can help you. Is that okay?'

'I think so,' I agreed.

Willam continued, 'Perhaps you would be kind enough to go through all your evidence in detail, both against this Douglas Jay, and what you have discovered during your recent visit to the United Kingdom.'

I started from the beginning with the request we had received from the US DEA to watch for a man carrying a camera bag.

Will interrupted, 'Yes, that alert came from us.'

I continued and described the evidence we had collected which had caused us to suspect Douglas. I described Tony Choizi's involvement. He stopped me there and asked if any other American detectives had visited the island.

'No, as far as I am aware we only ever had contact with Tony Choizi.'

I described Douglas's motorcycle accident and told him we suspected that someone had sabotaged his machine and, finally, concluded telling him about the drugs found in Douglas's safe. I then went through all that I had discovered in London.

Will had listened silently for an hour and half. He took a deep breath and said, 'There are some aspects of this which puzzle me. Much of your evidence against Mr. Jay is circumstantial.'

I agreed with him.

He continued, 'It is really only the discovery of drugs in his room that support the circumstantial evidence. But if he is the courier, we know he was only carrying the ketamine pills. So if the theory is correct and he was left with the undelivered end of his consignment, where did he get the heroin powder? Also why was he only left with such a small quantity of ketamine after he had made his deliveries?'

I was impressed.

Will asked me, 'Do you think Mr. Jay was using drugs personally?'

'Tony Choizi believes he had those drugs for personal use, but no, there was never any indication when he was on the island that he took drugs, and when the hospital tested his blood after the accident there was no sign of anything in his system. Also, remember we had had him under observation for practically twenty-four hours a day and his background and behaviour is not what you would typically expect from a drug user,' I responded.

'Ok, then we accept the drugs were not for his personal use. Another puzzle with these drugs is that you have proved that the two parcels originally suspected of being the means of delivering the ketamine were, in fact, perfectly innocent. If he were our smuggler, how then did he deliver the consignment if you had him under permanent surveillance, and why keep such a small part of the consignment back? It does not make sense.'

Again, I was impressed with his summary.

Will pursued another thought. 'The behaviour of Mr. Choizi is puzzling. He is the US officer in charge of the investigation into the Caribbean end of the smuggling operation and appears to have formed an early conviction that Mr. Jay is guilty without really questioning the evidence. Why would he do that?'

I wondered how he knew of the Caribbean end and that Tony was in charge, but let it pass for the moment. Will moved on and asked me, 'Do you have any view regarding who sabotaged the motorcycle?'

'No. We have recovered the hacksaw we believe was used and it has a very smudged thumb print on it which we have not yet identified.'

Will spent some minutes writing some notes before he concluded, 'In view of all the evidence you have collected, I am inclined to believe that those drugs were planted on Mr. Jay. I also think we can assume that whoever planted them also sabotaged the motorcycle. Mr. Jay is probably innocent so the question is, who gained by making him appear guilty? There are two possibilities.

'First, and most likely, the drug gang tried to silence him by arranging an accident that had fatal consequences, but why, if he was not involved with the gang? More likely they wanted to get him out of the way while they planted drugs and wanted to ensure you would find them and arrested him, so that the police would cease further investigations and thus allowing the gang to continue their activities unhindered.

'The second possibility is that the police planted the drugs.' He saw me about to object so added, 'It has happened before. Usually, in order to secure an arrest of someone thought to be guilty, but with insufficient evidence to secure a conviction. The problem with this theory is why sabotage the motorcycle?'

I thought of Tony's comments that he should not be resuscitated, and also that he did not care if Douglas was innocent or guilty; he just wanted a conviction. I kept quiet though.

Will congratulated me. 'You have been very thorough. Your work at Heathrow has added to our knowledge. We knew nothing of the woman and how they were arranging the transit route, and your contribution has given us more to work with.'

He picked up my pictures and notes that were on his desk and locked them in his desk drawer, saying, 'You understand that this episode is simply part of a much larger international operation to close a massive drug operation, and that what you have discovered here would jeopardise significant parts of the operation if it were to become general knowledge. I must insist you keep this information to yourself.'

'Will I hell!' I exploded. 'An innocent man is going to go to jail if this evidence is not presented and I intend to present it with or without your permission!'

Again, he spoke quietly, 'I am not threatening you Miss de Nouvelas, I am warning you that unless I have your assurance that you will respect our confidentiality I shall have no alternative but to arrest you and hold you until our investigation is concluded.'

Chapter 71

Douglas Jay; Monday 15th December

It is Monday. I have no idea what time it is and I feel like I am living in my own personal nightmare, where I am utterly out of control of my life.

I had not spoken with Joelle since last Thursday when she had phoned me, and although now I was hoping desperately that she was trying to help me I had no idea whether she had gathered more evidence that would help prove my innocence.

I thought back to last Friday when I had thought things were beginning to improve.

The doctors had seen me on Friday evening and completed their cognitive tests, and told me I was making good progress. They explained that I might get confused and feel a little disoriented at times and lose concentration, but that this would gradually pass and I stood every chance of making a complete recovery, but I needed to return for further tests in a month.

I did tell them that I had noticed certain weakness in my right hand and they said this was a side effect of the head injury. Dr. Leonard told me I should exercise my hand daily. 'Take up the piano,' he suggested, 'and the condition will gradually improve.'

They agreed I could be discharged the next day,

Saturday, but would need to attend an outpatient clinic the following Wednesday to have my wrist examined and the plaster changed.

Saturday was even better. Mary and Jasmine came to collect me. Mary had even bought me some clothes to wear as my own were still at the police station. They drove me back to their villa on St Martin's Point and showed me to an ensuite bedroom which Mary explained was one of their guest rooms, but I was to consider it my own while I was with them. It was a large room with a king sized double bed with lightweight duvet. After spending so much time in hospital, I was aware of how all the linen smelt clean and fresh to me. The room had a wardrobe and dressing table on one wall. The bed was against the back wall so that I could lie in bed and look out of the French windows and over the garden at the Caribbean Sea. There was a balcony outside with a lounger and a wicker chair.

Mary explained that she and Jasmine had bought me some clothes and other essentials but she also showed me another room, which she said had been her late husband's. He was about my size, and, she said, I was welcome to use any of the things in that room.

Jasmine came bouncing up and invited me to walk round the garden with her before lunch. I am afraid I only got halfway round before I was exhausted. I missed lunch and went to the room and slept most of the afternoon.

By the time I emerged, Mary had gone to the bar but Jasmine was still at home and told me she was staying to make sure I was OK. She asked if was hungry, which I was, and she prepared an early supper for the both of us. I went to bed that night feeling much happier.

Not much happened on the Sunday. I spent most of the day resting in the garden under the shade of a tree. The two women were conscientious in their care for me, and to my embarrassment kept asking me if they could do anything for me, asking if I needed anything. Eventually, Mary went to work but Jasmine stayed with me again.

This morning, Monday, I awoke late to a commotion going on downstairs. I could hear men's voices and Jasmine angrily shouting and I wondered what was going on. Mary knocked on the door and suggested I got dressed, as there were two policemen downstairs to see me. This was when the nightmare started.

I went downstairs and recognised DI Shrewd and Denzel. Shrewd told me they needed to ask me a few questions and invited me to come down to the police station.

Mary asked why I had to go to the police station. DI Shrewd said it would be better for all if I went with them voluntarily. He then cautioned me.

When we got to the police station I was escorted to an interview room where Shrewd asked me if I understood the caution. He turned on a tape recorder and proceeded to question me, asking first about the drugs found in my room.

'Are they yours? Can you explain how they got there?'

I said no, but, at first, tried to be helpful in answering their questions. However, when DI Shrewd said that they had reason to believe I was involved in smuggling of drugs I realised where this was leading and asked to speak to Sergeant de Nouvelas, but this was denied. I then told them I would not answer any more questions until I had a solicitor present. I had seen the TV programmes where the suspect replies to every question with 'nothing to say' but, by this time I was tired and getting confused so I just said nothing. After some more questions DI Shrewd arrested me and I was stripped, searched, and put in one of these underground cells, where I am sitting now.

Chapter 72

Joelle de Nouvelas; Monday 15th December

I sat silently running Inspector Ince's threat though my mind. I had no doubt that he was serious but equally I was not going to give up and go home empty handed so I said to him, 'If you arrest me you must realise that you will cause an international scandal. You may be able to keep it quiet while you detain me but, rest assured, that at the earliest opportunity I shall make as much noise about it as I can, and I do have the contacts that can make a lot of noise.'

I did not have any contacts but he did not know that. I continued, 'In any event you are being naive if you think I have not been submitting regular reports to my superiors detailing the evidence I have discovered this week, so even if you suppress me you cannot stop what I have discovered being revealed.'

Will looked at me again, nodding his head slowly. 'I think we can manage an international incident, but you are right about the difficulty of containing what you have discovered.' He twirled his pencil around his fingers and was obviously trying to resolve some inner conflict. 'If I trust you, can we make a deal,' he suggested.

'If it is sensible and I get what I want, then, yes you can trust me.'

We sat looking at each other for what seemed like hours. But eventually the silence was broken.

'Right then,' Will said, sitting upright. 'Here is the deal. I will tell you why this has to remain secret, and I will give you information regarding the identity of the man you saw in Heathrow and information regarding the contents of that camera bag. In return you will remove all the evidence of your investigations at Heathrow and here in Amsterdam from your files and keep it in a secret file, and only reveal it on a need to know basis and get my prior agreement before disclosing it to anyone. You will also sign our State Secrets Act before leaving this office.'

I was impressed again by his summary, and was beginning to realise that I had stumbled into something much larger than an illegal drug warehousing operation on Kaeta. I agreed to his request.

Will called in an assistant and asked him to write out a contemporaneous statement while he spoke to me, which he would sign and give me. When he started I just listened and did not interrupt.

'We can identify the man you saw in Heathrow as a partner in the Cordite Veterinary Group. That group have a contract with the Airport Authority in Eindhoven, under which, should any animals being transported through the airport require veterinary examination, they will attend. We know he has regular contact with a cleaner who works at the airport and we believe this is how he gets the drugs through the airport without detection.

'He travels about four times a year and to a number of international destinations and uses the camera bag to transport the drugs. He frequently changes aircraft en route using different transit points and stop-overs. He is very difficult to track and until you identified him at Heathrow we were uncertain how he was delivering the drugs as he usually manages to avoid discovery at his destinations, and even if he is found there is never any evidence of drugs.

'There is no doubt that the camera bag you saw being exchanged at Heathrow was the one he packed with thousands of ketamine tablets shortly before he travelled and we know that they were to be delivered in the Caribbean.

'We know this because we have an undercover police woman working as a veterinary assistant in the practice in Best and she saw him pack the drugs in that bag, and was able to look at his travel itinerary when he went to the toilet. Unfortunately the document was partly obscured and she did not want to move it and could only see that he was travelling via the Dutch Antilles. Incidentally, the camera bag is identical to the one you described as being found hidden in the aircraft.

'From the US FDA we received only an edited version of the evidence collected on Kaeta which identified the man Douglas Jay as our suspect carrying a camera bag. We now know that the bag Mr. Jay carried is not the one that was packed at Cordite Veterinary, which you identified as exchanged at Heathrow and carried on to the flight to Kaeta. As a result of your work at Heathrow it is clear that the identification of Mr. Jay as the courier was incorrect.'

He finished and asked if this statement was adequate to support the evidence I had already gathered.

'Yes. Thank you.'

'You understand that we are dealing with ruthless people here and disclosure could jeopardise our investigation, and worse, endanger our undercover policewoman.'

'Yes, you have my promise that I will only disclose this information to obtain Mr. Jay's release and I will ensure these files are marked "Secret".' The assistant left the office to type the statement.

Although it was not warm in the office, Will turned his fan on, pointing it away from us. 'There is something more I should tell you so you fully understand the situation. We have no proof of what I am about to disclose, only suspicions, so this is strictly for your ears only.' He leaned towards me and continued, 'In this investigation we are working closely with the US DEA. I mentioned that we received an edited version of the evidence you collected from them. That version was so heavily edited as to be misleading and leaving no doubt regarding Mr. Jay's apparent guilt. I will be investigating this aspect further with our contact on the Caribbean end of the investigation, Detective Tony Choizi.

'Now the point is that every time we feel we are getting close to the gang leaders, something happens to divert or disrupt our investigations. The evidence falls apart and we have to start all over again. I am afraid it looks like this is about to happen here. This makes me wonder if, somewhere in the various police departments involved, we have an informer who tips off the gang. If we can identify this woman you saw we may save something from this investigation, but I want to keep this known only to myself and my trusted officers.'

I realised what a responsibility he was now placing on me and promised I would not let him down.

'If you get chance to investigate this woman when you get home, please be discreet and report anything you find directly to me,' Will asked.

His assistant returned with a copy of his statement and a copy of the Dutch Secrets Act for me to sign. His assistant witnessed both documents. He passed his statement back to the assistant with my notes and pictures and asked him to make a copy before returning them to me.

'Now,' Will said, 'I assume you would like to visit Stripe Financing and return to London this evening.'

I agreed I would, so he took my ticket and gave it to the assistant and asked him to get me onto a flight back to Heathrow. The assistant soon returned with a new ticket and all the documents.

Will drove me to Stripe Financing via the hotel so I could collect my luggage. As we drove out of the red light area I observed that the exotic bars and twenty-four hour pole dancing clubs gave way to street cafes and more upmarket shops as we approached central Amsterdam. We headed south using a dual carriageway road built on stilts over the town towards Stripe's offices in a large, new skyscraper in the suburbs.

The interview at Stripe Financing was with one of the Presidents and was brief. Will introduced us and explained I had some questions. We were told that they had headhunted Douglas for the role at VP Ltd and were very pleased with the work he had done there.

'He substantially increased the value of our investment and made us a lot of money. We would like to work with him again when he returns from holiday,' he told us. He confirmed that they had agreed to pay Douglas a bonus in addition to what he received from VP Ltd.

'It was paid in four instalments: three interim payments of £50,000 payable on the successful completion of phases in the negotiations, and a final payment of £100,000 when the deal was signed.'

He also confirmed that they travelled to New York with Douglas on a number of occasions and at all times Douglas had been also accompanied by lawyers or accountants. 'They were strictly business trips with no time for sightseeing.'

When we had finished Will drove me out to Schipol

Airport. When we got there he said, 'I am sorry we got off to a bad start this morning but it was essential for me to decide whether or not I could trust you. Don't forget, please let me know how you get on and if I can be of any help to you do not hesitate to contact me.'

I had a couple of hours to wait for my plane so I went shopping in the departure lounge and bought Jasmine an iPhone for Christmas and the boys in the office whisky and cigarettes.

I got back to the Sheraton about eight thirty that evening and the receptionist gave me my old room for the night. I went across to the porter's desk to retrieve my luggage and he handed four message envelopes. When I got to my room one was from Mary, asking me to phone her and the other three from Bernie, asking me to ring him urgently, no matter how late.

Chapter 73

Joelle de Nouvelas; Tuesday 16th December

It was Tuesday and I was bored and anxious sitting in my hotel room with nothing to do until tomorrow. Last night I telephoned Bernie first, catching him still at work.

'Joelle. Thanks for phoning, things have moved on here since Friday and I urgently need to bring you up to speed,' he said as soon as we were connected. 'An attorney from the firm Peace Hood representing the US Drug Enforcement Administration turned up here late Friday afternoon and presented an Extradition Warrant for Douglas Jay to the court here in Kaeta Town. This morning, all hell broke loose. The Commissioner called me up to tell me that the court fixed an extradition hearing for 11.00am on Thursday this week and issued an arrest warrant for Douglas. He was discharged from hospital on Saturday and your mother took him back to your home.'

I interrupted, and told Bernie I had agreed that my mother should do that.

'That was not very clever, you are compromising yourself.' Bernie told me off.

I let it pass and listened to him as he continued, 'Denzel and Isaac camped outside your house all weekend. Nothing happened, Douglas did not go anywhere. This morning we had to arrest him.'

'Where is he now?' I asked.

'In the cells downstairs.'

'How is he?'

'Upset, confused and refusing to say anything. He has asked for you and he has asked for a solicitor.'

'I have got the evidence that proves he is not involved in any of this drug business.'

'Well then, you must get back here as soon as can, Thursday by the latest,' said Bernie.

'Is Tony Choizi on the island?'

'Not yet, but he telephoned me this afternoon and told me he was coming over for the hearing and would be taking Douglas back with him on Thursday afterwards,' Bernie said, 'and there is more – we found Zach this morning as well.'

'What is he saying?' I asked.

'Nothing, we have been instructed to just observe him, and to follow him if he moves, reporting anything back to Detective Choizi.'

'Why?' I asked.

'They think he may lead them to the ringleaders.'

I snorted, doubting that Zach even knew them. Bernie then instructed me, 'Send me the evidence you have found in case you don't make it back in time.'

'I can't do that. I will explain when I see you. I must go now and find a way of getting home.'

I did ring Mary next, but she just wanted tell me that Douglas had been arrested. I looked on the internet but the only direct flight to Kaeta was on Friday.

There was a flight to Barbados leaving at lunchtime on Wednesday which landed late afternoon, but sadly, much too late for me to catch the Wednesday Island Hopper flight. But there was an early morning Hopper flight on Thursday morning. It stopped at two other islands before Kaeta, but was scheduled to get to Kaeta at 10.00am. Unfortunately the Wednesday flight to Barbados was full and the website would not let me book a ticket.

First thing this morning I got the bus to the airport and went to the airline booking desk and explained my problem. At first they were apologetic but said the best they could do was put me on standby. I had to produce my warrant card and tell the sales assistant that under the terms of their landing rights in the Caribbean they had to give island Government Officials on urgent business travel priority. She said she would have to check with Head Office.

She came back and said, 'Yes, Sergeant, you are quite right, but unfortunately as this aircraft lands on Barbados and that does not apply. However the airline is anxious to assist you and is happy to accommodate you on this flight. Would you like me to also book a connecting flight to Kaeta?'

I agreed, and asked her to get me on the first available flight, which was the Thursday morning one. She issued me with a business class ticket and wished me a good flight.

I went back to my hotel. Firstly, I telephoned Will Ince and explained what had happened.

'You may explain the evidence to your senior officer,' he agreed. 'You will need to give the evidence to the court but you must insist that that it is heard in camera with only the presiding Judge, with evidence only disclosed to the senior attorneys. You and your senior officer can be present. Specifically, no other police officers can be allowed to see the evidence. Have you removed the evidence from open file as we agreed?'

'Yes,' I told him, thinking it was never actually on file in the first place. That was a bit of luck.

I started organising two files. One, the police file with the evidence I would present to court, the other, my personal file with that evidence but also including all my personal notes and suspicions. It was while I was making up this second file that I had a thought. There was smudged thumbprint on the hacksaw handle I had found and Merv had said only a small part of it was readable.

I telephoned Merv. 'Merv, can you get hold of the pictures you took of Douglas's safe when we found the drugs. The one showing the safe door open. Check that one for fingerprints. You should find yours, mine, Bernie's and Tony Choizi's. See if any of them match the second print on the hacksaw handle.'

Merv asked why and I told him to just do it.

After that I copied to disc the evidence file I had made for the Court and the one I had made for myself, went down to the hotel's IT centre, and personally printed off two copies of both files. I had nothing more to do now except wait for Wednesday lunchtime.

Chapter 74

Douglas Jay; Tuesday 16th December

Following my arrest yesterday I have been held in the police cells under Kaeta's police station.

This morning I was brought up from the cells for further questioning. I was taken into the same interview room as yesterday where DCI Strange was sitting accompanied by a PC and a well-built, coloured gentleman who introduced himself as David Rail and explained that he had been appointed by Mary de Nouvelas to represent me.

He turned to DCI Strange and asked for the interview to be adjourned as he had not had an opportunity to speak with me alone yet.

When Strange had left the room he explained that I was being held under arrest pending the granting of an extradition order made on behalf of the US Drug Enforcement Administration.

'I did not know that,' I said.

'The hearing is on Thursday, which does not give us much time,' he advised.

I asked him if knew where Joelle was and that I understood that she was gathering evidence which would show I was not involved.

'As far as I know, Joelle is in Europe somewhere. Mary

tells me she knows of your arrest but we don't know what additional evidence she has gathered or whether she will be back before Thursday.' He paused and pulled a note pad out from his briefcase. 'The evidence against you is largely circumstantial except for the drugs that were found in the room safe of the chalet you had occupied. Can you explain how the drugs got there? I assume they were not yours.'

'No, I can't explain how they got there and I can only assume that they were planted by someone to incriminate me.'

'I suppose we could say they were drugs for your own personal use.' David looked at me quizzically.

'No we could not.' I was little angry at the suggestion but tried to remain calm. 'I have never used drugs illegally and I am not starting now. Anyway if you say that surely it will just incriminate me further. I was told that some of the drugs found were KetVet pills made by my last employer.'

David agreed and then went through the other evidence which had been gathered and which was incriminating me. 'We have one thing up our sleeve,' he had noted. 'There was no evidence of drugs on the brown paper used to wrap the parcels, which it is claimed were the method by which the drugs were delivered. Joelle subsequently established that those parcels were brochures that you delivered.'

'That's right, the lady in the hotel gift shop asked me to deliver the brochures to the slave camp and sugar plantation.'

'That will be seen as unusual, why would she ask a hotel guest to run errands for her?'

'I told her I was going on an island tour and visiting the slave camp and sugar plantation and she asked me because she had been told to get the brochures delivered, but as she was the only person in the shop she could not leave it.

In fact I did not take the brochures on the tour as I only took my camera bag and did not have room.'

David made a note on his pad and then said, 'Yes, the camera bag. Do you know anything about the second camera bag found hidden on the plane?'

I thought for a bit, trying to remember if I knew anything about a second camera bag,

'No, I am afraid I don't remember any second camera bag.'

'Is that because you did not know of the bag, or you can't remember?' David queried.

'I don't think I knew but I can't really remember. The psychiatrist I saw last week warned me I may still suffer memory lapses and get confused.'

'No one has told me you saw a psychiatrist.' David looked at me.

'Yes, they carried out what they called cognitive tests before discharging me.'

'That's good, David smiled, 'that may help at least delay the extradition on medical grounds.' He summarised, 'We have got a chance of at least delaying the extradition pending further evidence. Most of what is here is circumstantial and if we can get hold of a medical report indicating you are not fully recovered that will help. Our problem is going to be those drugs in your room.'

He opened the door and told the PC outside that were ready to continue the interview. 'I will do all the talking. You say nothing.'

DCI Strange returned and immediately David said, 'You have insufficient evidence to imprison my client. I demand he is released into my custody immediately.'

'Sorry,' said Strange, 'can't do that.'

The police than repeated all the questions they had

asked me yesterday. I said nothing and David replied to them all, 'My client has nothing to say at this time.'

When DI Strange said the interview was concluded, David asked, 'I would like a copy of the medical report explaining the degree to which my client has recovered from the accident and his confused mental condition.'

Strange looked at Merv, who had joined the interview when the first PC left. 'What medical report?' he asked.

Merv shrugged and David launched in. 'You are telling me that you have arrested my client following a serious accident without first establishing that he was medically fit enough.'

DCI Strange shuffled uncomfortably and said he would obtain the report and pass a copy to David.

Nice one David, I thought, as David again asked for me to be released. For a moment I thought there might be a glimmer of hope but then Strange said, 'I am sorry; personally, I would like to accommodate your request, but I am under strict orders to hold Mr. Jay in custody as it is considered there is risk he will abscond.'

Isaac had given me a newspaper and some magazines to read and, later that day, when I was back in my cell, DCI Strange came in to see me.

'Don't get up,' he said as he sat down beside me. 'I am sorry we have to keep you down here but I have to comply with the court order.'

I said nothing and he continued, 'Mary has been in and told us that you have an appointment at the hospital tomorrow?'

'I have,' I replied.

'We are making arrangements to take you and Mary is insisting that she comes as well to make sure you are properly looked after. I spoke to Joelle last night and she says she has more evidence that will help prove you are not involved with this business. I don't know what she has got, she says she can't tell me over the phone, but she is trying to get back before the extradition hearing. It's going to be tight though as she can't get a plane out until tomorrow. Is there anything I can get you?'

'A more comfortable cell and something to read would be nice,' I replied.

Chapter 75

Douglas Jay; Thursday, 18th December

At quarter to ten this morning my suitcase was brought to me and I was invited to wear my own clothes for the extradition hearing. I chose a plain light blue shirt and cream cotton slacks.

At ten I was handcuffed to a PC and escorted to a police car and driven across the road to the island's courthouse and taken to an anteroom, where I was guarded by two police officers, while I waited to be taken into court for proceedings to begin.

I was very tense and anxious.

Promptly at 11.00am the handcuffs were removed and I was shown into the court. The courtroom had recently been refurbished and had plain white walls. The Judge sat at a table on a raised floor at one end of the room. The attorneys sat at tables in the middle of the room and public sat in seats behind them separated by a wood barrier. The dock was beneath and to one side of the Judge, while the witnesses had a table beneath and to the other side. I noticed there was a metal cage affair hidden above the dock, which I guess could be lowered when required. Fortunately someone had decided I did not require it. David Rail, my attorney, sat at his table, and the two attorneys representing the US DEA sat at their table. I saw Merv and Mary and DI Strange sitting in the public gallery.

Joelle was not in court.

The Judge walked in through a door behind his table, sat down, and announced that this was not a trial but a hearing of an extradition order and that he alone would deliver the judgment.

The senior attorney representing the US DEA, who I later deduced was Mr. Justin Cramp of a partnership bearing the same name, stood up and addressed the Judge. 'Your Honour, we apologise for the urgency here but time is of the essence in capturing the organisers of this drug smuggling gang. Detective Choizi has flight reservations to escort this prisoner back to the United States this afternoon and as the overwhelming evidence against this man was presented to the court with extradition papers. We submit that it is not necessary to go through all the evidence again and request that you grant the order now and save us all time and money.'

I was horrified but relieved what the Judge said, 'I decide proceedings in my court, not you, or detective Choizi, and I will not be rushed in my deliberations.' He turned to my attorney, 'What do you say?'

'The defense was not aware that an evidence file had already been submitted. We have here the Kaeta Island Police evidence file, which I note is considerable thicker than the evidence file on the desk there.'

The Judge halted proceedings for an hour to allow my attorney to read and consider the evidence file.

On resuming, he addressed my attorney first. 'Mr. Rail, is it necessary to go through the evidence in detail. My Lord the evidence file presented is light on factual evidence and makes a number of assumptions which are contradicted by the detailed evidence in the police files.'

'Please explain as briefly as you can,' the Judge instructed.

I was looking round the court and had seen Tony Choizi

sitting alone in the corner, but Joelle was still missing.

David looked at his note pad and started. 'First, the evidence file stated that the suspect was apprehended entering the country carrying the camera bag which contained drugs. The police file states clearly that the bags were searched but no drugs found. The police files also refer to a second camera bag found later hidden on the aircraft, which is not mentioned in the evidence files.

'Next, the evidence files state that traces of ketamine powder were found on the wrapping paper used to package the drugs for delivery. The local police sent the paper for forensic examination and that report shows no trace of any substance. Furthermore, the police subsequently discovered that the suspect packages did not contain drugs at all but sales brochures which Mr. Jay had been asked to deliver.'

David Rail continued to pull holes in the US DEA evidence files and concluded his argument by referring to the drugs found in my safe. 'The evidence file simply states that a quantity of drugs was found in the suspect's safe but offers no rational explanation for there being there. We know Mr. Jay is not a drug user himself so they are not for personal use. If Mr. Jay had delivered the drugs why would he hold back such a minuscule quantity? And why leave it openly in the safe anyway?'

The Judge asked the other attorneys if they wished to comment. After a tirade about David Rail simply trying to confuse and obfuscate the facts, they started to try and pick holes in his arguments.

'The brown paper wrapping was subject to sophisticated forensic testing in the United States where the traces of ketamine were found. It is not our job here to speculate on why Mr. Jay retained drugs in his safe; the fact that he did, combined with the other evidence against him is sufficient to prove his guilt.'

The Judge turned to David Rail and asked him if he had anything further to say.

'Your Honour,' he said, 'I would like it recorded that this extradition has been pursued by my learned colleague on the other table with undue haste, and the Kaeta Island Police have not had time to complete their investigations.'

Justin Cramp rose to say something but the Judge silenced him by saying, 'I shall start my summing up before we break for lunch and I shall consider my conclusion over lunch.'

He started his summing up by running through the documentation requirements to support a successful extradition request and noted that those requirements had been met. He then went through the reasons why an extradition order may not be approved by this court.

The final reason he listed was, 'If the person is not in fact a fugitive then the extradition will be refused. In this case this is the key point I must reflect upon. Both sides have presented a great deal of circumstantial evidence, some of which is contradictory. We have one actual event, and only one event directly connected with illegal drugs, and that is the presence of a packet of drugs in the bedroom safe of Mr. Jay. His defence team have implied that these drugs may have been deliberately placed there by a third party to incriminate Mr. Jay, but have produced no proof to this effect. I must give this evidence some weight in my deliberations.'

He paused and glared round the court. No one spoke and he continued, 'We will adjourn for a late lunch and reconvene at 2.30 this afternoon.'

Justin Cramp stood up and said, 'Your Honour, such a late start will mean Mr. Choizi will miss his plane.'

His Honour muttered as he walked out, 'He will have to get a later one then.'

Chapter 76

The day of the extradition hearing, I arrived at the airport in Barbados with a good hour to spare, thinking that if everything ran on time I should just make it to the hearing in time.

Ten minutes before take-off the indicator board was still reading 'wait in lounge' and I was beginning to worry. Ten minutes after take-off time I went to find someone who could tell me what was going on. I was told there was a technical problem with the aircraft that was being rectified and we would be boarding shortly.

I called Bernie to let him know what was going on. He was not available so I left a message for him. All I could do was sit and fret that I might be too late and the hearing would be over by the time I got back to Kaeta.

Some two hours later the flight was called, and the aircraft actually took off two and half hours late, and eventually we landed on Kaeta Island just under two and half hours late. I used my police pass to get through immigration quickly and tried to call Bernie but his mobile was off. I was close to panic as I drove from the airport into town. What if the hearing had finished before I got to the court?

I left my car at the police station and ran across road

clutching my briefcase with my evidence reports inside. Luckily I found Bernie inside the courthouse talking earnestly to a man in a suit.

Breathlessly, I asked Bernie if the hearing was finished.

'Not quite yet, we have just adjourned for lunch. Let me introduce you two.'

I shook David Rail's hand and Bernie asked me if I have had got anything.

'Yes,' I said, 'but it is a bit difficult to explain. Can we go somewhere private and I will show you?'

David showed us into a small anteroom. I took the two copies of the evidence files I had prepared for the court and put one each before Bernie and David. I had added a front sheet to each file. They both paused as they read the front page and looked questioningly at me.

I explained, 'It has to be like this because the Dutch have an undercover agent deep inside one of the supply point of the ketamine tablets. That in itself is secret and Dutch have not even told the Americans about her. Also, Willam believes that there may be an informer somewhere in the investigation team. He will not go into writing as he has no proof but that is why he wants this to remain secret.'

David asked the obvious question, 'If he is so secretive why has he shared this with you?'

'Because most of the information in that file came from my work at Heathrow this last week, when I went there to find further evidence in this Douglas Jay investigation. I threatened to go public with my information unless he allowed me to use this to prove Douglas is not the drug courier.'

They read the file, twice. First Bernie congratulated me and told me it was excellent work.

David said, 'This should get the extradition request dismissed if the Judge allows me up to present it. He won't like though. If he will not review this I will tell him that we intend to lodge an immediate appeal and try to halt the extradition that way.'

The court reconvened promptly at 2.30pm. The Judge looked questioningly at me sitting with Bernie and David Rail.

Douglas was looking at me as if he was trying to read my mind. I noticed his arm was in plaster and he looked pained. He was very thin and his clothes looked one size too big for him. He had the same grey pallor I had seen that very first time when I was sent to the airport to interview him.

Before the Judge could speak, David stood up. 'Your Honour, please could I approach the bench and speak with you privately for a moment?'

'Is this to do with the presence of that young lady on your table?'

'Yes, Your Honour.'

Permission was granted and David went up to the Judge with a copy of my report. There was absolute silence as everyone in the room tried to hear what David was whispering. The Judge picked up my file and said, 'Court is adjourned for fifteen minutes,' and he and David walked into his private chamber.

Justin Cramp and his junior immediately demanded that Bernie tell them what was going on.

'Can't say,' he replied.

'Who is that?' they asked, looking at me.

'My sergeant.'

'What is she doing here?'

'Can't say.'

The attorneys sat at their table fuming, muttering that this delay was intolerable

After five minutes David came out and told me the Judge wanted to talk to me in his chambers. This raised Cramp's anger level to the point of explosion.

David asked me to inform the Judge why it was so important that this information remain secret. I went through the explanation again.

When I had finished he looked at his watch and said, 'It is about 6.00pm in Amsterdam.'

He asked me to give his secretary Willam Inces's phone number and she put a call through. Luckily Willam answered the phone.

The Judge explained who he was and that he needed to verify what I told him. It was a brief call, and when he hung up the Judge sat silently in thought. His secretary interrupted him and gave him a note. He read it and smiled.

'The US DEA attorneys want know what is going on and are demanding to see me. Come, let us return to the courtroom.'

When we were all seated again, the Judge announced that the hearing would proceed to review new evidence.

There was a brief uproar which the Judge silenced, and then he asked which of the Cramp attorneys was the senior. The older man stood up, saying he was Justin Cramp and the Judge addressed him. 'You, me and Mr. Rail will retire to my chambers. Sergeant,' he looked at me, 'you will join us in case either of these two gentlemen wish to question you. The court will hear this evidence in camera. You will all remain in the courtroom until we return.'

As the four of us left the court pandemonium broke out, with everyone demanding to know what was going on. Douglas sat in silence watching me walk out of the room and I wondered what was going through his mind.

Chapter 77

Douglas Jay; Friday 19th December

I had watched Joelle leave the courtroom the previous afternoon with my emotions in turmoil; a mixture of anxiety, worry and perhaps a hint of optimism. I still was not entirely certain of Joelle's motives but I knew she was my only hope and I had to trust her to help me.

I had spent a stressful hour at lunchtime thinking about the morning's evidence. I had thought David had made progress as he went through the omissions in the DEA attorneys' evidence but then the Judge in his summing up seemed to dismiss a lot of the points made by David and fixed on the drugs found in my safe. I knew they had been planted by someone, but I had no idea who, and no one had asked me about the drugs. I had just sat silently through the morning's procedures. During that hour I had more or less convinced myself that the Judge was going to rule in favour of the extradition.

Things now, however, seemed to be changing. No one knew what was going on. Everyone, except DCI Shrewd and myself, was talking and asking if anyone knew what was happening. The remaining Cramp attorney and Tony Choizi were deep in conversation and looking concerned.

After about an hour the Judge and the other three returned, silently taking their seats. Justin Cramp looked sombre while Joelle was looking jubilant. The Judge wore no expression and, even though everyone in the room was silently attentive to him, he called the court to order, saying, 'I apologise to the court for keeping you waiting and for the unusual procedures I have taken during this review.' He looked round the room before continuing, 'Further to my comments prior to the lunch break I must inform you that the Kaeta Island Police have produced new and compelling evidence which, although it was presented to the court very late in the proceedings, it is of such significance that I felt obliged to review it, and take account of it.

'I am not a liberty to disclose and share that evidence in open court and I order that the file containing that evidence to marked and held "Most Secret". Furthermore any person revealing any information contained in that file will be held in contempt of this court and so charged and arrested.'

The Judge paused and allowed the general murmur of surprise to subside before continuing.

'I have considered all the evidence presented to this court and I find that evidence insufficient to establish Mr. Jay's involvement in this affair. Indeed were this a trial I would dismiss the case on the basis of lack of evidence, and order Mr. Jay's release.'

A wave of noise broke out through the court, mostly from the junior Cramp and Tony Choizi. Justin Cramp then looked stonily silent, but his junior jumped up and demanded to know what was going on. The Judge called for order and told the attorney to sit down or he would hold him in contempt.

He then continued with his judgement. 'Accordingly, I find the person in question is not a fugitive and the extradition order is denied. I shall inform the prosecutor of my decision and no doubt the police will consider whether they wish to pursue the charge against Mr. Jay.' He dismissed the court and walked out of the room.

I was ushered out of a side door where Joelle and DCI Shrewd met me and hurried me out through a back door and into the same Suzuki Escudo I had ridden in when I arrived on the island.

There was a lot of noise going on in front of the courthouse and Joelle had some difficulty negotiating through the crowd.

I never even got into the police station, as when we got into the police car park DCI Shrewd helped me out of the car and said, 'I am releasing you into Sergeant de Nouvelas's custody.'

Joelle hurried me across to her car and drove away. The whole transition from the court to Joelle's car had taken less that ten minutes and I felt dazed.

'Where are we going?' I asked Joelle.

'Home,' she replied.

'Am I free?' I queried.

'Not quite yet but I expect you will be by the time I get you home.'

We drove on in silence until I asked, 'Can you tell me what is going on?'

'I can't tell you at the moment,' Joelle replied, 'but when we get home I will tell you what I can.'

When we got back to Joelle's home, Windrush, she first phoned Mary at the Glass Bar to tell her and Jasmine what had happened. No sooner had she hung up, than her mobile rang.

'That was Bernie,' she told me. 'The prosecutor has agreed not to pursue any charges so you are free and it's all over.'

'Thank God,' I said, 'and I probably need to thank you

as well. Please tell me everything that has happened.'

We opened a bottle of wine and Joelle started to prepare a meal, and while she cooked she gave me a very edited summary of what she had done in London. She explained that it was connected with a much larger operation than just the smuggling on this island, and for that reason a lot of what was in that court file had to remain secret.

'I bet Tony Choizi is doing his pieces now,' she gloated.

'I thought you and he were friends,' I paused, 'or even more, he led me to believe.'

'Absolutely not,' Joelle replied. 'I loathe the man, he is just a disgusting letch.'

'But I saw you together in at the hotel.'

'What you saw was him making a clumsy pass at me. When I told you that I was working that night it was true. I was sent to the hotel to brief him on the surveillance operation we were running. He had just arrived that afternoon from the USA.'

'But wouldn't you do that in the police station – not at a hotel in the evening?'

'Normally, yes but I was out on another investigation that day and I did not get back until the evening, and after he had left for the hotel. He insisted that he wanted to talk to me and left instructions for me to meet him at the hotel.'

'I see,' I said, not quite sure what to say next, so Joelle continued.

'Honestly, Douglas, there is nothing going on between Tony and me and there never has been. He is a nasty person and I hope I never see him again.'

I did not know what to say but I think my pleasure must have shown.

Then Joelle challenged me. 'While we are clearing the air between us,' she said, 'what about you and that Jean Handley woman from the hotel?'

'Oh, that was nothing. She was on holiday here for a week and we just went to the hotel dance together a couple of times.'

It looked more than that to me,' Joelle grunted accusingly.

'Well, one thing led to another, but really, she was not my type and when I realised she was getting serious I tried to let her down gently without spoiling her holiday.'

'That was very gallant of you,' Joelle said jealously.

I repeated her words, 'Honestly, Joelle there is nothing between Jean and I. I told you she is not my type at all.'

'Have you decided if you have found your type yet?'

'Yes, I think I have.'

Joelle blushed and bustled around her cooking.

We were silent for a while and then Joelle said, 'I must tell you about the best bit. When we went to the Judge's chambers this afternoon, the attorney was jumping up and down and telling the Judge he could not operate like this and he could not be silenced in this manner. The Judge said he could and would and threatened him, saying, "If you tell anyone then I will arrest you for contempt and at the same time an arrest warrant will be issued in Holland and you will be extradited to Holland to face charges there." The attorney told him he could not do that and the Judge said, "Try me and see."'

We ate dinner and finished the wine and I fell asleep in a chair. Joelle woke me and sent me to bed.

I slept in late again this morning and raised voices downstairs woke me. This time I could hear Joelle's voice but not quite what she was saying. I experienced a strong sense of déjà vu as Mary knocked on the door and said, 'You had better get dressed Douglas. The police are downstairs to see you again.'

Once again, Shrewd was there with Isaac. He cautioned me and very apologetically arrested me again. Joelle insisted on coming with us to the police station.

Chapter 78

Joelle de Nouvelas; Friday 19th December

Bernie put Douglas in the back seat of the police car and I got in next to him before Bernie could say anything. Isaac drove and Bernie sat in the front passenger seat.

We moved off in silence and it was Douglas who spoke first. 'Please, can someone tell me what is going on? What am I supposed to have done now?'

I put my hand up to stop Douglas from saying any more but repeated his question.

'Yes Bernie, what is going on?'

'Late yesterday evening, in fact just before the courts closed, the US DEA, lodged an appeal against the decision to deny the Extradition Order on the grounds that the decision was not legally sound and that the additional evidence presented late deliberately omitted a witness statement that directly connected Mr. Jay with the drug distribution ring.'

Joelle and I looked at each other in horror and I blurted out, 'That's impossible!'

Joelle asked, 'What witness and where did this so-called statement come from?'

'I don't know yet. We were told that the statement would be presented to the court this morning.'

I whispered to Douglas, 'Say nothing and ask for your attorney when you get to the police station. I will try and sort this out.'

When we arrived at the police station Douglas was led away by the duty sergeant and I went upstairs with Bernie. Tony Choizi was sitting in Bernie's chair looking smug.

'Arrested the villain then?' he asked.

We ignored him and Bernie asked him what he wanted.

'Just making sure that our drugs lord is safely behind bars,' he replied, as he turned and addressed me with one of his leers. 'Unfortunately the appeal process apparently will take some time to organise, so, Joelle, you have the pleasure of my company for a while yet.'

I turned and walked out of the office.

Shortly after, while I was talking with Merv, Tony walked out and stopped by me desk. 'I will be staying at the Hotel Glass Bay – come over and have a drink with me anytime.' He walked off.

'Will you?' Merv asked.

'You are joking!' I continued before he could answer, 'Tell me what has happened here while I was away.'

'That woman you identified boarding the plane, Elizabeth Bruce.'

'That was not her real name,' I commented.

'Yes well, we identified her arriving at the airport. She had no camera bag with her, just a wheelie-bag and wrote on her immigration form that she was staying at the Atlantic Lodge Hotel. I went over there to check but they had no reservation for anyone by the name of Elizabeth Bruce. I showed the picture around but no one recognised her. It would appear that she did not go to that hotel. I also checked the passenger manifest for the returning flight a week later and her name was not on the list, and we looked at the CCTV pictures of the departing passengers but we could not see her.'

'I don't suppose we will find her now,' I said, hoping that Willam Ince would have more luck.

Merv then said, 'You asked me about the prints on the hacksaw blade.' He went to the evidence table, which had not yet been cleared, and picked up the hacksaw and the photograph and brought them over to me. 'As you thought there are a number of prints on the photograph. I have identified yours, mine, and Bernie's but there is this one here that we can't identify. I compared it to the smudged print on hacksaw but there is just not enough of a clear print to make any comparison. Also if you look carefully at the handle it is quite clear that the handle has been wiped, but because this thumb print is right down near the blade it had only been smudged and not completely removed, but it was obviously made by whoever used the saw for cutting.' He held his hand as if to cut with the saw to demonstrate.

The WPC from downstairs walked into the room and asked for someone to assist with the questioning of the prisoner. I thought for a minute that she meant Douglas as she said, 'It's another drugs bust. This one's name is Zachariah Farthing.'

I looked up with interest and said I would do the interview. *Zachariah*, I thought, *Zach, could it be?* 'Give me a few moments and I will come down,' I said.

On his mobile, I rang Denzel who was on surveillance duty at Zach's sister's house in Grumble. 'Denzel, have you seen Zach this morning?'

'No, not so far, but that's not unusual, he spends half the night drinking beer and he does not get up till about lunch time.'

'Go down and knock on the door and see if he still there.'

'I can't. My instructions are just watch, stay out of sight and report what he does.'

'Denzel, I am instructing you to go and see if he still there.'

Denzel grumbled, 'That American detective won't like it, he was here yesterday and told me make sure I was not seen.'

'Denzel, I take responsibility, just do as I say.'

As he walked down to the house he told me, 'There was a bit of excitement here this morning. Apparently someone stole a motor yacht from the marina last night.'

I heard him knock on the door and a woman's voice ask what he wanted. He asked for Zach and I heard the woman then ask who wanted to know. Denzel informed her he was the police and I heard the woman say, 'No, he left last night.'

I did not wait for Denzel, I just hung up and rushed downstairs to interview Zachariah Farthing.

Chapter 79

The custody PC handed me a slim arrest file as I walked into the custody suite and entered the interview room where Zachariah Farthing was sitting with the WPC.

I introduced myself and then slowly read the file. There was not much in it. The coastguard had received a report of a motor yacht drifting about half a mile off St Martin's Point and had gone out to investigate. As they approached the boat they identified it as the one that had been stolen. Zach was the only person aboard and he told them was delivering the boat for the owner. They searched the boat and found it had run out of petrol. They searched Zach and found six ketamine tablets.

I was with him for about an hour but he stuck to the story that he was delivering the motor yacht to St Martin's for the owner and had run out of fuel, and the tablets had been given to him by a friend for his personal use. He did not know the name of the friend and flatly denied he had ever worked at the Zip Line. I finished the interview. Zach was taken back to his cell and I told the WPC to check the story with the motor yacht owner.

When I went back upstairs Bernie called me into his office and handed me a couple of photocopied sheets of paper. 'David Rail just got these from the court,' he told me, as I started to read.

The first one was signed by Tony Choizi and witnessed by one of the attorneys.

It went through a preamble about this statement being true and then told us that Tony had visited the suspect Zip Line operator on the Wednesday 16th December as he was concerned that the local police had not arrested and questioned him.

I looked at Bernie and asked, 'I don't suppose you have in writing his instruction to only watch Zach?'

'No,' said Bernie grimly. 'It was all verbal over the phone.'

I continued reading but all Tony's statement told me was that he had questioned Zach at his sister's house in Grumble, where Zach admitted that he was the contact at the Zip Line for the drugs operation, and he was hiding at his sister's house, fearing arrest once he realised that the police were on to the drug smuggling operation.

Zach's statement, dated the same day, was written in the same hand as Tony's statement but signed by Zach and witnessed by Tony.

It said that Zach had made this statement of his own free will and that it was all true. He admitted that he was the contact at the Zip Line. His job was to collect the drugs from the carriers and take them to the storeroom, where the individual shipments were consolidated until there was a large enough quantity to smuggle them out by motorboat. He did not know where they went. He was contacted by text and told where to deliver the consolidated shipment. He identified Douglas Jay, not as one of the drug carriers, but said he was more important than that. Zach said Douglas told him he was visiting the island to check that the drug smuggling and storage was operating well and that as far as he, Zach, was aware, Douglas was one of the bosses.'

'I don't believe this for a second,' I told Bernie. 'Tony has written this out and got Zach to sign it.'

'You might be right but it will be difficult to prove it,' said Bernie. 'In one stroke they have made all the circumstantial evidence irrelevant and can now rely on that statement and the drugs in Douglas's room to prove guilt.'

'Unless we can prove that Zach's statement is a lie,' I said.

Bernie replied, 'That won't be easy, you are talking about another policeman here, and you will need a lot of evidence to cast any doubts on the validity of these statements.'

'Unless Zach retracts and makes a statement that he made the first confession under duress.'

'Even that won't be enough. Choizi's attorneys will say that we got the retraction under duress. You can be sure they will have thought of that angle.'

I left Bernie wondering what to do. I took a walk around the cathedral grounds and hatched a plan. First I needed a private word with Zach.

I told the custody PC I needed to talk with Zach off the record. I should not really do this, he cautioned, but let me into Zach's cell anyway.

'Right Zach,' I said. 'This conversation is off the record and I want you tell me what really happened.'

'I have told you,' he said.

'Don't take me for a fool. We can easily check out your story and have you identified, so come on, tell me what is going on. I have seen the statement made to the American detective and we both know it is a pack of lies.'

I have come across people like Zach before. They are not particularly clever but have a good sense of self-preservation, and a good threat is usually enough to get them to see sense, so I said to Zach, 'I don't know how the American got you to sign that statement, but if you don't tell me the truth I will see that you go down with Douglas Jay and get extradited to America with him. If you tell me the truth now we will only charge you with the theft of the yacht and possession of drugs for personal use. You have no previous convictions so you will probably get off with a fine and a suspended sentence. Your choice.'

Zach started talking. 'He said he would help me escape if I signed the statement. He said that not only were the local police after me but the drug gang was as well for taking some of the drugs and that they would kill me when they found me. He said if I could get to Bermuda he would see I was looked after.'

I encouraged Zach to talk further. 'He was lying. He would have arrested you as soon as you appeared and he does not know any more about the drug gang than we do, and we have no reason to think they are after you.'

Zach thought about this and started to say, 'Okay, I will tell you. The American came to see me yesterday afternoon and threatened me like I said, and I agreed to sign that statement when he promised to look after me in Bermuda. The first bit about what I did at the Zip Line is more or less true but the bit about Douglas Jay was what he told me to say. He wrote the statement and made me sign it, then he signed it. He told me to wait until the middle of the night then steal to boat and get away. It was just bad luck the one I picked had no fuel.'

'Did you know who Douglas Jay was? Had you ever seen him before?' I asked, and added, 'and why did you date the statement for Wednesday?'

Zach replied, 'I might have seen him, I saw a lot of people at the Zip Line, but I don't remember him and how would I know who he was? The American dated the statement, not me.'

I got Zach taken up to an interview room and called

the WPC to join us. I told her that Zach wished to make a statement and invited Zach to repeat what he just told me. When he had finished I gave him some paper and a pen and asked him to write it all down. This he did in round childlike, but very legible handwriting. When he finished he signed the statement and I asked the WPC to witness and date it. I then took the statement away and told the WPC to return Zach to his cell.

'What about your promise?' he queried.

'Don't worry,' I said, 'you will stay here on the island.'

It was quite late in the afternoon before I got back upstairs. I sat at my desk and thought through my next move. I looked at the thumbprint on the hacksaw handle and compared it with the unidentified print on the picture. Merv was right, they might possibly match but the print on the handle was so smudged it was impossible to tell.

Bernie came out of his office and spoke to me. 'Where have you been all afternoon? Tony came into the station again to tell me that Zach had disappeared and that we employed monkeys who could not guard a peanut in a cage. "Good job I got the statement before he disappeared," was his parting shot.'

I don't think I had ever seen Bernie quite so irritated before so I asked him if he would like some good news.

'Go on,' said Bernie. 'Make my day!'

'Zach has not disappeared. In fact he is in a cell downstairs and I am just about to charge him with theft of a motor yacht and possession of illegal substances.'

I did not tell him about the statement sitting on my desk, which I was about to photocopy for the next step in my plan.

Chapter 80

Douglas Jay; Friday 19th December

I could not believe what was happening. I was arrested again.

I remember asking what was going on but Joelle indicated I should be quiet and she took over. I was glad she had come with us and sat next to me, holding my hand; that gave me some comfort as I sat in the car. I was beginning to feel quite confused and physically sick. I don't much remember that journey, and only vaguely recollect arriving at the police station and being charged with drug offences again, and taken down to a cell. It was hot and stuffy in that cell and I lay on the bunk and must have gone to sleep.

I don't know what time I woke up, but I did feel better and my head was a lot clearer.

I tried to remember what DI Shrewd had said in the car, but it had gone, and all I could remember was that I had been charged with another drug-related offence. I wondered what would happen next. I wondered what Joelle was doing now. *I hope she is trying to get this sorted out*, I thought. I thought about last night and what we had said to each other and reflected that if this business ever ended and I was not in prison, we might actually get together. But I then sank back in despair, wondering what was going on and what would happen to me. My only comfort now was Joelle, and I thought, *if I go to prison I wonder if she will wait for me.*

After lunch I was taken up to an interview room where David Rail and DI Strange were waiting with another PC.

Strange asked me how I felt and if I understood what had happened.

I said I was OK, but had no idea what was going on. He explained that the Extradition Order was to be reheard, at a date yet to be agreed, probably after Christmas.

I asked to see Joelle and was told that she was not available at the moment.

Then Strange asked, 'What do you know about a statement that you visited the island to check on the distribution network here?'

'Absolutely nothing, except that it is a lie. I have nothing to do with drugs and I have told you before that I am just on holiday here.'

'The American detective has a signed witness statement implicating you.'

I repeated, 'It is a lie.'

Strange asked a few more questions, to which David replied, 'My client has nothing further to add to what he has just told you.'

When the interview finished David said he was going to apply for bail. Strange nodded and said he would not object.

I was taken back to the cell, where I sat on my bunk with my head in my hands feeling very low. Later in the afternoon Joelle found me like that, and sat next to me, putting her arm round my shoulders and giving me a little hug. She released me, saying, 'Don't worry, I have plan but I must go before the shops shut.'

Not long after she had left DI Strange walked into the cell and gave me my shoelaces.

'Come on,' he said, 'David Rail has managed to get a bail hearing this afternoon. We are due in court in ten minutes. You won't try to run away will you?'

'No,' I assured him. He did not bother with handcuffs and told me it would be quicker to walk.

As we crossed the road he said, 'Douglas, I am really sorry you are being put through all this again. I can't find Joelle, I thought she would want to come to the hearing with us but she has disappeared again.'

'She just came to see me and said she wanted to get to the shops before they closed,' I told him.

He looked surprised and said, 'I wonder what she is up to now?'

We entered the courtroom just seconds before the Judge walked in. David Rail was at his table and the Cramp junior at his. It was the same Judge who had heard the extradition application the previous day.

The Judge cut the preamble and said, 'David Rail has applied to bail Mr. Jay. Has anyone here any objections?'

The Cramp junior got to his feet, saying, 'We object, Your Honour. The prisoner is a foreign national and will almost certainly abscond to escape justice.'

His Honour asked DI Shrewd, 'Do the police hold Mr. Jay's passport?'

'Yes, Your Honour.'

The Cramp junior stood again and said, 'A man with Mr. Jay's underworld drug connections will have illegitimate ways of leaving the island, Your Honour. I must insist he is held in custody.'

The Judge addressed him sternly. 'Sir, you will withdraw that remark. In my court we presume innocence until guilt is proved, and if you insist on insisting I will arrest you for contempt.'

The Cramp junior was suitably silenced and humbled. The Judge addressed DCI Shrewd again. 'Do the police have any objections to bail being granted?'

'No, Your Honour.'

'In that case I shall grant conditional bail. The prisoner will surrender his passport, he will reside at an address on the island to be advised to the police and he will report daily to the police station in Kaeta Town. Surety is set at $50,000. If Mr. Jay does not have that much money available on the island I will accept surety posted by an appropriate resident of the island.'

The Judge turned to me and asked, 'Do you have a residential address on the island and do you have available $50,000?'

I did not like to give Joelle and her Mary's address without asking them first and I certainly had not got $50,000 available on the island so I answered, 'No Sir.'

'You will therefore remain in police custody until you can find an address and raise the surety.' He adjourned the court.

David Rail, DCI Shrewd and I walked back to the police station together. Shrewd said to me, 'Don't worry we will get you out of the cell just as soon as I can track down Sergeant de Nouvelas. The Judge only ordered you to be kept in police custody, not jail, so I can release you now into Joelle's custody.'

'Thank you,' I said. I had a growing respect for DCI Shrewd. He seemed a fair and reasonable man. My only problem was that Joelle had disappeared and no one knew where, so I was heading back to a cell.

Chapter 81

Joelle de Nouvelas; Friday evening,
19th December

I left the police station early and on my way out went down to see Douglas. He was looking very miserable, and I would have liked to spend a little more time with him, but I wanted to get to the shopping mall with the chandlers and hardware shop before it closed. When I got to the shop I went straight to the DIY tools section and, I was right, this was the shop that sold the hacksaws with the yellow handles. I picked one up and went to the till to pay, and asked the assistant if they sole many of these little saws.

'Quite a few,' he told me.

'Can you remember a customer who bought one of these two or three weeks ago, a fat American?'

'You must be joking, I can't remember the last customer let alone two or three weeks ago.'

Never mind, I thought, *it was a bit of a long shot*. I headed for home.

The first thing I did was to write out some notes for my private evidence file. I did not think I was in any real danger but as a precaution I had told Mary about the file and said that should anything happen to me she should give the file to Bernie Strange.

I had a shower and considered whether to wear my hair up in a bun but decided against that. I carefully put make-up on, and then went to the wardrobe. I selected a body hugging, low cut, white blouse and tight black trousers, and a pair of black high-heeled shoes. I looked at myself in the long mirror and thought, *Nice, this should do the trick, but I need one last thing.* Out of my jewellery box I selected a gold chain and locket that my father had given me. It hung very satisfactorily on my chest, drawing the eye to my cleavage. I thought guiltily of Douglas sitting miserably in his cell while I was getting all dressed up for another man.

It was time to go. I checked I had everything in my black leather shoulder bag and walked out to the Toyota. I was heading for Hotel Glass Bay and as I drove I thought about the times I had driven this road last month, ostensibly to see what Douglas was up to, but secretly I had quite enjoyed meeting him.

I got to the hotel and first went into the ladies to change my trainers for the high heels. That done, I headed for the beach bar. He was there, sitting at a table overlooking the beach, beer in hand, just as he said he would be. He looked surprised as I walked over to him. I noticed he could not keep his eyes off me. *Good*, I thought; I wanted to distract him and put him off guard.

'Joelle.' He tried to stand up, but not being the most graceful of men managed to get stuck between his chair and the table. When he had extricated himself he caught my arm and gave me a kiss on the cheek and invited me to sit down.

'How nice to see you, can I get you a drink?'

'A Setting Sun cocktail please.' I knew that was only a small champagne with orange juice, and not too alcoholic, as I wanted to stay reasonably sober for the evening ahead. He brought the drink over and sat down opposite me, unable to keep his eyes off my chest.

'I must admit I am surprised to see you, I did not think you would take up my offer so soon, but good, you have and we should have a real good evening. You will be joining me for dinner I hope?'

Avoiding that invitation I said, 'Let's just talk for a bit first.'

'Sure, what would like to talk about? Did I tell you about this apartment I am looking at in Bermuda? Hey, if I get it you should come over and stay, that's a great idea.'

'No, you did not tell me, and we should get to know where we stand with each other before we start making plans.' I could see his mind was racing now, wondering where this was going.

Time to start my play, I thought. 'Tony, I want you drop these charges against Douglas Jay and let him go. You know as well as I, that he is innocent.'

'If I do that what is in it for me, are you going to persuade me?'

I could read in his look and exactly what sort of persuasion he had in mind so, thinking, *I am going to enjoy this*, I said, 'Yes, that is exactly what I am going to do.'

'And what did you have in mind?' He was getting excited now, thinking of the possibilities, so I reached into my bag and pulled out the hacksaw and put it on the table in front of him, saying, 'This.'

He looked at it with surprise and this told me exactly what I wanted to know. He recovered his composure quickly and said, 'Are you a sadomasochistic or something, because that's fine with me, honey.'

'No, this is the saw that was used to cut the cable on Douglas's motorbike which caused the accident which nearly killed him. We are looking for the person who did that to charge him with attempted murder.'

He shrugged, saying, 'Don't know what you talking about. Nothing to do with me.'

'I found this saw thrown into the bushes near where Douglas parked his bike. It was not very clever throwing it away like that.' I waited for a response but Tony said nothing. I carried on, 'The murderer wiped the handle clean but in his haste he missed a thumb print here, right at the base of the handle, and I have identified that thumb print. It is yours.'

Tony was not leering at me now. His eyes had narrowed to slits and his mouth assumed a nasty sneer. 'I don't know what you are talking about,' he said as he picked the hacksaw up and threw it into the sea.

'There, what are going to do now, you have lost your evidence.'

'Yes,' I replied, 'I want you drop the charges against Douglas, go home and never come back here again.'

'Can't do that,' he said, smiling now, 'I have a witness statement saying he is involved in the drug ring, one of the bosses actually, and you can't get to the witness because he has disappeared.'

'Tony, you are a stupid man. Do you really think I would come down here and threaten you, without sorting out all the loose ends and organising backup?'

Tony looked round warily, I had him rattled now.

'Zach is safely tucked away in the cells at in Kaeta Town Police Station and has made a statement withdrawing the confession given to you, and saying you coerced him into making a false statement.'

I put the copy of Zach's statement on the table. Tony picked it up, went pale and tore it up.

'That was only a copy – I have the original safely locked away. Oh, and by the way, that saw you threw away

I bought this afternoon; the actual saw you used is safely locked away in the evidence room.'

Tony scowled at me and started to swear, calling me a bitch, amongst other names. I interrupted him and said, 'You have two choices. Arrange for all the charges against Douglas to be dropped and the appeal withdrawn or I will arrest you for attempted murder and perverting the course of justice, and have a good dig into all your other activities and see what we can find. And don't think you can just disappear. If the charges against Douglas are not dropped by Monday lunch time all this evidence will go to the court and Douglas will be released and a warrant issued for your arrest.'

Tony looked really ugly now as he rose, telling me I was fitting him up and had not seen the last of him, and then walking out of the room. I was banking on him not working out the flaw in my threat; why give him the opportunity to escape, why not simply arrest him now?

Chapter 82

Joelle de Nouvelas; Monday, 22nd December

It is Monday morning and I am sitting at my desk in the police station. This morning should be when I find out if my threat to Tony Choizi worked.

After Tony walked out of the bar last Friday I did not see him again. I left the bar and went to my car as soon as Tony was out of sight. I sat in the car and started to shake and I realised how tense I had been; I had to sit for a few minutes to recover before I was able to drive. I wanted to be with Mary and Jasmine and I headed for Glass Bar. As I arrived there I suddenly had a wild thought that Tony might be there, but he was not.

Jasmine looked at me as I walked in and asked, 'Where have you been mother, all dressed up like that?'

'I had a bit of police work I needed to finish off.'

'What, dressed like that?'

'Yes, I had to meet someone and I needed to impress.'

Jasmine looked quizzical and said, 'Well, you are certainly dressed to impress.'

Mary walked out of the kitchen. She did not say anything, just gave me one of her old fashioned looks. I got a drink and sat with Mary and Jasmine and they told me what sort of day they had. Jasmine and I went home early that Friday evening and as we walked out Sean called across, 'Joelle, the police station are looking for you, I took a message; can you call in as soon as possible?' I did not feel I could face another problem that evening. *I will call in the morning,* I decided.

Next morning I realised I had turned my phone off and left it in the car. I went to retrieve it and immediately it rang, with messages from Friday evening: three from Bernie, one from the police station and one from David Rail. Essentially they were all the same, telling me to contact Bernie urgently. I was about to phone him when he rang me. 'Joelle, where have you been? You disappeared yesterday and no one knew where you were.'

'I had some personal business I had to sort out,' I explained.

'Well it does not matter now. Douglas Jay was granted bailed yesterday, and I want to release him into your custody while he sorts out his bail conditions. Can you meet me in the police station, say in half an hour?'

I agreed. When I got to the police station Bernie was already there in his office with Douglas, who looked terrible, and said he had not slept the previous night. Bernie signed a custody paper and Douglas and I left immediately after and went home.

The rest of the weekend was quiet. I felt bad because I should have taken the messages on Friday, and then Douglas would not have had to spend another night in a cell. He was preoccupied worrying about his arrest, and telling him it would be sorted out and not to worry did not seem to help him.

He came into the police station with me this morning and we were waiting for Bernie to arrive and then we were going across to the court to sort out the bail conditions. Douglas would be staying at Mary's house with us and I was going to stand surety for him.

It did not take long to sort things out at the courthouse and after, I offered to take Douglas home. He refused and said he would get a taxi. So, I am sitting at my desk waiting to see what happens.

Just before lunch Bernie stuck his head round his office door and beckoned me inside. 'Bit of a surprise here,' he said. 'A court messenger has just delivered a note from the Judge. Apparently Justin Cramp went to court this morning and withdrew the appeal. They are no longer seeking to extradite Douglas. They have decided they have no case to prosecute as Zach has changed his statement. I better ring Tony and tell him.'

He phoned Hotel Glass Bay and was told Tony had checked out early Saturday morning and had taken a taxi to the airport.

Bernie looked puzzled. 'This is very strange, when I told Cramp on Friday that Zach had changed his statement they told me they were still going to prosecute and that the statement made in custody was worthless, as he would say anything if he thought it would be to his benefit. Now Tony Choizi clears off.' He gave me a knowing look, saying, 'I don't suppose this is anything to do with your Friday night disappearance has it?'

I smiled and replied, 'Well, we can release Douglas now can't we?'

Bernie agreed.

Chapter 83

Douglas Jay; Thursday 25th December

It was Christmas morning and I was sitting on the terrace in the sun drinking orange juice and planning the day with Joelle, Jasmine and Mary.

This was not how I had imagined I would spend Christmas at all. Last week I thought I would probably spend Christmas in jail and prior to that I had contemplated spending Christmas at Hotel Glass Bay, but when they said they were fully booked I had expected to be back in England on my own, with the highlight of the day being a visit to the local pub for a Christmas pint.

This was much better. Joelle's attitude towards me had changed completely. She had come rushing home last Monday lunchtime to tell me I was finally free and the Americans had gone home. We both burst into tears and ended up hugging each other. We then spent the rest of the afternoon explaining the past couple of months and Joelle told how she had been instructed to watch me as they suspected I had smuggled drugs. I had to agree that initially the circumstantial evidence had built up, not helped by some of my actions, where, unwittingly, I had appeared to incriminate myself. She explained how she had found it increasingly difficult to maintain a professional distance and not to get personally involved with me.

It was Mary, she told me, who had first cast doubts on

the evidence and how, despite the pressure from Tony Choizi, after the accident she had gone back over the evidence and concluded that I was an innocent bystander. She told me about Tony Choizi; what an unpleasant man he was, and what she had gone through with him. That made me feel guilty and I started apologising to her for doubting her motives.

Monday afternoon had cleared the air between us but it was then like two strangers meeting. We had to get to know each other all over again. Initially I was not used to this smiling, kind and considerate woman, who kept trying to nurse me. She was not at all like the moody, preoccupied person I had known. As for Joelle, she apologised all over again, more than once, telling me she now had to keep reminding herself that I was friend, not a potential criminal.

That Christmas morning it was Jasmine who finally broke the ice between us, joking and laughing and teasing both Joelle and myself about our growing relationship that was obvious to everyone except Joelle and I.

The weather that morning was glorious, the sky was blue with some fair weather clouds just beginning to build. The air was clear, and while it was not yet too hot it was clearly going to get warmer under the sun. The sea was a deep, inviting, turquoise colour. Joelle proposed we spend the day on the beach and suggested Three Sisters Bay.

Jasmine was getting excited about opening presents, which reminded me that after I was released I had completely lost track of the date, and it was Jasmine who had told me Christmas was only two days away and this year we had all got presents from England.

I was shocked when she said, 'Mum's got you one as well and it's quite heavy.'

I did not want to be left out and needed to do my own Christmas shopping, but how?

I remembered that when Jasmine had been looking at my photographs she had said she would like a camera, and so I had asked Joelle to buy her one for me to give her. I showed her my little Canon Ixus and asked her to try and find one like it.

On Christmas Eve I persuaded Jasmine to help me buy some gifts for Mary and Joelle, and we took a taxi into Joseph town. We found Mary an antique wall clock to replace the old plastic one in Glass Bar. But Joelle was proving difficult. I did not want to give her anything too personal, not yet anyway, and the best we could come up with was some scent. Jasmine told me what to get, but on the way home I had a brainwave. Jasmine thought it was a great idea so we rushed back to the house.

Eventually, that Christmas morning we agreed a plan. Mary had bought a large chicken to roast, and said she wanted to cook a traditional English Christmas lunch for me. Joelle would help Mary get the lunch ready, preparing the vegetables, and putting the chicken in the oven to cook ready for when we returned from the beach for a late afternoon Christmas dinner. Jasmine and I would make sandwiches, beers and Cokes to take down to the beach. Jasmine declared I could not use a knife properly with only one hand, so she made the sandwiches and sent me off to find the drinks and load up the car.

When we were all ready I announced, 'Just one thing, I think this present might be useful on the beach.' I gave Jasmine the camera, which she was delighted with, especially as I had charged the battery so she could start to use it immediately.

We drove to the beach but could not get the car right down the narrow access path, so we had to walk the last half-mile. That was a bit tricky for me with broken ribs and one arm in plaster up to the elbow. The girls split the picnic up between them to carry. I offered but they said an invalid could not also carry stuff.

'It's not you we are worried about,' Jasmine told me, 'but you could drop the bag and spoil the contents.' After I had stumbled a bit and nearly fallen, Joelle gave her bag to Jasmine to carry and announced that she could not look after me and carry a bag as well.

Jasmine pulled a face at me as I told her she was a clever dick and carrying both bags served her right. We soon managed to make it to the beach with Joelle fussing around me telling me to be careful. We spread out towels on the sand and lay down enjoying the heat from the sun. Soon, the girls decided to go into the sea. Me, I lay in the shade, even though I took a bit of teasing from Jasmine and Joelle. I don't like getting sunburnt!

We spent the best part of the day on the beach. The girls lying in the sun, getting too hot and jumping into the water to cool down and then back in the sun again. I spent the day lying in the shade, snoozing and watching the three girls, but mainly watching Joelle and thinking how gorgeous she looked in her bikini. That afternoon it was like having a family again for the first time in years.

We got back to the house about four in the afternoon. Joelle and Mary cooked the dinner. Roast turkey with all the trimmings, and Mary had even found a traditional Christmas pudding from somewhere. Mary insisted we did it properly and sat down at the dining room table.

Their dining room was magnificent. It was a large wood-panelled room. It was simply furnished with, on one wall, an antique mahogany sideboard, in which the best china was kept, while on the opposite wall was a pair of large open French windows looking out over the garden. An eight-seat antique mahogany dining table stood in the centre of the room.

Mary explained that the furniture was English and had been brought out to the island by a plantation owner to furnish his new home when he settled on the island. Her husband had bought the items at an auction just after independence, when a lot of the big estates had been broken up and sold.

I was sat at the head of the table and presented with the chicken to carve. I waved the knife and said to Jasmine, 'I thought you did not trust me with a knife?'

Joelle smiled as she replied, 'Ah but, carving is a man's work.'

Although my right hand still tended to shake a bit sometimes, I thought I could manage tolerably well as I held the knife and concentrated on keeping my right hand steady, but in the end I had to give up and give the bird to Mary to carve.

Joelle opened a couple of bottles of wine and we pulled the crackers before we tucked into the meal.

After dinner we exchanged presents. Mary loved the clock. Jasmine was annoyed that the battery on the camera was flat and she could not take any more pictures, but the iPhone Joelle gave her grabbed her attention.

Joelle gave me a present to unwrap. I was absolutely delighted with the two books and told her they would be invaluable. Joelle explained that she had an ulterior motive in giving me that present and she made me promise to help her restore the car.

It was my turn and I gave Joelle two parcels. She opened the small one first and told me it was her favourite perfume, then, she unwrapped the larger present and held up a leather seat base. She gave me a puzzled look and asked, 'What is this for?'

I showed her the cigar burn on the seat panel. 'This is

the seat out of the old Princess. Jasmine helped me get the cover off yesterday and for your Christmas present I shall send that off to the car trimmer I know in England and get him to match the leather and replace the damaged panel. I am sorry I could not organise that in time for today, so this is the next best thing.'

Fortunately, Joelle was delighted and told us all it was a wonderful present.

'Actually,' I said, 'Jasmine did all the work, I just stood there and told her how to do it.'

After dinner and when we had cleared up Jasmine went off to her room to play with the iPhone and Mary decided she needed an early night.

The evening was still warm and as there was no moon it was very dark, but the stars were numerous and amazing. The air hummed with squeaks as the night insects emerged, and in the distance we could faintly hear music and voices from a Christmas party in full swing. Joelle and I took our drinks out to the veranda and sat in friendly silence, just looking at the stars. After a while Joelle turned to look at me and asked me if I remembered the sunset we had watched that evening sitting on the terrace outside Glass Bar.

'I remember it well. I thought you were going to get all romantic,' I told her.

'I nearly did,' she confided.

She was silent for minute, and then she said, 'You know that dinner date you asked me for, and I never gave you an answer?'

'Yes, I remember.'

'Is it too late to say yes, please?'

Epilogue

Douglas did take Joelle out to dinner. They went to the New Year's Eve Dinner Dance at Hotel Glass Bay. The event was fully booked but Joelle used her influence to get two tickets. The Hotel was delighted to see her and Douglas, and reserved for them the best table on the dining room veranda overlooking the sea, and even served a complementary bottle of French champagne.

Dress was formal. Joelle wore a long, simple, white, strapless evening dress with her gold chain and white high-heeled sandals. She went to the hairdressers in the afternoon and wore her hair up that evening. Mary found her husband's old dinner dress suit with its white jacket. She had to alter the trouser waistband as Douglas had lost a lot of weight, and had the suit cleaned for the occasion. Mary cried when she saw them walk out to the taxi, they looked so happy together. Jasmine wondered wistfully what it would be like to actually have a proper father.

Douglas stayed at Mary's house for another four months while he recovered from the accident. Joelle had to work, but took as much time off as she could in order to spend time with Douglas. Jasmine started to teach Douglas to play the piano, initially with his right hand to help him recover its normal use. Mary continued to run Glass Bar and gradually the events of November and December receded into a memory, and life resumed a normal and happy rhythm.

Joelle always took the time off to take Douglas to the hospital every week for a check-up. His arm and wrist healed well and the cast was removed at the end of February.

Over that period, Douglas, Joelle, and Jasmine started to restore the old Princess. With his arm and wrist in a plaster cast Douglas could not do very much, but showed the two girls how to go about dismantling the car, taking notes and pictures as they went along.

By mid-April the hospital had declared Douglas recovered and discharged him.

By early May Douglas was feeling very well. He had put on weight and, having resumed early morning running, was as fit as he had ever been. With some regret he realised he could not continue to enjoy hospitality from this family for much longer, and so he reluctantly took the decision to return England to sort out his affairs and decide what he was going to do with his life.

Joelle, Mary, and Jasmine took him to the airport to say goodbye. Jasmine made him promise to come back soon. Joelle made him promise to keep in touch and write to her. Mary just hugged him and told him to look after himself.

Joelle and Douglas did keep in touch. They wrote occasional letters to each other but also discovered how easy it was to contact each other using the internet.

What they did not know was that back in Florida a storm was brewing. The Dutch Police were furious that the investigation on Kaeta had been a fiasco, and were attempting to hold the US Drug Enforcement Administration responsible. An investigation had started and Tony Choizi was busy looking for a scapegoat.

The End

About the Author

The author writes under the pen-name, John de Caynoth. He retired following a successful business career to assist his wife running their equestrian training business and started writing to exercise his imagination and prove he could actually do it.

At school John was not considered to be the brightest child in the class, mainly because he could not spell. His school savior in class 3b was the English teacher, Mr Benson, who told John that he would not give any more detentions for poor literary skills and gave him the choice of using the full spectrum of the English language, or constraining his writing to those words he could cope with. He chose the later option.

John also enjoys photography, his particular delight being equestrian photography and his pictures have been used to illustrate books written by his wife, Claire Lilley.

His other great enjoyment is the restoration of classic cars and he currently has three vehicles to work on!

John and Claire and live in a picturesque 350 year old thatch cottage, with Sammy their standard poodle, on the edge of Salisbury Plain in Wiltshire.

John de Caynoth
17th July 2015

Printed in Great Britain
by Amazon.co.uk, Ltd.,
Marston Gate.